# THE (MOST UNUSUAL) HAUNTING OF EDGAR LOVEJOY

*Roan Parrish*

sourcebooks casablanca

Copyright © 2025 by Roan Parrish
Cover and internal design © 2025 by Sourcebooks
Cover design by Sarah Brody/Sourcebooks
Cover art by Jillian Goeler
Internal design by Tara Jaggers/Sourcebooks
Internal images © derketta/Getty Images, Jana Salnikova/Getty Images

Sourcebooks and the colophon are registered trademarks of Sourcebooks.

All rights reserved. No part of this book may be reproduced in any form or by any electronic or mechanical means including information storage and retrieval systems—except in the case of brief quotations embodied in critical articles or reviews—without permission in writing from its publisher, Sourcebooks.

No part of this book may be used or reproduced in any manner for the purpose of training artificial intelligence technologies or systems.

The characters and events portrayed in this book are fictitious or are used fictitiously. Any similarity to real persons, living or dead, is purely coincidental and not intended by the author.

All brand names and product names used in this book are trademarks, registered trademarks, or trade names of their respective holders. Sourcebooks is not associated with any product or vendor in this book.

Published by Sourcebooks Casablanca, an imprint of Sourcebooks
1935 Brookdale RD, Naperville, IL 60563-2773
(630) 961-3900
sourcebooks.com

Cataloging-in-Publication Data is on file with the Library of Congress.

Printed and bound in the United States of America.
VP 10 9 8 7 6 5 4 3 2 1

*For my haunted love
and my little ghost cat*

# 1

# Edgar

Beyond the beaded curtains of the Never Lounge was another world.

Light spangled every surface and caught in hazy shafts of perfumed smoke that plumed from the stage. Velvet-flocked walls, a cascade of velvet curtains, the velvet shred of a horn bellying low…the darkened club embraced Edgar before his eyes could adjust.

Someone called his name, and he blinked away the haze until he could pick out the familiar form of Helen Vang waving him over to the high-top table they were sharing with Veronica Deslonde and Greta Russakoff. Empty glasses, bottles, and cigarette packets littered the tabletop, and they whooped a greeting as he joined them.

Edgar steeled himself for the discomfort of socializing and tried to smile.

Helen turned to Veronica and held out their hand. With a humph, Veronica pulled a bill from her cleavage and handed it to them.

"You just cost me ten bucks," Veronica said, but she kissed his cheek with as much welcome as she always did, the delicious honey-smoke scent of her calming him.

"I never doubted you," Helen crowed.

Greta snorted and whispered, "They changed their bet three minutes ago," as she hugged him hello.

"I come to stuff," Edgar grumbled. But he didn't grumble too loudly, because it wasn't true, strictly speaking.

Carys, Greta's partner, approached with an armful of drinks. Her eyes widened when she saw him. "Oh wow," she said, sliding the drinks onto the table. "You showed!"

But she elbowed Edgar teasingly, and he tried to relax.

"Yeah, yeah."

"Get you a drink?" Carys asked.

"No, thanks."

"Edible?" Helen proffered an Altoids tin covered in glitter, and he waved it off.

"I'm good."

As Edgar's eyes adjusted to the dim light and his friends' conversation picked back up around him, he began his habitual scan of the room.

The trick was to keep your gaze steady but unfocused, letting your eyes pick up on anything that unusual. The brain snagged on standout things more easily that way. Of course, at a queer burlesque show in New Orleans, there were standout things everywhere Edgar looked.

Lava lamps on the lip of the proscenium glowed with orange, pink, and violet globules that drifted, broke, and recombined in hypnotic pulsations; ostrich feathers riffled in the breeze of the overhead fans. Performers slunk through the crowd, eyes and mouths exaggerated or erased, hair pomaded slick or piled high, rhinestones and sequins and glitter twinkling in the light, bootheels and tap heels and high heels click-clacking a chaotic rhythm that underlaid the music's driving moan.

The atmosphere caressed every sense, and a tingle began in Edgar's inner thighs and flushed through him.

It was seductive, but allowing himself to be seduced meant his guard would be down, so he shook it off and forced himself to breathe evenly as he resumed scanning the room, searching, as ever, for things that shouldn't be there.

*Creatures* that shouldn't be there. Because they shouldn't exist at all.

What he usually caught first was a glimmer—light catching their nonforms differently than the living, because they weren't made of the same corporeal stuff. But in the dark, he couldn't depend on that.

If not a glimmer, then sometimes it was a mirage—the air between him and the entity wavy like the hottest days of August. But with the stage lights and dim houselights and the smoke and dust motes catching in both, right now he couldn't depend on that either.

A familiar itch of panic sparked, and Edgar inhaled through his nose and exhaled slowly through his mouth, noting the glowing red exit signs as beacons of escape.

The conversation had moved to the new flavor that Helen, Veronica, and Greta were developing for Lagniappe Lemonade, the cocktail business they'd developed the year before. Edgar worked for them part-time, delivering the bottles of artisanal hard lemonade made with New Orleans–grown lemons and herbs and sweetened with the honey from Veronica's bees. He'd quickly learned that Helen, Veronica, and Greta were as close as family, and—used to it from his own sister—he'd welcomed their sibling-esque meddling and prying with equanimity.

It was why he had come tonight. They invited him to things often. Dancing, dinner parties, game nights. He rarely attended, citing his other job or a family obligation or—as often as it was believable from someone they teased for having no social life—other plans. But he'd wanted to see the queer burlesque show that some of Helen's friends were performing in. The boldness of burlesque had always intrigued him.

Now that he was here though, he regretted it. Even as he tried to remain calm, the air became thick in his throat, and his ribs clutched at his heart.

"Bathroom," Edgar mumbled and made his escape.

He wound through the crowd, careful not to brush up against anyone if he could help it. If there was one of *them* in the crowd and he touched it by mistake, ice would slide down his spine and twist his gut.

The bathroom was nearly as crowded as the club, but the second a stall opened up, Edgar sank down on the toilet seat and cradled his head in his hands. He considered calling Allie and letting her calm him down, but he'd been trying not to do that as much anymore. His sister had enough to take care of—like growing a whole person while she ran her own business. He didn't need to throw his panic attacks into the mix.

The thing about seeing ghosts was that there weren't a whole lot of resources out there for dealing with it. You couldn't tell a therapist because they'd think you were crazy, couldn't dial a hotline or hire an expert for advice because they didn't have any, couldn't pop a pill to make them disappear. Edgar knew because he'd tried all those things and more over the years.

Absent these solutions, Edgar had developed his own tools for coping with his unique problem, hiding in bathroom stalls chief among them.

Edgar took slow, deep breaths, keeping his eyes open to avoid being startled.

Instead of calling Allie, he opened the video feed that he'd set up to check on the new kitten arrivals at the cat café where he worked. As he watched, his pounding heart slowed, and his breathing evened.

*I hate this. I just wanted one night.*

"You okay in there, dude?" a voice said. When no one else responded, Edgar cleared his throat in what he hoped was an affirmative noise. The bathroom door opened and closed again, leaving him in relative quiet.

"I hate this," he whispered once he was alone. He opened the stall door, making sure to avoid the mirror—you never knew what might be reflected behind you—and left the bathroom to rejoin his friends.

At the table, Helen now had their arm slung around the waist of a fat red-haired guy with a glorious beard.

"But it takes place in four timelines, each one year apart," they were saying as Edgar approached. "Oh, Edgar, good, this is Isak, my friend who's performing in the second act. Cat café," Helen said, pointing to Edgar.

"I need another cat," Isak said, his eyes wide and sparkling.

He screwed up his nose. "Not *need*, like, *require for blood sacrifice* or anything. *Need* like *caaaats*." He drawled the word with the worshipful delight of a cat lover.

"There's a form to fill out for adoption. Don't write anything about blood sacrifice on it, and you'll radically increase your chances of success," Edgar said.

Belatedly, he remembered to smile, and then Isak laughed.

"Ha! I couldn't tell if you were kidding."

"Edgar's never kidding," Greta told Isak.

"Or," Veronica proposed, "is he always kidding?"

Edgar cringed. "We open at nine," he said. "I'm gonna grab some water. Get y'all something?"

Confirming that everyone had a full beverage, Edgar made his second escape. He didn't have it in him to meet anyone else.

He ordered a sparkling water with lime from the preoccupied bartender and wedged himself between the bar and the wall so nothing could sneak up on him. The wallpaper was an ornate pattern of orchids and foliage, blue-black flocking on an oxblood field. Edgar traced a bloom with his fingertip, some areas of the velvet soft with age and dust, others brittle enough to crumble onto his fingertips.

"It's a reproduction."

Edgar startled back around.

"The wallpaper. It's not the original. People ask sometimes."

The person who'd spoken wore a smoking jacket in peacock colors, a vee of creamy skin just visible between the parting edges of the silk.

"Oh," Edgar said intelligently, distracted by the stranger's beauty. A curl of their light brown hair fell over one bright blue eye smudged with black eyeliner.

"The original was modeled after a Jean-Baptiste Réveillon in Paris, but this replaced it after a fire in the seventies." The alluring stranger smiled. "I'm Jamie. I use they/them pronouns."

"Hey. Edgar. He/him." Flustered, Edgar dropped his gaze and blinked at the wallpaper. "Are you an interior designer?"

Jamie smiled, revealing prominent eyeteeth and charming dimples. "Nope. Just a casual wallpaper historian."

Jamie's nose crinkled, and Edgar was captivated.

"I perform here, so I've heard a lot of conversations about this place. You know, the tourists who are following online guides and tours and stuff? They come in here all the time wanting to see the original wallpaper because it was featured in this cult movie from the sixties."

Edgar knew the type. "Um. Are you performing tonight?"

Jamie raised one dark eyebrow. "Mm-hmm. You sticking around?"

Heat kindled in Edgar's gut at the idea of seeing stunning Jamie take off their clothes onstage, followed immediately by guilt.

Jamie's eyebrow rose impossibly higher, like maybe they knew what he was thinking, and Edgar hesitated. The thing about being able to see ghosts was the question it raised—that if ghosts existed, what other creatures considered mythical were real? It was hard to dismiss the possibility of vampires, werewolves, aliens, or troublingly attractive strangers who might be able to read your thoughts.

"Can you read minds by any chance?" Edgar asked, then shook his head. "Just kidding. Yeah, I'm here with my friends."

"Not generally, but I think I can read yours right now," Jamie said. Their voice was half flirtation, half amusement. They put fingers to their temples and closed their eyes, in the pose of a performative fortune teller. Their soft lashes fluttered in the dim light. "You're wondering if it's weird to be talking to someone you're about to see almost naked onstage. Then that makes you picture me naked, and you feel bad about that. But you realize I choose to do it, so you're wondering if it's shitty to feel awkward because that kind of implies that I don't have agency. Am I close?"

Edgar blinked, narrowing his eyes to make sure there was no discernible glimmer or mirage in the air between them. He contemplated whether there was any socially acceptable way to touch Jamie and make sure they were real.

"Is that what everyone thinks?" he asked.

Jamie shook their head. "Most people stop at the picturing me naked part."

The bartender finally slid Edgar's drink across the bar to him.

"So, um." But Edgar couldn't think of anything to say.

Jamie gave him a small smile and gestured to his drink. "May I?"

Edgar handed it to them, holding his breath against the moment their fingers would touch. When they did, Edgar nearly let out a sigh of relief at the brush of warm, rough fingertips. A fine frisson ran through him, more delicate and complicated than the vertiginous slide of ice down his spine.

Jamie's full lips lingered on the rim of the glass, and they signaled to the bartender, who poured them a whiskey.

They seemed utterly at ease. Edgar took a deep breath and squared his shoulders in an attempt to find a similar self-confidence but ended up nervously scanning the club again. When he refocused on Jamie, they were watching him curiously.

"So what is your act like?" Edgar finally managed.

Jamie threw back the whiskey, squeezed their eyes tight

against the burn, and then grinned. "You're just gonna have to stick around and find out, Edgar."

They winked and disappeared into the crowd in a swish of silk and curls.

Edgar gaped. He supposed he had until the end of the show to come up with something more impressive to say.

# 2

# Jamie

There was always a moment, about two minutes after Jamie Wendon-Dale took the stage, when performance shifted to embodiment. When the audience fell under their thrall and changed from observers to participants in creation. It was the moment they waited for every time they performed.

In stark contrast, the dressing room where they prepared was always pure chaos—a minefield of curling irons and stiletto heels, cobwebbed with stockings and wigs, the entire thing dusted in glitter so fine it clung to clothes and hair for days.

"Who's the guy?" asked Deon, handing them a shot of tequila.

"What guy?" Jamie asked, wanting to keep the frisson of attraction they'd felt for the handsome stranger for a little while longer.

Deon, understanding, simply clinked her glass to Jamie's, and they both drank.

But Marie, midway through donning her towering Marie Antoinette wig, chimed in. "The hottie who looked like he was gonna cry. Ugh, can you help me, please?"

Jamie, who had just started slicking back their hair, held up hands covered in gel and considered that description. Deon sprang up and held the wig straight so Marie could pin it in place.

"I just met him," Jamie said casually.

They wouldn't have described Edgar that way, but there *had* been something that drew Jamie to him. A vulnerability that made Jamie want to crowd him against the wall and soothe and interrogate him in equal measure.

Jamie looked at their reflection in the mirror as they lined their eyes with kohl. Was there a sparkle in them that wasn't usually there? They reapplied deodorant, adjusted the straps and buckles of their costume, and absolutely, positively did *not* wonder what the handsome stranger from the bar would think of their act.

"Now, put your hands together for The Count!" the announcer said as Jamie stood in the wings.

Whoops came from the audience, and a flurry of hands patted Jamie's back as the music began. The lights hit first, and that rush of time speeding up, tugging at their every motion. But the difference between a good performer and a great one was their response to being hurried. Great performers treated time like it was infinite, like they'd never leave the stage, believed the audience would be happy to watch their slightest movements forever.

Jamie aspired to it.

They'd started doing burlesque at the behest of a friend and quickly realized that burlesque functioned just like their day job: designing haunted houses. Both used concealment to draw an audience in and the promise of revelation to lead them exactly where Jamie wanted them.

It had been what attracted them to horror movies as a child. Even when they were too young to understand the films, they'd been captivated by this interplay between what is hidden and what gets revealed. The wicked special effects hadn't hurt either.

Halloween costumes became an avenue of expression for them, then fashion. But burlesque specifically had healed something for Jamie, allowing them space to experiment with how they presented their body.

As The Count, Jamie strutted and splayed, menaced and seduced, stripping off their cape and using it as a prop. They bared their fangs and swirled the velvet fabric. The music whirled and coaxed, the lights dimmed and spun, and excitement rushed through Jamie.

They bit down on the blood capsule in their mouth and let the streak of red hit their snow-white shirt. The crowd cheered and whistled, and slowly Jamie stripped it off, letting the red streak their ribbed white tank too.

Jamie couldn't see the crowd with the spotlight on them, but they felt the energy building. Jamie had them. They were in.

They faced the wings and caught the comically large wooden stake the stage manager threw. For a moment, they played it to the audience as if they were scared of the object. Then they quirked an eyebrow and reconsidered the stake, grinding on it rather than fearing it. The crowd went wild.

They twisted and inched the tank up their torso, revealing more and more skin.

Finally, blood-streaked clothing on the stage and velvet pasties that matched the cape covering their nipples, Jamie turned to the cheering audience. They held the stake suggestively and thrust their hips forward. A gong sounded just as the stake ejaculated a spray of red confetti directly into the audience.

The closest table shrieked and laughed, brushing at the glitter in their hair and clothes. Jamie swept a low bow that allowed them to grab their costume from the stage. Then they exited, heart pounding and stomach light, to enthusiastic applause and whistles.

# 3

# Edgar

Edgar was captivated. Jamie moved like molasses, slow and sinuous and sweet. Edgar scripted things he could say to them after—compliments, flirtation.

"You okay there, bro?" Helen asked and elbowed him in the ribs.

"Huh?"

"You're practically drooling," they said.

Edgar couldn't look away. He didn't want to miss one second. He did, however, clamp his mouth shut against any drool, even though he was pretty sure Helen was joking.

Onstage, Jamie raised their arms, and bright red blood burst from their mouth and trailed down their pale skin. Edgar gasped. A table close to the lip of the stage burst into riotous applause at the blood, and Edgar glanced at them for just a second, envious of how close they were to Jamie.

That was when he saw it.

A creature that had once been human and was now a rotten, twisted echo of one. The ghost's skin was mottled gray and yellow, and the hair a brittle shock of matted straw. Where its eyes had once been, blank pools of jelly quivered. Its mouth gaped around black teeth and a tongue swollen to twice its natural size. Edgar didn't know how it could see him through those gelatinous eyeballs, but he felt it like a fist in his throat. Then the slow freeze slipped down his spine, and Edgar scrambled out of his seat.

"Hell, yeah," Carys cheered beside him. Then she slid out of her seat to stand too, clapping wildly. The rest of the audience followed suit, and Edgar realized that Jamie had finished performing.

"Wanna go meet them?" Helen was asking. "I'll introduce…"

But Edgar's head was swimming, and his hearing was going in and out to the precipitous beat of his heart.

Jamie was right there, gorgeous and so alive, bowing to the uproarious audience and scanning the crowd—surely not? But possibly?—attempting to look for him. And between them, impossible, the ghost.

Edgar glanced away for a second to see everyone at the table staring at him, as if they knew.

"Edgar?" Helen prompted. "Do you want to?"

The ghost had moved a table closer, as if it were magnetized to Edgar.

"I gotta go," Edgar slurred, patting his pockets for his phone and wallet. "Sorry, thanks, sorry," he mumbled in the direction of the group, never taking his eyes off the ghost.

Then, before it had a chance to get any closer to him, Edgar fled the Never Lounge, ran into the dark streets of the French Quarter, and didn't stop until he hit Canal Street.

# 4

# Jamie

The server led Jamie to the table where their mother, father, and sister sat and took Jamie's to-go coffee cup, which they'd drained on the way to the restaurant in an attempt to caffeinate themselves into coherence after only four hours of sleep.

When Jamie had gotten offstage after their performance last night, they'd been so excited to find Edgar in the crowd. They'd felt a connection with the handsome stranger and couldn't wait to talk with him more. But when they'd changed out of their costume and gone to look for him, he was nowhere to be found.

*Yeah, because he wasn't flirting with you; he was just awkward,* insisted the voice in Jamie's head.

What Jamie *had* found was a voicemail from their mother,

requesting Jamie's presence at breakfast—not brunch, because by then Jamie's mother would have had to put out a dozen fires—to discuss something important.

Jamie's mother was a force to be reckoned with. She'd found politics later in life and approached it with the zeal of a convert. No resting on laurels or hoping things worked out for Blythe Wendon—nope, she gave a hundred percent effort a hundred percent of the time. On the plus side, 8 a.m. nearly guaranteed them privacy, so Jamie wouldn't have to watch their mother grasp awkwardly to introduce them to any friendly constituents.

Jamie's mother rose to kiss them on the cheek, a glancing peck that was more breath than contact.

"So," their mother began before Jamie had sat down. "Emma has some news."

Once, Jamie and their sister had been close. Only two years younger, Jamie had watched Emma intently, sure they'd follow in her footsteps, and Emma—although she'd sighed huffily and rolled her eyes—had seemed to enjoy the captive audience. Emma, not their mom, had been the one Jamie watched apply makeup, tweeze her eyebrows, shave her legs. When Emma had her first crush, Jamie listened to her enumerate the charms of the floppy-haired second clarinet with such ardor that they fell a little in love with him themself. When the boy broke Emma's heart three months later by making out with her best friend, Jamie cried with her, raged with her, and held a grudge against this so-called best friend long after Emma had moved on.

When Jamie came to understand they were trans and nonbinary, Emma had been the first person they told, assuming that all those years of being an Emma devotee would be enough to inspire reciprocal support.

It had been a miscalculation.

Emma held out her hand and waggled her fingers.

"Dave proposed," she said. There was a squeal of delight in her voice that reminded Jamie of sitting curled up on Emma's bed all those years ago while she gushed about Nathan Jones, the cheating clarinetist.

This wasn't unexpected, but Jamie had held out hope that Emma would tire of dull Dave before he had the chance.

"Congrats, Emma," Jamie said automatically. "That's so great."

They tried to infuse their voice with sincerity. But it was hard to muster enthusiasm for a lifetime spent with a guy who'd once pulled his phone out to check the status of his crypto while people were singing him "Happy Birthday."

"The ring was his grandmother's," Emma said, her hand still extended in Jamie's direction.

"It's a stunning ring," Jamie's mother declared before Jamie had a chance to respond.

When the waiter came to take their orders, Jamie asked for a Bloody Mary with their pancakes, suspecting they'd need it to get through what threatened to be a lot of talk about weddings. When the drink was slid before them, they could've sworn the waiter shot them a sympathetic look. It was confirmed when they took a sip and tasted the amount of vodka.

"Have you and Dave chosen all your uh…?" Jamie grasped for the appropriate terminology. "Wedding-related stuff yet?"

"I have a Pinterest board," Emma said, phone already in hand.

"That's a good segue," Blythe said, cutting off Emma's Pinterest show-and-tell. She stacked her used half-and-half containers and brushed something invisible from her husband's collar. "This wedding will be…an event for the whole family as well as for your sister. You know how these things are when you're in the public eye. No avoiding it. And of course, my family represents me. So I'd just like to make sure that any…scrutiny… is met with a…"

She seemed to search for the perfect turn of phrase, as if words were a spell that you had to get exactly right to conjure their intended effect.

"Met with a united front," she concluded.

Jamie gulped Bloody Mary. They'd learned the hard way that when their mother used corporate politspeak, it meant they were about to suffer.

"A united front, yes," Jamie's father echoed.

That was mostly what Hank Dale spent his time doing. When it wasn't his wife he was echoing, it was his bosses, his golf partners, and his favorite news podcast.

"And what precisely is the front that you want me to unite around?" Jamie asked.

"There's so much to do," Blythe said, ticking them off on her fingers. "Flowers, catering, music, colors, transportation." She waved off what Jamie suspected would've been another hand's worth of items she could've named.

"Yeah, I'm happy to help," Jamie said hesitantly. "Whatever you need, Em."

Their mother's satisfied smile made Jamie feel good for the first time since showing up.

"Well, that's great," Emma said, searching out a bite of kiwi in her fruit salad. "Because I was hoping you would be my maid of honor?"

The words settled in Jamie's gut like concrete, *maid* soaking up the vodka they'd drunk, leaving Jamie terribly, recklessly sober. They caught the waiter's sympathetic eye and signaled for another Bloody Mary.

Recklessness wasn't something that was received well in the Wendon-Dale family. *Plan, prepare, execute.* That was their mother's motto and had been for as long as Jamie could remember. Spelling words and multiplication tables? Memorizable. Two term papers due the same day? Plan to write one the week before. Not sure you're in love with your boyfriend anymore? Make a pros and cons list and proceed accordingly.

No excuses. No room for mess or chaos or indecision.

No room for Jamie.

*Do you still think of me that way? After all this time, after everything I've explained, do you still look at me and see a girl I've never been?*

"I, um… Yeah. But can we please not call it the maid of honor? Since, you know, I'm not a maid."

The second Bloody Mary landed in front of Jamie, and they took a deep gulp to drown the rest of the words that wanted to come out.

"Oh, tell her the best part," their mother said delightedly. She had cut her eggs Benedict into identical square bites. "Them," she corrected herself absently, spearing a bite.

The rage simmered in Jamie's throat and heated their ears. *At least she corrected herself,* their peacemaking side nagged. But Jamie was already checking out. When you realized someone wasn't really speaking to *you* but to some fantasy they've constructed of you, it was pretty hard to invest in anything they were saying.

It was like this every time: an internal fight between the part of Jamie that cared about their family and wanted to be loved by them and the part that screamed to let their true feelings out, even if that meant alienating their mother and, by extension, their father, who would never stick up for Jamie if it meant disagreeing with his wife.

"We got the sculpture garden at the art museum!" Emma said. "It's going to be perfect."

"They had a cancellation, so we snapped it up," Jamie's father said.

How long had their family been planning this without mentioning it?

"That's...that'll be really pretty, Em."

"God, I can't believe we're trying to plan a wedding in three months," Emma said, turning to her mom. The *we* meant that Emma and Blythe had a shared file of documents, spreadsheets, and to-do lists that they consulted daily. That was what it meant to plan anything with Blythe, and for just a moment, Jamie was envious. To be on the receiving end of something their mother planned felt as close to a warm hug as they could get from her.

"You have the date, then?" Jamie asked.

"November first. We lucked out with that cancellation. They didn't have any availability until next May, and I can't wait that long," Emma said, eyes soft.

"Yes, it'll be all-hands-on-deck until the wedding," Blythe said with finality.

Jamie stuffed a bite of food in their mouth to buy time.

*Are you fucking kidding me? You misgender me, ask for my help, and plan the wedding so all the work needs to be done in my busiest month of the year?*

"Yeah, that's, um. That's not really going to be a time when I can help with the wedding much," Jamie said. "Since the haunted house opens to the public in October, I work time and a half. As you know," they added.

Jamie's mother waved them away. "You can get time off to help your family with your sister's wedding, surely." It was the same certainty she'd had when Jamie's schedule interfered with an event during her election campaign. And they could understand why, since Jamie had gone through the tortures of the damned to get time off as requested.

But that had been two years ago, and Jamie wasn't as easily cowed anymore.

"Actually," Jamie said, still trying to keep their voice steady, "I committed to the job, and—"

"I'm sure you'll work it out," Blythe said, definitive. "And if not, there are other jobs."

Creating the premiere haunted house in the New Orleans area was Jamie's dream job, and their boss would replace them easily and without a second thought if they asked to take time off in the month before Halloween. But Blythe didn't care about that. In the Wendon-Dale family, Jamie's work was an embarrassment. Dropping out of college to pursue it? Well, Blythe still hadn't forgiven Jamie for that.

There was no arguing with their mother when she had her mind made up. She refused to acknowledge any conflicting information or opinions. They'd simply have to figure the schedule out somehow. For now though, all they wanted was to get the hell out of here because they didn't think they could deal with one more instance of being disregarded.

Jamie looked to Emma instead.

"I'm really happy for you, Em. I'll try to help out however I can, but you're not going to be able to count on me for a lot during October. If you'd like to ask someone who has more bandwidth to be the, uh, whatever of honor, that's fine with me."

Emma frowned, like she couldn't compute someone turning down a family demand. It certainly wasn't common, not in their family.

"Well, maybe I can ask Meredith," she mused. "You know how Meredith is. She was really upset when I said I picked you."

Jamie didn't, and they didn't care. "Sounds good."

"My roommate. Mer. You remember Meredith."

Their parents were both looking at Jamie as if they'd said they didn't remember who the pope was. Jamie was ninety-nine percent sure they'd never even seen a picture of this person, but they gave a noncommittal nod to keep the conversation moving forward.

"She'll be good with all the planning. She was secretary of our sorority."

Relief flooded Jamie at being let off the hook. They could just imagine pulling an all-nighter because they had to plan a fucking bachelorette party.

Emma went on, "And I swear I'm not gonna be all bridezilla about this. Like, I'll make sure all the bridesmaids will look good in the color I choose. And I won't pick any dress you would hate either. God, remember Shawna Kinkaide's wedding?" Emma asked, turning to their mom. "She had me wear that lime mermaid dress? Yikes." Emma shuddered.

Heat clawed up Jamie's throat and finally exploded.

"Dude, I'm not wearing a fucking dress!"

Jamie's mother looked around the restaurant to make sure no one had heard her offspring curse.

The second Bloody Mary metabolized all at once, and Jamie became acutely aware of their heart and how hard it was pounding. There was a strange ringing sound in the restaurant. No, in their ears.

"How about I wear a tux, okay?" Jamie offered weakly.

"It's not black tie," Blythe snapped, sounding horrified.

"A suit, then," Jamie offered. "You tell me the color, and I'll take care of the rest."

There was an awkward silence at the table—the kind Jamie had gotten used to after coming out to their family.

"Whatever," Emma sniffed.

"We'll figure it out," their father soothed, placing a placating hand on his wife's arm.

A familiar shame settled over Jamie, a shame that stiffened their spine, squared their shoulders, and lifted their chin, just like it had when they were a child.

"Yes," Blythe said. "We certainly will."

It sounded more like a threat than a reassurance in her mouth.

Jamie took a bite of cold pancake. It stuck in their throat.

# 5

# Edgar

Things were not going well, for entirely mundane reasons—a depressing reminder that while being haunted was Edgar's biggest problem, it wasn't the only one. Edgar had gotten splattered with muddy water by a passing truck, popped a tire on his bike, and torn the hem of his shirt while fixing it, and it was only 3 p.m. So when he approached the next address for delivery and the sign read *BAINBRIDGE ANTIQUES*, it was just confirmation that today was not his day.

"Come on," he muttered and double-checked the address.

Antique stores, estate sales, museums—those places all held objects likely to be connected to the dead. That meant a far greater likelihood of a ghost hanging around.

With a sigh, he heaved the box of Lagniappe Lemonade

bottles from the trolley of his bike. He'd just square his shoulders, keep a tight grip on the box, and get out as quickly as possible.

After the bright sun, Bainbridge Antiques was so dark that for a moment, Edgar could hardly see anything. As his eyes adjusted, he found himself in a narrow entryway lined with art and furniture. Quiet hung over the place. Edgar didn't want to disturb it—or anything in it—so he picked his way carefully down the serpentine hall. The layout was like a beehive, with furniture and mirrors dividing the space into cells and corridors that led to who knew where.

Edgar followed two faint voices down the rightmost path and came to the center of the maze, a stack of luxurious rugs illuminated by dozens of softly lit crystal chandeliers.

"Delivery for Mr. Bainbridge," Edgar said when a stooped white-haired man came into view. "Where would you like it?"

"Oh, hello, dear boy," the man said delightedly. "Hmm." He looked around him as though even he wasn't entirely sure where anything was.

"And I'll just need your signature." Edgar shifted the heavy box from one arm to the other to pull out his phone.

"Have you ever tried this beverage?" Mr. Bainbridge asked. He peered up at Edgar, eyes sparkling behind his spectacles. "I must admit, I was beguiled by the packaging."

But before Edgar could answer, a figure emerged from behind a large mirror. Someone Edgar hadn't expected to see again after their meeting at the Never Lounge the weekend before. *Hoped,* but not expected.

Jamie.

Dressed in Carhartts, work boots, and a white undershirt, they looked nothing like they had at the club, but Edgar would've recognized them anywhere.

Edgar had watched Jamie's burlesque performance with an ache in his throat that he couldn't explain. Every twist of Jamie's hips and drape of their arms had felt like magic, and the look on Jamie's face as they performed…well, it had made Edgar wonder if that was what Jamie would look like in the throes of passion.

Now, given a second chance, Edgar drank them in greedily, his heart starting to beat faster. The weight of the box he held became irrelevant.

"Well, hello there, stranger." Jamie's voice was music and their grin even more engaging than Edgar recalled. "Remember me?"

*Yes*, he thought. *I haven't been able to get you out of my mind.*

Edgar's throat went dry, and his tongue insisted on attaching itself to the roof of his mouth.

"Hi," he managed to choke out, more growl than word.

*Get it together, man.*

"Well, how lovely. Everybody's friends," Mr. Bainbridge said with tangible delight. Edgar couldn't help but like him.

"Did you wanna put that down?" Jamie asked mildly, and Mr. Bainbridge fluttered into action.

"Yes, of course, forgive me, dear boy."

Edgar carefully put the box down on the floor and held out his phone. Bainbridge swapped his wire-frame glasses for a pair of metal pince-nez he fished from the breast pocket of his vest.

"You use your finger as the pen," Jamie explained when Bainbridge squinted down at the phone.

Bainbridge did and beamed. "Well, isn't that remarkable." He brandished his finger like he was wondering what other unexpected things it could do.

"Do you want it in your office, Carl?" Jamie asked.

"Yes, yes, much obliged, dear human."

Jamie grinned and waited for Edgar to shoulder the box, then led the way through the maze of antiques.

Edgar's mind raced as he tried to think of the right thing to say to explain why he hadn't waited to see Jamie after their performance, so much so that he almost smacked into Jamie's back as they made a quick left into the office.

Bainbridge's desk was covered with papers but for one cleared spot that held a sandwich wrapped in wax paper, and every other surface was crowded with so many boxes and objects that Edgar could hardly turn around.

"Maybe here?" Jamie moved the sandwich to the windowsill, and Edgar placed the box on the desk.

"So, um," he began, shoving his hands in the pockets of his khakis. "You work here?" Edgar asked.

"No. I was picking something up from Carl." Jamie had a lovely voice. Soft and a bit rough but musical. Edgar wanted to keep asking questions so they wouldn't stop talking.

But before he could, movement flickered in Edgar's periphery. He whipped his head around so quickly his neck kinked, every muscle tensed and ready to run, and searched for the creature.

*No, not now. Please, not now!*

From the top of a bookcase stuffed with old leather-bound volumes and objects of fascination, it leapt, landing on the desk with a solid *thwump*.

A cat. A fucking cat.

Edgar sucked in a breath through his nose and tried to convince his heart that this was not a convenient time to explode.

"Jesus fucking Christ." Jamie put a startled hand to their chest. "Gertrude, not cool! You okay? She's a devil."

"Fine," he croaked. The adrenaline faded, leaving him with shaky muscles and drenched armpits. He reached a trembling hand out for the cat to smell, but she wasn't interested. "I should…" Edgar cocked his head toward the door, not trusting his voice further.

"Lemme walk you out. It's a bit of a labyrinth."

Edgar trailed behind Jamie, shielding his eyes from the bright sun as they adjusted from the dimness of the shop.

"Sooo," Jamie drawled. Their voice was still casual, but they looked uncertain. "I hoped I'd see you after my act."

*They'd hoped!*

"Yeah, uh."

Edgar raked a hand through his hair. They were staring at each other, and Edgar's heart pounded. This was the moment to say something smooth and flirty. Explain that he'd wanted to stick around after Jamie performed. Maybe come right out and ask Jamie on a date.

"I'm really sorry about that. I wanted to see you too—I meant to see you. But I started feeling…unwell."

Instantly, Jamie's expression changed to sympathy.

"Shit, sorry to hear that. I hope my act didn't make you sick," they added.

"No, no, the opposite. Your act was…stunning."

A delicate blush rose in Jamie's cheeks. Edgar's mind was flooded with what else would make Jamie blush.

"Wow. Thanks. I… Thank you."

"I wanted to talk with you again, after," Edgar clarified. "I didn't want to leave."

Jamie smiled. "I wanted to talk to you too."

Edgar's heart hammered. They had wanted to talk to him! They had wanted him to stick around! *Say something good*, his brain demanded. *Say something suave and flirtatious!*

"You ever been to a cat café? I work at one."

*Yeah, nope, not that.*

But Jamie's face lit up.

"That's adorable. Where is it? I wanna go."

*Yes! Accidental success.*

"Yeah? You should come. I'm there nine to one on weekdays and all day on Saturdays."

Edgar couldn't believe how well this whole awkwardly blurting random facts thing was working out.

*Don't get your hopes up. People say things all the time that they have no intention of following through on.*

But then Jamie smiled, and Edgar was made of hope.

"I'm gonna come," Jamie said. It sounded like a threat. Like Jamie was giving him a chance to change his mind. But Edgar hoped it was a promise.

# 6

# Jamie

Jamie drummed on the steering wheel to the rhythm of the new Garden Gate single, and Amelia tossed boiled peanut shells out the window while they drove out of town in Jamie's trusty truck. Well, trusty-ish.

"It's clearly meant to be," Amelia was saying through a mouthful of peanut. "Everyone knows when you run into someone again, that means it's fate."

"Is *that* how you ended up dating Cassandra for three months, or—?"

"Shuddup. But actually, kinda."

Amelia's lazy, appreciative grin meant she was fondly remembering the hurricane of a woman that that had left her heart—and her apartment—in a state of ruin the year before. Jamie admired Amelia's ability to extract the positive from even the worst situations. It had been one of the things that drew Jamie to her. And now, more than a decade after Amelia sauntered into Jamie's second-period AP chemistry class and slid into the empty seat beside them, it was still something Jamie appreciated.

Jamie squinted into the sun as their phone indicated the turn. "This should be it."

Jamie and Amelia got out of the truck, and Amelia spat a peanut shell into the drain with admirable precision. Before them loomed an old textile factory. What was once a clanking ode to modern innovation was now still, abandoned to elements both human and natural. Windows had been cracked by branches and bricks, doors wrenched open by vines and crowbars.

Jamie grabbed the flashlight they kept in the glove compartment for explorations such as these.

The friend of an acquaintance who'd given Amelia the tip about this place had mentioned a broken first floor window hidden by a copse of trees, and Amelia crowed with excitement when she found it. Despite the oppressive heat, they both wore long pants and sleeves for protection against everything from broken glass to the flesh-eating parasites that it amused Amelia to pretend she'd contracted, so they made it through the window without incident.

The smell of mildew, decaying wood, and the strangely sweet scent of rot hit Jamie immediately.

"You're lucky I love you," Jamie muttered, but they were vibrating with excitement. They loved exploring. Jamie and Amelia's friendship had solidified in abandoned places like this, after all.

This was no lark though. This time, they weren't just exploring, as they'd done so many times; they were scouting locations for a scene in Amelia's film. The space needed to look dilapidated, be big enough for fifteen actors, and be free—hence the *abandoned* part.

Once inside, they moved slowly and quietly, making sure they didn't disturb anyone. Just because buildings had been abandoned by the people who once owned them didn't mean they weren't inhabited. And Jamie never wanted to intrude on someone's home.

Jamie shone the flashlight around the room. A rat ran from the light, skittering along the wall to disappear into another dark corner. "Jesus, ick."

A massive tangle of machine parts was covered in tarps that had fallen to tatters, draping the machines like skin stretched over a metal skeleton. It was eerily beautiful, and Jamie snapped a picture with their phone.

"Are you gonna see him again?" Amelia prompted.

Finding out that Edgar had left the Never Lounge because he hadn't felt well and not because he'd been avoiding Jamie had made Jamie's hope that there might be something between them bloom again. He was as awkward as he was handsome, but Jamie had approached him at the bar because he'd seemed interesting. Out of place. There had been something about him that struck Jamie as deep loneliness, even though he had been at the club with friends.

"Yeah, I'm gonna go to the cat café where he works."

"Oh, shit, that's so cute," Amelia said.

Jamie wholeheartedly agreed. "He just seems…"

Jamie found they couldn't finish the sentence, but Amelia had been Jamie's best friend long enough that she raised her eyebrows and finished it for them.

"In need of saving?"

"What? No!" Jamie said immediately.

*No more savior shit!* they'd promised themself after they finally broke up with Jason.

"Mm-hmm," Amelia said doubtfully.

Jamie searched for how to explain the combination of uncertainty, intrigue, and surprise that had animated Edgar.

"He seems like a time traveler who's ended up here and doesn't want people to know that he's from another time."

Amelia paused her scouting in corners, intrigued. "Hmm. Time traveler from the future or the past?"

Jamie laughed. "The past. He looks around like everything about the world shocks him."

"I kinda like a time traveler for you, actually," Amelia said. "Such chance for interesting conversation. You can explain our modern customs to him."

"You know who I'd *like* to explain modernity to? Emma, who asked me to be her maid of fucking honor."

Jamie's words hung in the air. They hadn't texted Amelia about this before because they were embarrassed they hadn't stuck up for themself more at brunch.

"What the fuck?" Amelia said, sounding gratifyingly disgusted. "What are you gonna do?"

"Hire a lot of queer strippers for the bachelorette party, that's for sure."

Amelia giggled appreciatively. "God, she'd be so mortified."

Jamie relished the image of their sister's horrified face.

"You wanna be my date and keep me sane by making fun of everything with me?"

"Of course. Unless…" Amelia waggled her eyebrows. "You and the time traveler." She bumped her fists together.

Jamie flipped her off, but they couldn't deny the frisson of excitement that shot up their spine at the unlikely possibility.

They shone the flashlight up wooden stairs that they wouldn't trust with their weight, and Amelia shook her head, moving back into the main room. "This isn't the place. Let's go."

✦ ✦ ✦

*Just because someone is hot and looks cute around cats does* not *indicate something fundamental about their personality. So don't you dare base a whole-ass crush on the juxtaposition of muscles and kittens*, Jamie lectured themself as they approached Take Meowt Catfé three days later.

But the first thing they saw inside was Edgar with a cat perched on each of his broad shoulders.

"Oh, this is really bad," they muttered.

"Welcome to—" Edgar began. Then his eyes widened. "Oh, wow, hey. You came."

Edgar's cheeks flushed, and he turned his chin so the black cat on his right shoulder could rub its cheek against his. The small orange cat on his left shoulder, possibly aggrieved at the momentary lack of attention, took that opportunity to try and climb onto his head.

It was one of the more adorable things Jamie had ever seen. And really who was to say that being hot and looking cute around cats couldn't mean *something*?

*Just no spontaneous crushes.*

"Need a hand?" Jamie offered. It looked like the orange one trying to climb his head was digging its claws into his scalp.

"No, they're good. They won't fall off."

A pang in Jamie's gut said that their self-directive had been ineffectual.

"Come on in, and you can meet everybody," Edgar said.

*I am only human,* Jamie thought and let themselves off the hook.

The space was bright and open, and a few people sipped drinks and chatted as the cats went about their business around them. One whole wall was built of a pyramid of boxes for climbing, and several huge cat trees held snoozing cats with tails ticktocking lazily over the sides of their perches. A large cat with magnificent gray fur stood on the counter as though it worked there.

"This is Henrietta Rampart." Edgar indicated the orange cat on his head. "And this is Basket," he said of the black cat, making a face as he said it. "I did *not* name her. Ridiculous name."

"Oh?" Jamie asked.

Edgar dropped his chin, which resulted in him being nuzzled by both cats. "It seems undignified."

"Dignity's in the eye of the beholder," Jamie said and raised their knuckles to Basket. "Hey, buddy."

Basket purred and rubbed her jaw against their knuckles.

"Just be prepared, becau—"

Henrietta took their proximity as an invitation and launched herself from Edgar's shoulder to Jamie's. She weighed practically nothing, but her claws dug into their skin.

Jamie held still as Henrietta made biscuits on their cheek.

Edgar and Jamie stood, cats on their shoulders, facing each other.

"Well this is extremely weird," Jamie said.

"Yeah."

Jamie took in Edgar's appearance beyond his adorable kitten epaulette.

Edgar wore khaki pants, a blue-and-white-striped T-shirt, and black sneakers. His dark brown hair was thick and cut short. There was nothing about his person that gave insight into his personality, interests, or style. But his brown eyes were intense, and his handsome face seemed permanently poised on the edge of wariness.

"You can meet the other cats?" Edgar suggested.

"Please. Should I leave her here?"

Henrietta purred and nuzzled their ear.

"It's cute you think you have any control over her."

*Cute!*

Edgar was a gentle giant. He handled the cats with utter care and dignity.

"Milkshake and Taco are getting adopted this week," Edgar said, scritching under the chins of two tortoiseshell kittens.

"That's great," Jamie said, but Edgar sounded conflicted.

"Yeah. I'll just miss them."

"Must be heartbreaking to work with cats if you miss them all when they leave?"

Edgar bit his lip. "A little."

Jamie's heart was spared melting because at that moment, a bullet of white fur shot across the room and began to run in circles around Jamie. They tried to turn and watch it but quickly got dizzy.

"Um. Should I…be alarmed?"

"No. He'll calm down in a minute. This is Robert McBride."

*Let me guess, you named him.*

"How do you pick their names?" Jamie asked.

Edgar frowned, regarding the cat. "He just seemed like a Robert McBride."

"Okay, if you could rename the cats whose names you don't like, what do they seem like to you?"

Edgar sat down on the floor next to Jamie, careful not to jostle Basket. Robert McBride lost interest in zooming around and flopped in the middle of the floor like a rag doll.

"Well, I thought she seemed like an Addie." He patted Basket's head. "I would've named Milkshake and Taco…Sabrina and Freya. That guy in the corner? Snowball? I would've named him Leo Virginia."

Jamie grinned. "Sounds like a porn name."

Edgar gave a quirk of the lips that might someday grow up to be a smile. "Shit, you're right."

The other group in the café left, and Edgar rose to see them out.

"Thanks for coming in," he told them. "We get new cats all the time, if y'all want to stop back."

They promised they would.

*He tries hard to get the cats placed in good homes even though he misses them when they leave.*

"Can I get you anything?" Edgar offered Jamie. "A coffee or something?"

Jamie stood, careful not to step on any cats. "How about a date?"

Edgar frowned. "I don't think we have any. Though maybe with the smoothie stuff—"

Jamie huffed out a laugh. "Edgar. Do you want to go out on a date? With me?"

Jamie had the pleasure of seeing something like wonder cross Edgar's face. They were already planning how they'd relate their total smoothness to Amelia when they told her this story later. Then Edgar's brow furrowed, and he dropped his chin.

*Well, fuck. Not smooth. Not slick. Just rejected. You sure read this one wrong.*

Jamie said quickly, "No worries. You're not interested. It's cool. Um, want to show me more cats?"

Jamie moved toward the back of the café, away from Edgar. Rejection stung, but it was better to know sooner rather than later. And at least they could drown their sorrows in cute cats before making a dignified exit, never to see Edgar again.

"No, wait." Edgar followed them. "I'm not...not interested. You just surprised me."

Jamie's heart flip-flopped. "Oh. No worries if you don't want—"

"I do." He sounded sure of himself now. As certain as he'd been that Basket was not a suitable name for a cat.

"Well, okay, great," Jamie heard themself say. "How about dinner?"

After a slight pause, Edgar nodded.

"Saturday night?"

Another pause and a flicker of worry in his face before he said, "Okay."

Jamie hesitated. "Are you okay?"

"Yes, definitely," Edgar said quickly, but a line appeared between his eyebrows that didn't go away. "I'm really looking forward to it."

Jamie tried to take people at their word, so they said, "Okay, great. Me too."

They exchanged phone numbers, and Jamie found themself looking for excuses not to leave. They pet every cat on their way to the door, but too soon they were in front of it with no excuses left.

"Hey, Jamie," Edgar said. It was the first time he'd said their name, and it sent shivers through them. "I'm really glad you came by. Thanks for asking me out."

And this time, there was no hesitation, no flicker of unease. Edgar was smiling—softly, subtly, but smiling nonetheless.

Jamie beamed. Feeling brave and reckless and full up with joy, they blew him a kiss on their way out the door.

# 7

# Edgar

"All your clothes are tragic," Allie said. Edgar had rested the phone on his dresser to FaceTime with her and was now regretting it. Once upon a time, his sister would've come over to help him pick out an outfit, bringing what she would insist was the perfect article of clothing from the store. But now, eight months pregnant, she wasn't as effortlessly mobile.

"I wish I could bring you this jacket we got in the other day. Pure seventies delight. With fringe."

"Sorry I'm not the brother you can dress up like a doll."

"You *being* a doll is worth your disinterest in fashion," she assured him. "Besides, I'm sure he'd never let me now. He won't even text me back."

"Me neither. Maybe the white button-down. The restaurant's pretty nice."

"Did you go look at it?"

Edgar hesitated. "Yes."

"I thought you were trying not to do that anymore?"

"I am."

He knew she'd let it go because she was good like that.

"I just want things to go well," he explained. "So I wanted to be prepared."

"And?"

"I didn't see anything outside, but it's not really like I can go in and be like, *Hello, good people. I'm just here looking for ghosts. Enjoy your oysters.*"

Allie snorted. "They'd think you were doing some kind of larping thing."

"Yeah, maybe." Best case scenario.

"I gotta pee. Be right back."

"You're good. I'm gonna get going."

"The white button-down will look great," she said, giving him the same thumbs-up that she'd given him since they were kids. When she'd walked him to the bus stop for his first day of school. When he'd won the science fair in seventh grade. The first Christmas after their dad left. When Poe ran away. The thumbs-up meant *Everything is going to be okay*. And while Edgar knew it wasn't magic, it was still comforting.

✦ ✦ ✦

Edgar crossed Rampart into the French Quarter and let himself enjoy the way the streets teemed with life. He avoided Bourbon

Street and turned into the alcove where the restaurant's iron lace gates stood open to the street. The hedges that secreted the space from passersby twinkled with fairy lights, and terra-cotta pots of birds of paradise flanked the entrance.

It was beautiful. And Edgar wished he could appreciate it instead of every sculpture and plant registering as a threat.

He let his gaze relax and scanned the area. Nothing but people enjoying their food.

"Hey!"

Edgar startled, so intent on looking for ghosts, he hadn't noticed Jamie approach.

"Shit, sorry," Jamie said and put a comforting hand on his arm.

Jamie looked amazing, in tight black trousers, pointy-toed black boots, and a pale pink velvet vest. Their hair looked like they just rolled out of bed, and their blue eyes glowed.

"Wow," was all Edgar could say.

When Jamie smiled, their gazes locked. Edgar could see now that Jamie had a light spray of freckles under their eyes. He wanted to kiss them.

"Hi," they said. "Shall we go in?"

Edgar followed Jamie inside, admiring the play of their muscles beneath tattooed skin.

"Wendon-Dale, for two," Jamie said, and a man dressed in all black led them to a table in the corner of the dining room.

Edgar couldn't remember the last time he'd been to a restaurant like this. A napkin-in-your-lap, would-you-like-to-see-the-wine-menu, very-good-sir place.

Jamie seemed perfectly at home, making polite small talk with the maître d' and ordering water for the table.

Edgar had scanned the place when they walked to their table, but now that they were seated, he had the opportunity to check things out more thoroughly. The huge painting of a shipwreck on the nearest wall, the drape of white tablecloths on each table, the freestanding ice buckets for champagne. Chances were that to everyone else in the restaurant, the decor spoke of luxury. To Edgar, however, it was just a collection of lines and textures he had to ignore so that he could search for beings that shouldn't be there.

"You want to see the wine list?" Jamie was asking him, holding out a slim folder.

"Not for me, thanks. Go ahead though," he told Jamie.

Jamie ordered a glass of white wine and thanked the waiter. "I was worried you might not show," they said with a wry smile.

"What? I would never do that."

"Well, I don't really know you yet."

"I guess that's what dates are for," Edgar said.

They pored over their menus instead of talking, though Edgar wasn't really seeing the words in front of him, too occupied with trying to divide his attention between Jamie and keeping a vigilant watch on his surroundings. As a result, he pointed to something when the waiter came and instantly forgot what he'd ordered. Then, with no business left to attend to, they were left in silence once again.

Edgar searched his mind for questions to ask on a date. Suddenly he regretted the amount of time he'd spent scoping out the restaurant, wishing he'd spent it memorizing conversational topics instead.

"So," he began, hoping that somehow when next he opened his mouth, something interesting would come out. "What do you do?"

*Oh, excellent. Truly inspired. Definitely not the most banal question of all time.*

But Jamie's eyes lit, and they leaned in. "I'm a haunter. I design haunted houses. Well, any haunt, really, but my main gig is working on House of Screams, the haunted house just outside the city. D'you know it?"

Edgar's brain screeched to a halt. *Haunted houses?* Haunted, like, by ghosts. His first date in forever… The first person he was excited about in forever. And their job was making the world scarier? His heart sank.

"I'm not familiar," Edgar managed, flustered, hoping his voice sounded normal.

Jamie's expression suggested it had not.

"Are you nervous?" Jamie's expression was so kind it made him squirm.

"Yes," Edgar said. "That obvious?" But he knew it was.

"Yeah, pretty much," Jamie said. "Can I ask why?"

Even putting aside his experiences with ghosts, Edgar had never been good with people. He hadn't needed to be, because he'd had his siblings and Cameron and Antoine, a built-in friend group that had accepted him as he was. It was only after losing Antoine, then Cameron, then Poe, that Edgar realized how unusual such acceptance had been.

"Because I don't really do this. Dating thing. Talking thing. People can never tell when I'm kidding. Sometimes it takes me a long time to think of what to ask because I don't want to intrude, but then people think I'm not interested in them. Um." *I get distracted looking for ghosts and may need to flee at any moment. Just your ordinary haunted shit.*

Jamie looked thoughtful. "How do you feel about truth or dare?"

"Um. The game?" Edgar asked.

"Yeah, y'know, sleepovers and middle school parties. Truth or dare."

*Poe and Allie and Cameron and Antoine, kicking rocks and running wild, daring each other absurdly. Jump over that fallen log, steal a pack of gum, sneak into the church at midnight, jump off the highest branch and into the—no, don't think about that. Don't think.*

"It's definitely been a while."

"The people I work with," Jamie said, "they dare each other constantly. It's silly, but when I started doing it to connect with my coworkers, it actually worked. Might help break the ice?"

Edgar was worried. The truth? Forget about it. Truth made people angry and resentful. Truth made people think you were crazy. Truth made everyone leave.

But Jamie was sitting across the table from him, and they looked stunning. They had asked *him* out. They seemed to maybe, possibly like him. And Edgar hadn't been able to get them out of his head since the moment they met. The thought of Jamie's face falling if he said no, of Jamie curling away inside themself, felt unbearable.

"Nothing big," Jamie assured them. "Just to get to know each other. And you get three skips. So if there's anything either of us doesn't want to do or questions we don't want to answer, we can use a skip. Okay?"

Edgar narrowed his eyes. "You just made up that rule, didn't you?"

"Yes. What do you think?"

And Edgar, who hadn't told the truth to anyone outside his family since he was twelve years old, agreed.

Jamie's smile was as rewarding as he'd thought it would be.

"Fun. Okay, you go first."

"Truth or dare?" Edgar asked.

"Truth," Jamie said.

Edgar ran through questions in his head, but they all sounded like a kindergartner's attempt—favorite color, number of siblings, middle name. Books. He could ask about books or movies. Yeah, movies were good.

But what came out of his mouth was, "What does it feel like to do burlesque?"

Jamie's eyes lit up. "Oh, man. It's amazing and terrifying and sexy and exhilarating. I started last year. My friend Ramona sent me a cryptic text saying to go to this burlesque performance. I thought she was gonna meet me there, but when I showed up, it was a performance and info meeting for people who wanted to join the troupe."

Jamie gave a wry smirk and rolled their eyes at the thought of their friend.

"But I stayed because I was curious, and the performers were amazing. I'd only seen cis folks do burlesque. Seeing queer and trans bodies of all shapes and sizes onstage performing…it made me feel like maybe my body could be, like, appreciated?"

Jamie traced the edge of their bread plate with a fingertip, deep in thought, and Edgar thought of a dozen questions that it was too soon to ask.

"I appreciated it," Edgar said softly. "You're so…" Edgar frowned, searching for the right words. Jamie's performance had been titillating and sexy, confident and a tease. Face-to-face, they were just as glamorous, just as sexy, but sweeter, more accessible. "Sorry. What were you saying?"

Jamie's eyes were soft with appreciation.

"Thanks, Edgar. At the beginning of my transition, I went through a period of worrying that my body was…too complicated? It felt like people looked at me as if I was a mystery to solve rather than a person."

Edgar leaned in subtly.

"But what I learned at that performance is that burlesque is all about the tease. The whole point is to choreograph a routine that *creates* mystery around certain parts of your body that you may or may not choose to reveal to the audience later. And that really appealed to me—the power of being the one to create the mystery rather than being at the mercy of others trying to solve it."

"You're like the author of the mystery instead of the reader," Edgar said.

"Exactly."

"Were you nervous about the, er, nudity part?"

"Yeah, for sure. But there was this trans performer there, and he explained that he doesn't even take off much. He makes it feel as if he does because of how the routine is choreographed." Jamie's elegant fingers trailed along the belly of their wineglass. "It's all about building up the tension to the point that even the revelation of a bare shoulder or thigh can feel legitimately titillating to the audience. Same principle as haunting, really."

Jamie's eyes were shining, and Edgar thought that he could happily sit in this restaurant all night and listen to them talk. Even, it turned out, about haunted houses.

"How so?"

Jamie sipped their wine. "We're always trying to figure out how we can create the biggest impact with the smallest stimulus. It's all about manipulating how someone experiences the environment. Distracting them with something over here." Jamie held up their wineglass. "While over there"—they raised their other hand and put it under the table—"something is setting up to *getcha!*"

When they said *getcha*, they tapped Edgar's knee with their empty hand, and he startled a bit, even though he'd anticipated it.

"And the more on edge the audience is, the less it takes to push them over. A sudden noise. A puff of air. A change of texture." Jamie scratched his thigh lightly. "A bright light. That's all it takes to make some people scream."

Edgar felt fairly certain he would be one of the people in question. His skin felt electrified, and his mind supplied images of Jamie making him scream in less terrifying but equally potent ways.

"Watching people get scared exactly like you planned, performing burlesque. Both make me feel like a god."

As Jamie said this, the waiter arrived with the food. He slid steaming plates in front of them with a "Bon appetit" and a slight bow. Jamie declined another glass of wine.

"What did you get?" Edgar asked.

"Lobster ravioli. Wanna try?"

"Sure. Do you want to try…?" Edgar realized with horror that he had no idea what he'd ordered.

"Blackened Cajun redfish with polenta," Jamie offered, raising an eyebrow.

*Just tell them the truth and don't be weird*, Edgar instructed himself.

"I, um, I was so nervous earlier that I guess I didn't pay attention to what I was ordering," he admitted and was rewarded with a soft smile.

Jamie put a hand on Edgar's. A gentle, comforting pressure that demanded nothing. "I was nervous too," they confessed. "I thought you were wishing you were anywhere but here. You seemed really distracted."

And damn, there was that hint of vulnerability that tugged at Edgar's heart. He hated that he'd made Jamie—lovely Jamie—feel that way.

"No. Definitely not. I...was just anxious. I'm having a really good time."

Jamie held out a forkful of lobster ravioli for Edgar. The pasta was fresh, the lobster buttery, and the crispy breadcrumbs on top added the perfect amount of crunch.

"Damn. That's really good."

"You sound surprised."

Edgar tried to remember the last time he'd been on a dinner date. (He couldn't.) The last time he'd shared bites of food with anyone. (Allie finishing his pancakes when he went to the bathroom didn't count.) The last time anyone wanted to get to know him. (Nothing came to mind.)

"Just hungry, I guess."

He made Jamie a bite and passed it to them.

"Yum. Spicy."

Edgar tried his own food. It was indeed spicy. Sweat broke out at his hairline. *Damn.* He would never have ordered this on a date if he'd been paying attention.

"It's good," he said, wondering which was grosser: wiping off sweat at the table with his napkin or allowing it to eventually drip down his face.

He compromised on subtly blotting at his forehead with his napkin and cleared his throat.

"Sorry. I'm..." He downed half his water and cleared his throat again.

"Are you okay?" Jamie asked, tone suggesting they were ready to spring into action at any moment if his answer was no.

"Yeah, fine," he croaked. "Just a little spicier than I imagined."

Jamie's expression was part suspicion and part... Could that be tenderness?

They reached over and swapped the dinner plates, taking the fish for themself.

"You don't have to do that," Edgar protested. "You ordered what you wanted. It's not your fault I'm an enormous spice baby."

Jamie grinned at *spice baby* and gestured that Edgar should eat.

"That's really nice of you," he said, mortified. They ate in silence for a minute, and Edgar collected himself. There had been something he wanted to know. "Truth or dare?" he asked.

"Truth."

"Why did you ask me on a date? I know I was awkward when we met."

"All *three* times we met," Jamie teased. They buttered a piece of bread slowly. "I don't mind awkward."

They seemed to choose their words carefully.

"I thought you were hot when I saw you at the club," they said slowly. "I saw you standing at the bar, and you looked so...remote, I guess. Like you were in another dimension, peeking through into this one."

Edgar felt a pang of sadness at the confirmation that he seemed as isolated as he felt.

"And I guess I wondered what was going on in your dimension and whether you might come far enough into this one to connect." Jamie's expression was warm. "But honestly? I knew I wanted to ask you out when I saw you with the cats. You treated them with such dignity and care. I...hoped that was how you'd treat me if we were ever together."

Edgar could see that it had cost Jamie something to admit this.

"Anyway, I had to get you in a noncat environment so I wouldn't be distracted by how fucking *cute* it is to see a big muscular Superman guy cuddling a bunch of damn kittens."

Edgar choked on his bite of ravioli. "Superman?"

"*That's* the part that stuck with you about what I said?"

"Sorry, I just... No one's ever referred to me that way before."

"Why did you accept?"

"Because I thought you were lovely," Edgar said without thinking. "At the show, when I first saw you, I couldn't take my eyes off you. And you were captivating onstage. I, um, I was really sorry I couldn't stick around after to talk to you more."

Jamie's blue eyes went soft, and it gave Edgar the courage to continue.

"I would, you know."

"Would what?" Jamie asked.

"Treat you with dignity and care. I mean. If we. You know."

"Yeah?" Jamie asked.

They reached their hand across the table, palm up, and Edgar took it. Rough fingertips and soft palms, like sand and velvet. What would it would be like to have someone to hold hands with while he walked through the streets? Someone to squeeze his shoulders after a hard day?

"Thanks. I would too." Jamie's voice was just breath. They stroked the back of his hand with their thumb, and Edgar's pulse pounded. Jamie broke the charged silence. "Truth or dare?" They made an adorable face. "And you should really choose *dare*."

"Okay, dare," Edgar said, wanting to please Jamie even though it made him nervous.

"I dare you to order two desserts." They winked at him, and relief flooded Edgar.

"That's about the speed of dare I'm up for," he said with a smile.

He ordered lime cheesecake and grapefruit sorbet. Jamie ordered gingerbread panna cotta and beignet bread pudding.

"Now we both get to try four," Jamie said as the waiter left.

Edgar returned their smile. He would gladly have ordered ten desserts to make Jamie happy. In fact, seeing Jamie smile was quickly topping Edgar's list of favorite things, displacing such old standbys as watching a cat's paws twitch with dreams and not having to leave his apartment.

"What's your favorite dessert?" Jamie asked.

But before Edgar could answer, cold trickled down the back of his neck, like someone had cracked an egg made of ice. Edgar froze, time slowing down as he became horribly aware of his own body and of the presence of another that shouldn't be there.

As slowly as he could make himself move, Edgar turned to look behind him.

A torso and head were sticking halfway out of the wall. The face was an unseeing mask of terror. Once, it had been a man, but now it was a screaming echo—empty and desperate and terrified. Sweat soaked Edgar's armpits and back, and the ringing in his ears drowned out the conversation around him. All of a sudden, he couldn't breathe. He was alone in the world of this creature.

It reached out a rotting hand and grazed Edgar's hair, the sensation like cobwebs and insects and the dark secret things that no one should know.

Edgar jumped out of his seat before he realized he was moving.

"Are you okay?" Jamie asked, expression concerned. They rose also, reaching a hand out to Edgar.

It was gone. The wall was just a wall. Edgar touched his hair, half convinced he'd come away with a handful of cobweb and dirt and writhing beetles, but of course there was nothing there.

"Can I help you, sir?" asked their waiter as he appeared with dessert.

"No. Thanks," he choked. "I'm okay. Sorry."

The waiter inclined his chin gravely, the picture of decorum, and placed the desserts on their table.

"What's wrong?" Jamie asked, still clearly concerned.

Edgar pressed his hand to the empty wall. He managed to get a breath and cleared his throat. *Fuck.* What explanation could he possibly give Jamie that didn't make him sound delusional?

"Um. Spider."

He lowered himself back into his seat, wincing as sweat seeped into the back of his underwear.

"Oh, yikes," Jamie said, apparently accepting this explanation. "Are you arachnophobic?"

Jamie, Edgar assumed, wasn't afraid of spiders—or anything.

"I, um. It just startled me. Sorry to be a freak."

"No problem. Wanna switch seats?"

Jamie seemed as sincere as they had when they'd swapped dinners, and it made Edgar's throat tight.

"No, I'm fine. Sorry." The last thing he wanted was to watch the ghost touch Jamie, even if Jamie never knew it was there. Edgar inched his chair around the table so it was closer to Jamie's and farther from the wall. "We can share desserts easier this way," he said.

Jamie accepted the excuse without comment, and relief washed over Edgar.

He sat on his shaking hands and surveyed the desserts, wishing more than anything to return to the camaraderie they'd been sharing before the undead interruption. "So what've we got here?"

Jamie took a bite of the gingerbread panna cotta and groaned. "This is amazing. Really creamy but great ginger flavor." They pushed it over to Edgar. "Do you like gingerbread?"

Edgar didn't, but he said, "It's okay."

Jamie tried the next dessert, and their eyes went wide. "Oh, damn, this one's even better. Do you like beignets?"

Edgar started to lie, then realized that Jamie's preference for the truth probably transcended the game they'd been playing. Yeah, he couldn't tell the truth about seeing ghosts, but at least he could be honest about his taste in food.

"I don't have much of a sweet tooth."

Jamie's eyes went wide. "But you ordered… Oh, that was only because I dared you."

"No."

"It's okay, I get it. Thanks for being honest."

"No, it wasn't. I promise."

Jamie frowned. They didn't look at all convinced. "Then why?"

"I figured you probably dared me because *you* thought it would be nice to taste four of the desserts. And I wanted you to be able to."

"That's sweet," Jamie said. "But just so you know, you're allowed to speak even during dares and say, like, *Hey, Jamie, I don't like dessert, so it'll all be for you.*"

"I just wanted you to have what you wanted," Edgar explained. It came out sounding much more intimate than he'd intended.

Jamie regarded him intently, and for a moment, like at the

club when they first met, Edgar felt terrified that Jamie could read his mind. They looked at him as if they saw far more than he meant to reveal. Just as he felt like he'd drown in their eyes, they quirked an eyebrow.

"Well, I certainly can't allow food to go to waste, so." They pulled the cheesecake and sorbet toward them and dug in.

A lightness fluttered in Edgar's chest. Joy at Jamie's joy. Envy that he didn't share it. Hope that perhaps someday he might.

"This cheesecake isn't very sweet at all. Want to try?"

Edgar took a small bite. It did taste sweet to him, but not as sweet as most desserts. It was pretty good.

Jamie tried the sorbet.

"Ooh. Kinda sour. Really good. Wanna try?"

"Okay." He ate a bite, and the grapefruit sourness made his mouth pucker, then gave way to a mellow sweetness that was more fruit than sugar.

"I like that," he said, surprised.

Jamie pushed it in front of him. "So no beignets and coffee for you, huh?"

"Nah. Powdered sugar is like sweet chalk. And it squeaks."

"More for me, then. *If* we ever go out for coffee, that is," Jamie teased.

Edgar pictured how it could be. Walking hand in hand with Jamie, each sipping their coffee as they wandered through the Garden District or along the river. Jamie would carry a bag of beignets, munching as they went. Maybe he would lean over to kiss them and come away with the faintest taste of sweetness from their tongue.

"We should," he murmured.

"I'd love that," Jamie said softly.

They acquitted themself admirably but couldn't quite finish all four desserts and relinquished the remains to the waiter in exchange for the check. Jamie slid their credit card into the envelope before Edgar could even offer to pay.

"So what do you say, Edgar I-don't-know-your-last-name-yet? Wanna come with me on the second half of our date? Or do you want to take off?"

Edgar hadn't known there *was* a second part to the date, but he definitely wanted to go on it. "Yes."

Jamie cocked their head.

"I mean, yes, I want to go on the second half of our date. Are you sure I can't split—"

Jamie waved him off and accepted their credit card back from the waiter.

"It's my pleasure."

"Lovejoy, by the way. My last name."

Jamie snorted. "Of course it is."

Outside, the balmy evening air settled around them. The quarter was coming alive with evening revelers, the afternoon bands that played for shoppers and tourists along Bourbon Street giving way to partiers wielding radioactive-colored cocktails in bright plastic go-cups of different shapes—purple voodoo punch, pink fishbowls, green hand grenades, and daiquiris in every color of the rainbow.

"So, um, where are we going?"

"You'll see," Jamie said with a grin. They walked with purpose.

Edgar did not appreciate surprises. Surprises meant unfamiliar places, and sometimes unfamiliar places meant ghosts. But since he couldn't say that, he said, "It's weird to be down here on a Saturday night. Usually I avoid the quarter like the plague on weekends."

"Same. Once, I had to pick something up for work the morning after St. Patrick's Day, and I knew Bourbon Street would be deserted because everyone was so hungover, so I cut down it. And oh boy, what a mistake. Just puke and pee and wigs and beads, and even the street was sticky, and it was ick. *Very* gross."

They shuddered.

"But we have a good reason for being here, and I promise it doesn't include cocktails that look the same color coming back up. God, sorry, I don't mean to keep talking about vomit on a date."

Edgar smiled. But as they crossed Rampart, all humor drained from Edgar as he realized where they were.

Jamie grinned at him. "Here we are." And they gestured to a sign that announced what the second half of their date would be.

A ghost tour.

# 8

## Jamie

Jamie was tipsy with excitement as they walked through the French Quarter with Edgar by their side. Every time their shoulders bumped or their fingers grazed, Jamie felt a frisson of possibility.

Had there been some strange, awkward moments during dinner? Yes. But Jamie chalked it up to first-date nerves on both their parts. They couldn't wait for a time when Edgar felt comfortable enough to let his guard down. Hopefully, a little bit of kitschy haunted fun would help. An excuse to stand close in the dark, to whisper, lips grazing cheeks, to hold hands.

"Here we are," Jamie said as they approached the sign that announced *FRENCH QUARTER GHOST TOURS*. "I signed us up for Carys' ghost tour! I know she's a friend of yours, so I thought—"

The expression on Edgar's face brought Jamie up short. He looked like he'd retreated to the dimension he'd been in when Jamie first saw him at the Never Lounge.

Their stomach fell. Edgar clearly thought it was stupid, and no wonder, since they were locals and this was mostly a silly tourist thing. Or maybe Edgar was one of those people who considered horror lowbrow, like their parents.

Disappointment and humiliation warred.

"We don't have to do this," they backtracked. "I thought it'd be fun, but…"

Edgar was chewing on his bottom lip so hard Jamie worried for it, but he didn't answer.

"Edgar?"

"No, yeah," Edgar said, voice rough. "It's okay. Yeah, it'll be fun. I just wasn't…expecting it."

He was clearly lying, but Jamie didn't know why. What they did know was that they hated lying. You couldn't trust a liar, even if they were lying for your benefit. Jamie had learned that the hard way.

"Are you sure? Because it seems like you're not into it. Which is okay, but please tell me."

"No, it's cool. Really. Thank you. For planning our date."

Jamie wasn't entirely convinced, but when they asked one more time if he was okay and Edgar promised that he was, Jamie took him at his word. Edgar bumped Jamie's shoulder with his own. It was a charming, jejune gesture that made Jamie think of childhood best friends, siblings, and maybe also partners who'd been together a long time and could communicate complex thoughts through a single gesture. It filled them with warmth.

"Okay," they said, allowing their excitement to trickle back in. "Have you ever done one of these before?"

"No, never."

"I've gone on a bunch of them, as research for haunts. The tour guide makes all the difference. That's why I picked Carys, really, in addition to the fact that we both know her. Did you know the tour guides do their own research into the supernatural history of the city?"

Edgar shook his head. He watched Jamie intently.

"The first one I ever went on was a vampire tour, when I was nine or ten. My parents and my sister weren't interested, but I begged them to take me. I was hooked. My family had to tell me to shut up about vampires five times a day for the next six months."

"The birth of a haunter, huh?" Edgar said.

"Yep. My parents are probably still cursing the day."

"They're not into it?" Edgar asked.

Jamie's expression no doubt said there was a lot to discuss, but they only managed briefly, "Supremely not into it."

Before they could say more, Carys came outside to gather everyone for the tour.

"Hey," she said to Jamie and Edgar. "Thought I saw a couple familiar names on the roster. It's so good to see you guys."

"I've heard you're the best," Jamie said, and Edgar gave a wave.

"Oh yeah? Did my very objective girlfriend tell you that?" Carys asked.

Jamie waggled their eyebrows in confirmation. She turned to Edgar. "Can't believe I'm seeing you twice in one week, Edgar. It's nice."

"Thanks, you too," Edgar said, ducking his head.

"All right, everyone, gather around," Carys announced, raising her voice to include the rest of the group milling around the meet-up spot. "Let me orient you briefly, and then we will set off into the dark and thrilling world of the haunted French Quarter."

Just the phrase *dark and thrilling* was enough to get Jamie excited. But Carys was a great speaker, and she held the tour group in her thrall. She managed to make everything she was saying sound like a secret she imparted to them and them alone, and she wielded her black lace parasol like it was an extension of her arm. Jamie would happily have followed her around all night, hearing creepy stories in her smooth voice.

Edgar, to the contrary, did not seem to be having fun at all. In fact, Jamie got the feeling he was actively trying not to listen to the stories on the tour.

He looked the opposite direction of everywhere Carys pointed, his gaze darting around, eyes following each passerby as if he were searching for someone he would only vaguely recognize. At one point, he looked so pointedly away from the tour that he tripped over a Cthulhic tangle of beads, hair extensions, and a discarded shoe on the corner of Bourbon and Ursulines. Jamie caught his elbow and steadied him. Edgar gave an apologetic smile, but his eyes were manic.

"Dude. Are you okay?"

"Uh-huh." Edgar gave Jamie's shoulder a squeeze. "Sorry. I'm a klutz."

Jamie had seen no indication of that up until now, but they supposed Edgar would know. "Okay, well. Just…don't die on Bourbon Street. It's undignified."

Edgar nodded in agreement, and Jamie succumbed once more to Carys' melodic voice as she told them about the ghost of a young girl in a long white dress holding a gray cat that people had reported seeing since the 1880s.

But ten minutes later, Edgar grabbed Jamie's arm. For a moment, Jamie thought their plan of holding hands during the scary parts was coming to fruition. But when they turned to Edgar, his face was stark with a terror far greater than Carys' tale warranted, no matter how well told.

"What's wrong?" Jamie asked, resting their hand on Edgar's where it clutched their arm.

Edgar blinked fast, schooling the fear from his face. His eyes came into focus, and he dropped Jamie's arm.

"I'm good," he croaked, then cleared his throat. "Sorry about that."

Jamie frowned. Edgar had looked sincerely terrified. Earlier, when Jamie had mentioned being a haunter, Edgar had gone tense. Jamie had put his response down to nerves, but what if Edgar was genuinely frightened? Some people simply weren't cut out for horror, no matter how tame. Jamie just wished he'd be honest about it.

"Hey. I shouldn't have booked this without asking you. If it's too scary, just tell me. We'll take off. Go get a drink or something."

"No, no," Edgar said quickly. "You're fine. It's... I just... Ha ha. Yeah. I guess I got...startled?"

Jamie narrowed their eyes. Edgar was clearly lying, and Jamie loathed lying. But he was lying so *badly*. Incompetently, really. Was that better or worse? Was it some macho thing about not admitting he was scared? That certainly wasn't attractive.

"If you say so," Jamie said.

For the next few blocks though, Edgar seemed fine. They stopped in front of the old Ursuline Convent, and Carys said, "Let me tell you the tale of the filles à la cassette, young girls who arrived from Europe in the eighteenth century and whom locals believed to be vampires."

Edgar inched back against the wall they stood near. It looked like he was trying to press himself through it. Just as Carys was getting to the good part—Jamie knew this story well—Edgar jerked away and clutched at the plaster behind him, eyes wild.

Something was very wrong.

"Edgar." Jamie moved in front of him, not wanting to startle him.

"I'm okay. Sorry, ha ha."

But Jamie wasn't going to accept Edgar's dismissals anymore. "No. You're obviously not. Come here."

They took Edgar's hand and tugged him around the corner and away from the tour. Edgar slid down the wall into a crouch. Jamie knelt in front of him.

"What's wrong?" they asked as gently as they could.

Edgar shook his head. "Nothing. Sorry."

"Listen," Jamie said. "I'm really worried about you. I get that we don't know each other that well so you might not wanna tell me what's up with you. And that's okay. But please don't lie to me. I don't—lying is not okay with me. It makes me feel like I can't trust you, and if I can't trust you, I don't want to be around you. I don't mean to be harsh, but it's nonnegotiable."

"I get it. I, um. Something is wrong. With me. But, uh. I don't want to talk about it."

Relief that Edgar wasn't going to keep lying swept through Jamie. Sure, they wished Edgar would trust them enough to tell them what was wrong. But honesty was a start.

"Okay," Jamie said. "Thank you."

Edgar nodded miserably. "I guess we should find the tour?"

"No way. This is clearly not enjoyable for you, and a date is supposed to, like, not be horrible."

"I wouldn't know," Edgar said with a ghost of a smile.

When Edgar said that he hadn't dated in a while, Jamie's first thought had been, *How is that possible?* Now though, they had more than an inkling of how it was possible. Something more than first date nerves was definitely going on with Edgar.

"Come on. Let's get out of here."

Edgar frowned. "What about Carys? We can't just leave."

"I'll text her. She'll understand."

Edgar bit his lip.

"I won't tell her you were scared, if that's what you're worried about."

Edgar frowned but acquiesced.

Jamie stood and held out a hand. Edgar took it and let Jamie haul him up. His palms were slick with sweat.

Jamie put a hand on Edgar's back and walked them toward a bar with a quiet back patio that tourists didn't know about.

"Is this okay?" they asked Edgar when they got there.

He nodded as he trailed in after them, looking diminished.

"Here, you sit and save the table, and I'll get us drinks. What would you like?"

"A ginger ale, please."

Jamie squeezed his shoulder. "You're okay if I leave for a minute?"

"Yeah." Then he added, "I promise."

Jamie made their way to the bar and ordered drinks. They texted Carys, apologizing for ducking out early and assuring her it had nothing to do with her excellent tour-guiding.

**Obviously**, she replied with a winky emoji.

Then they had nothing to do except ponder what the hell was up with Edgar. Was he on drugs? His behavior was erratic and confusing enough. In witness protection and constantly on the lookout for his old life coming after him? Surely, witness protection would pick a more common name than Edgar Lovejoy, wouldn't they? Perhaps it was garden-variety mental health stuff, and Edgar was simply having a rough day. Or week or month.

But most likely was that the obvious solution was the right one: Edgar wasn't really that into Jamie romantically, and he didn't want to hurt Jamie's feelings.

It had happened before. Cute, sweet, cis gay guys who thought Jamie was hot but turned out not to want a relationship with a nonbinary person. It stung, but not as much as it would after two or three dates.

The bartender slid a ginger ale and Moscow mule across the bar top and only charged them for the cocktail. Jamie thanked her, tipped for both drinks, and made their way back to Edgar.

It was a warm night, and the cold drinks felt good in their hands.

Edgar had chosen a table in the farthest corner, next to a small fountain and half-hidden by huge potted ferns. Careful not to startle him, Jamie approached by skirting the edge of the patio. They needn't have bothered though, because Edgar had his chair pushed so tight against the fountain that nothing could sneak up on him except a shower.

They handed him the ginger ale and sat down.

"Thanks."

"No problem."

They sat quietly for a minute, sipping their drinks.

Jamie said, "So. This thing that you don't wanna talk about."

Edgar tensed.

"Are you physically safe? Like, do you need medical assistance or anything?"

Edgar shook his head, looking mortified. He was quiet so long that Jamie thought he wasn't going to respond. They decided they had about five minutes, or the time it'd take to drink one drink, before they needed to bounce and nurse their disappointment.

But then Edgar said, "I'm not trying to be mysterious. It's just…I can't really explain."

"Well, you are," Jamie said. They were hit with a wave of exhaustion as disappointment replaced excitement. "Listen, Edgar, I've really enjoyed spending time with you tonight. But if you're not interested, *please* tell me. It's… I get that it can be awkward to let someone down, but it's so much kinder, honestly, than—"

Edgar grabbed Jamie's hand in both of his. His fingertips were cold from the icy glass, and a shiver ran through Jamie despite the heat.

"I'm interested," Edgar said quickly. "I had a really good time. Before the…anyway. But I don't know if…I'm just not sure I'm any good for you."

Jamie sighed. That was such a classic cop-out.

"What about you do you think would be bad for me?" they asked.

Edgar blinked. "I…can't tell you?"

Jamie got up. "Okay, I get it." They didn't know *what* they got precisely, but they knew this move. This was the I-don't-want-to-be-the-bad-guy-so-I'm-going-to-make-you-do-it move.

The scrape of a chair, and then Edgar's hand closed on their elbow.

"Wait, please," he said, eyes darting around anxiously.

"Dude. This is officially not feeling good to me. You get, like, one more sentence, and then I'm gonna go."

The part of Jamie that was crushing on Edgar hoped that he

would find the one perfect sentence that would convince them to stay.

And for a moment, Edgar looked like he was going to oblige. He opened his mouth, his eyes wide and panicked, as if he too were searching for that one perfect sentence. Jamie waited, their heart poised on the precipice, ready to be scooped into Edgar's arms or tumble over into the free fall of disappointment.

"I'm sorry," Edgar whispered.

# 9

## Edgar

Edgar's best friend died when he was twelve, and it was all Edgar's fault.

No one would admit it. Quite the contrary, in fact. They all insisted it was a terrible, tragic accident. They said it when the paramedics came and at the hospital, when Edgar wouldn't let go of Antoine's hand. They said it at his funeral and the wake that followed. All these brokenhearted adults, unable to see the truth.

But Edgar knew. He knew it was his fault the same way he knew that he was in love with Antoine—a bone-deep feeling that no adult logic could shake.

Antoine and his older sister, Cameron, had always been there, two doors down. Cameron was Allie's age, Antoine was his, and Poe toddled around after them, generally happy to be included, even when they ordered him around. The five of them had been inseparable.

Somewhere along the way, Edgar realized he felt differently about Antoine than Allie seemed to feel about Cameron. He loved the way Antoine's clever hands turned dandelions to flower crowns as they sat sprawled lazily in the summer grass, reading comic books and planning their own. The way his warm brown skin drank in the sun and his thick lashes fluttered as he drifted off to sleep. That he moved worms off the sidewalk after it rained to keep them from being stepped on.

How he never—not one time—made Edgar feel like a freak.

Antoine and Cameron had understood that the Lovejoys would always rather hang out at their house than at their own. They'd been privy to enough fights between Edgar's parents to understand why. Analytical Cameron had applied her belief in scientific principles to the matter, but Antoine accepted ghosts the way he did a retconned plot in a comic book—it was just the new normal, and he didn't want to waste any time dwelling on what used to be.

Walking to school a week after Antoine's death, Edgar had seen his friend leaning against the bodega where they had always met up for the rest of the walk. A lightning bolt of relief struck him first, and then a hot rush of longing to throw his arms around Antoine's skinny shoulders and smell the scent of fabric softener that always clung to his clothes, the warm scent of shea butter on his skin, and the bright hint of apple always on his breath.

Then he'd seen Antoine's face. A blank, dead face with no trace of the sweet, smart, funny boy who'd been Edgar's everything. That was when the choking cold had come.

And it had never really left, just twisted into a shiver that lived in his shoulders. Made him hunch them to his ears. One more layer between Edgar and the world.

He hadn't told his siblings about seeing Antoine because every time someone said Antoine's name, Allie and Poe looked at Edgar with such naked pity that it made him want to cry. He didn't tell Cameron for obvious reasons. The waterlogged horror haunted his dreams for months, until he had trouble recalling what living Antoine had looked like. And when the other ghosts came, there was a shade of Antoine in every one.

# 10

# Jamie

Every Saturday morning since Jamie had moved into Carl and Germaine's guesthouse, they had enjoyed coffee, fruit, croissants, and gossip with the couple. Jamie loved to sit on their back porch, shaded with banana leaves. They'd breathe in the scent of flowers and sip the strong chicory coffee that Germaine brewed with cinnamon, molasses, and a pinch of salt and lightened with cream, the way his mother had made it and her mother before her. With croissant flakes on their fingers and the taste of butter on their lips, the three of them (and whichever friends of Germaine and Carl's had stopped by) would talk until the heat of the day drove them inside.

This morning, when Jamie opened the screen door to the porch, Carl and Germaine were already sipping coffee with their friend Muriel. Jamie loved Muriel, though they found her a touch intimidating. She was elegant and beautiful, with a long fall of salt-and-pepper hair, which she caught up with ornate pins or braided over her shoulder in a complicated plait. Today, it was piled on her head in knots and secured with what looked like silver spoons. Knowing Muriel, they might be actual silver. Once Jamie had admired a pocket watch she wore, and she'd given it to them on the spot, saying she'd love for them to wear it. The next day, Carl had told them it had belonged to Muriel's grandfather and was probably worth a mint.

"Dear Jamie!" Carl greeted them enthusiastically. One of the things Jamie loved most about Carl was how genuinely excited he was at all times to see someone he liked.

Indeed, moving in with Germaine and Carl had been the best thing that had happened to Jamie in the last year. Jamie was fairly sure their own parents loved each other, but it was in a language Jamie didn't speak—a language of obligation, appearances, and dismissal of anything that didn't conform to their desires. It wasn't dissimilar from the way they loved their children.

Germaine and Carl, however, loved one another the way Jamie wanted to love and be loved. Theirs was a love of delight, curiosity, and mutual growth, and watching it gave Jamie hope that someday they might live with a partner who saw them clearly, adored them, challenged them, and gave them grace when they failed to live up to those challenges.

It was from Germaine and Carl that Jamie had learned something else too: that without honesty in a relationship, you had nothing.

"Late night, huh, kiddo?" Germaine asked, raising an eyebrow and pouring them a coffee.

Jamie kissed Carl's cheek, took the cup and saucer from Germaine, and kissed his cheek, then sat next to Muriel on the wicker love seat.

"Hello, darling. Lovely to see you," she said and kissed both their cheeks.

"You too, Muriel. It's been a while."

She sighed. "Yes, I've been unusually busy the last few months. And you know how I like to be nocturnal in the summertime," she lamented, the latter directed at Carl and Germaine. Jamie could certainly see why though. Summer in New Orleans was brutal, and some days melted even the hardiest.

Muriel regaled them with her work on a new initiative to bring gardens to schools in the city and the work that her friend Greta was doing to facilitate it.

"Carys' partner? I actually saw Carys last night."

Germaine's deep brown gaze focused on Jamie. "I thought you had a date last night?"

"I did," Jamie said.

"And?" Germaine demanded. He was patient about everything except gossip.

Jamie groaned and slid down in their seat.

"Do tell, darling," Muriel encouraged, passing them the plate of pastries.

Jamie took a bite of rich, buttery croissant and a sip of milky chicory coffee and settled in to tell them all about the mysterious, sweet, borderline disaster that had been their evening with Edgar Lovejoy.

✦ ✦ ✦

Jamie crawled back into bed with a third cup of coffee after Muriel took her leave. They cranked the window air conditioner as high as it would go and settled in for an afternoon of sulking and horror movies.

Muriel, Germaine, and Carl had listened intently to Jamie's description of the date and had agreed that something was definitely up with Edgar. But when Muriel left, she had lingered over her goodbye to Jamie, saying with uncharacteristic gentleness, "I hope you give him another chance."

When Jamie asked her to elaborate, she wouldn't, simply kissing them on the cheek with a vague eyebrow raise and an even vaguer, "You just never know, do you?"

Jamie, generally of the opinion that they did know, had said nothing. But now, watching as a brother and sister duo were shish-kebabbed by a cursed sword and trapped in a demon dimension, they found their thoughts drifting back to Edgar.

There had been moments—only a few, but they'd been there—when Edgar was truly present and had been sweet, generous, and interested. Moments when his eyes had gone soft at something Jamie said or did. Moments that had made Jamie imagine second dates, walks by the river, kisses, and curling up together after a hard day. And it had been those moments that made it so hard to walk away from Edgar at the end of the night. Jamie had learned from experience that if someone couldn't make it through a first date without setting off their alarm bells, then it was best to leave it be.

But Muriel's words drifted through Jamie's mind as they snuggled deeper into bed. Lulled asleep midmovie by the daily afternoon downpour, Jamie awoke a few hours later to the following texts:

**Edgar**: Hi, Jamie, it's Edgar. You probably don't want to hear from me, but I want to apologize for being so weird yesterday. And for not telling you why. It's just pretty personal and not something I talk about. Usually.
**Edgar**: Anyway, sorry for being a crap date.

Twenty minutes later, he'd sent another text.

**Edgar**: Is there any chance you'd give me another shot? Maybe you could come over and we could watch a movie?

Ten minutes after that, another.

**Edgar**: But not a scary movie, please 😊

As Jamie read through the messages, they started to smile, and by the time they got to that one, they were grinning. Edgar was just so damn *sweet*.

A final text came through as they held their phone.

**Edgar**: Okay, I'll leave you alone now. Thanks for considering 😊

Edgar had acknowledged his alarming behavior, said it was personal, and apologized. Everyone had struggles and things they didn't like to share. Jamie could respect that, as long as Edgar didn't keep his secret forever.

A moment from their date came back to Jamie then. Edgar's explanation for why he'd ordered desserts even though he didn't plan to eat them. *I wanted you to have what you wanted*, he'd said. That didn't sound like someone inconsiderate.

Jamie had cultivated a habit of truthfulness because so many people in their life had wanted them to lie. It was a slippery slope, and Jamie didn't intend to be one of the people who ended up at the bottom of it, trying to climb their way back from a lifetime of self-erasure. But Edgar wasn't Jamie, and he deserved time to feel safe enough to open up.

Jamie texted, I know just the G-rated movie.

Edgar's response was immediate: Thank you for giving me another chance. That sounds really great.

Jamie's cheeks ached, and they realized they were grinning at their phone again.

They were pretty sure that meant they'd made the right decision.

✦ ✦ ✦

The House of Screams crew worked in a large warehouse near the tangle of the Pontchartrain Expressway and the river, building set pieces that they'd take to the site of the haunt once the space was available. It was incredibly humid and stuffy inside and always smelled like sawdust kicked off a table saw, hot from the blade. On a sunny day like today, the warehouse baked you no matter what you did, making the entire crew grouchy and irritable.

This Friday, the day of Jamie's second date with Edgar, in addition to being hot and stuffy and grouchy, it was one of those days that seemed to have been cursed from beginning to end. Tools broke, a delivery of lumber got stuck under a bridge because the truck was too tall, and the trusty coffee machine that lived on the paint cabinet finally perished.

Marty, their fearful leader, was in rare dudgeon thanks to the setbacks—particularly the coffee machine, toward which he'd demonstrated more tenderness than toward his children. And when Marty wasn't happy, nobody was happy.

He caught Jamie as they came back from lunch. "I need you to go pick up the chandelier for the drawing room in Pearl River tonight," he said.

"Uh. Tonight? Could they deliver it?"

"No. A buddy's doing me a favor."

"Dude, ordinarily I would, but I have plans tonight. Since it's your buddy, maybe you could pick it up?" they asked hopefully.

"No can do." He gave no further explanation.

"Marty, seriously. I have a date. Can someone else do it?"

Marty's eyebrows were bushy, aggressive things, and now they drew together in a V Jamie recognized. This was not going to go well for them.

"If you're only interested in working during certain hours, I know lots of guys who would be thrilled to have your job."

There was no arguing with that. "Yeah, okay, no problem," Jamie said.

"I'll text you the info," Marty said. "Don't let me down."

"*Fuck!*" Jamie said after Marty had walked away.

*See, Mom, this is why I can't just get some time off for the wedding.* Their mother had texted multiple times in the last few days to remind Jamie of their responsibilities.

Jamie grabbed their phone and texted Edgar before they got back to work.

**Jamie**: I'm really excited to see you tonight, but my boss sprung a last-minute job on me. Is there any chance I can compel you to come on a random road trip with me instead of watching a movie? I'll bring snacks!

Jamie would just have time to shower off the filth and make groceries before it would be time to go to Edgar's. If Edgar was willing, that was. He took long enough to respond that Jamie worried he'd back out—and they couldn't blame him. Going on an errand wasn't most people's idea of a good date. But finally, just as Jamie was finishing for the day, he replied.

**Edgar**: If you'll be there, then I'd love to go.

Jamie's heart fluttered.

✦ ✦ ✦

"We're picking up a haunted chandelier?" Edgar asked when Jamie explained, sounding horrified.

"No, no. Not haunted," Jamie assured him. "A chandelier *for* the haunt. My boss needs it to be picked up now, apparently. Asshole," they muttered.

"Oh. Okay."

"Sorry to change our plans," Jamie added, feeling a bit flustered now that they were face-to-face.

"It's okay. Thanks. For giving this another shot. I—just thanks."

"You're welcome." Jamie opened the passenger door for Edgar. He smelled wonderful, like tea and plants and something darker. "Hi," Jamie said for the second time.

"Hey," Edgar rumbled, and Jamie felt the softest touch to their hair.

Jamie forced themself to leave the touch and get in the truck. They pointed it toward the I-10, and then they were on the road.

Jamie loved to drive. They felt powerful and free behind the wheel, and now that they were on the road with Edgar, picnic in a bag between them, they found they didn't mind the trip.

"Thanks for doing this with me," they said.

"You're welcome," Edgar said. "I thought…"

"What?"

"When you texted before. When I saw your name, I thought…I thought you were probably cancelling." He sounded resigned.

"Nope," Jamie reassured him. "I'm excited to try again."

*Please, please don't make me regret it*, Jamie added in their head.

"Me too," Edgar said softly. "I just thought maybe…you know…"

"Yeah. People ghost," they said.

Edgar coughed and fiddled with the air vent. Jamie spent the first few minutes with one eye on the road and the other observing Edgar, watching for sudden movements, expressions of terror, or any of the other behaviors that had appeared on their date the week before, but when none were forthcoming, Jamie relaxed and let their gaze settle comfortably on the road. Edgar seemed a bit tense, yes, but Edgar always seemed a bit tense.

Once they got out of the city, there were few cars on the road, and the swamp grasses that crept toward the highway rippled in the breeze. A large bird soared overhead.

"Broad-winged hawk," Edgar murmured, pointing at it.

"Are you into birding?" Jamie asked. That was pretty adorable.

"I love birds," Edgar said. "All animals, really. I wonder if her nest is around here."

"Well, I'm glad this doesn't totally suck for you," Jamie said, relieved.

"It's perfect. If I could drive, I'd come out into nature all the time."

"You can't drive? City boy," Jamie teased.

"I can, technically, but I don't. What about you?" Edgar asked. "Did you grow up in New Orleans?"

"No, Metairie. We came into the city a lot, but it was a really different vibe. My sister and I always used to talk about running away and living in New Orleans when we were younger though."

They'd sit on Emma's bedroom rug, heads swimming with all the exciting things they'd seen and done that day. They'd plan what colors they were going to paint the intricate details of their wooden Marigny houses. Emma had been in a purple phase and always chose lavender, but Jamie had dreamed up something different every time.

"Yeah? You and your sister close?" Edgar asked.

"No. Not anymore."

The admission sent a pang of loss through Jamie. The pain had been sharp once, but it had dulled over time.

"How come?"

Jamie sighed. Ever since Emma had announced her engagement, the wedding had been a constant presence in Jamie's life. At first, they'd thought it might be fun to pick out expensive shit that someone else was paying for with Emma, but it quickly became clear that this was not going to be a sibling-bonding opportunity. To the contrary, the family text thread had been activated, and Jamie was getting two or three texts a day that seemed to presume their familiarity with things like the distinction between nylon and silk organza but never asked how their day was going.

Jamie even tried responding off thread to Emma a couple of times: to connect over something their parents had said that was just *so* their parents or to tell her that they'd driven past the art museum and caught a glimpse of the gardens and thought of her. But those texts had received nothing but likes, so Jamie had stopped and gone back to watching the texts about flowers keep rolling in.

"She's on track to be exactly what my parents wanted us to be. She's going to graduate law school, clerk for a judge, and become a politician like my mother. Which is great, if that's what she actually wants to do. But it's hard to tell. My folks…there are things that are acceptable to them and things that aren't. Emma's choices are acceptable."

"Let me guess," Edgar said. "They think your choices aren't?"

"Yup. They'd never come out and say it—far too Southern, of course. But let's just say that when I dropped out of college, my mother cried, and my father said I had ruined my life." They snorted. "As you might imagine, building haunted houses wasn't on my parents' list of acceptable professions for their child to have."

"But you love it, right?" Edgar asked.

"I really do. I guess I just wish they could be happy for me. That they could see it's a real art. Not that they've ever come to any of the haunts I've worked on."

They said it lightly, but it stung. Jamie knew that if they had been an architect or a speechwriter, an astronaut or a neurosurgeon, their parents would have attended every opening, promotion, and blastoff. They would have bragged casually about them to people who didn't care because they were so brimming over with pride that it spilled into every conversation. They would have asked a hundred annoying questions because they wanted to be able to picture precisely how their Jamie had the world by the throat.

Jamie swallowed hard. A lizard skittered across the highway. Warm fingers closed around Jamie's where they rested on the gearshift. The gesture offered sympathy and comfort, but the touch of Edgar's skin made Jamie break out in goose bumps. They were very glad they had decided to give this another try.

✦ ✦ ✦

Jamie parked the truck on the gravel turnoff outside the address Marty had texted them. It was a post-Katrina-built cottage perched on pilings covered in flaking white paint.

The man who answered the doorbell was white, with deeply tanned skin and flyaway blond hair. "You Jamie?" he said to Edgar in a Cajun accent.

Edgar pointed at Jamie, while Jamie replied, "That's me."

"Marty say you don't need wiring?"

"No, it's not going to be lit, just used for atmosphere," Jamie explained.

"I get it for ya."

He left the door open but didn't invite them inside. Jamie shrugged at Edgar.

Edgar surprised him by whispering, "I dare you to go into this guy's house, hide in his shower, and jump out at him next time he goes in the bathroom."

Jamie snorted. "I think if I did that, then you'd find my body in the nearest bayou wrapped in a shower curtain. So with great regret, I must forfeit the dare."

Edgar's eyebrows waggled in an exaggerated gesture of victory.

The man was back in a few minutes with an armful of dusty white fabric. He peeled back the corner to reveal a twist of aged brass, then thrust the whole bundle into Jamie's arms. "Me, I'd take off. Storm's coming."

He closed the door before Jamie could say thank you.

"Well, that was ominous," Jamie said.

Edgar pointed at the sky. "I think he meant it literally."

As they got in the truck, the first drops of rain smacked the roof.

Five minutes later, it was pouring.

# 11

# Edgar

Summer in New Orleans came with two hours of pouring rain every afternoon, but this was no predictable afternoon shower. It was a storm with thunder, lightning, and driving rain that menaced them off the road after ten minutes.

Edgar's palms prickled with sweat. Rain hit the truck, and thunder cracked, cacophonous.

"Gonna be another three or four hours, looks like," Jamie said, tapping at their phone. "There's a motel seven miles from here. We could try and get there, wait it out? I realize it's rather forward for a second date," they added jokingly, clearly trying to lighten the mood.

Edgar breathed in through his nose and out through his mouth, searching for an island of calm in the storm of panic.

Ever since he'd texted Jamie to ask for another date, Edgar had been debating with himself about what would happen if Jamie found out his secret.

*They'll think I'm a freak and in need of psychiatric intervention. And then they won't want to be with me.*

*Allie told her ex-boyfriend, and he didn't try to have her committed,* he disagreed with himself. Of course, he hadn't tried in any other way either, so maybe not the best example.

*If they don't think I'm crazy, then they won't believe me.*

*They make haunted houses for a living,* he'd argued with himself. *They might believe you.*

*Fine, even if they do believe me, they'll eventually get tired of the fact that I can't go anywhere. That I don't have any friends except my sister because I have this huge secret. That I'm a fucking basket case. And then they won't want to be with me. So same outcome either way.*

"Motel's good," Edgar croaked.

Jamie's eyes were on him instantly.

"What's wrong? Are you—what's it called? Storm-phobic?"

*Astraphobic,* his brain supplied, but he didn't risk verbalizing it. Edgar managed a nod, and Jamie's hand landed on his shoulder, a warm comfort.

"Okay, I've got you," Jamie said.

Edgar ached for it to be true.

Though the motel was only seven miles away, it took them nearly half an hour to get there. Mercifully, navigating the road required all of Jamie's attention, leaving Edgar to white-knuckle it with his eyes squeezed shut so tightly that he gave himself a headache.

By the time Jamie swung the truck into the motel's parking lot, the rain was coming down so hard the name of it was illegible.

"Wait here, and I'll be right back," they said and ducked outside.

It was agony alone. Edgar wanted his eyes closed so he couldn't see anything in the lightning. The electricity got ghost ions all hopped up or something, he'd concluded over the years, so when lightning struck, ghosts seemed more corporeal, more terrifying. But he wanted his eyes open in case anything appeared close to the car. As a compromise, he kept them squinted, which made his headache even worse.

Jamie was back five minutes later, soaked, brandishing a key on a blue plastic fob like a prize. "Best room in the house," they announced and pulled the truck around to the back of the motel. "Grab the picnic, would you?"

Edgar did, and by the time he got out of the truck, Jamie had the door to their room open. Edgar was only outside for a few seconds and still got soaked. Jamie ran back outside.

"What are you—" Thunder crashed, and Edgar winced. He pressed his back to the wall, every muscle tense, and scanned the unfamiliar room. Lots of brown, but no ghosts. A flash of lightning made him wince.

The door slammed open, and Jamie returned a minute later carrying the sodden bundle of the chandelier.

"If I don't have this come Monday morning, Marty will fire me. I'm not taking any chances," they explained, locking the door behind them.

The struggle to keep breathing at a nonhyperventilatory pace required all of Edgar's energy.

Jamie frowned and placed the chandelier on the floor, then crossed to Edgar.

"Hey," they said gently, so gently. "It's going to be okay. I've got you. I won't let anything happen to you."

The deepest, most hidden part of Edgar thrilled at this promise. Even though it was made in ignorance, it was what he wanted. To be taken care of. Protected. In all his debate with himself over the past week, that was the card he never played because it was too much to wish for. Too scary to hope for. And far too much to ever ask. What would it feel like if he told Jamie the truth and they could actually help him?

Edgar didn't have any idea what that might look like, but he thought it might start off feeling very much like Jamie's warm hand on his arm, Jamie's calm voice in his ear.

"I can see you're really scared," Jamie continued, and Edgar realized he'd closed his eyes against another flash of lightning. "Maybe panic-attack scared? Just concentrate on breathing, okay? I'm right here, and I'm not going anywhere. Do you want to sit down? Want a shower? Want me to distract you? Or maybe just shut up?"

It was this last that made Edgar open his eyes. He didn't want Jamie to ever shut up. He wanted Jamie to keep talking to him all night long.

Lightning flashed outside, and Edgar caught a glimpse of something in the storm that shouldn't've been there.

Edgar flinched away from the window and crouched on the floor. Jamie looked scared.

*Fuck, no, please not now!*

This date was Jamie giving him a second chance. If he fucked this up, he knew Jamie wouldn't give him a third. Jamie, who cared about the truth and being themself and wanted him to do the same.

He knew if he put Jamie off again with an excuse, it would have to be good enough that they believed him. But fear had wiped his mind of anything useful. He risked a glance at the window. If it had been a ghost he'd seen, it was either gone or about to ooze through the wall at any moment.

Jamie turned and looked where Edgar was looking. They turned back to him, looking confused and worried. Edgar couldn't stand to see them worried, couldn't stand to see the trust they'd given him fade away. *Fuck!*

"Edgar?" Jamie said softly. "What's going on? Do you need me to get help? Call someone for you?"

Edgar shook his head, trying to make his voice work. He had never thought he'd tell anyone the truth, not after the way his father had behaved. But he hadn't reckoned with meeting someone he liked as much as Jamie either. Someone he wanted to *know* him. Someone he wanted to spend time with. And spending time meant seeing him see ghosts. There was no way to hide it from Jamie, he was realizing. No way to hide it and still get to be with them.

*Fuck, fuck, fuck! Am I really going to do this?*

Edgar swallowed hard, reached out, and caught Jamie's hand.

*Thank you*, he wanted to say. *Thank you for being wonderful and for caring. Please don't leave when I tell you the truth. Please don't give me that look—the one that means,* Oh, dear, he's insane. *And he looked so normal.*

"I, um."

Jamie looked instantly relieved that Edgar had formed words.

"I need to tell you something about me. Um."

His tongue went thick in his mouth, and his throat was dry. But he focused on Jamie's freckles and their kind blue eyes, lashes spiked with rain.

"I see ghosts."

All these years of shoving it down, swallowing it, and chewing on it had worried it smooth, and it slid right out of Edgar's mouth like a stone.

A rush of adrenaline roared in his ears, leaving him dizzy.

"Sorry," Jamie said. "Can you repeat yourself? I think I heard you wrong."

"You didn't." Edgar swallowed a woozy giggle.

Jamie nodded slowly. "Just to double-check, I heard you say that you see ghosts?"

"Correct," Edgar said.

"Huh," Jamie said simply. Then their face lit up. "Ghosts are real? Wow, sorry, not the time. So you… Wow."

Jamie's mind seemed to be going a mile a minute, but they hadn't yet said that they thought Edgar was crazy. Or a liar. So that was good.

"You…you believe me?" Edgar had to ask.

"Are you telling the truth?"

"Well. Yeah."

"Then I believe you."

And that, apparently, was that.

They stood staring at each other in the aftermath of his confession. Edgar didn't know what he'd expected to happen the first time he told someone. A musical swell or explosion of fireworks? That he'd suddenly transform into a different person?

But he was still just him, dripping rain onto brown motel carpet with absolutely no idea what to do.

"I don't know what to do now," he admitted and winced.

Jamie took charge, steering Edgar into the bathroom and turning on the shower.

"I'm going to get some food set up while you take a shower.

Get warmed up, get out of these wet clothes. Then you can have something to eat. You'll feel better," they said with the absolute certainty of someone who didn't see ghosts.

But as he stood in the shower letting the hot water stream over his cold skin, Edgar did feel better.

*I am no longer a person with a secret,* he thought as he lathered his hair.

*There isn't a huge, uncrossable gulf between me and every single other human on earth except my family,* he thought as he rinsed it.

*Someone knows the thing about me that I wake up in the middle of the night and clutch to me like a hobgoblin,* he thought as he dried off and wrapped the towel around his waist.

The partly fogged mirror created the illusion that half of his face was gone. Did the part he could see look different though? Younger? Unburdened? In all the self-debate, he'd never actually thought about how it would *feel* to tell someone.

He remembered what Jamie had said they felt like performing burlesque. *Like a god.*

Maybe this was how they felt.

✦ ✦ ✦

Edgar made his way out of the bathroom to find Jamie putting the finishing touches on a truly impressive spread of food.

"Shower's free," he said, suddenly feeling awkward and exposed with only the rough towel slung around his hips. Probably this was no big deal to Jamie, who did burlesque and dated regularly, but he had to fight the impulse to cover himself with his hands.

When Jamie looked up, their mouth fell open at the sight of him.

Flustered, Edgar apologized for his state of undress, explaining that there were no robes.

"Fuck," Jamie said, still staring. "You're really fucking beautiful, Edgar."

Edgar flushed. He knew that working the delivery job over the last year had strengthened his muscles. He'd noticed his shirts fitting tighter. But Jamie was looking at him with heat, appreciation.

Desire.

An answering heat flushed down his throat and across his chest, and suddenly the absence of anything between them but the scratchy towel felt like a liability.

Flustered now by his body as well as his mind, Edgar felt utterly overwhelmed.

Jamie cupped his cheek. The cool of their palm grounded him. Edgar let his eyes flutter shut, hiding.

"Too much?" Jamie asked quietly.

*God, no*, Edgar groaned internally. *I'm scared of fucking everything up, but you make me feel brave.*

He shook his head. When he managed to open his eyes, Jamie was biting their lip, eyelids heavy. They made a low sound in their throat. Edgar's heart hammered. He wanted Jamie to crush him safe against this wall and do whatever the hell they wanted to him. It was an almost overwhelming urge. Edgar swallowed hard, his dick swelling at the thought.

"Will you be okay out here if I take a quick shower?" Jamie asked, voice thick.

Edgar made himself nod, even though the idea of Jamie leaving him was physically painful. They gave him one last heated look, then walked into the bathroom.

"Oh fuck." Edgar slumped against the wall.

He'd never responded to anyone this way before. His knees were shaking, he was trembling, and his heart was racing. It was a set of sensations that Edgar usually associated with the aftermath of seeing a ghost. If you didn't pay attention to the erection straining the front of Edgar's towel, that is. But he was paying a *lot* of attention to it.

What was happening to him? Did he have an I-just-confessed-to-the-person-I'm-falling-for-that-I-can-see-ghosts kink?

*More like a Jamie Wendon-Dale kink.*

# 12

# Jamie

J amie's mind was reeling. Edgar was intensely hot and saw ghosts.

The ghost part explained a lot: Edgar's haunted hypervigilance, his impulse to guard his secret, his terror at the ghost tour—god, Jamie could kick themself for that one. And honestly, after some of the, er, creative possibilities that Jamie's brain had spat out late at night, this explanation was a relief.

But even though Jamie was desperately curious to hear everything about ghosts, it was the *intensely hot* part that currently occupied them. Edgar was gorgeous, yeah, but it was how he responded to Jamie that made them burn for him. Desire, vulnerability, need.

He'd practically come undone at the touch of Jamie's hand on his cheek. They couldn't wait to see what touching him elsewhere might do.

Turning off the shower, Jamie wrapped a towel gone stiff with bleach around their hips. Even two years after top surgery, twenty years of thinking of their chest as something to hide, twenty years of it being sexualized, made the act of casually going without their shirt feel like breaking the rules. But this was what they'd had to do: practice until the feeling receded. Until they could deny indoctrination by sheer stubborn habit.

Breathing in through their nose and out through their mouth, Jamie took control. After a minute, their posture relaxed, and their shoulders settled. A few more minutes after that, and breathing was once more automatic.

Jamie pretended they were onstage at the Never Lounge, controlling the crowd with confidence and power. Power was a mindset, and Jamie breathed into it with their whole body. Only when they were full up with it did they walk out of the bathroom and back to Edgar.

He was hovering around the food, the old tube television tuned to a nature program.

Outside, the storm still lashed, but inside room 3A, they were comfortable and dry.

"I'm glad I don't have to spend my whole life constantly terrified of predators," Jamie mused as the camera closed in on the terrified liquid eyes of an ibex while a puma burst from the scrubby brush.

Edgar mumbled something noncommittal as he selected a piece of fried chicken, but he wouldn't meet Jamie's eyes.

"Do you feel like that?" they asked him.

Edgar appeared to shrink into himself at the question, all his physical strength and size useless in the face of a noncorporeal threat.

Suddenly Jamie wanted to jump on him, to tip his chin up and look directly into his eyes. They wanted the *real* Edgar. The Edgar that wasn't trying not to scare them away.

Jamie insinuated their knees around Edgar's and leaned in. "Tell me," they said softly but with command. "I want…I really fucking want to know you, Edgar. Tell me?"

"Yes." Edgar was looking at Jamie's palms on his thighs. "I feel like I'm always at the watering hole just waiting for a fucking tiger to appear and rip me to pieces."

He said it in a rush and then squeezed his eyes shut.

Jamie moved slowly but deliberately. They straddled Edgar's knees and wound their arms around his neck. They were the same height like this, and Jamie could feel the shuddering breath that Edgar took. But he didn't push them away. He rested one hand gently at Jamie's lower back, keeping them there. With the other hand, Edgar pinched the bridge of his nose like he had a headache.

"Have the ghosts ever hurt you?" Jamie asked gently. "Are they dangerous?"

When Edgar's eyes fluttered open again, they were the eyes of a child waking from a nightmare. The eyes of a man who didn't believe in hope but wanted so badly to be wrong.

"I don't know," he said.

"But you're scared they will?"

"Jamie," Edgar said in a voice so small, it seemed to come from somewhere deep and choked inside him. "I'm scared of everything. All the time."

Jamie threw their arms around his shoulders and squeezed him tight.

"Being scared sucks so much," they said, stroking Edgar's hair.

With a groan, Edgar's head fell forward and *thunked* against Jamie's sternum. They could feel his warm breath on their chest. Jamie pressed a kiss to the top of Edgar's head. They cradled him in their arms, and it felt so right. Even though their towel was damp and their hair was cold and the room smelled of mildew and cold fried chicken, Edgar's presence rendered those things unimportant.

They tilted Edgar's face up and kissed his forehead, the bridge of his nose, the curve of his cheek. They pressed a gentle fingertip to the teardrop above his upper lip and stroked the thin skin behind his ears. When his eyes fluttered shut, Jamie kissed his eyelids.

"I wanna kiss you so fucking bad," Jamie said, voice rough with desire. "It doesn't have to be anything more than that, but I—"

"Kiss me, please. Fuck, please, just—"

Jamie caught Edgar's mouth in a kiss. At first, it was sweet, but at the tension in Edgar's thighs and his hand at the small of their back pressing them closer together, Jamie's control snapped. They opened their mouth to the velvet swipe of Edgar's tongue. The kiss deepened, and Edgar moaned, the sound ripping through Jamie with a jolt of lust. They cradled Edgar's face and feasted on his mouth until he was writhing beneath them.

Heat pulsed between Jamie's legs, and they wanted to press into Edgar, feel him from the inside. But they forced themself to end the kiss.

They were both breathing heavily, looking into each other's burning eyes.

"Jesus," Edgar murmured, sounding surprised.

Jamie kissed him again. This time, their tongues met and tangled, their lips barely containing the kiss. Jamie moved closer, and their nipples brushed Edgar's chest. They shivered at the delicious sensation, and Edgar's arms tightened around them. Desire burned in Jamie's gut. They threaded fingers through Edgar's hair and pulled gently.

Edgar shuddered and then froze. Jamie did it again. Edgar's nipples hardened, and he shut his eyes.

"Mmmm." Jamie pressed against Edgar, helplessly turned on.

Edgar pulled them closer, and their lips reunited. This time, the kiss was slow as honey and hot with promise.

Jamie trailed kisses across Edgar's jaw and sucked lightly at the skin of his throat. Edgar's hips bucked, and Jamie felt his erection.

"Sorry, I—" Edgar began, but Jamie clapped a hand over his mouth.

"Shut up," they said. "You're fucking exquisite. Don't apologize."

Edgar swallowed, and then he pressed a kiss to Jamie's palm.

It was as if, denied the ability to explain, Edgar let his body speak for him. He slid the hand at Jamie's back slowly down their spine to the swell of their ass. Jamie's breath caught. Even through their towel, they could feel the strength in Edgar's hands, feel how gently he applied it.

Fuck, fuck, fuck, Edgar's responses were driving Jamie wild. They replaced the hand over Edgar's mouth with their mouth, and as they both melted into the kiss, Jamie tightened their hand in Edgar's hair again. This time, they tugged a bit harder and longer. Edgar gasped and shuddered, pulling Jamie to him and burying his face in their neck.

"S-stop. I—"

Jamie gentled their hand and stroked Edgar's hair. "Are you okay?" they asked with a soft kiss to Edgar's cheek.

"Uh-huh. It's been a really…really long time, and I just…" He shivered.

Jamie eased off his lap. For a moment, Edgar looked bereft. Then he saw the hand Jamie held out to him, and his expression eased. He took it, and Jamie led him to the bed.

They were relieved Edgar had called time-out, because they weren't sure they could have.

"Cuddle with me?" they asked.

Edgar hesitated a moment, looking lost, as if he wasn't sure Jamie was serious. They got beneath the covers, wincing as the wet towel bunched beneath them. They pulled it off and dropped it on the floor.

When they patted the bed beside them, a flush burned high on Edgar's cheeks, but his eyes were soft. "Yeah. Okay."

He lay on top of the covers for a moment, then got underneath as well, shedding his own towel.

"C'mere," Jamie said and put out an arm.

Edgar arranged himself so he lay on his side with his head resting on Jamie's shoulder and draped his arm across their stomach. Jamie gathered him in so they could stroke his hair.

"You're…" Edgar began, but he seemed unable to finish the sentence. He trailed off and began tracing patterns on Jamie's skin.

Jamie grabbed a handful of his hair. They didn't pull, just squeezed, and Edgar's eyes fluttered. He squirmed. Finally, he looked at Jamie.

"I'm?" Jamie prompted.

"You're very hot," Edgar said.

"You're very hot too," Jamie said. "We're not gonna go any farther tonight. Just kissing."

Edgar bit his lip. "Thanks."

"You have permission to keep grabbing my ass though," they added with a grin.

In one effortless movement, Edgar switched their positions, pulling Jamie onto his chest so his large hand could cup Jamie's ass.

"Good to know," Edgar said, and Jamie laughed.

"Your enthusiasm is appreciated by my ass."

"Your ass is appreciated by my…uh…enthusiasm?"

"Is that what the kids are calling it these days?"

Edgar kissed Jamie's lips gently, sweetly.

"Hey, can you reach my phone?" he asked.

Jamie contorted themself to snag the phone from the windowsill where Edgar had plugged it in.

"Checking the weather?" they asked. The storm seemed to have quieted a bit. Or maybe they'd just been too distracted by Edgar to notice it.

Edgar shook his head. Jamie traced Edgar's ribs, the planes of muscle smooth between each curve of bone. Edgar balanced his phone on his stomach and tapped the screen, revealing something pixelated and dark.

"What am I looking at?"

"You'll see."

Edgar tapped a settings panel and then something that looked like a switch, and the image onscreen brightened and resolved.

"Oh. My. God. Is that…?"

"Yup."

Edgar settled back, and Jamie snuggled closer. Edgar's phone was showing a streaming video of the interior of the cat café. He'd just turned on a light from his phone, and the cats were clearly visible. Some snoozed, some played, and one ran directly into the wall.

"Oh, Basket, get it together," Edgar mumbled.

"You tap into the security camera and watch the cats? That's the sweetest thing I've ever heard."

"Oh, well. Um. Not exactly. I installed the camera. So I could watch them. And a smart plug so I could turn the lights on to see them better."

Jamie blinked. Was it possible for a heart to explode from sheer adorableness? If so, theirs was currently at risk. "Gah," was all they could manage, and they squeezed Edgar tight.

They watched the cats, and Edgar narrated the video—where this one had been found or how that one liked to spend its time. He knew them all well.

Eventually, Jamie got up to pee and put the remains of the food away. They turned off the lights as they slid back beneath the covers.

"You didn't get to eat your cake," Edgar murmured sleepily into Jamie's neck. His phone lay on his stomach, a cat snoozing in the foreground, paw twitching in dreams.

"I'll have it for breakfast," Jamie said and kissed his cheek. They picked up Edgar's phone and moved to put it on the side table, but Edgar caught their hand.

"Will you leave them on?"

Jamie nodded and put the phone back where Edgar could see it. They imagined him waking at night, alone and scared or sad, soothed by his friends on the screen.

They put their palm against Edgar's chest to feel the beat of his precious heart.

✦ ✦ ✦

Sometime in the night, the storm broke. When Jamie awoke, it was to the Louisiana sun peeking through the blinds, the hum of the air conditioner, and a large man spooning them from behind.

Edgar. The motel room.

In the fresh light of morning, Jamie took stock of the situation and found that they wouldn't change a thing. Edgar's arms were warm and heavy, his breath sweet on the back of Jamie's neck. The bed was surprisingly comfortable for a roadside motel, and Jamie wished they were here under more romantic circumstances. But since they weren't, they carefully extricated themself from Edgar's arms.

After a quick shower, they slung a clean towel around their waist and went to wake Edgar. But Edgar was already up.

"Ugh, they're still damp." He plucked at jeans strewn over the chair, T-shirt drooping over his arm.

"They'll dry pretty quickly in the sun."

Edgar nodded but stared at his shirt.

Jamie crossed the room to him. "Are you okay?"

Edgar nodded again but didn't meet their eyes.

"Weirded out?"

Edgar nodded a third time, and Jamie forced themself to let go of the dream of coupledom that had lasted the length of their shower.

"No worries," they said, injecting their voice with a hearty dose of chipper. "The chances of us being stranded together again are vanishingly small. I won't hold you to anything."

Jamie squeezed Edgar's shoulder as they walked past him to claim their own clothes. A quick, fraternal gesture to reinforce this new distance. This was fine. This was perfectly fine. Last night, Edgar was vulnerable, horny, scared. And this morning he…wasn't. That was allowed. It was all fine.

"Hmm?"

Jamie looked up at Edgar with their friendliest smile. Their sunniest, most self-sufficient, I-don't-require-anything-from-you-so-you-don't-need-to-deny-me smile. Once, that had been their default expression. One that projected nonthreatening, no-strings-attached opportunity. It excluded no one and included no one, so it was inoffensive. Insulated. Safe.

Now though, it felt alien. Like slipping back into their seventeen-year-old self when visiting their parents and watching that same self cease to exist the second their door closed behind you.

Edgar scowled. "I said, I don't feel weird about you. I feel weird about me."

Jamie's gut unclenched. "Wait, what?"

In one step, Edgar loomed over them. "Where did you go?"

"When?"

Edgar ran a finger over the corner of their mouth. "You smiled all weirdly, and then it was like you were gone."

*It was hot, dude, except… You're great, only… You made me come really hard, but…*

"I'm here," Jamie said. "Now what did you mean about feeling weird about you?"

"I… When you… I really liked when you… And I guess I didn't know that I…but I…I really did…"

*Oh.* Relief rushed through Jamie, along with a new understanding. Edgar wasn't giving them a kiss-off. He was processing how much he liked being topped.

Jamie let the desire show in their eyes, and Edgar's face went slack.

"You really liked it when I...what?" Jamie teased. They crowded Edgar back until his shoulders hit the wall.

Edgar sucked in a breath. He had a freckle on his left eyelid and another at the corner of his mouth, and Jamie promised themself that they would find every other freckle he had.

"Truth or dare?" Jamie murmured against his lips.

"How do you go from zero to so fucking hot in one second?"

Gratified, Jamie just smiled.

"Truth," Edgar whispered.

Jamie had been expecting him to say *dare*, but this was sweeter. It was his truth that Jamie wanted most.

"You really liked it when I what?" Jamie repeated.

Edgar looked at Jamie so deeply it felt like he was crying. When he spoke, it was in a voice so low and thick, it was mostly breath and want.

"Pulled my hair." He shuddered. "Bossed me around. When you took charge. When you took...care of me."

There was no sound in the world for Jamie except the whispered confession. Edgar—strong, scared, lonely Edgar—wanted someone to take care of him. And Jamie? *Fuck*, Jamie wanted to be the one to do it.

They swallowed thickly but managed to get out, "Why does that make you feel weird?"

Edgar shrugged, but Jamie could practically read his thoughts in the air. *Because I'm not supposed to. Because it makes me feel weak. Because, because, because.*

"Maybe *weird* is the wrong word," Edgar said. "Maybe I'm just...surprised."

"Surprise isn't too bad," Jamie ventured.

Edgar's smile was sweet and warm. "Yeah. Not so bad." Then

he reached for Jamie and tangled their fingers together. "Kiss me?" he asked.

Jamie obliged, and when they pulled apart, breathing heavily, the alarm on Edgar's phone chimed.

"Checkout time," he said in a voice that registered his disappointment.

Jamie swallowed their own, kissed him chastely on the cheek, and backed away. They stole glances at each other as they gathered their things and packed up the food.

Once outside, the heat instantly turned their damp clothes warm and muggy, a particularly undesirable microclimate that made Edgar pull his shirt off as soon as they got to the truck.

Feeling intoxicated with glee, Jamie did the same, loading the chandelier into the back and tucking their shirt around it for protection.

"Just have to drop off the key." Jamie held it up.

"I can do it," Edgar offered.

Jamie looked down at their bare torso and took a deep breath. "No, it's okay. I can do it."

They spun on their toe before anxiety could change their mind.

The office was so dark that the woman behind the desk probably couldn't even see Jamie's scars. But that didn't stop them from feeling triumphant as they pushed the key across the counter.

*I did it! I did it! I did it!* pounded through Jamie's head to the beat of their damp boots on the pavement, and they slid behind the wheel of the truck with a grin.

"You're a fucking badass," Edgar said. Then they held up the bakery cake and a plastic spoon.

"My life's perfect right now," Jamie said.

For a moment, they regretted the comment, not wanting to come on too strong. But with the sun falling on the bare skin of their chest, the promise of cake for breakfast, and a sweet, fascinating, gorgeous person in the passenger seat with the road ahead of them, nothing had ever been more true.

# 13

## Edgar

3:14 P.M.

**Edgar**: Dude, please don't ignore Allie's texts. She gets really worried and then she asks me to text you. So this is me, texting you. Are you doing okay? Could you please text A back?

4:02 P.M.

**Edgar**: But if you're not doing okay, you can tell us that too.

6:37 P.M.

**Edgar**: Poe? ARE you ok?

8:49 P.M.

**Edgar**: If something's wrong I can help. Well, I can try.

8:54 P.M.

**Edgar**: You used to text me back, dude. What did I do, I don't get it? If you tell me why you're pissed I could at least apologize.

11:06 P.M.

**Edgar**: Remember the time we got Stu Mandeville to give us beers during Mardi Gras and we were so amped but then it turned out beer is disgusting?

12:21 A.M.

**Edgar**: Remember how we used to tell each other everything?

12:58 A.M.

**Edgar**: Night bro. I hope you're okay. I love you.

※

Allie handed Edgar the bowl of batter and the spatula and collapsed onto the barstool in slow motion, hand on her belly. "I'm gonna need you to make these, actually."

"How's the—what fruit or household object is it this week?"

Allie had an app on her phone that told her the size of her fetus as compared to inanimate objects, and it amused her deeply. "It's the size of a cauliflower, and believe me, it fucking feels like I've got one lodged in there."

Edgar melted butter in Allie's cast iron pan, the same one their mother had used to make pancakes. The batter sizzled as it hit the pan, heat holding it together.

After their mother died, Edgar had worried that the pancakes would never taste the same again. She'd always said there was a special ingredient in there, and he'd never thought to watch and see what it was. Then Allie had slid a plate of pancakes in front of him and Poe one day, and they had tasted exactly like their mother's. Years later, when he'd told Allie how glad he was that she knew the secret ingredient, her face had gone soft. *Aw, Edgar,* she'd told him. *The secret ingredient she meant was love. These are straight off the back of the box.*

But Edgar was pretty sure that wasn't the whole truth, because he'd made the recipe off the back of the box himself, and they hadn't tasted like his mom's or Allie's.

Still, he watched the bubbles like Allie had taught him and flipped the pancakes when they were a perfect golden brown. He loved the smell of them on the griddle and the sweet scent of syrup hitting their warm, buttery surface.

When he set them in front of Allie, she inhaled the steam with closed eyes.

"Damn, I love pancakes," she said. "The baby loves pancakes too."

"Any movement on the name front?"

Allie spoke through a huge bite. "No. Names are weird."

Edgar snorted. "Tell me about it."

"Whatever. Edgar's a dream compared to being a girl named Allan."

They exchanged speaking looks.

"Come on, you have to have some ideas."

"It's a lot of fucking pressure to choose a name for another person without ever having met them," Allie insisted.

"Yeah. You should probably just leave them nameless until they can decide. I'll call them Lovejoy until then."

"Maybe we can just call them 'It,' like the Stephen King book," Allie mused. "Or Pennywise. Do you think their teachers would call CPS if I named them Pennywise? Penny for short."

Edgar didn't dignify that with a response.

"God, they're gonna be in school one day," Allie said. "They're gonna have a personality and things that annoy them and stuff they love. And it'll be on me to not crush their fragile little spirit. Fuuuuck."

Allie shoved another bite of pancake in her mouth.

"On me too," Edgar added. "I'm here, Al. You know I'm gonna be here for you and little Lovejoy, right?"

Allie frowned, then started to cry. She waved Edgar off.

"I know, thanks. That's so nice. Ignore my face." She wiped at her eyes. At a certain point in her pregnancy, Allie's emotions had begun to overflow and leak out her eyes—at least, that's how she'd described it when it happened the first time and Edgar, concerned, had wrapped her in his arms.

"You're the best brother, you know that?"

"Well, I'm the one who stayed," Edgar said.

*You're my favorite Lovejoy*, Antoine had whispered in his ear, the sweet scent of apples on his breath, before wading deeper into the bayou.

"What if I'm making a huge mistake?" Allie's voice was softer, more uncertain than he'd heard it since the night she showed up at his apartment with a positive pregnancy test.

"It's not too late," Edgar offered. "Adoption."

"I know. I just can't stand the thought of…what if they *do* see ghosts and they grow up with some normie family who makes them feel insane? Can you imagine how much worse it would all have been if we'd grown up with only Dad? How long do you think we would've lasted before we believed him that we were actually crazy?"

Their father's voice still lived in Edgar's head and spoke to him sometimes in the aftermath of an encounter when he was shaking and terrified: *Coward. There's nothing fucking there. You look like a fool. Weak. Pathetic.*

"I talked to Cameron the other day," Allie said.

Edgar's heart started pounding. Cameron's parents had sent her to a science boarding school in Atlanta for her final year of high school, and she'd gone to college and medical school in Boston after that. She and Allie had always stayed in touch, but Edgar had only seen her a few times, when she'd visited for the holidays or her parents' birthdays. She'd always been warm to him, but he'd never been able to enjoy seeing her because all he could think was, *It's my fault your brother died, and you should hate me.*

"She sends her love. She's also back for a while. She's doing her residency here."

Edgar's stomach leapt with excitement because he loved Cameron, then crashed at the realization that his squirmy guilt might mean he would be a nervous wreck any time he saw her.

"Wow," was all Edgar could manage.

After they ate, soporific with pancakes and heat, they collapsed onto Allie's bed.

"Do you ever talk to Lincoln?" Edgar asked.

"Absolutely not. If I'd known how quickly he'd bounce when he heard about the baby, I would've gotten knocked up sooner."

"You're not worried he might, I dunno, want custody later or something?"

Allie snorted. "No. He's terrified of me now. I told him if he changes his mind down the line, I can command ghosts to haunt him."

Edgar grinned. "So what's the freak meter at today?"

Even though Allie saw ghosts just like Edgar did, her emotional and physical reactions to it were different.

Allie sighed, settling into the mattress. "It's at a four today, but it was pushing seven yesterday."

"You see something?"

She nodded. "I dunno, man. There are *so many* things you're entirely responsible for when you have a baby. They don't know anything about the world or life. They don't know how to do anything. I'll be filtering how they experience and understand the world and keeping them alive. But on the other hand, I have zero control over their brain, their feelings. Everything that makes them *them* is just a huge mystery. So even if they inherit…you know, is that the biggest thing that will affect their life? Probably not."

Edgar frowned. "It's the biggest thing that affects *my* life," he said.

Allie was quiet, but they both knew her thoughts on the matter. That his problem wasn't seeing ghosts but rather his *reaction* to seeing ghosts.

"Yeah. I know."

Eight months ago, a knock on the door woke Edgar at midnight, and when he'd peered through the peephole, he'd seen a positive pregnancy test held up in front of his sister's shocked face. He'd wrapped her in a blanket on the couch, put the pregnancy test in a plastic bag, in case for some reason she wanted it later, and made her a cup of tea.

"Do you know if you want to have the baby?" he'd asked, and she'd said she didn't know. There were all the usual things to consider, but there was, of course, an added complication: knowing what she knew about their family and the likelihood that her kid would be able to see ghosts, did she want to bring them into the world?

They'd talked until the sun rose, by which time her answer was no. She'd scheduled an abortion, and Edgar had planned to take her. She'd had one two years previously and knew it was a great option for her.

But then she'd changed her mind. She'd been talking to their aunt and mentioned the burden that she wanted to protect her child from. Only Alaitheia had said, *You think of this as a burden? For me, it is my greatest gift.* And that perspective had changed everything for Allie. Not just about any future children but about her own experience with ghosts.

Edgar had always been envious of Allie. Her encounters were less startling than Edgar's. For Allie, ghosts faded into visibility rather than bursting in. They were less detailed. But also unlike Edgar, Allie experienced the apparitions as having a clear desire—a reason for being there. And that distinction meant that she felt more empathy toward them and less fear.

When Allie told Edgar she'd decided to keep the baby, he had also sent up a silent promise: that if this new Lovejoy experienced ghosts the way he did, he would do everything he could to help prepare them so that they would never feel the terror that he lived with every day.

"Do you remember Poe's first time?" Allie asked.

Edgar groaned. "Oh, man, that little punk. He was so casual about it."

"Right?" Allie went on to speak in her Poe voice. "'*This* is what you're scared of?'" She grinned. "What a dick. If my kid is that much of a dick at age nine, can you please adopt it?"

"Absolutely not. I dislike children."

"I know." Allie reached for his hand and gave it a squeeze. "And even so, you're still gonna help out. You're such a gem. Hmm," she mused. "Uncle Edgar. I like the sound of that."

"I don't. Can't it call me Edgar?"

"Sure." She squeezed his hand again. "Can we just take a little nap?"

"Yeah, sounds good. You'll be the second person I shared a bed with in twenty-four hours…"

Allie jerked upright. "You *what*?!"

Edgar smiled tranquilly.

"Tell me every fucking detail, or I'll tell my kid to call you Uncle Eddie."

"You wouldn't."

"No. But you'll tell me anyway, won't you?"

And settling back into the soft pillows that smelled like his sister—rosemary and eucalyptus and the rich scent of old leather—he told her about Jamie.

✦ ✦ ✦

When Edgar got to Helen and Veronica's house to start his delivery run the next day, Helen narrowed their eyes at him.

"What's wrong with you?"

It was a verbalization of what he assumed everyone was always thinking about him, but it was startling to hear it spoken aloud.

"Um. Nothing?"

"Exactly. Usually, you look like you're about to cry, dissociate, or have a panic attack. But right now, you look strangely neutral, which I'm assuming is your version of glowing."

"Have I mentioned lately that I enjoy the particular way in which you're rude?"

"You have. Well, not lately. But really, someone only has to say it once, and I extrapolate it to every encounter I have with them."

Edgar smiled.

"Holy crap, a real smile. Are you on drugs?"

Edgar shook his head, and they leaned in.

"Do you wanna be? Cuz V and Greta started growing weed in the backyard, and they're, like, super good at it."

"I'm okay, thanks."

"Oh, right. You're about to go deliver our product, packaged in glass, on a bike, to our important customers. Of course you can't have weed."

They said it loudly, and Edgar turned around. His hunch was correct. Veronica stood in the doorway, one eyebrow raised.

"Quit telling literally everyone that we're growing weed, bro," she said. "Edgar doesn't even smoke."

"I'm impressed," Helen insisted.

Meanwhile, Veronica was looking at Edgar with her brow furrowed. "Did you win the lottery or something?" she asked finally. "You look all…" She gestured in the air toward him.

"Right?" Helen exclaimed. "That's what I was saying. He doesn't look like he's about to cry or puke or run away!"

Veronica snickered. "You're an asshole, but you're not wrong."

"Is that really what I look like?" Edgar asked.

"Yes," Helen said immediately.

"Kinda," Veronica concluded.

Edgar hoped he didn't look as mortified as he felt. "Okay. Well. I'm gonna grab the stuff and get going. Have a good one."

"See ya!" they chorused.

Edgar took the bike around to the back entrance where they stored the boxes of Lagniappe Lemonade and checked the clipboard for the printed delivery route. As he loaded boxes onto the bike, he could hear Veronica and Helen talking in the kitchen.

"—our employee," Veronica was saying. "He could sue us!"

"Aw, Ronnie, he's not gonna sue us."

"Not the point. We all like him, but he hasn't returned our overtures of friendship. You can't force someone to be your friend."

"I know," Helen grumbled. "I just feel like…he seems so fucking lonely and sad all the time. And I don't want anyone to feel like that. Especially another queer person."

"I know, boo," Veronica said. "But think about it from his perspective. Maybe to him, we're being the creepy bosses who make personal comments about him and try to get him to do drugs."

"Ugh. Yeah, from that perspective, we suck. Okay. I'll be the picture of professionalism henceforth."

"I hope you and Henceforth will be happy together. Pass me that pipe. Wait 'til you try the new strain Greta and I…"

Veronica's voice trailed off, and Edgar figured they'd gone into the living room. He sighed. Was that really how he seemed to people?

*Isn't that how you feel? Why wouldn't people be able to see it?*

Usually, that would be the point at which Edgar went on his delivery run and never spoke about their interaction ever again. But Jamie had taken his nod in the hotel room as a complete rejection of their night together until he'd explained. He genuinely liked Helen and Veronica. He didn't want them to think otherwise.

Edgar leaned the bike against the house and went back into the kitchen, then through to the living room. Helen and Veronica were passing the pipe back and forth and looking at a spreadsheet projected onto the large television.

He knocked on the doorframe, not wanting to startle them.

"Hey!" Helen said, a bit too chipper. "Everything okay with

the bike? And the lemonade? Just all the professionally relevant things…"

Veronica snorted and shook her head.

"I like you both," Edgar blurted. "I heard you talking in there, and I just want you to know that. I don't think you're creepy. I don't feel pressured to do drugs. I'm not gonna sue you. And I—actually, I am in a good mood today. So. Thanks. For noticing."

Helen's grin was wide and sunny, an instant reward. Veronica's smile was softer, more knowing.

"Yes, I *knew* it!" Helen crowed, punching the air. "I knew you liked us, and I knew something was different today." They elbowed Veronica in the ribs. "I'm always fucking right about this shit." Then, to Edgar, "Spill!"

"Huh? Oh. Um."

"What my dear business partner meant to say," Veronica drawled, "is that we'd love to celebrate any happiness or good fortune with you, should you choose to entrust us with the information."

Helen snorted. "Yup. That's exactly what I meant to say."

They patted the couch next to them.

"I… The lemonade…?"

"Omigod, it's fine, you can take ten minutes and tell us what's changed your whole personality."

"But no drugs for you," Veronica said and blew the smoke away from him.

"I don't like weed," Edgar said. "It makes me paranoid."

That was an extreme understatement. The one and only time he'd tried smoking pot, he'd seen a ghost and been convinced that it was going to slide inside his skin and puppetize his body. Then for the rest of his life, he'd be trapped in there, conscious but unable to tell anyone because the ghost would have control. He had sworn a solemn oath on that day—the next morning anyway—never to touch another mind-altering substance.

And like most of the rules that Edgar made for himself, he followed it scrupulously, out of fear of the alternative.

"Great, more for us. Now spill."

Edgar was unsure whether Jamie would want him to say anything yet. Unsure of what he *would* say. Where did they stand? What even were they?

"I… Maybe I'll keep it to myself for now," Edgar said. "But thanks. And sorry. For making you worry that I didn't like you. Because I do."

Helen had their arms wrapped around their torso like they were hugging themself in lieu of hugging him. They shivered with joy and leaned against Veronica. "Yay, he likes us!"

Veronica patted them on the head.

"Double yay: something to speculate about as soon as he leaves!"

Veronica raised an eyebrow and nodded.

Edgar turned to leave, then hesitated. "What is it exactly that makes me look like I'm about to cry? Or, um, puke?"

Veronica grimaced and said nothing.

"Just your face, basically. And your whole expression. Expressions. All of them. And your bearing and demeanor. Also your voice. And there's a real funk around you like, if I could read auras, I bet yours would be whatever color funky auras are."

Veronica closed her eyes slowly, but she didn't seem irritated with Helen; she seemed to agree on such a deep level she didn't want to admit it.

"Great. So everything about me."

Helen made a finger gun at him. "Bingo. Ooh!" They turned to Veronica. "Should we do a bingo night?"

"Yes, absolutely. Queer bingo. Disco ball, queer shit as the boxes on the cards. Perfect idea."

Edgar decided to take this opportunity to slink away.

"Come to bingo night!" Helen and Veronica both yelled at him as he walked back through the kitchen, eager to start his route and distract himself from how people perceived him.

# 14

# Jamie

Jamie climbed the back steps to Edgar's apartment, fizzing with anticipation. This stretch of Annunciation Street was quiet and unassuming, mostly residential, with a sandwich shop on the corner. The air smelled of muffulettas, sweat, and the magnolias that tented the sidewalk. The sun was setting, which meant the streets would soon come alive. After a busy week at work, without any time to connect with Edgar, they'd had to settle for memories of their night together in the hotel room. Now, Jamie couldn't wait to make new ones.

The door swung open, golden hour light painting Edgar's skin the color of honey, setting his eyes aglow.

"Hey. Come on in." His voice sounded low and intimate, and

Jamie could've gotten lost in his eyes. They followed him inside, relieved to be out of the oppressive heat.

"Hi. Hello. How are you?"

The intimacy in Edgar's voice had been replaced by flatness, which Jamie associated with Edgar's nerves. His vulnerability awoke a longing in Jamie. A deep, tangled desire to make Edgar certain of something. Certain of Jamie. They shivered despite the heat, remembering how Edgar's eyelashes had fluttered when Jamie told him what to do.

Jamie took a slow, deliberate step toward Edgar. Edgar didn't move. Jamie crowded him. Edgar sucked in a deep breath.

"Can I hug you?" Jamie said softly.

At Edgar's nod, they leaned in and wrapped their arms around him. For a moment, Edgar froze; then he softened into Jamie's touch. When his arms came up and he returned the hug, they melted together, chest to chest. Edgar's arms were strong, his body warm and solid. He slowly squeezed Jamie tighter and closer, as if he wanted to absorb them into his own body, wanted them to never let go.

When Edgar's palm cupped the back of Jamie's head, caressing their hair, Jamie let out a deep sigh and burrowed their face more deeply into Edgar's shoulder.

"I could stay like this forever," Jamie said, only it came out like "Mcuhstayhmfrver" because of the whole nuzzling situation. They were pretty sure Edgar got the idea though, because he squeezed even tighter.

Jamie stroked Edgar's back and shoulders and breathed him in.

"Do you want something to drink?" Edgar asked when they untangled.

"What've you got?"

"Oh. Um. Water?"

"I'd like water, then."

Edgar *did* smile, Jamie was learning. It was a subtle tightening of the skin around his eyes and at the left corner of his mouth that they hadn't initially noticed. A small, private smile that was for himself. The smile of someone used to being alone.

"So this is the kitchen," Edgar said, handed them a glass.

The kitchen was dated but clean, with brown-and-white-flecked linoleum and brown countertops. The walls, ceiling, and cabinets were painted a pleasant light blue, which lent a much-needed lightness. Five-gallon water jugs were stacked in a corner, an Audubon society calendar hung on the refrigerator, and aloe plants grew on the windowsill.

"Living room." Edgar led them through the shotgun house.

Jamie didn't realize it until they stepped into the living room, but they'd expected Edgar's apartment to be sterile and lacking personality, like his clothes. Instead, the apartment was a beautiful, curated space. There was a thick circular rug on the floor and a large bookcase crammed with worn paperbacks. An air conditioner hummed in the beside an extensive record collection. Art lined the walls, gallery-style.

The large sectional and worn leather recliner faced the fireplace and mantle, above which hung a large painting done in pinks, oranges, yellows, and teals. The backs of three heads and the ocean stretching beyond them, kicking up spumes in the surf. The sunlight spilled over everything, gilding hair and sand and the circling gulls like a benediction.

"Wow," Jamie said. "That's fantastic."

"My mom painted it."

It was the first time Edgar had mentioned either of his parents.

"She's really talented."

"I think so too."

"Are y'all close?"

Edgar's face did something complicated, and he stared at the painting as if the answer lay inside its brushstrokes.

"No," he said finally. "We used to be. It was me, my brother, my sister, and my mom against the world. Well. Against my dad and the world. But she…" He touched the edge of the canvas where a bright spot of blue sky bloomed. "We don't see her anymore. She was in a hospital for a while, and now…well, she's not really in touch with reality these days. Bathroom's through there."

Jamie squeezed his shoulder, a silent agreement that they were done with the subject.

Though as dated as the kitchen, the bathroom had been arranged with care. A thriving fern hung in front of the window, reclaimed wood shelves hung in the place of a medicine cabinet, and a tangle of driftwood claimed the windowsill.

Past the bathroom was the bedroom, which was minimally decorated. A large bed, a heavy antique dresser that had seen better days, and an old peeling steamer trunk were the only furniture, and the walls were mostly bare. Above the bed hung another painting in the same style as the beach scene. In rust, ochre, violet, and gray, a lone figure stood looking at a barge traveling down the Mississippi. The figure appeared to be made from the same material as the muddy water, as if they could drift through each other.

The painting made Jamie desperately sad for Edgar's mother and for her children.

Other than the painting, the only decoration was a complicated macramé wall hanging and a few potted plants. The effect was peaceful. Where the kitchen was practical and the living room was expressive, the bedroom was a quiet sanctuary. The light blue walls added to the calm.

Suddenly, something dawned on Jamie.

"It's haint blue," they said. "The walls, the cabinets, the rug…"

Haint blue was the color of porch ceilings all over the South. It was tradition now but had originally arisen from the association of blue with water and the belief that ghosts couldn't cross it. By painting the entrance to your home blue, you tricked spirits into thinking it was water so they couldn't pass.

Edgar had taken care not to invite anyone in.

"It's to protect you. So the ghosts can't come in here?"

Edgar frowned. "It probably doesn't do anything. But it makes me feel better."

"It's a nice color," Jamie said. "Whether it does anything or not."

Edgar snorted. "I actually don't like it much. Maybe I'm just sick of it. I dunno."

Jamie reached for his hand and gently tugged him close. "Maybe it's time to repaint," they offered softly.

"Maybe," Edgar said.

They'd moved closer and closer as they spoke until they were shoulder to shoulder.

"You smell good," Edgar murmured as he pressed a kiss to Jamie's neck.

The touch of his lips sent a pulse of heat through Jamie.

"Do that again."

Edgar pulled Jamie closer and did as they said. His fingers searched for Jamie's, and he clasped their hand. A surge of pure tenderness rose in Jamie.

"C'mere," they said and guided Edgar's mouth to theirs.

They kissed Edgar slowly, savoring his mouth. Edgar kissed

tentatively at first, sweetly. Fuck, was he sweet. But when Jamie pressed a thumb to the corner of his mouth, Edgar curled his tongue around it and then kissed Jamie like he wanted to consume them.

Needing more access to Edgar, Jamie pushed him down on his back on the bed and straddled him. Edgar's mouth dropped open in surprise, then he let out a shuddering breath.

Jamie inched their hips forward experimentally and pressed slowly into Edgar's erection. Edgar's throat flushed, and color burned high on his cheeks. His dark hair was in disarray, and his lips were plump and pink with kissing. He looked debauched.

"You should see yourself," Jamie said. They traced the line of a dark eyebrow, the hollow of a cheekbone, the swell of his mouth. "You're fucking stunning."

Edgar shuddered, and Jamie felt his cock swell. A look of confusion touched Edgar's face.

"I can feel how much you like it when I tell you how hot you are," Jamie purred, intrigued. Edgar ducked his head. "Or is it when I tell you how gorgeous you look when I debauch you?"

Edgar clutched Jamie's ass with both hands as his hips pulsed.

Their beautiful Edgar wanted permission, wanted his pleasure to please someone else as well. He wanted to feel cared for, protected, safe.

"Can I take these off, baby?" Jamie plucked at the button of Edgar's pants.

"Please. Yours too?"

Their pants were tangled together at the end of the bed so quickly that Edgar laughed.

"I am a professional after all," Jamie said. "Well, I'm an amateur. But whatever."

Edgar pulled them back down on top of him. "I defer to you in all matters of clothing removal, amateur or profesh—Mpf."

Edgar smiled into the kiss, then their tongues tangled, and he moaned.

"I really like the way you kiss," Edgar said, pulling away, breathless after a while. His lips were obscene.

"How do I kiss?" They kissed him again, deeply, for data.

Edgar regarded Jamie through eyes heavy-lidded with lust, their lips a breath apart.

"You kiss like everything's going to be okay," Edgar said. He instantly looked embarrassed, like he hadn't meant to verbalize that.

Jamie burned for this man. They wanted to devour him, make him scream, make him theirs. Fuck, they wanted everything.

Jamie kissed his burning cheek. "Thank you. I really like the way you kiss too."

Jamie encouraged Edgar to take his shirt off and stripped off their own as well. They made no attempt to hide their admiring stare.

"What do you like in bed?" they asked, tracing his rib cage with their fingers.

"I, um, I like to get fucked." He flushed so beautifully. "And apparently, with you, I really like when you, um, tell me what to do, and…"

"What else?" Jamie murmured. They touched his nipples and watched his eyes flutter closed.

"I like to p-pleasure people. Watch them come."

Jamie couldn't resist kissing him.

"What do you like?" he asked.

"Mmm. I love kissing. And touching. Can I touch you?"

When Edgar nodded, they cupped his cock and gently stroked him.

"And you're in luck," they said. "Because I would love to fuck you and tell you what to do." They took his hand and guided it between their legs. "Touch me like this."

They slid out of their underwear and showed Edgar how they liked to be touched and where. When they were so turned on it felt like they'd explode, they pulled away, groaning.

Edgar's whole chest was flushed, and he was breathing heavily. He looked about to protest, but before he could, Jamie said, "Take your underwear off."

Edgar hesitated for a moment, then lifted his fingers to his mouth and touched his fingertips to his tongue. He shuddered as he tasted Jamie.

Lust blazed through Jamie.

They managed to drag Edgar's underwear off while kissing the hell out of him. When they were both gloriously naked, they looked at each other in appreciation.

Edgar lifted a hand and traced a scar on Jamie's chest, then pulled it away.

"Is that okay?" he asked.

"Yeah," Jamie said, happy he'd asked. "Right here"—they put their hand over his to show him—"is pretty numb. But I can definitely feel when you touch me here." They put his hands on their nipples.

Edgar leaned down and kissed their nipples. They stroked his back and slid a hand into his hair. He sucked lightly, and Jamie hissed in pleasure. They tightened the hand in Edgar's hair, and he sucked harder. Jamie imagined encouraging Edgar to stay like that for hours, feasting on their body until they exploded.

Jamie's breath quickened, and Edgar shifted over them. They both groaned when their hips aligned. Edgar kissed a line up

Jamie's throat and sucked lightly at the skin behind their ear. Jamie was on fire. They couldn't wait any longer.

"Lie on your back," Jamie said breathlessly. Edgar obeyed immediately.

Jamie straddled Edgar and wrapped a hand around his cock. Edgar gasped, throwing his head back into the pillow.

"Jamie, Jamie, Jamie," he begged, breath ragged.

Jamie's nipples tingled, and their head was buzzing. Edgar put a bracing hand on their chest as they swayed above him. His eyes drank them in, and they felt like a god.

"Show me how you like it," Jamie said.

They stroked him once, then released him, and watched him mourn the loss. Jamie moved their hand between their own legs and stroked themself instead. They were swollen and leaking. Edgar reached for his erection, but his eyes were glued to Jamie. Jamie noted details for later—Edgar liked it a little rough on the downstroke and slower than Jamie would've thought.

They touched themself while they watched him, the pleasure building exquisitely.

"Jamie," Edgar said after a little while, voice strained and low. He was close.

"You're so fucking sexy, Edgar. Are you gonna come for me?"

Edgar groaned desperately but held off.

"What do you want, gorgeous?" Jamie asked.

"T-touch me?" Edgar begged. "Please."

Jamie scratched their nails lightly down Edgar's chest. His breathing was ragged, and Jamie's wasn't much better.

"Here?" Jamie teased.

Edgar looked horrified, and Jamie smiled. They trailed a finger lightly down his chest to his stomach.

"P-please." Edgar was clearly on the edge. He could've brought himself to orgasm any time he wanted to, but he hadn't. He wanted Jamie to be in charge of it.

Jamie leaned over Edgar, chest brushing the wet tip of his cock. He gasped.

"Edgar," Jamie said. They kissed his cheek, and he shook. They kissed his lips, and he groaned into their mouth. "Tell me what you want."

"Make me come? Please? I want…I… Please."

Fuck, he was exquisite.

Jamie reached between them and grasped the base of his cock. Edgar let go immediately.

"Don't stop," Jamie said. Edgar started to stroke himself again.

Jamie sat up again and closed their hand over his, learning his rhythm. They clenched as arousal rolled through them. Edgar had placed himself utterly in their hands. They tightened their hand over his and kissed his neck as they stroked him.

Quickly, Edgar was writhing on the bed, pushing up into Jamie's hand. Jamie ground their hips forward as their arousal grew.

Edgar squeezed his eyes shut and came with a silent roar, the muscles in his neck cording and his thighs bunching. Edgar held them to his broad chest as he shuddered and gasped.

After a minute, he said, "Will you finish like this?"

At first, Jamie wasn't sure what *this* meant, but then they realized Edgar wanted them to come in his arms. Something flipped pleasantly in their stomach.

"Okay."

Edgar murmured something into their hair that they couldn't

make out. Jamie settled on top of Edgar, then touched themself, rolling their hips as the pleasure grew. Edgar stroked down their spine and cupped their ass in both hands, encouraging them to thrust more forcefully.

"Grab my ass harder," they said.

Powerful hands squeezed their ass, and Jamie stroked themself until they exploded, the orgasm coming in waves of pleasure that rocked them.

"Fuuuck," they groaned finally, going limp on top of Edgar.

"Jamie," Edgar murmured.

Jamie gathered him up in their arms and pressed a tender kiss to his temple.

"I think you killed me," he said softly.

"Terribly sorry for the inconvenience," Jamie murmured. They rolled onto their side and propped their head up on their hand. "How are you doing?"

Edgar couldn't meet their eyes. Jamie straddled them.

"Hey. How are you doing?" they repeated gently.

Edgar covered his eyes with his arm.

"Good," he said. "Like...so good I don't know what to do."

Jamie's lips pressed gently to his, and they kissed him until he wrapped his arms around them. "It was really good for me too."

Edgar's eyes lit up at that, and he cupped Jamie's cheek. "You sure?"

"Very sure," Jamie said and kissed him softly on the lips.

They were drifting in a languorous postorgasmic haze, on the edge of falling asleep, when Edgar's stomach growled loudly.

"Sorry," he said.

"You don't have to apologize for having bodily needs, babe," Jamie teased. "Let's get some food."

Edgar seemed reluctant to get out of bed; Jamie related. But Edgar's stomach growled insistently.

"Good lord," Edgar muttered and finally stood, leaning over to kiss Jamie before going to the closet.

He pulled a navy blue robe from the closet and put it on.

"Would you like something else to wear?" he offered. "I know my stuff's not really your style."

"May I?" Jamie tapped the dresser.

"Sure. Just be careful because it's a little—"

As Jamie opened the drawer, one side of it slid out of the track and slumped into the drawer below it.

"Broken," Edgar finished.

Jamie snorted. "Whoops."

They heaved the drawer back onto its tracks.

Edgar jumped in. "Better let me."

As he pushed the drawer in, the one beneath it groaned and sagged into the one below it.

"The bottom one works," Edgar said, stepping away from the entire armoire.

"Congratulations," Jamie said.

Edgar slid an arm around them and kissed the side of their head before addressing the drawer. While he did, Jamie moved to the closet, running their fingers over the row of khaki pants, plain button-down shirts, and drab sweaters. The clothes in the armoire were more of the same: T-shirts and polos and sweatshirts in solid, muted tones with the occasional stripe.

For themself, Jamie chose the black-and-white-striped T-shirt that Edgar had been wearing the day Jamie asked him out at the cat café. It was the only garment they'd seen that didn't make them desperately sad.

When they pulled it over their head, they found Edgar watching them intently. He brushed hair out of their face and kissed them tenderly.

"Looks good on you."

"Thanks." Jamie smiled. They fished out their phone. "Do you want to order something?"

"Um. I have cereal?"

"Cereal's good."

They made for the kitchen, and Edgar caught Jamie's hand, walking next to them. In the kitchen, they took any excuse to touch as they found cereal and milk, passed silverware, and pulled out chairs. Their knees found each other under the table, and they held hands as they ate. Jamie felt utterly serene.

"Did you have a favorite cereal as a kid?" Edgar asked, pouring more on top of his milk.

"Not really. My parents were going through a health food phase when I was a kid, and they made our granola. It was very dry. What about you?"

Edgar, his mouth full, tapped the box. Jamie wasn't sure why they found it adorable that he still bought the same cereal he'd liked as a kid.

"Do you have a favorite color?" Jamie asked.

"That peachy color in the sunset when the clouds are backlit."

"I love that color too," Jamie said. "You don't have any clothes that color though. Do you not like to wear it?"

Edgar looked down at his cereal. "I don't really wear many bright colors. I like them, but…" He trailed off and took another bite.

"Is it because you don't want to seem…queer?"

Edgar huffed. "No, everyone knows I'm gay. My family knew when I was, like, twelve."

Jamie wasn't going to press Edgar to say more but didn't really understand.

"You're going to think I'm ridiculous," Edgar said softly after they'd eaten in silence for a little while.

"I already think you're ridiculous," Jamie said. "In the best possible way." They squeezed his thigh.

"I don't want them to notice me," Edgar said softly.

Had Jamie underestimated how shy Edgar truly was?

"Dude, you're incredibly hot. I'm afraid your clothes aren't..." Jamie broke off as the pieces clicked into place. It wasn't other people whose notice Edgar was trying to elude. "The ghosts."

Edgar nodded. "I don't want to draw attention to myself. Sometimes it seems like if I lie low, then they don't see me as much."

"Yeah?" Jamie imagined Edgar might have done many of these sorts of experiments over the years.

"Well. I don't know. But I figure better safe than sorry."

*But you haven't felt safe, have you?*

"Honey," Jamie said, turning to face Edgar. "It's not your fault that you see them. That they find you."

"Maybe not. But if I make myself uninteresting to look at, then maybe they...maybe they'll get bored of me?" Edgar's voice had gotten soft, and he was addressing the cereal bowl.

Jamie kissed his shoulder, his cheekbone, his hair. "I don't know how anyone would ever get bored of you."

Edgar's eyes were so soft, and he pulled Jamie to him, stroking back their hair. "I hope you won't," he said.

Jamie melted against his shoulder. "Well, I think you're hot as fuck no matter what you wear. And especially when you don't wear anything at all." They slid their hand under the hem of his shirt and stroked the soft skin of his back. They loved the way

Edgar always leaned into their touch. "If you ever want to find clothes that you like instead of ones that make you invisible, I'd love to help."

"My sister would be ecstatic. She manages a vintage store," Edgar said.

"Oh? Which one?"

"Magpie Vintage over—"

"Oh, off Magazine? I've been there. It's great."

Visions of thrifting with Edgar danced in their head.

"I wouldn't even know where to start," Edgar hedged, but he sounded intrigued.

"You could leave it all to me," Jamie assured him. "If you want."

Edgar looked at him shyly. "Okay. Let's do it."

# 15

## Edgar

When Edgar opened the door to Magpie Vintage, early Riven was blasting on the stereo, and a half-full rack of clothes stood in front of the cash wrap.

Allie grinned when she saw him and turned the music down.

"Yay! Okay, I'm all ready for you. I pulled some pieces I thought you might be interested in and some that I have no clue about but that are about your size. Anything you want, just put it behind the counter on this rack. I'll use my employee discount and ring it up tomorrow. Cool?"

"Yeah. Thanks, Al."

She waved him away. "In exchange, I only require one thing."

"Oh god, what?"

"I wanna stick around for a few minutes and meet Jamie."

She made prayer hands. "Please, please, please. You've never had a boyfriend before, and I'm so happy for you. Do you call them your boyfriend?"

Sweat trickled down Edgar's spine. The music was too loud, he had no idea what to call Jamie, and the clothes Allie'd pulled looked flashy and bright, like they were screaming, *Look at me, ghosts! Here I am!*

"I—"

But before Edgar could respond, the bell tinkled, and Jamie walked through the door.

An unconscious smile tugged at the corner of his mouth, and he ducked his head to avoid grinning like a fool. Jamie's mere presence made him happy like nothing ever had before.

"Hey, Lovejoys!" Jamie said as they swept into the store. Their combat boots added an inch to their height, and their denim vest had an eye painted on it the exact blue of Jamie's own eyes. Everything about them was beautiful and interesting.

Did Jamie feel their own warmth? Could they bask in the kindly, sunny disposition of *Jamieness* the way Edgar did? What would it feel like to be the battery of your own joy?

"It's nice to finally meet you," Allie said. "I love what you're wearing, and I'll greet you in approximately three minutes when I finish extricating myself from this chair."

Allie had a precise process for getting up that Edgar had learned not to interfere with, no matter how much it looked like she wasn't going to make it.

Finally she got to her feet and greeted Jamie with a hug.

Edgar had always thought of his sister as larger than life. She was capable, strong, had basically raised him after their father left. It was only looking at her now that he realized she was shorter than

Jamie. The hand she pressed to her lower back dug in. She had a tangle in the back of her hair, and the hem of her shirt was frayed.

Allie showed Jamie the clothes she'd pulled. Edgar went around the desk and lowered the shade on the side window for privacy.

It had been a hard week. Two ghost sightings in the same afternoon had sent him rushing for home, and he'd narrowly missed being sideswiped by a car while he was on his bike the next day. In swerving, he'd toppled a whole crate of Lagniappe Lemonade, bottles smashing in the street and the scent of honey going sickly sweet on the sticky cement.

Helen and Veronica were understanding and glad he wasn't hurt, but Edgar felt awful. Then when he'd turned a corner walking to the cat café, he'd walked directly into something that felt like cold water dumped down his back. The ghost was a blur of purplish lips and gray skin, but its parts weren't where they should have been. It was stretched tall and thin, looming above him.

An encounter like that would usually shake him. But this time, owing to the week he'd already had, Edgar found himself crouched on the sidewalk, arms over his face. The murmurs of concern from passersby and a bracing *Hey, man, I think you had a little too much*, accompanied by an extended hand, had been so overwhelming and mortifying that he had pretended not to hear or see them, curling into a ball, trying to make himself as small as possible.

The smaller you were, the harder it was for them to find you.

The smaller, the plainer, the quieter. The less you affected the fabric of the world they shared, the less likely you were to bring them down on you.

Right?

Edgar had always thought so. But three times this week, he'd encountered them. And all three times, he'd been walking alone, quiet and plainly dressed.

Maybe he'd have had four encounters if he'd dressed or acted differently. Or five. Or twenty.

But maybe, just maybe, trying to make himself invisible didn't accomplish anything at all.

Edgar had gone home, only able to relax once the door to his apartment closed tight behind him and the only creatures that existed in his world were the cats he watched on the video monitor. He'd taken a long shower, then stood naked before the mirror, wondering.

In the present, Jamie and Allie were still talking. "Did Edgar ever dress in any specific style?" Jamie was asking.

"When he was eight, he got into dressing monochromatically, from head to toe. And for a while, he swiped all my good band shirts, even though he didn't listen to any of the bands. But not really. Our house was pretty chaotic. There wasn't much money for clothes besides school clothes, and we mostly fended for ourselves. As long as he was dressed and got to school…"

"I bet he looked pretty cute no matter what he wore."

Allie winked. Oh god, what would happen if his sister and his…whatever Jamie was…became friends?

Allie sighed wistfully. "He was honestly the cutest kid. He had this infectious giggle, and he'd get Poe going, and they'd both roll around like puppies."

Edgar tried to remember a time when he'd done anything unselfconsciously. When he'd rolled around on the floor with no awareness of his surroundings or what was out there waiting for him.

For the first time in years, he missed Poe so much it choked him. Poe had been younger and smaller but fierce. Much fiercer than Edgar.

"Poe always won when we wrestled," Edgar remembered.

"Yeah," Allie laughed. "Because you were trying not to hurt him, and he was trying to win."

Edgar hardly had time to register this information, because Jamie's eyes narrowed, and they looked between Allie and Edgar.

"Your brother is named Poe?"

Allie and Edgar nodded as they always had when people noticed.

"And you're Allie."

They nodded again.

"So you're Edgar, Allie, and…Poe. Is that—that has to be on purpose, right?"

"Yes," Allie said. "Our mom was a big fan."

At the same time, Edgar said, "Our mom was in a cult."

Jamie's expression froze at the word *cult*, their blue eyes so wide and bright that Edgar almost laughed. Being the subject of Jamie's fascination was a heady drug.

"We didn't grow up in the cult," Edgar explained.

"It was when she was younger," Allie clarified. "But she was out by the time I was born. Mostly," she added.

Jamie's eyes got wider.

"She and our dad met there. Anyway, they asked everyone to choose a new name when they joined, one better suited to who they wanted to become, and Mom chose Lenore. So she named us to fit with her. My legal name is Allan—with an *a*."

Jamie blew out an impressed breath. "Damn. I would really like to be invited over to hear many stories from y'all's childhood."

"You've got it," Allie said. "Now, as much as I deeply—and I do mean *deeply*—want to watch Edgar try on clothes he wouldn't ordinarily wear, I'm at the end of my ability to remain upright and will now drag my ass home."

"Want me to walk you?" Edgar asked. She did look more tired than usual.

Allie gave him a quiet smile. "No. I'm good." She turned to Jamie. "Listen. I am going to *need* some photographic evidence that this happened. Please. In fact." She pulled out her phone. "Lemme give you my number so that you can text them to me."

Jamie brandished their phone in what was clearly a promise.

When the door finally closed behind Allie, Edgar let out a sigh. He adored his sister, but he'd been looking forward to seeing Jamie all day.

Jamie held out their arms, smiling softly, and Edgar walked into them. He nuzzled into Jamie's scent—something zingy and delicious—and breathed deeply for what felt like the first time in days.

He and Jamie had texted all week, but Edgar hadn't wanted to focus on the bad shit. Now though, in Jamie's arms, he let the waves of the week break over him.

"Hey, hey," Jamie murmured, stroking his back. "You okay? What's up?"

Trying to keep it light, Edgar said, "Just a ghost-heavy week."

Jamie squeezed him tighter. "I'm so sorry. Want to tell me about it?"

Exhaustion swept over Edgar at the idea of describing the incidents. One of the loneliest things about his encounters was that to tell someone about them was to relive them, with no real sense of relief.

"No thanks. Not just now. I'm okay."

Jamie pulled away enough to examine his face. "Yeah?" They didn't seem convinced.

"I'm ready to try on clothes, so."

"Okay. Let's see who Edgar Lovejoy is."

They pushed the rack of clothes in front of the door so no one could see in, and Jamie changed the music to something Edgar didn't know. It was low and smoky and seductive. It reminded Edgar of Jamie.

Jamie asked questions. A *lot* of questions. Mostly questions to which Edgar didn't know the answers—"How do you want to feel in your clothes?" "What makes you feel powerful?" "How do you want others to perceive you?"—but just having Jamie's full attention on him was intoxicating.

Between questions, Jamie wandered around the store muttering, pulling things from racks and off shelves and adding them to the pieces Allie had left them.

Finally, they turned to him.

"Okay. I think we should just try a lot of different things, because you have no idea what you want. Right?"

Edgar felt a pang of anxiety. "Right."

Jamie clapped, eyes shining. "This is gonna be so fucking fun. I want you to close your eyes, and I'm gonna hand you stuff to put on."

Edgar didn't like to close his eyes. Closing your eyes was how you got snuck up on.

"Why?"

"Because I want you to get the full effect of the whole outfit on you as opposed to forming opinions about the individual pieces in the abstract."

For the first time, Edgar was struck by how much thought Jamie was putting into this. He'd gotten the sense this was a fun excuse for Jamie to dress him up, see how he'd look. And he'd been fine with that. More than fine. Jamie's eyes on him, no matter the reason, were very welcome. But although he had no doubt Jamie was having fun, this was something more.

Jamie dressed to express themself—gender, personality, interests, style, opinions. It was something that had drawn him to Jamie when they'd first met, the sense that Jamie knew exactly who they were and had no interest in hiding it.

Now Jamie was trying to give Edgar the chance to stop hiding. The chance to show himself to the world instead of trying to be invisible. It was a scary but intoxicating proposition.

Edgar looked around. He'd never seen a ghost in Allie's shop. She'd never seen a ghost here. It would probably be okay.

"Okay," Edgar said and forced his eyes closed. Jamie's warm hand on his cheek was calming, and he pressed into it.

"Thank you." Jamie's voice was velvet, and Edgar shivered. "Okay, here's outfit number one."

Jamie handed him the garments one at a time, and Edgar changed, his equilibrium off with his eyes closed. Jamie caught him a few times when he would have lost his balance, hands lingering a bit longer than necessary.

They adjusted his waistband and grazed his hip bone. Fingers ran through his hair and sent frissons from his scalp through his whole body. He thought about the other night, when Jamie had touched him so sweetly, he'd wanted to scream.

A whiff of Jamie's delicious scent, and then a gentle kiss feathered across Edgar's cheekbone.

"Okay. Open your eyes, and look in the mirror."

Edgar blinked blearily as his reflection came into focus. Only he didn't look like himself at all. Seafoam-green joggers ended in elastic at his anklebones, and his feet were shoved into too-small black-and-white-checkered sneakers. The shirt reminded Edgar of old pictures of Breton sailors, with its wide neck, three-quarter-length sleeves, and thick horizontal navy and white stripes.

At first, he couldn't tell why he looked so different; then he realized Jamie had pushed his hair forward where he always combed it back. It was just long enough to fall over his forehead, and it made him look both younger and less somber.

"Wow, I look…"

"Damn," Jamie said, eyes drinking him in. They cleared their throat. "So what do you think?"

"I like how you did my hair."

"Oh, good. I just thought I'd try it. But if you train your hair that way after you shower, it'll start doing it on its own."

Edgar imagined himself as a head of hair and Jamie training him into what they wanted him to be. It made his chest heat.

Flustered and at a loss for anything to say, Edgar blurted the only thing that came to mind. "You can see my—" He touched his collarbones. "It makes me feel…" Vulnerable. "Weird."

Jamie kissed his cheek softly and went back to flipping through the rack.

"Exposure doesn't have to feel vulnerable. If you choose when and how you let people see you, it can feel powerful."

Edgar considered what it would feel like to dress for Jamie rather than for the ghosts. What it would feel like to someday, just maybe, be able to believe something like *exposure doesn't have to feel vulnerable.*

"Like burlesque?" he asked, remembering Jamie's description

of the power they felt when they chose to reveal their body for the audience.

"Exactly. Okay, what else do you think?"

"I don't really like the color of the pants. It reminds me of a baby's room or something? But I like the elastic at the ankle. That would be convenient for biking especially."

Jamie was nodding, listening intently.

"The shoes are too small, but I would maybe wear them if they fit. Especially in the summer. They'd be cooler than boots."

He stared at the shirt. Kept coming back to it.

Jamie put their hands on Edgar's shoulders.

"Why don't we put the shirt over there and revisit it later?" Jamie suggested.

"Um, okay."

Jamie leaned in until their lips were an inch from Edgar's. "Can I tell you something?" they murmured.

Edgar's heartbeat sped. "Uh-huh."

"This shirt looks so hot on you. It's the tiniest tease, but it reminds me that you have a body underneath your clothes and that I want to reveal it." They kissed the corner of his mouth. "To strip your clothes off and see everything they hide." They kissed his cheekbone, lips lingering sweetly.

Heat pulsed at the base of Edgar's cock. "What…what happens when you look at the clothes I usually wear?"

"Oh, I want to do the same thing. I just want the clothes to land in a donation bin rather than on your floor."

Edgar laughed and groaned at the same time, erection making the pants suddenly far too tight.

Jamie's eyes traveled down his body, and they bit their lip. "All right, next outfit."

They tried on outfit after outfit, and they were laughable, ugly, fine, and silly by turns. But something started to happen the more clothes Edgar tried on. At some point in between the drop-crotch shorts (laughable), the neon orange jacket (ugly), the gray plaid trousers (fine), and the lavender and brown paisley (silly), Edgar stopped evaluating the clothing based on how different each piece was from what he usually wore. His polo shirts and plain-colored T-shirts didn't have to be the yardstick if he didn't want them to be.

When he opened his eyes to find himself in a utility kilt and beret, Edgar laughed. "This is fun," he said. "I can't believe I'm actually having a good time doing this."

"Wow, thanks," Jamie said, feigning offense. "So you're into the kilt, then?"

"Absolutely not. I look ridiculous. Besides, I'm not even Scottish."

"Noted. Are we keeping the beret?"

Edgar shot them a look, and they laughed.

"Okay, okay. Next step: I want you, using everything that we have learned here tonight, to put together an outfit of your own."

"Yes, sir," Edgar muttered and made his way into the bowels of Magpie Vintage.

What had he learned about his style? He didn't like anything scratchy or stiff or that had tight collars. He disliked the color purple. And there was something a little bit—dare he say *sexy?*—about the idea of titillating someone with his body.

The number of choices was so overwhelming that Edgar finally picked a rack, closed his eyes, and ran his hand along the clothes until he felt a texture he liked and pulled it out. The T-shirt was worn soft and had the characters from *Super Mario Bros,* on it. Edgar smiled. When they were kids and their dad had brought home a vintage Game Boy, Allie had said they were like Mario and Luigi. Poe had demanded to be Wario instead.

He found black jeans and a pair of sneakers and brought the armful back to Jamie, who was on their phone. They slid it back into their pocket when they saw him.

"Good job," they said, and Edgar's stomach thrummed with warmth. "I'm gonna close my eyes this time, and you tell me when you're dressed so I can get the full picture."

"Uh, I don't think it's gonna be that good." Edgar eyed the jeans and T-shirt. Not creative. Not that much different than what he usually wore. "I don't think I did a very good job. Maybe I should try again."

"You can try as many outfits as you want, but this is just to see. You're not getting graded or anything."

"No, I know." But Edgar wanted Jamie to feel like he'd listened, like he'd tried.

"Please show me this one?" Jamie asked, blue eyes soft. There was no way Edgar could deny them. He didn't want to.

"Okay, yeah. Sure."

Jamie smiled and closed their eyes.

He pulled on the jeans first. They were a little snug in the crotch and short in the leg, but they zipped. The shoes were uncomfortable. When he pulled on the T-shirt, it was clearly too small. But instead of stripping it off and looking for a larger size, Edgar pulled it taut over his chest and stared at himself in the mirror, wondering what Jamie would see when they looked at him.

"You can open," he murmured.

"Will you tell me about what you chose?" they asked, voice giving nothing away as they looked him up and down.

"I, um. The jeans are too short. This shirt was soft, so I picked it. But it's too small."

"Is it?" they asked, voice neutral again.

The shirt was tight. It skimmed the waistband of his jeans; his biceps strained at the fabric.

And Edgar couldn't look away from himself. "Isn't it?"

Jamie moved in front of him. They tugged the sleeves up so the hems were above the swell of muscle and bent to cuff his jeans.

"The shoes suck," Edgar said.

Jamie stood beside him. They slid an arm around his waist and tucked their hand into Edgar's back pocket. Then they pointed at the mirror.

"If you saw those two walking down the street, what would you think of them?"

"I would think…" Edgar stared into the mirror. "I would think they were gay."

"Would you think that one's shirt was too small?"

"No, I'd just think it was tight."

"Why?"

"Because he wanted to look good for his—" Edgar cut himself off, heart thumping in his ears. He felt a bit dizzy all of a sudden.

"Finish the sentence," Jamie commanded softly. They looked at him steadily, eyes warm, expression telling him that however he finished the sentence was okay.

"Boyfriend?" Edgar said, so low his voice was barely more than breath.

"Yeah?" Jamie asked, turning Edgar to face them. Their eyes burned, and there was a flush high on their cheekbones. "Is that what you want?"

Edgar had lost track of whether they were referring to him or to this hypothetical couple he was seeing on the street, but the answer was the same in either case.

"Yes."

Then Jamie was kissing him and kissing him. He was pressed back against the cash wrap, and a pile of folded clothes toppled to the floor.

Edgar was burning up. Jamie's clever hands slid up his back and down his pants. He'd never felt anything like this before—the vulnerable squirming electric shiver of being the object of desire. Visions flooded him. Of wearing an outfit that would make Jamie look at him and think of sex. Think of undressing him. Think of revealing inch after inch of flesh to their ravenous mouth. An outfit that Jamie would want to tear off him after they shoved him against the wall and—

"Jesus Christ, you just got so hard," Jamie groaned. "What are you thinking about?"

Edgar was lightheaded with lust and confusion and fear and want and *maybe*. "You, um, looking at me."

"Hey, hey, c'mere," Jamie said. The tone of their voice had shifted instantly from lust to comfort. "You look like you're about to fall over."

Edgar kept his eyes shut and let Jamie ease him down to the floor. The lights in the shop were suddenly far too bright, and the music pounded in his temples.

"How do you sit in this shirt?" Edgar muttered as inches of his back were exposed.

"Hotly," Jamie said. They knelt before Edgar, looking concerned. "Did you see…something?"

Edgar shook his head. He hadn't seen a ghost. He'd seen a

version of himself that it had never occurred to him to want. But now that he'd seen it—*did* he want it?

"Can you tell me what's up, babe?" Jamie sank to the floor beside him. They were awkwardly leaning their backs against the cash wrap, the fallen clothes making an uneven surface.

When Edgar opened his eyes, Jamie's fingers were intertwined with his, and Jamie's soft blue eyes looked concerned.

"I don't exactly know." Edgar spoke slowly, trying to figure out what he meant as he went. "I never thought of myself like this. Like a…like…"

"The object of someone's desire?" Jamie offered gently.

"Yeah, exactly. How did you know that?"

Jamie smiled at him fondly. "We teach women it's their job to make themselves desirable so they can be chosen by a man, and we teach men it's their job to choose. It's more complex when you're queer or trans though. The categories blur. Who does the desiring, who's the desired. It's not bound to gender."

Edgar nodded, mind racing. He knew all this, of course, but knowing it and feeling it weren't the same thing.

"And what do you prefer?" Edgar asked.

Jamie smiled. "I enjoy being the object of another person's desire when I'm in the mood for it. And I also find it hot to do the choosing. It all depends on my mood. And the other person's, of course."

Jamie began gathering the fallen garments and refolding them. Edgar got the impression they were giving him a chance to collect himself.

Edgar thought about how he'd felt when Jamie told him how hot he looked, how debauched. The squirming humiliation that was quickly replaced with relief when he let himself let go of the feeling that there was anything he was supposed to want, to need, to be.

"I think I like it," he said softly. But of course Jamie heard him. They knelt in front of him and lifted his chin.

"You like being the object of my desire?" they purred. "You like turning me on with how hot you are? How much I want you?"

His breath came shallower, and suddenly he wished he hadn't said anything, because Jamie was looking at him like they saw him. Like they really saw the writhing agonized *need* deep in his guts and liked him anyway. Maybe liked him more because of it.

"You…you like it that way too?" Edgar asked, feeling silly, because hadn't Jamie just said so? He closed his eyes.

"I do, Edgar. I like *you*. A lot."

Edgar opened his eyes, needing to tattoo this moment on his heart for later when he was once again unsure. Afraid of the world and of himself and of the things he wanted from Jamie.

"You know I don't give a shit about your clothes, right?" Jamie said.

Edgar was confused.

"You're so fucking hot, Edgar. I just want you to like what you wear because you deserve it. Because you deserve to express yourself and not be afraid. That's all I want."

"Easier said than done," Edgar joked. But it didn't come out sounding the way he'd intended.

Jamie slid a warm palm up his spine and rubbed his back. Then they tugged at the hem of his T-shirt, which had ridden up.

"Well, FYI, I am very much in favor of adding this shirt to your wardrobe. Even if you only wear it at home. For me."

A fizz of energy rushed from Edgar's stomach to his chest.

He'd never imagined himself wearing anything like this, but now he was already imagining the next time he'd wear it for Jamie.

For his boyfriend.

## 16

## Jamie

"Sorry, sorry, sorry," Jamie huffed as they hurried toward their sister, picking their way through the maze of clothing racks, poufs, handbags, and precariously large floral arrangements. "I'm so sorry," Jamie said again. "I had to cross the 10."

Emma hung up her phone and shot Jamie an unimpressed look.

When she'd texted to invite Jamie wedding dress shopping with her, Jamie had been touched. Was it possible that Emma wanted their opinion more than it had seemed in the family text thread? It had sowed a tiny seed of hope that maybe they could connect after all.

"I can't wait to see these dresses." They looked around, trying to remember the names of Emma's many friends, but didn't see them. In fact, they didn't see anyone familiar. Jamie had imagined a scene like in a movie, where Emma came out it progressively larger dresses, and when she found the right one, they'd all cheer for her and toast with champagne. But apparently that was just in the movies.

"Is Mom not coming?"

It wouldn't be unusual for their mother to have cancelled last-minute, pulled into this or that work crisis, but given Blythe's excitement when they'd met for breakfast, Jamie thought family would've trumped work on a day like today.

Emma shook her head. "She's already seen them."

Jamie was confused. Had the cheering and champagne toasting already happened without them?

"So this is…just to show me?"

"You said you wanted to see!" Emma sounded exasperated, and Jamie already regretted driving across town on their lunch break.

"Emma, I do want to see the dresses. I just thought other people were going to be here. It's not a problem."

Emma's irritation turned to excitement, and she grabbed their hand. "Okay, be right back."

She rushed off down a hallway marked *Brides*.

Jamie pulled out their phone and flopped onto a fluffy-looking couch, wincing when it was harder than it had looked.

**Amelia**: Dude, what about the abandoned Six Flags?

Amelia's text was followed by a sheaf of photographs that presented a tangle of nostalgia, rot, and impish reclamation. Graffiti decorated the SpongeBob SquarePants ride; a purple, green, and yellow carousel had been relieved of its horses; the skeleton of a roller coaster stood against the summer blue sky, weeds taller than Amelia's head choking the structure.

**Absolutely perfect!**, Jamie texted back.

They zoomed in on the photograph to see the details of the graffiti.

"Excuse me." The woman who'd spoken wore all black and stood with her hands clasped behind her back like a docent.

"Hi," Jamie said.

"If you'd like to come with me, I can take your measurements while you wait for your sister."

Her voice had the lulling, unflappable quality that Jamie associated with post-op nurses and childcare professionals. It said, *I am very good at making sure everyone remains calm*. It filled Jamie with anxiety.

"Oh, I'm not getting a dress, so I don't need to be measured," Jamie said in the case-closed-thanks-bye voice they'd perfected for moments such as these.

"Of course, yes. I will be measuring you for your suit. Your sister explained everything."

Jamie fumed. This was why Emma had invited them for this special private viewing. It wasn't her desire to share this moment with Jamie, nor was it because she valued their opinion. It was an ambush. Emma and their mother wanted them in a woman's suit—the kind bridal boutiques made out of taffeta for mothers of the bride, in iridescent fabrics called shit like "perfect pearl" or "evening solitude."

Jamie would rather don a hair shirt.

They managed a "No, thank you" through gritted teeth.

"I'll let you and your sister discuss it," the woman said and faded silently into the background.

Emma swanned down the hallway, grinning, and for a moment, Jamie remembered her wrapped in their mother's wedding dress when they played dress-up as children. She had always wanted to be the bride.

Her smile faltered when she saw Jamie's face. Her eyes cut to the woman who'd approached Jamie, and guilt flickered in her expression. She opened her mouth and shut it again, chewing on her words. Jamie waited.

"I just thought it would be easier for you," Emma said finally. "You always say how busy you are, so I thought you could kill two birds with one stone."

"And did you also think that when I told you I'd get a suit in the color you requested, I was planning on getting fitted for it at a wedding dress store?" Jamie kept their voice low, not wanting to attract attention. "I'm pretty sure you didn't think that, Em."

She put her hands on her hips. "Why do you care who makes your suit?"

"I care," Jamie said, voice quietly poisonous, "because the suit that they'll make at a place like this will be a woman's suit, and I do not want a woman's suit. Obviously."

"They're very good at what they do," Emma sniffed. "I'm sure it will fit you excellently."

"It's not about that, and you know it. What the hell is wrong with you, Emma? I told you I'd take care of it, and it would be in the color you requested." Jamie hissed. "Why do *you* care who makes my suit?"

They'd meant it as a rhetorical question because Emma was being intentionally thick, but then Emma bit her lip.

"Wait, why *do* you care?"

Emma's shoulders slumped. "Fine. Mom suggested that we

have the shop make you a dress in addition to the suit in case you'd change your mind and wear it."

"Mom suggested," Jamie echoed.

They could imagine their mother and Emma, picking out fabric for the dress they secretly wanted to see Jamie in. Discussing what silhouette would flatter Jamie in the way they hoped. Jamie felt like they'd swallowed a snake. It writhed in their guts and tried to slither up their throat until they couldn't speak.

"Come on," Emma said. "It's not a big deal. It's just to have the option."

How old would Jamie have to get before their family saw them as themself rather than the frustration of what they'd hoped for?

How much would they need to achieve before their family valued their dreams and goals?

And the question that really made the snake writhe: Did Jamie care? Was maintaining a relationship with their family worth the disrespect they would have to tolerate?

As Jamie contemplated this, Emma went on, defending their mother like she always did and finally lathering herself into, "Besides, it's not even about you. It's *my* wedding."

"Emma," Jamie said, exhausted. "You get that I'm nonbinary, right? And you get that asking me to wear a dress when I'm not a woman feels really bad to me, right?"

"I've been a really good sport about all that stuff," Emma hissed, leaving Jamie wondering how she could possibly have gotten that impression. "So yeah, I thought maybe you could just give me a break for this one day so I can have my wedding the way I want it. But I guess that's too much to ask."

Once, tears would have pricked Jamie's eyes, but now the ball of betrayal, disappointment, and shame rolled down their throat and settled in their gut. Emma had never accepted them. She'd just been playing along until the moment it inconvenienced her too much, and now she wanted them to tuck themself away.

"It is too much to ask," Jamie told her. They let Emma hear their sadness. "Going against the deepest parts of yourself. It's far, far too much to ask of anyone."

Emma gaped. Jamie realized that if this was the way they left it, this could be the last time they ever saw Emma. Her in her wedding dress, midafternoon, standing in front of the sign that said *Brides*. The ball of emotion threatened to come back up.

"You look really beautiful in that dress," Jamie said. They just had time to see Emma's expression soften to confusion before they walked away.

✦ ✦ ✦

Later that evening, Jamie knocked on Edgar's door, desperate to lose themself in Edgar's sweet embrace. Part of them had thought that Emma would text or call to apologize, so they kept their phone on vibrate in their pocket all afternoon at work.

She hadn't.

Edgar answered the door smiling shyly. He'd styled his hair the way Jamie had at the store. Jamie touched it gently as they stepped inside.

Edgar's smile disappeared.

"What's wrong?" he asked, cupping Jamie's shoulders.

"It looks really good," Jamie said.

"Jamie."

Their throat ached with the threat of tears.

"Bad day," they choked out before they found themself enveloped in the warmest, most comforting hug of their life. Enfolded, enveloped, they slumped a little and let Edgar take their weight.

"Do you want to talk about it?" Edgar asked, stroking their hair.

Jamie sighed and let Edgar ferry them to the couch.

They told him about the bridal shop and Emma and their mother's plan. Edgar's fists were clenched the whole time Jamie was talking.

"I wish..." Jamie said, then shook their head.

*Winners don't wish; they work!* Their mother's phrase popped up uninvited in Jamie's mind.

"Wish what?" Edgar asked.

Jamie lifted his fist to their lips and kissed it. Edgar unclenched his fingers.

"I wish I had a sister like yours," Jamie said. "A partner in crime. Like it was Emma and me as a team calling each other to talk about whatever irritating shit our parents did. Instead of it feeling like the three of them are a team and I didn't get picked."

"I hate thinking of you being left out of your own family like that," Edgar said.

"I don't get why they act like they want me to be so involved in this wedding stuff, but they don't want my real opinion. So why ask me?"

Of course, that probably wouldn't be an issue after today.

Edgar murmured soothing sounds, but Jamie didn't want to think about this anymore. All they wanted was to be taken out of themself.

Jamie wrapped their arms around his neck, kissing him hungrily. Edgar smelled so good, and his arms were strong, and his chest was warm, and Jamie just wanted to feel loved instead of judged or manipulated.

Jamie kissed Edgar's throat, loving the way Edgar pressed into them. They sucked on his skin until Edgar gasped and his knees shook. He clutched at Jamie's shoulders to stay upright.

"I want you," Edgar said, eyes begging.

"Yes, whatever you want. Tell me."

Jamie's heart was pounding with the desire to take Edgar apart with pleasure. To control this man whose whole life felt out of control. To keep him safe.

Edgar took Jamie's hand and led them to the bedroom. He stripped out of his clothes, and Jamie drank in the sight with appreciation. Then he lay down on the bed, ass up, and looked at Jamie.

"Would you fuck me?" Edgar asked. "Hold me down?" His lashes fluttered with effort. "M-make me come?"

Liquid fire slid through Jamie's veins, and they groaned. Edgar clenched his eyes shut.

They walked over to the bed, admiring the broad planes of Edgar's shoulders and the delicate curve of his lip in profile against his pillow.

"You're so beautiful," Jamie said. "And fuck yes, I will."

Jamie traced the curve of Edgar's spine from the nape of his neck to the crack of his ass, and Edgar shuddered, goose bumps rising on his skin though the evening was warm. His ass was round and plump, and Jamie wanted to give it a swat and see how it jiggled, but that was for another time.

Ditching their pants, Jamie climbed in bed next to Edgar and kissed the path their fingers had just taken. Edgar shuddered and trembled as their lips moved over him, and when Jamie licked back up again, Edgar's muscles tensed.

"You okay?" Jamie asked.

Edgar groaned in response.

They nipped at Edgar's ass and were rewarded with him raising it for their thorough investigation.

"God, you're so fucking hot," Jamie muttered. "Turn over?"

Edgar did, revealing that his face and throat were flushed pink. His erection strained against his stomach.

Jamie straddled Edgar's waist, and they kissed deep and desperate, tongues entwining, lips feasting, until they were both breathing heavily. They ground their crotch into Edgar's hip, loving the exquisite pressure.

"Jamie, Jamie," Edgar said.

"What's up, baby?"

"Please, fuck. I need you. It's been so long and I…I need it. I need you."

Edgar's eyes were wild, and he was writhing on the bed. Seeing Edgar like that had Jamie nearly lightheaded with lust.

"I've got you, baby," Jamie said.

Edgar's cock was hard and wet at the tip. They wanted to drink down his nectar and then blow his mind. Instead, they ran a fingertip over the precome beading there and rubbed it between their fingers.

"You need this?" Jamie said, voice low and rough with want.

"So fucking bad."

Jamie felt like electricity held together by a fragile skin. "You like to get fucked hard by a big cock, Edgar?"

Edgar nodded slowly.

"You sure?" they teased.

"Yes, god, please fuck me," he said, looking into Jamie's eyes.

Jamie groaned, lust making them throb. They pulled out the

strap-on from their overnight bag and held two dildos up to Edgar—one of an average size, the other a bit larger and with a wicked curve.

"Lucky boys get to pick," they said. "So which is it gonna be?"

Edgar's eyes flew back and forth between them and then up to Jamie. He swallowed hard, then pointed to the larger of the two.

*Fuck*, they couldn't wait to see Edgar's face when they slid inside him.

Jamie slid their underwear off and stepped into the harness, tightening the leather straps around their hips.

They lubed their cock and knelt between Edgar's legs.

"You want this?" Jamie teased Edgar's hole with the tip.

Edgar moaned wildly and let his knees fall apart. He looked wanton and beautiful, cheeks flushed, dick straining against his belly.

Jamie pressed inside him slowly, feeling the smooth muscle giving way as they pressed deeper.

Edgar let out tiny little gasps, and Jamie watched closely as they pushed in deeper. Edgar shifted his hips, and they both groaned as Jamie slid inside him.

"Right there. Oh, fuck. Right there."

Jamie fucked Edgar until his eyes rolled back in his head. He squirmed and strained, cock so hard it bounced against his stomach.

"Please," Edgar begged weakly.

"Turn over," Jamie said.

He groaned and threw his head back, then flipped over onto his hands and knees and looked backward over his shoulder at Jamie.

They slid back inside him, and Edgar found the angle that made him gasp, and then they moved together.

"Touch your cock," they instructed. "But only a little bit. I wanna see."

Edgar's groan was the sweetest reward Jamie had ever won. His hand rose tentatively from the bed to close around his leaking erection. The second he made contact, he melted against Jamie, groaning and saying mindless things about how gorgeous Jamie was and how sexy.

While he stroked himself, Jamie kept fucking him, seeking out the angle that made him moan.

"So close," Edgar gasped. "Please, please, please, Jamie."

Jamie had never heard someone sound so close to desperate tears. They fucking loved it. They felt glorious and powerful, and they couldn't wait to hear what sounds Edgar made when he came.

"Get on top," Jamie said.

Edgar's eyes were wild with lust, and they did it without question. Jamie settled on the bed, and Edgar straddled them, reaching behind himself to guide Jamie back inside.

"Now. I want you to fuck yourself on my cock however you like, and play with yourself until you come."

Edgar lowered himself, wincing, back onto Jamie's cock. Then he pushed deeper and froze.

"You okay?"

"Jamie." Edgar's voice was full of worship.

His eyes fell shut, his head fell back, and he began rising and slamming himself down on Jamie. Jamie thrust up to meet him, heat swirling between their legs.

Edgar rode them like a man possessed. Finally, he started dropping his weight down on Jamie's hips, and his eyes rolled back in his head.

"Oh, oh," he gasped in tiny breaths. *Please*, he mouthed again and again.

Jamie lifted their hips, feet on the bed, to give Edgar more contact, and Edgar took it.

"Yes, baby, yes, fuck yourself; that's it," Jamie murmured.

They reached up and tweaked his nipples, and he hissed. Jamie did it again.

"'M gonna come. Oh god. Jamie."

Jamie took Edgar by the waist and steadied him so they could thrust harder. One moment, Edgar was riding them, head thrown back. The next, Edgar's mouth fell open in a silent scream, every muscle tensed, and then he was coming in great strangled gasps.

"Oh my fucking, oh god, oh shit," Edgar said as the orgasm racked him.

He fell forward onto Jamie and kissed them avidly, his breath still coming in gasps. Then he groaned and buried his face in their neck.

Jamie smiled then and stroked up and down Edgar's back. No sex act had ever made them feel more powerful, and tears pricked at their eyes.

Eventually, Edgar reluctantly lifted himself off Jamie's cock, wincing a little. Then he lay next to Jamie and put an arm around their waist.

Edgar was sexy and sweet *and* he liked to cuddle after sex? The total package.

They lay that way for a few peaceful minutes, and then Edgar asked, "What would you like me to do for you?"

"Hmm. Lie on your back?"

Edgar did, watching Jamie remove the strap from under orgasm-heavy eyelids.

Jamie straddled Edgar's thick thigh and squeezed the muscle between their own.

"You're so gorgeous," Edgar murmured as they began to roll their hips.

Tendrils of delicate lust danced through Jamie's belly, up and down their thighs, and pooled at their groin.

Edgar's hand fell on their back, pulling them closer. He murmured how sexy they were and how hard they'd made him come. Jamie's lower belly began to tremble with the prelude to orgasm.

They ground their hips harder into Edgar and felt the pleasure begin to unfurl. It was a murmuration, notes of pleasure striking and moving in swooping formations until Jamie's head was spinning and they couldn't hear anything but the pulse of their own blood.

The orgasm broke over them like a wave. The pleasure was so sweet and so shattering that Jamie couldn't do anything but let it drown them.

"Fuck," they groaned, collapsing into Edgar. They settled into his side.

Soft fingers stroking their hair and neck brought them back to the present.

Edgar murmured worshipfully. "You're so fucking hot. Thanks. For letting me see you. And for, uh, you know."

"Fucking your brains out until you came screaming?" Jamie suggested casually.

Edgar groaned at that and reached for Jamie again, rolling them underneath him and kissing them until they started to get turned on again, and then they pushed him away and buried their face in his neck.

Edgar tightened his arms around them.

"This is perfect," Jamie murmured, then nestled their face back into the curve of Edgar's neck.

"Perfect," Edgar mumbled and ran their fingers through Jamie's hair until they drifted off to sleep feeling safe and warm.

# 17

# Jamie

9:08 A.M.

**Emma**: Hey. I wanted to apologize for last week. I thought about it, and I shouldn't have gone along with Mom's idea to make you a dress. It sucked of us.

2:23 P.M.

**Emma**: I should have said that to Mom, and I shouldn't have had that idea in the first place. I got carried away with the whole vision and forgot that it's not all about me. I'm really sorry, Jamie.

6:57 P.M.

**Jamie**: Thank you for the apology. I really appreciate it.

7:02 P.M.

**Emma**: I was talking to my (gay) friend Thomas. He's in fashion, and he told me that an old classmate of his is now a menswear designer and is going to be doing a pop-up in a few weeks. I'd like to pay for you to have a suit made by him. Anything you want. It doesn't have to be for the wedding.

7:10 P.M.

**Emma**: I don't know why I said he was gay. I panicked. 😬

7:49 P.M.

**Jamie**: That's a really kind gift, Em, thank you.

7:49 P.M.

**Jamie**: LOL I didn't know you had any gay friends 😆

7:50 P.M.

**Jamie**: Also how you put it in parentheses haha

7:58 P.M.

**Emma**: I'll tell Thomas, my GAY FRIEND, to set it up 😂

7:59 P.M.

**Jamie**: Thanks, I'll show my GAY ASS up!

8:04 P.M.

**Emma**: 🖤

✦ ✦ ✦

A week later, when Edgar and Jamie were half an hour into a movie, cuddling on the couch, Edgar's phone rang. He shot Jamie an apologetic look, then answered. He froze comically, one hand on the way to his face.

"I'm on my way," he said tightly. "Don't worry, everything is going to be fine. Text me your room number when you get there?"

Jamie leaned in, trying to hear the voice on the phone, but Edgar hung up and stared at them.

"Allie's in labor." His voice was urgent, but he didn't move.
"Holy shit!"
"I have to go to the hospital."
But he was frozen to the spot. Jamie cocked their head.
"Are you…okay?"
Edgar nodded.
"That was the most un-okay nod I've ever seen."
Edgar nodded again,.
"Can I drive you?" they offered.
"Um." A long time passed. Jamie peered into Edgar's eyes. Rapid calculations were clearly going on behind them.

Jamie took Edgar's phone from his hand and slid it in his pocket. They rested their hands on his shoulders and leaned in. "Edgar? Look at me."

Edgar's eyes focused slowly on Jamie.

"Let me drive you to the hospital. I'd feel better if you weren't driving. Okay?"

"I don't drive," Edgar reminded Jamie.

"Of course. Even better then. Do you need to bring anything?"

Edgar shook his head. "Just a second," he mumbled and went into the bathroom.

"Are you having a panic attack?" Jamie asked through the door.

"I don't think so," came the shaky reply.

Jamie hadn't seen the sick expression Edgar got when he was scared of a ghost, so that was good at least.

Oh, shit. The ghosts. Of course. Jamie had never considered it, but Edgar's particular ability would probably make hospitals one of the worst places to be.

When he came out of the bathroom, Jamie asked, "Babe, are you worried about seeing ghosts at the hospital?"

Edgar raised haunted eyes to Jamie. "I'm worried about my sister," he said. "But now I'm also worried about ghosts."

Jamie winced, wishing they hadn't mentioned it. "Shit, I'm sorry."

Edgar put a hand on the back of Jamie's neck, fingertips brushing sensitive skin and sending a shiver to the roots of their hair. "I'm worried about ghosts all the time. I never, ever forget that they're all around me. You didn't make it worse. It's always terrible."

Edgar sounded so matter-of-fact that it broke Jamie's heart. Knowing that Edgar had to deal with this all the time. That even when he wasn't seeing a ghost, he worried about seeing one. That the threat of fear lurked within every moment of joy. That it wasn't something that would ever go away.

But all they could do was nod and lead the way to their truck.

"Jamie?" Edgar said when they'd buckled their seat belts. "Thanks for tonight. And for coming with me. It's better when you're there. Here."

Jamie leaned over the gearshift and kissed Edgar, soft and sweet. Even if they couldn't make the ghosts leave Edgar alone, at least they could be there for him.

"I'm glad."

✦ ✦ ✦

The hospital was a maze of elevators, fluorescent lights, and garbled announcements squeaking loudly over the public address system. Two nurses at two different information desks had already directed Edgar to other floors to speak to other people. Apparently they were in the wrong wing.

Edgar was polite and biddable, but he wasn't aggressive enough to get results. When the third nurse sent them away, Jamie pulled up the hospital on their phone and tried to find the correct wing. It seemed to be above them and to the left.

Jamie grabbed Edgar's hand and tugged him toward the stairwell.

"Other way, sir!" the nurse called after them, but Jamie didn't stop. They jogged up the stairs and were met by a doctor coming down.

"Are you looking for someone?" the doctor asked.

When Edgar didn't say anything, Jamie said, "Yeah, his sister is having a baby."

The doctor nodded. "Go through the double doors up there, take your first right, then your second left. They won't let you in unless you're on the list though."

"But…" Edgar began.

"Okay, thank you!" Jamie called, hooking their elbow through Edgar's.

They found the maternity ward where the doctor said it would be, but the nurses at the front desk stopped them. "Who are you here for?"

Edgar began to open his mouth, but Jamie cut him off.

"We're here for Allie Lovejoy. This is the baby's father, and I'm the mother's doula. What room should we go to, please?"

The nurse narrowed her eyes like she might ask more questions; then someone yelled something from behind her, and her nostrils flared. "You got ID?" was all she said.

They showed their licenses, and the nurse waved them down the hallway. It was moments like this that Jamie was grateful they'd legally changed their name, even if Louisiana didn't allow them to change the gender on their ID.

"Thanks," Edgar said and reached for Jamie's hand.

When they found Allie, she seemed comfortable. She smiled but shot Edgar a look. "I told you not to come yet, dude. You're gonna be waiting forever."

Edgar scuffed his toe and looked at the floor, hands clasped behind his back, and Jamie imagined they were seeing Edgar the way he'd been as a child.

"I didn't want you to be by yourself," he said, taking her hand.

"She's not by herself," a voice said from the door.

Jamie turned to see a short Black woman standing there, holding a bottle of water.

"Hey, Edgar," she said. "Been a long time."

Edgar's eyes went wide, and a slow smile crept across his face. "Cameron, hey. I—hey. Welcome back."

He moved to her stiffly but relaxed when they embraced.

Cameron handed Allie the water and turned to Jamie. "You Jamie?"

"Yeah." Jamie was thrilled that they had rated a mention. "Nice to meet you."

"I'm Cameron. I've known these two forever."

They shook hands. Now wasn't the time to ask Cameron what the Lovejoys had been like when they were younger, but Jamie wanted to later. Cameron sat in the chair next to Allie's bed and pulled a paperback out of her bag.

Edgar and Allie exchanged information in a sibling shorthand that Jamie had never shared with their sister.

"I guess it'll be a while," Edgar said apologetically to Jamie.

"I'm good," Jamie assured him. They squeezed his shoulder and felt the muscle relax.

Soon, Allie was drifting off, and Cameron stood and motioned them out the door. They trooped to the family waiting room and found a cluster of seats.

Cameron reached into her bag and pulled out a manila envelope, which she handed to Jamie.

"If you need a distraction."

Inside the envelope were dozens of crossword puzzles. Actual newsprint ones, razored from the paper itself.

"Don't you want to do them?" Jamie asked, not wanting to waste Cameron's stash.

"I do them. But my grandmother sends them to me every week, so I have a lot. Go ahead."

"Awesome, thanks."

Cameron said she was going home to shower and change and pick up Allie's phone charger and would return.

"Take care of her while I'm gone," she instructed Edgar.

"I always do."

Cameron regarded him for a moment before giving a single nod. The second she was gone, Jamie turned to Edgar.

Edgar leafed through the crossword puzzles, then stood up and paced the waiting room as he spoke.

"We grew up with her and her brother. They lived across the street when we were little. She and Allie kept in touch after she moved, but I haven't seen her in a while."

Edgar kept pacing for a while before dropping into the chair next to Jamie's. He pointed at the crossword.

"*Eiderdown.* Forty-three across."

Jamie inked in the letters and rested their other hand on Edgar's thigh.

As they were debating the square shared by twenty-five across and sixteen down, someone ran through the door.

"Where is she?" he bellowed.

Edgar's head snapped up, and he stood, crossword puzzle floating to the floor.

The man wore faded black jeans and an elbow-cracked black leather jacket. He was smaller than Edgar and slighter, with the same dark hair falling in a tangle of waves down his neck. His brown eyes were ringed with kohl.

Edgar swallowed audibly, and Jamie almost missed the word he choked out.

"Poe."

# 18

# Edgar

"Eddie. Where is she?"

It was the first time Edgar had heard his brother's voice in three years, other than a saved voicemail that he played sometimes: *Happy birthday, bro. Hope it's a good one.* And no one had ever called him Eddie except Poe.

Edgar had texted Poe on the way to the hospital and once they'd found Allie's room but hadn't heard back from him and certainly hadn't expected him to be close enough to be here this quickly.

Questions swamped Edgar: *How did you get here? Where have you been? Why haven't you answered any of my texts recently? Why didn't you call?*

But then he registered his brother's face. Edgar had been so caught up in trying to map the changes the last few years had wrought in Poe that he hadn't noticed Poe's eyes were wild. His mouth was slack on the left side where a small pucker of scar tissue—the result of an ill-conceived fence-climbing adventure when they were children—tugged it out of line with the rest of his face. He looked terrified.

"Are you okay?" Edgar asked.

"Allie? Is she—she's okay?"

"She's doing fine. Didn't you see my messages?"

Poe fumbled in various pockets and frowned. "Um. Yeah, no, I... Okay."

He visibly forced his breathing to level out and tucked his hands in his armpits before slouching in the doorframe.

His hair was long and his frame lithe now rather than skinny, but Edgar could still see the little boy who'd shoved his hands under his arms so no one would see them shaking.

"She's sleeping right now," Edgar said, trying to infuse reassurance into his voice. Poe would never accept outright comfort. "But I'm sure she'd want to see you."

"Yeah. Okay." Poe didn't move. "Well, I'll let her sleep. As long as she's okay."

Edgar took a step toward his brother, wanting so badly to fold him into his arms, feel the solidity of Poe's body for himself, prove to himself that he was actually here. But Poe didn't unfold. He leaned a tiny bit closer to Edgar and allowed his shoulders to be clasped for just a moment. He felt rigid beneath the leather jacket, muscles bunched like a panther ready to run. Edgar let him go and sat back down.

"This is Jamie," Edgar said, having momentarily forgotten they were here. "My...boyfriend." He tried the word out nervously. It tasted sweet on his tongue.

"Hey, Jamie, they/them. Nice to meet you, Poe. I've heard…a sprinkling about you." Jamie smiled their warmest smile and stood, holding a hand out to Poe.

Poe looked Jamie up and down. "Hey, Jamie." He held out his fist to bump, the sleeve of his jacket hanging halfway over his hand.

Jamie bumped fist to leather casually and sat back down beside Edgar, pressing their shoulder against his as if they could pass on Poe's gesture.

They sat in a triangle of silence until Poe asked Jamie, "So are you the one who got my brother to wear a color?"

"I wear colors," Edgar grumbled.

"Yeah," Jamie said emphatically, and Edgar's heart leapt at their defense. "Beige is technically a color, because it has shades of yellow and brown in it."

Edgar grumbled wordlessly this time.

The right corner of Poe's mouth tugged up. Jamie wouldn't know, but they'd just elicited a rare genuine smile.

"Where are you living?" Edgar asked.

Once, there had been no one in the world closer to Edgar than Poe. Edgar's mind knew they weren't close anymore, but his body still recognized his brother's, still retained the comfort born of years and years of flopping onto the couch together or the floor; of bumping shoulders to get the other's attention and taking bites of food off the other's plate; of falling, finally, asleep.

How did you go from sharing popsicles and socks with someone to not knowing what state they lived in?

Poe grinned, showing teeth. This was not, for him, a smile. It was a confrontation. "Guess."

Anger kindled so quickly Edgar frightened himself with it. "How could I guess?"

Jamie was looking between them quizzically. "Is this a bit?" they asked.

"Nope," Poe bit off as Edgar said, "He's just being a dick, like usual."

"So, um. Where do you live then?" Jamie asked.

Edgar could see Poe weighing whether to poke around in Jamie's clockwork and learn what made them tick. He glared at Poe.

"Nashville. For the moment."

"Cool. Are you into the music scene?" Jamie asked.

"On that note," Poe said, "I gotta piss." He stood up and loped off down the hall.

Jamie turned wide eyes on Edgar. "I can *see* why Allie didn't ask him to be her birth partner."

The comment was so not what he had expected, and the notion was so absurd that Edgar let out a bark of laughter.

"How are you? You looked pretty, uh, shocked to see him."

Edgar nodded blankly. He felt like he was drifting closer and closer to the ceiling. "Been a while," was all he could manage.

A warm hand cupped the back of his neck.

"Sweetheart," Jamie said, low and gentle, and Edgar shivered, wanting nothing more than to be back in his living room with Jamie, head in their lap on the couch, as Jamie played with his hair.

A few minutes later, Poe came back, slipping his phone in his pocket. He hesitated at the door. "Y'all done talking shit about me, or should I give you another minute?"

"We're done," Jamie said lightly.

Cameron came back into the waiting room, clothes changed and carrying Allie's weekender.

"How's that puzzle coming?" she asked warmly.

"Oh, uh. We got a little…" Edgar began.

"Distracted," Jamie finished.

Poe stood up to face Cameron. "Guilty," he said, scuffing his heel against the linoleum. "Hey, Cam."

Poe had always idolized Cameron. Hell, so had Edgar.

Cameron looked Poe up and down, and her expression said everything that Edgar wished he could say: *Where the hell have you been? Why the hell haven't you called your siblings? What the hell is wrong with you?*

For a moment, he thought Cameron was going to say it all out loud. But her face went soft, and she said, "Uh-oh, it's the Poe-Poe. Everyone hide your contraband!"

Edgar sputtered out a laugh. Poe, being the youngest, had gone through an irritating tattletale phase when he wasn't included in their hijinks.

"That was one time!" Poe exclaimed.

Cameron and Edgar snickered.

"This one time," Cameron told Jamie, "we had stolen a bottle of liquor from their aunt's bar and were all gonna try it. Little Poe-boy here—"

Poe looked pained at the introduction of yet another old nickname.

"—ran to tell their daddy on us. Turned out we'd grabbed a bottle of mint schnapps by mistake, so maybe that was a blessing in disguise. I couldn't brush my teeth for weeks without the taste of mint making me gag."

"What did your dad do?" Jamie asked.

Edgar remembered the grip on his skinny upper arm and his father's sweat, which smelled of sour mash and the applejack brandy he liberally added to his beer.

"Probably confiscated it to drink himself," Poe drawled.

Edgar shut his mouth.

"You gonna give an old friend a hug or what?" Cameron said to Poe.

"I stink," Poe said. "Been on the road."

Cameron narrowed her eyes and shrugged. "I'm gonna go check on your sister," she said. She got a few steps down the hall before turning back around. "Y'all coming?"

They scrambled after her, Poe falling into step with Cameron and saying something too quietly for Edgar to overhear.

A hand reached for Edgar's. Jamie. Their sweet, comforting presence had been a source of stability the whole night. Now, rays of sun were beginning to peek through the windows.

"You don't have to stay," Edgar told Jamie. At the flash of hurt in their eyes, he quickly added, "I mean, I want you here. I just…I know it's been a long time, and you have a life and work and…"

"It's Saturday," they said. "And I'm right where I want to be." They lifted their joined hands and kissed Edgar's knuckles.

Cameron knocked softly, then opened Allie's door. She was groggy but awake, a nurse checking her vitals. It wasn't visiting hours, but Edgar guessed that since Cameron was a doctor, no one questioned her right to be there.

Poe hung back by the door, and it took a minute for Allie to notice him.

"Poe?" she said. He stood a little straighter, and her eyes watered. "Get over here, you asshole."

Poe walked woodenly to her side and let Allie pull him into a hug. The moment she let him go, he moved back, staring at her like he could drink her in.

"Where the fuck have you been?" she demanded. "And why are you constitutionally incapable of returning a phone call?"

Poe opened and closed his mouth like a fish. "Sorry," he mumbled.

"Ugh, shut up, never mind. I'm so damn glad to see you."

She looked on the edge of tears, and Edgar took her hand.

Allie looked between her brothers. "I'm having a baby. Can you fucking believe it?" She giggled. It was a sound as familiar to Edgar as his own voice, the burble of her laughter enveloping him in warmth. "We see ghosts, and I'm having a fucking baby," she said, her laughter turning manic.

Poe snorted. "Dad abandoned us, and Mom went crazy, and you're having a baby," he said, then sputtered out a chuckle of his own. He and Allie looked at each other and laughed even harder.

Allie had a contraction and swore a blue streak, then went right back to laughing. For some reason, this struck Edgar as being absurd.

"Poe ran away from us the second he could, I'm a basket case, and you're having a baby!"

He joined in his siblings' laughter, and something broke open inside him. Having Poe back had shifted a missing piece back into place. They were a triangle once more, balance restored.

Allie's contractions were coming more and more frequently. Cameron installed herself by Allie's side and took her hand.

"Distract me!" Allie demanded.

Edgar scrabbled for something to say, but his mind was blank. Poe's expression said he could think of many things to say, but none of them were appropriate. Cameron watched them with an expression that clearly said, *Get it together and distract your damn sister!*

Finally Jamie spoke, their tone so natural and calm that the tension in the whole room relaxed.

Allie had another contraction. And another. And then it was on.

Edgar stood, shoulder blades pressed against the painted cement wall, and watched as a creature tore its way out of his sister's body in slow motion. He couldn't imagine how anyone could experience such a thing without being ripped to shreds.

"I can't believe I did this! What is wrong with me? I regret everything! How did you let me do this?" This last was snarled at Cameron, who had the calm of those regularly faced with the insides of other people's bodies and equipped with the knowledge to fix them.

"You are *not* dragging me into this mess," Cameron said. "One day, it was, 'I will never be in that mess,' and a year later, you were like, 'Will you be my birth partner?'"

"I *know*!" Allie said, then devolved into grunting. "God, why didn't I have a home birth?"

"Because insurance wouldn't cover it," Cameron said calmly. "And because your apartment would end up splattered with baby gore from front door to kitchen if you tried to give birth in there," she added.

"Fuck, I gotta move," Allie groaned. "My place is, like, twenty square feet."

Poe snickered. "I can't believe you still live there. Remember how you had to saw your bed in half to get it up the stairs?"

"No one say another word about my tiny hideous apartment!" Allie commanded. "Say nice, sweet, gorgeous shit about the beautiful fucking world I'm bringing this kid into!"

Then her eyes went wide.

"Oh my god. I'm bringing a kid into the world. This terrible world. Where they won't have civil rights. Or health care. Or breathable air. Oh my lord, what have I done? Cameron! Keep it in there!"

"Yeah, I'll get right on that," Cameron said.

"Oh my god. Oh my god," Allie said over and over again. "I'm gonna ruin its life. Somehow. Oh god! Fuuuuuck."

Poe edged toward Edgar and pressed himself against the same wall. The zippers of his leather jacket scratched against the wall as he trembled.

"You okay?" Edgar asked, never taking his eyes off Allie.

"Uh-uh," Poe said, his eyes on her as well.

Jamie was listening to something Cameron said, then they went into the bathroom to get water for Allie.

"They're nice," Poe said, nodding his chin at Jamie.

Edgar nodded. "They're everything."

Poe's zippers rattled louder against the wall.

"Are you scared for Allie or the baby?" Edgar asked. He knew better than to put an arm around Poe for comfort.

"Allie."

"Me too."

"It'll be weird to have a baby around. It's been just us three for so long," Poe said.

"Weird to have you around," Edgar replied. "It's been just us two for so long."

Poe nodded. "I know."

They stood in silence as nurses and doctors came into the room and swarmed around Allie.

"Do you know what she's gonna name it?"

"No. I don't think she knows."

"Usher," Poe said.

"Ligeia," Edgar retorted.

"Dupin," Poe said. "Do you know the sex?"

"No."

"Did she—"

"Dude, why don't you ask Allie?"

"I don't wanna bother her. She's in the middle of having a fucking baby."

Edgar snickered. Poe elbowed him in the ribs the way he'd done when they were children. Poe had the sharpest elbows in the whole world.

"Ow, dammit."

He elbowed Poe back, but his leather jacket protected him, and he just squirmed away. Then, under his breath, Poe began to chant, "Go Allie, go Allie, go Allie, go," the same cheer they'd yelled at her high school basketball games. She'd only stayed on the team for two seasons. After Dad had left, their mom's behavior had rapidly gone downhill, and Allie had quit basketball to get a job—first at the po'boy joint on the corner, and then at Magpie Vintage. But she'd been pretty good, and Edgar, Poe, Cameron, and Antoine had been in the bleachers for every game, cheering her on.

Cameron shot them a look, but that just made Poe raise his voice. Then Edgar found himself joining in, and they chanted it together.

"Go Allie, go Allie, go Allie, go!"

Cameron snorted and shook her head.

"Are they," Allie gasped between attempts to expel her offspring, "doing a"—*scream and push*—"basketball"—*swearing, swearing, swearing*—"chant right now?"

"If we had a sanitary garbage can, you could try for a

three-pointer," Poe suggested mildly. His eyes danced with an infectious humor. "A padded sanitary garbage can."

Cameron cut them a withering look. "You all never did know shit about basketball. It would obviously be a two-pointer." She grinned, and the smile hit Edgar like stepping into the warm sun on a cool day.

"Would you assholes shut the fuck up!" Allie yelled. "My baby will *not* be a fucking two-pointer. It will *obviously*—" She grabbed the plastic side of the hospital bed with one hand and Cameron's hand with the other. As she screamed and squeezed, Cameron winced. "Be a slam fucking dunk!"

Poe snorted. Cameron chuckled and patted Allie's hand. Edgar grinned. His family. They were all back in one place. It had been so long that he'd forgotten what it felt like. And now, to have Jamie here with them? It was more than he'd ever let himself imagine.

Jamie's eyes found Edgar's, and even from across the room, he could feel their attention, their support.

Then Allie began to do something Edgar could only describe as impossible. He forgot that Poe was back. He forgot that Cameron was there. He forgot that he was quickly falling for Jamie and was terrified he'd mess it up. He even forgot to be afraid that a ghost would appear. All he could do was watch as his big sister brought a fucking *person into the world*.

A person who was going to have a whole life, full of love and fear and failure and joy and hope.

At some point, Poe had migrated up to the bed. A nurse wiped goo out of the baby's nose and mouth. Jamie was bending over Allie and taking pictures of the tiny gunk-smeared creature. Cameron had her hand on Allie's brow and was stroking her hair back, smiling down at the baby.

The doctor and two nurses inspected the baby, wrote something down, then handed them back to Allie.

Edgar stood, back against the wall, and watched as the blood poured from Allie. No one seemed to notice, too focused on the baby. But bright red blood came so fast. Too much, surely? Life draining out of her. Someone should do something? Why weren't they helping her?

A nurse put a hand on his shoulder.

"Do you need to sit down?" he asked quietly.

Edgar pointed at the blood.

"Perfectly normal," the nurse said. "I know it looks like a lot, but we just need to stitch her up, and she should be fine."

Edgar didn't believe him.

This was all it took to become a ghost, really: flesh rending. To a bullet, to a knife, to disease, to a fist, to despair. Humans were just future ghosts walking around. Allie would be a ghost. And Poe and Cameron. Edgar would be a ghost someday. And Jamie.

Jamie.

The nurse had moved to stitch Allie up, and Jamie, the future ghost—no, no, Edgar could *not* think of them that way, because what was the point of living if you were just waiting to die, so *stop it*—took his hand.

"Are you okay?" Jamie asked, sliding their arm around Edgar's waist.

Edgar tried to speak but couldn't. Something was swirling around in his brain that he couldn't examine too closely or it would slip away.

It was something so simple that it complicated everything he'd ever believed: ghosts were just people; people would become ghosts. His mind shied away from it, but something in his gut held fast. A baby *just* arrived in the world was like a ghost just gone from it. Both of them were helpless and confused and didn't know how to do anything. Both were just trying to figure it out the best they could.

Edgar's vision tipped, and the next thing he knew, he was lying on the floor, head in Jamie's lap.

He blinked and saw concerned faces looking at him. "Did I...?"

"You didn't faint," Jamie whispered. "Just got all shaky and nonresponsive, so I made you lie down."

"Oh."

"Are you not good with the sight of blood? If so, you kinda picked the wrong seat."

"I'm okay," he said. It would be too much to explain right now, when he didn't even understand it himself. "I'm good."

He got to his feet with effort and walked over to his sister. His head was still swimming, and his head was buzzy, but he bent over and looked into the face of this brand-new person in his family.

"I can't believe you just did that," he said.

Allie looked up at him. "No shit, me neither," she said peacefully.

"Have you decided on a name?" one of the nurses asked. She wore a beautiful blue headscarf over her box braids and seemed to have a voice made for speaking to people who'd just shoved babies out of themselves.

"Roderick Usher," Allie cooed.

"Umm," Edgar said.

"What the fuck?" Poe exclaimed.

"I'm kidding, I'm kidding," Allie said. "God, you should see your faces."

Jamie snickered.

"I haven't decided yet," Allie told the nurse.

The nurse smiled good-naturedly and put a clipboard down in front of Allie. "If you'll just fill this out at your leisure," she said calmly.

"Do you want me to do it?" Jamie asked, waggling a pen.

"Thanks," Allie said. "I don't know if this is one of those weird medical bonding things or if I'm just too tired to hold a pen, but I can*not* let go of this thing." She indicated the baby.

Jamie smiled at her and took the clipboard. "Okay." They asked her a few questions, then. "Um, sex?"

"Female," Allie said.

"I'd love you to have a daughter named Roderick Usher, to be honest," Poe said.

"I dunno if they'll be a daughter," Allie said. "So I'm going to use they/them pronouns for them until they tell me what they prefer."

"Oh, right, cool," Poe said. "That makes sense."

Edgar was watching Jamie. They were cradling the clipboard to their chest, and their expression was a complicated mix of joy and pain.

Edgar crossed the room and enfolded them in his arms from behind, pressing a fierce kiss against their head. He held Jamie as they answered the rest of the questions on the form, their usual neat block capitals just the tiniest bit shaky.

It was full daylight now, and the sun fell on the new member of Edgar's family like a kiss. He and Jamie, Poe, Cameron, and Allie made a circle around the new baby, this new person just arrived in the world, as if they could protect them with the sheer force of love they shone down.

They couldn't protect the new Lovejoy from everything. Edgar knew that they'd have their own battles and triumphs and loves and losses. The world was a harsh and scary place. But they could sure as hell try and make the world just a little bit better for them.

# 19

# Jamie

The tunnel narrowed, and Jamie was trapped in the dark. They pushed at the heavy forms crushing them but found no way to free themself except turning back or moving through them. The air was warm and close. The muffled sounds of screams and scratching came from all sides. Jamie's heart started to pound. Finally, after what felt like a Homeric journey, they pushed their way to freedom. But as soon as they were free of the maze, the ceiling began to dip lower and lower.

CRAWL IF YOU WANT TO SURVIVE, the sign said in glowing drips and fingerprints. Jamie dropped to their knees and crawled. Something brushed their cheek, and they flinched away. Spiderwebs. There was no light, no sense of which way was out. With multiple people attempting to escape, it would be even more difficult to navigate. They tried to climb over a body-shaped obstacle on the floor, but the ceiling was too low, the wood rough and dusty, and they ducked back down to find another route to freedom.

Finally, a faint glow emanated from ahead. Jamie followed it, the scent of fog and sawdust thick in their nose. The tunnel opened just enough that Jamie could stand, and then they were hurrying toward the exit. They cleared the door in a rush of relief. Just as the feeling swelled, a terrifying figure strafed them, trailing bandages, eyes glowing holes. The smell of metal and rot lingered in their wake, and the second act of the haunted house commenced.

"Dude," Jamie said to Dante, who stood in the doorway. "That's really working."

Dante, one of Jamie's favorite coworkers, nodded and smiled, his white teeth gleaming in the darkness. "Cool. What's left?"

"I think we could fill the sandbags a little more, especially at the top. We should get Maurice to go through and see where they hit him."

At six four, Maurice was their gauge for whether the illusion was maintained for tall people.

Dante agreed.

"And I know it messes with the texture, but we're gonna need to pad the ceiling in the crawl-through tunnel. If anyone freaks out and sits up, they'll get brained."

"Spray foam or sheet, do you think?"

"Spray would be faster and easier to do but harder to strike. Sheet would take longer to put in but come out easily. Your call when we do most of the work."

"Spray," Dante concluded immediately. Striking the haunted house was the worst part of their job, and Jamie would've made the same call. "Now about those spiderwebs…"

✦ ✦ ✦

Edgar's invitation had come as Jamie was driving home from work: **I know this is maybe not fun, but I'm at my sister's. Any interest in coming over and hanging out?** Jamie was exhausted and smelled like haunted ass, but they hadn't seen Edgar in a week, so they turned around at the next block.

Allie lived in the Irish Channel, not far from Magpie Vintage. Jamie threw their truck into park and sniffed tentatively under their arms. Not good. Outside, the day was turning to evening, but a few honeybees still feasted on the wisteria. They hummed along lazily, pollen-drunk and dizzy. Outside of Allie's place, it smelled of jasmine, fry oil, and beer.

It was Poe who opened the door, Edgar fast on his heels.

"Hey," Poe said, looking frazzled. "Welcome to hell."

Edgar elbowed him, his eyes warm on Jamie's. "Hi. Come in. Thanks for coming."

Edgar shifted his weight from foot to foot like he couldn't decide whether to kiss or hug Jamie in front of his brother. A pang of hurt clanged in Jamie's gut at the rejection. They'd certainly dated people before who claimed to care for them, as long as no one was watching.

But when they looked into Edgar's eyes, all they saw was longing. He wasn't ashamed of Jamie—he just didn't know how to behave, and he was looking to Jamie to show him.

Jamie fixed their eyes on Edgar and stepped forward, sliding a hand around his waist and the other on his shoulder. They kissed him gently on the lips.

Edgar leaned into the kiss and buried his fingers in Jamie's hair. The feeling in Jamie's stomach twisted from hurt to glee as they felt Edgar's yearning. Jamie's presence wasn't a burden. He wanted them—needed them. And it felt really, really good.

"Sorry I smell so bad. I was crawling around in a bunch of—soft, cheerful, uh, dirt," they concluded, not wanting to inadvertently plant any seeds of fear in Edgar's fertile mind.

Edgar squeezed their shoulder in thanks and turned and walked into the living room, Jamie and Poe trailing after him.

Jamie leaned close to Poe. "So what's this about hell?"

"I dunno, dude. If you like babies, it's probably great. But I… do not."

Allie sat on the couch with the baby in her arms. They wore a plain white onesie and had a shock of dark brown hair that stuck up like a fledgling crow's feathers. Their brown eyes were round and heavy lidded, and they blinked up at Jamie, Poe, and Edgar with interest.

Jamie preferred older kids who could draw weird pictures of monsters and make hilariously inappropriate comments in polite company, but Allie's baby was pretty darn cute.

Jamie began to ask Allie how she was doing when the baby puked on her stomach and all over the couch cushion. Niceties dispensed with, the adults sprang into action, then, once everything was clean again, flopped onto the couch together.

"Here's the thing," Allie said once she'd changed. "This baby is clearly a demon sent here to collect my soul. But I love them so much that I guess I'll let them do it? Nice knowing you."

"I know you're kidding," Jamie said. "But could demons exist?"

Allie shrugged and gestured to the baby, who was burbling adorably in her lap.

Jamie looked to Edgar.

"I don't know," he mused. "Since there are ghosts, there could just as well be demons."

"Vampires?" Jamie asked hopefully.

"Who knows?" Allie said mildly. *Disturbingly* mildly. An excited shiver went through Jamie. "If you ask some people, there are vampires, werewolves, witches, everything. That's New Orleans for you. But even if that's true, I've never seen them. At least not that I was aware of. I'm not sure how I'd know for sure."

"Vampires would be rad," Poe said slowly.

Jamie imagined Allie's baby as a mini vampire who'd suck her dry while breastfeeding and shivered, filing the image away for next year's haunted house.

"What did your mom and her family think? Were there theories?"

Jamie had asked Edgar before, surprised that he didn't have a more cohesive theory about what he saw, only to realize that answers were not something Edgar's mother had ever offered. She had been trying to survive, trying to raise her kids in a difficult situation, and she had spent her energy making sure they knew their experiences were real.

"What you have to understand about our family," Allie said, "is that they aren't the most trustworthy sources of information."

"That's an understatement," Poe said wryly. "They're all drunks, druggies, and crazies. Like our aunt Alaitheia. She hasn't been anywhere except her bar or her apartment in ten years, and she hoards broken pottery in shoeboxes."

"She does mosaic art," Allie said. "It's not like she collects it for no reason."

"Mm-hmm," Poe said dubiously and shot Jamie a look.

"Does she see ghosts too?" Jamie asked.

"Oh yeah," Allie said. "She doesn't hide it either. She'll talk to them when people are around and everything."

Jamie was confused. In all the conversations with Edgar about his experiences, he'd never mentioned an aunt who sounded like she could be a resource for him. But why?

"People think she's faking it," Poe said.

"She's cultivated a certain reputation, sure," Allie said. "But it's better for people to think you're eccentric than dangerous, isn't it?"

"I would think that it would be pretty acceptable in New Orleans?" Jamie asked.

When Edgar stiffened beside them, they realized how that might sound to him.

"Shit, Edgar, I didn't mean it like that," Jamie said. They slid a hand to his thigh and squeezed.

"No, you're right," Poe said emphatically. "As we've tried to tell him forever."

"You don't speak for me," Allie cautioned.

"What 'forever' is this?" Edgar asked sharply. "Because you haven't been around to tell me *anything* in six years."

"Yeah, well—"

"Poe!" Allie warned. "I'm begging you to shut up before you make a fool of yourself."

Poe made a theatrical bow of assent and then flipped them both off.

"Um, so," Jamie said, "where's your aunt's bar? Would I know it?"

The siblings exchanged speaking glances. After a moment, Allie answered.

"Le Corbeau, over in the Marigny."

"Le Corbeau," Jamie said, rolling the familiar name around on their tongue. "Wait, the old Rondeau place?"

Allie cut a glance over to Edgar, who was looking at Poe with a narrowed gaze. Finally, Edgar turned to Jamie and said, "The Rondeaus are our mother's family, on her mother's side."

Jamie's mouth fell open.

The Rondeaus were legendary for anyone who'd grown up in New Orleans. Stories of their preternatural abilities were passed down from generation to generation by those who believed the family's powers were genuine. Others believed the Rondeaus had made up their abilities to strike fear into the hearts of those who might wrong them. Still others claimed the Rondeaus' power was real but only granted to them in exchange for horrible acts of fealty.

Things fell into place with a *click* in Jamie's brain: Edgar was probably far more powerful—and far more tortured—than they had understood. Even though they had believed Edgar about what he experienced, Edgar never really described his encounters unless Jamie specifically asked. He'd say, *It wasn't a great week for ghosts* or *Pretty gnarly encounter earlier*. And Jamie, not wanting to make him relive the horrors, tried to offer comfort without fully comprehending what Edgar was going through.

Edgar hadn't told Jamie he was a Rondeau because he hadn't wanted Jamie to know. Because if Jamie knew, they'd understand how bad it was. And if they understood that…what? What was Edgar so afraid of? Did he think Jamie wasn't strong enough to handle it? That they would leave?

He had to know Jamie would never think he was crazy. Learning that some of the things they'd been fascinated by since childhood were *real* had been a dose of magic directly into Jamie's veins. Unless *that* was the problem? That Edgar worried Jamie would want him for his hauntings and not for himself?

Edgar's hand found theirs, touch tentative. He was seeking comfort but didn't want to presume. Did he really think Jamie's feelings were so conditional? Jamie was trying not to be offended when Edgar pulled his hand away.

*It's not about you, dude. His father rejected him for this. It's not a referendum on your character; it's a fucking trauma response.*

Jamie grabbed Edgar's hand tightly and looked at him. In Edgar's eyes was the same fear and shame and longing they'd seen when Edgar wanted them to tell him what to do in bed. The fear that the most personal, vulnerable parts of him might be rejected in the moment he trusted someone enough to reveal them. They squeezed Edgar's hand and let their eyes communicate: *I got you.* Edgar visibly relaxed.

"We don't exactly advertise it," Poe was saying. "Since people believe we sacrifice virgins and all that."

Edgar said, "When we were kids, our mom would tell us stories about ghosts she saw. How this one was juggling and that one was walking a dog."

"She was trying to prime us not to be afraid," Allie offered. "She thought if we got used to knowing there was something there that we couldn't see, then maybe we wouldn't be so freaked out when we started to see them."

"Did that work?" Jamie asked.

"No," Edgar said, shivering, as Allie replied, "Kind of." Poe just narrowed his eyes.

"I was twelve, my first time," Allie said. "Walking home from the river with a friend, I laughed at a parrot on a woman's head. My friend asked what was so funny, but when I pointed at her, my friend didn't see anyone there. And even though the ghost itself didn't look scary, I would have been super freaked out to realize my friend couldn't see her if I hadn't been prepared for it."

"It wasn't necessarily your first time, though," Poe pointed out. "Just the first time you were aware what you were seeing wasn't alive."

"True," Allie allowed.

"What about you, Poe?" Jamie asked.

"Uh. I think I was like nine or ten? I don't really remember. But it was near the aquarium, and there was this guy dressed in old-fashioned clothes, juggling. He looked like he came from one of those Depression-era traveling carnivals, y'know? At first, I thought he was entertainment for people going into the aquarium or something, but then he disappeared while I was watching."

Jamie turned to ask Edgar the same question, but before they could, Edgar turned to Allie and abruptly asked, "So have you picked a name yet?"

The conversation then devolved into more absurd suggestions—Idont, Dontyou, and Cantwee Lovejoy, among many awful others—and Jamie sank into the sweetness of being included in the intimate family gathering.

But even as they enjoyed cheesecake and sibling razzing, Jamie didn't forget that Edgar had dodged their question. And Jamie wanted to know why.

# 20

## Edgar

A few days after revealing that he was part of the Rondeau family, Edgar found himself walking hand in hand with Jamie toward Le Corbeau. Once they'd found out about the connection, they'd immediately begun speculating about what answers Aunt Alaitheia could provide to Edgar's many uncertainties.

"I can't believe you haven't asked her before," Jamie said for the third time, squeezing Edgar's hand excitedly.

Poe snorted from beside him. "You'll believe it after you meet her."

But nothing could quell Jamie's delight at meeting another member of the Rondeau family. "She must have such amazing stories!" Jamie kept saying.

Edgar didn't think revealing that those stories had terrified him as a child would do anything to dampen their excitement.

"She's kind of..." Edgar trailed off as he thought about how best to describe his aunt.

"Infuriating," Poe suggested.

"She can be a bit...vague," Edgar admitted. He hadn't seen her in years, but he doubted that had changed.

Poe muttered something under his breath that Edgar couldn't hear and pushed the front door open, the cool dark beckoning them in from the heat of the day.

Once, Edgar had been a frequent visitor. Before his father left, he, Poe, and Allie had done their homework in the polished wood booth at the back while their mother and aunt talked away long afternoons. Cameron and Antoine knew to find them there and would often join them, sneaking glances at Aunt Alaitheia until one of them (usually Cameron) worked up the courage to ask her for a potion. His aunt would look deeply into Cameron's eyes as if searching for the truth of her, then mix drinks for the table that always seemed to be exactly what they were craving at that moment.

But after...after his father left and Antoine was dead, the visits to the bar stopped. Aunt Alaitheia would appear at their front door on the nights when their mother was at her worst. The sisters would climb out on the balcony, close the window behind them, and talk long into the night.

After their mother had lost too much of herself to have anything left for her children or anyone else, Aunt Alaitheia had been the one to lead her, hand in hand like frightened children, out of the house for the last time.

Le Corbeau looked just like Edgar's memories of it. In fact, it didn't look all that different than it had a century before, in the oldest pictures Edgar had seen. It had weathered Katrina as it had every storm that had come before it, though whether the rumors of otherworldly intervention were to be believed, even Edgar wasn't sure.

"Wow," Jamie murmured as they walked through the heavy wooden doors. Edgar had to admit the place had ambiance.

The elegant curve of the long wooden bar was polished to a mirror shine. Behind it was a huge ornate mirror, de-silvered in spots. Glass shelves held a rainbow of bottles, some familiar and others unlabeled, concocted in-house from family recipes passed down with the bar and only available to those who knew to request them. The wood plank floor was worn smooth in places from a century and a half of dancing, stomping, and sweeping, and the walls were painted a glossy midnight blue that made the place feel cool and dark, even when the sun blazed outside.

Aunt Alaitheia was tall and broad-shouldered. Where his mother had colored her hair to cover up the bit of gray in her temples, Alaitheia's rioted down her back and over her shoulders in a kudzu of gray curls. Her brown eyes were as keen as Edgar remembered, but the neon pink glasses on a chain around her neck were new. She raised them to her eyes and peered at them.

"Nephews," she said, crossing to them. "What a surprise. Congratulations on a new generation of Rondeaus."

"How'd you know that?" Poe asked suspiciously, arms crossed over his chest.

"Our family gift has many uses," she said. Then she winked at Edgar and added, "And your sister texted me."

Edgar had forgotten Allie's soft spot for their aunt.

Aunt Alaitheia leaned in to examine Jamie, and Edgar froze,

praying she wouldn't do anything weird or rude. But she simply regarded them for a while and smiled. "You must be Jamie."

"Must I?" Jamie quipped. "Just kidding, sorry. It's really nice to meet you. Guess I'm a little starstruck," they added sheepishly.

"Starstruck? By little old me?" But her wink was conspiratorial and appreciative, and Jamie grinned back at her like they'd understood everything she'd implied. "How is your sister getting along?" Alaitheia asked, gesturing them to follow her to the booth in the back corner where they'd spent so many afternoons.

"Pretty well," Edgar said, not knowing how to talk to this aunt he'd never really gotten to know.

His mother's sister. She had to know things, right?

They sat in the booth, and Aunt Alaitheia waved a languid hand to the man behind the bar.

"I remember when your mother had Allie," Aunt Alaitheia said in a faraway voice. "She was such a sweet baby. She just wanted to be carried around all day and be with the people she loved. You know, when your mother was pregnant with her, she constantly craved pancakes. We must've been to every twenty-four-hour diner in the city."

The bartender set down a tray before Aunt Alaitheia. It contained four Pontarlier glasses, a glass fountain with two spouts, four slotted spoons, a bowl of sugar cubes, a bottle of absinthe, and a pitcher of water.

"Do you remember when she was pregnant with Edgar?" Jamie asked, leaning in to accept the glass of absinthe she prepared for them.

"Oh yes. She craved grilled cheese and Bloody Mary mix. You"—she turned to Edgar—"were a serious baby. Allie was a toddler at the time, and she would drag you around like a stuffed animal."

"What about me?" Poe asked softly.

Aunt Alaitheia paused, regarding him. Her eyes darkened for an instant, but the shadow was gone as soon as Edgar noticed it.

"Little Po'boy," she said. Poe made a long-suffering face. She seemed to consider her words carefully. "You wanted to be wherever your brother and sister were. You wanted to be just like them."

That didn't seem unusual for a youngest child, but Poe scowled like she'd insulted him.

Aunt Alaitheia finished passing out the absinthe. Jamie was sipping theirs slowly and with relish. Poe tossed his back like a shot, then scraped the green sugar sludge from the bottom of the glass with his finger and sucked it clean. Aunt Alaitheia downed hers in two sips. Edgar stared at the cup before him.

He had long avoided anything that might make him less aware of his surroundings. The night of the last day of his freshman year of high school, Edgar had gone with some friends to a party. It had been in the gymnasium of an old elementary school in Tremé, shuttered after the damage from Katrina had proven too costly to repair or rebuild. Ivy had crawled into every crack in the intervening years, pulling the walls apart. The windows were boarded up and the doors padlocked, but that was nothing to local youth in search of a place of their own.

A first floor window had been pried open, where overgrown vegetation blocked the view of it from the road. Crows cawed at them from telephone wires above, but the only other people around were a knot of guys dealing on the corner, and they didn't care.

That night, Edgar had been celebrating. It had been a difficult year. His father had taken off eight months before, and they didn't know where he was. It wasn't precisely a surprise. He and Edgar's mom had fought all the time—about her drinking, about his yelling, about whether she and her children actually saw ghosts or she'd raised them with a dangerous fiction he couldn't abide. His relationship with his kids was just as volatile. Whenever any of them mentioned something *queer*—his word—he went off, telling them never to talk about their mother's nonsense to anyone else. Telling them they hadn't seen anything. That they just wanted their mother to approve of them.

As for Edgar's mother, she'd taken his father's absence as a boon at first—cooking foods he'd disliked and playing records he'd despised. She cuddled them near her on the couch and told them they were better off without him because he was trying to convince them that she was crazy, that they were all crazy.

When three months had passed with no word or sign, she'd seemed to realize that he wasn't coming back. That was when she got sad. She told them their father was a good man, a caring man, and he'd left them because he'd been jealous of what they shared. That he'd felt left out of his own family. Edgar hadn't missed him much. Hadn't missed wondering which version of his father he'd get—the distant, scornful shadow who only wanted to be left alone, the jocular dad who wanted an audience for his stories, or the furious bully who berated them for being like their mother. Allie hadn't wanted him to return either.

Poe had mourned his loss deeply though, and looked for him everywhere, convinced that if he could just tell their father that he was welcome, then maybe he'd come home. Edgar and Allie didn't tell their mother about Poe's search, and they told him not to say anything either. Because that had been when the sadness had given way to something more confusing.

In the last few weeks before her breakdown, she'd begun to talk to Edgar and Allie fervently after Poe was asleep, warning them of threats she'd never mentioned before, about shadowy figures and arcane conspiracies and people—no, things—that meant them harm. Her drinking and drug use, always robust, had intensified since her husband had left. Whether the substances were the cause of her paranoia or the result, Edgar didn't know.

His father was gone; his mother was blinking in and out of sanity; Allie had just graduated. So for the next year, before Poe started high school, Edgar would be alone at school for the first time in his life.

He hadn't said much about any of that to the friends he'd come to the party with. Charles and Babette had befriended Edgar after winter break, and he'd gratefully let them. They were the kind of friends who told him where they were going and when to show up and assumed he'd be there. And he always was. Because he hadn't had real friends since Cameron and Antoine... and he didn't like to think about them anymore. Not after what had happened.

Charles and Babette had hugged him and pulled him inside. His classmates were gleeful, having cast off the mantle of the academic year with nothing yet to replace it. They drank, they danced, they celebrated, and Edgar tried to lose himself in all of it. Caught between carefree Charles and confident Babette, he'd drunk whatever they gave him, the world blurring around the edges.

Was this how his mom felt—floaty and detached and able to forget? Was this freedom from fear or responsibility worth leaving her kids on their own?

He could see how it might feel that way.

The party raged until the wee hours of the night, and when Edgar had stumbled outside, the air had been thick with unspent rain and the streets dark, the streetlamps in Tremé much farther apart than they were in the Bywater. Babette had made pronouncements to the moon, grin effulgent and curls painted silver. Charles bubbled with laughter. Edgar felt vaguely ill but optimistic, the latter a feeling he hadn't had in a long time. They'd walked, arm in arm, in the neutral ground on Ursulines Avenue and hurried beneath the I-10 where a woman with a sweet smile had collapsed onto a mattress with a needle in her arm and an old man waltzed with no one.

Babette and Charles danced to the music pouring out of the bars as they crossed Frenchman Street, then peeled off at Esplanade, waving their goodbyes and gleefully promising to meet for beignets and coffee the next morning to plan all the things they'd do that summer.

Edgar's face hurt from smiling so much, but there was a lightness in his bones and looseness in his joints, like gravity was acting on him less than usual. He could imagine how tomorrow would go: he'd wake late, make his way lazily to the café where he, Babette, and Charles would take their pastries to go, sunglasses firmly in place, then find a spot in the rocks by the river. They'd sip coffee weedy with chicory and dust the rocks with powdered sugar from every sweet bite. They'd make plans. They'd dream up adventures. They'd laugh. Friends.

But Edgar never made it to the café. He didn't leave the house for the next month.

Because as he drifted drunkenly home, his future before him like a bowl of sugar cubes waiting to melt on his tongue, something moved in his periphery. Edgar cocked his head. The

Friday night merriment in the Quarter and along Frenchmen Street drifted downriver some nights, mixing with locals on street corners and outside bars, so Edgar assumed it was a tourist who'd wandered away from his group.

An explosion of hydrangeas made Edgar sneeze, and when his eyes opened, something was right in front of him.

He stepped into the ghost, and the nauseating sensation that had rolled through him was ice and heat and damp and bone-dry and *wrong*. Edgar had reeled back, losing his footing and falling, catching himself on his hands. His palms stung, but all he cared about was the looming, grotesque *thing* that looked like it could pull him apart and climb inside him, drag him screaming to hell, or obliterate him so entirely that Edgar would cease to exist.

It had been a man once, but now it was a lolling, shredded monstrosity, with eyes that burned into Edgar like twin moons, all reflected light and nothing inside.

Edgar didn't know how he'd gotten to his feet and run away. But three blocks later, he glanced over his shoulder at a dead run and saw nothing there. He had a stitch in his side and felt utterly, painfully sober.

It was the second one he'd seen. Only he hadn't been sure the first time. Maybe seeing Antoine Valliere one last time hadn't been a ghost but a wish.

This time, however, he had no doubt.

Edgar fell to his knees and puked, only noticing that the pavement had grated his palms to blood when he left red smears on the thighs of his pants. He had a wriggly, tremblesome feeling in his knees, and his stomach attempted to flee his body by way of his throat. His head pounded, and his skin crawled. When he had finally dragged himself upright and made for home, he'd looked over his shoulder every other step, convinced something crept along beside him, hiding in every shadow.

He hadn't had a drink since.

"Edgar!"

He startled back to awareness. Poe had called his name, and Jamie was squeezing his shoulder, looking concerned. Aunt Alaitheia watched him with narrowed, curious eyes.

"Where'd you go, dude?" Poe demanded.

Edgar blinked, having no intention of answering his question.

Aunt Alaitheia took his glass and downed the absinthe in a few long swallows.

"Now then," she said. "What brings the Lovejoys back to Le Corbeau?"

It was Jamie who broke the silence. "You know how Edgar, Allie, and Poe see ghosts?"

Aunt Alaitheia was still for a moment, then nodded.

"Well, I guess we—oh, sorry, I'm Edgar's boyfriend, by the way. I don't see ghosts." They grinned.

"Don't you?" Aunt Alaitheia said softly. And before Edgar could ask what the hell that was supposed to mean, Jamie grinned.

"Nah. I create them though. I mean fake ones. I make haunted houses."

"I know," Aunt Alaitheia said.

"For real?" Jamie asked, clearly impressed. "Are you psychic too?"

"Sometimes," she said. Then she winked at them. "But Allie told me."

"Jesus, does she send a newsletter around or something?" Poe muttered.

"Edgar has all these theories," Jamie continued, undaunted. "But he doesn't know much for sure. Ghostwise, that is. So we were wondering if you had some insight into how it all works. How they work. Ghosts…" They trailed off.

"That's a big question," Aunt Alaitheia said.

"Yeah, I guess it is," Jamie replied.

"What did your mother tell you?" she asked Edgar and Poe.

Poe snorted. "Fuck all."

"She always said it was different for everyone," said Edgar. "We tried to ask her, but she said it was like life or god or love—we had to decide what they meant for ourselves."

"Like I said: fuck all."

Aunt Alaitheia looked resigned. She poured them all another round of absinthe and, once more, downed Edgar's herself. Then she leaned toward them, tracing patterns on the table with a wet fingertip.

"All I can tell you is what I believe," she said. "Your mother and I did not agree on everything, not by a long shot." There was a hint of bitterness in her voice, like wormwood. "But we do agree that the experience is different for everyone. What you think of ghosts depends on how you think of death. And, I suppose, on how you think of life."

Suddenly Edgar wished they hadn't come here. What had he been thinking when he'd allowed Jamie to give him hope his aunt might have answers that his own mother had never given him, answers that he'd never been able to figure out on his own? There were none here, just more questions: *What really happened between you and Mom? Why did you always come for her but never for us? What do we actually know about you?*

"For me," Aunt Alaitheia said, eyes taking on a faraway look, "death is a liminal state, somewhere between life and nothingness. For some, it feels like an instant; for others, decades, centuries, millennia. Time has no meaning outside of life. Duration is only significant as a concept when there's an opportunity for something to end. So a ghost doesn't know that a piece of it has persisted past the point of physical death. In its mind, it isn't *lingering*, because you'd have to understand time to know that. It doesn't sense that passage of minutes or days any more than it can feel temperature without a body. It's an echo, a presence that implies absence."

Jamie was nodding, rapt. Poe was making a face Edgar recognized best from the times he didn't get to pick the movie they'd watch as kids.

"What do they want?" Edgar asked, wishing to leave the realm of theory and enter the practical.

"I don't know," Aunt Alaitheia said. "Perhaps they have as many different desires as living humans do."

"Why can we see them?" Poe asked, leaning in.

Aunt Alaitheia shook her head. "I don't know. The Rondeaus have always had the gift—or the curse, depending on who you ask. We're different from other people. We see more. Maybe ghosts sense that. Maybe that's why they're drawn to us."

"Well, what can we do to make them back the hell off?" Edgar asked.

His aunt's expression held more pity than Edgar was expecting, and it made him want to disappear.

"Oh, darling," she said. "You have had a rough time of it, haven't you?"

*You'd have known that if you ever bothered to ask about us.*

Edgar stared at the tabletop. It was buffed shiny, but the wood was deeply scarred and stained, a record of the years. He hadn't realized how angry he still was. His aunt had been the one person who knew their circumstances, and she hadn't done anything to help them.

Jamie put a hand on his knee.

"They terrify him," Jamie said. "They jump out at him and melt through walls to startle him, and if they touch him, he feels cold and ill, and they won't leave him alone. Do they have… unfinished business? Something that they need him to help with before they move along?"

"Horror fan, are you?" Aunt Alaitheia said.

"Well. Yes."

"I've never found that interpretation very compelling," she said. "Mainly because I don't think ghosts experience time linearly. I don't think they would be invested in getting revenge on a person or revealing a secret, because that involves understanding that something in the past is still affecting the present."

She raised the absinthe bottle, the green liquor glowing where light shone through it, and offered it to Jamie.

"That stuff's strong," they said but motioned for her to fill their glass again. Poe did the same. For the third time, Aunt Alaitheia drank both her own and the one she poured for Edgar.

"One hundred and forty proof," she said in agreement. "Just like Mama made it."

"So you think they're detached from their human lives and are what—just popping up wherever, with no rhyme or reason, and we see them because we're fucking cursed?" Edgar demanded.

It came out sounding childish and irritable. But once the question hung there between him and Alaitheia, he found that anger burned through his veins. She had never once tried to help them when their mom had left them alone for days at a time. Or when, Edgar's junior year of high school, his mom had brought home Marcus, who took over their house for a year, treating it like a bachelor pad, leering at Allie and ordering Edgar and Poe to bring him beers or fetch him cigarillos from the corner market.

Here she sat, apparently as unbothered about ghosts as she had been about him, Allie, and Poe for all those years.

"You're saying that after they die, there is no right or wrong? What the hell good does that do me?! Even if *they* have no intentions or don't understand their existence, *I* still experience the consequences. And they're *awful*."

His voice broke. He was breathing shallowly and blinking fast, trying to keep from crying. Jamie rubbed his leg, a reminder that he wasn't alone anymore.

His aunt's expression was somber but curious. "You feel malice from them?" she asked.

"Hell yes, I feel fucking *malice* from them. They're *ghosts*! They shouldn't *be* here! It doesn't make any sense."

He slumped in his seat.

Aunt Alaitheia regarded him calmly, her expression calculating.

"What is it that you believe then? What explanations have comforted you by making sense?"

Suddenly, Edgar felt like a child. *Sense*. What did that even mean? So little in the world made sense. People spent their lives amassing money and did nothing good with it. People hurt one another constantly. They destroyed their home planet with no thought to the future. They were hateful and capricious and selfish and unkind. Nothing made sense. Why should ghosts be any different?

He squeezed his fists together, fingernails cutting into his palms, the way he had as a teenager, so full up with feelings he needed a way to keep them inside.

"I guess I don't have one," he said finally. "We came here because I hoped you might know something. But I guess not."

Poe lurched across the table and grabbed the absinthe bottle. He put a sugar cube directly into his mouth, then swirled a pull of liqueur like mouthwash and swallowed. His cheeks were flushed and his dark hair wild.

"See, that's always been your problem," he said to Edgar. "You think sense equals good and nonsense equals bad. But most people just want whatever makes them feel not like shit in the moment. They're acting out of desperation or desire or whim." He tossed back another absinthe, eyes wild. "*You've* decided that ghosts are an aberration because they scare you. Being scared of something doesn't give you the right to try and obliterate it. When people try to do that, we call them villains."

Edgar blinked, stomach gone hollow. It was more than he'd heard Poe say at one time since he'd left New Orleans six years before. Shame rolled through him, and he couldn't find a single thing to say. Was Poe right about him? Was he so sunk in his own fear that his whole worldview had been constructed on it? Was he a villain? Maybe he was.

"I agree with you," Jamie said to Poe, and fear lanced through Edgar. "But your brother isn't trying to control anyone. He's not trying to obliterate ghosts. He's just trying to get through the day."

Jamie squeezed Edgar's leg.

"You're talking about his fear like he has control over it. But ghosts appearing for him might as well be like, like…a seizure disorder or something. A stimulus causes a reaction that has really negative effects on him. It's something so unpredictable that he's constantly afraid of it happening, even when it's not. So there's the terror of when he *does* encounter a ghost. But the other three-quarters come from your brother being stone-cold terrified to leave his fucking house most days because he *might* encounter them."

Jamie's voice was getting more heated. They leaned in toward Poe. "It's a disability! He's in a state of constant fear. He can never enjoy himself because he feels like the second he lets his guard down, that's when he's at the most risk."

Poe was listening calmly, eyes narrowed in the suspicious *I'm not sure I buy this* expression that had infuriated authority figures since Poe was little.

"Maybe you should try an antianxiety med, bro," he said mildly.

Jamie knelt up on their chair, impassioned. "Yeah, okay, maybe he should!" They shut their mouth and cut an apologetic look to Edgar. "But I don't get how you can have no sympathy for your brother. What, when you see ghosts, you're super chill about it? You're like, *Hey, ghost dudes, like my cool leather jacket that I wear when it's a hundred and four fucking degrees*? Seriously, *how* are you wearing that in New Orleans in the summer? Anyway, I'm curious. Are you just super brave or have no startle reflex or what?"

Poe didn't reply, but Edgar didn't think Jamie had really expected him to.

"Just maybe start with a little damn sympathy before you lump your terrified brother in with villains and hate-mongers."

When Jamie sat back down, Edgar could feel them trembling with anger. That their anger was on his behalf warmed his heart. The only person in recent memory who'd stuck up for him was Allie.

Poe gazed steadily between Jamie and Edgar. Aunt Alaitheia watched them as if from a far distance but said nothing.

Poe nodded as if in conversation with himself. He pushed himself up, palms on the tabletop, too-long jacket sleeves slapping zippers against the wood.

"I'm gonna go. Aunt, a pleasure. Jamie, I like you."

He turned to Edgar. There was concern in his expression but also resignation. "I do have sympathy, Eddie," he said. "But ask yourself this: Can you remember a time when you *weren't* afraid? Even before the ghosts? Because I can't."

# 21

# Jamie

Jamie's head was reeling by the time they said their goodbyes to Alaitheia. The sun beat down relentlessly, and the rain-wet streets nearly steamed as the afternoon storm burned away. Jamie plucked at their sweaty shirt.

"Seriously, how does he wear that leather jacket in this heat?" they grumbled, not really expecting an answer.

They didn't get one. Edgar seemed lost in his own world.

"Do you want to go to my place?" Jamie asked. "Germaine and Carl will have cold drinks, and their balcony is shady."

Edgar assented, and Jamie led them slowly through the streets.

"I don't even go in my apartment when the sun's out if I can help it," Jamie said, keeping up a steady stream of chatter as they walked in an attempt to distract Edgar.

They told him about how they'd come to live in Germaine and Carl's guesthouse after Jamie's landlord had changed their house from a long-term rental into an Airbnb, one more in a long line of people who cared so much about making a buck for themselves that they didn't care that short-term rentals had radically driven up housing prices, especially in Black and lower-income neighborhoods.

"There it is," they said.

Every time the white columns and broad wooden planks of the Marigny house's grand porch came into view, Jamie felt how lucky they were to have ended up here.

"Wow. You live here?"

It was the first thing he'd said beyond murmurs of agreement with Jamie's disgust at the housing market.

"Well, I live in the guesthouse around back. But yeah. Here, we can cut through this way to the back balcony."

They flicked the side-gate latch, then led Edgar around the rosebushes that hugged the house and into the garden. The backyard was like an oasis thanks to years and years of strategic planting. Germaine and Carl had created a space invisible to neighbors and hidden from anyone passing by on the street.

Jamie glowed with pride when Edgar said it was beautiful. It hadn't been their design, but they'd certainly spent enough hours out here being Carl's hands and, more importantly, his knees.

Above them, on the balcony dripping with bougainvillea and ivy, dressed in white linen, lounged Carl and Germaine.

"Come up, kiddo," Germaine called down.

They climbed the helix of the iron stairs to the second floor. The breeze from the three fans on the balcony ceiling kept the heat from settling, and the icy pitcher of drinks between them made Jamie's mouth water.

Carl was squinting at Edgar.

"I know you," he mused. Then he turned to Germaine. "Do I know him?"

"Got me, darlin'." He stuck out his hand. "Germaine Fell."

"Edgar. Lovejoy. Nice to meet you." They shook hands, and Edgar turned to Carl. "We met at your shop, sir. I delivered a box of Lagniappe Lemonade for a party you were having?"

"Of course, dear boy, of course," he said. "Jamie's beau."

"We prefer *paramour* or *inamorata*," Jamie joked.

Carl smiled and gestured for them to sit down. Carl was never happy unless everyone was seated with a drink in hand.

Jamie got them settled and made Edgar a nonalcoholic version of Germaine's concoction.

They enjoyed the breeze and the respite from the heat for a few minutes, then Germaine rose and stretched.

"Well, I think it's time for a nap. What do you say?" He held a hand out to Carl, who blinked owlishly up at him.

"A nap? You don't—"

Germaine cleared his throat and kicked at Carl's shoe.

"Yes, yes," Carl said, nodding and rising, "wouldn't a nap be just the thing!"

Then Jamie and Edgar were left alone, Jamie rolling their eyes fondly at their hosts.

*There's no time for subtlety when you're old*, Carl had told Jamie once. *You stop trusting people to understand, because if they don't, you've wasted precious moments of the life you have left.*

Edgar fixed Jamie with an intense look.

"Was my brother right?" he asked. "Am I a coward?"

"No, you're not a coward. On the contrary, I know how much bravery and strength it takes just to exist in a world where you have good reason to be scared all the time."

"God." Edgar slumped, looking utterly exhausted. "It's all so fucking *hard*. Where do you get the energy to fight the world again and again?"

"Aw, babe." Jamie wanted to wrap Edgar in their arms and squeeze the fear from him like poison. "The alternative is giving in and not living the life you want, and that's so much worse."

"It's not fair," Edgar said, and his voice was small and choked.

Jamie ached for him. But a tendril of worry also crept in. They didn't want to sound like they were siding with Poe and blaming Edgar for his fear, but they'd listened intently to the conversation at Le Corbeau and hadn't come away with any answers except this: Edgar's fear, if left unchallenged, was going to make his life smaller.

That was his choice to make, of course. But Jamie hoped he'd choose to try and dig. Because if he didn't, Jamie wasn't sure there was a future for them.

"It's really not," Jamie echoed. "It's so unfair and it sucks, and I hate watching you suffer."

"But?" Edgar prompted, sounding resigned.

"But," Jamie added slowly.

"You can say it," Edgar interrupted. "You agree with Poe. I should just deal with the fact that I'm a coward and I'm ruining my life." He looked disgusted with himself.

*Whoa, where did that come from?*

"Hold on," Jamie said. "I do not think you're a coward. Don't put words in my mouth." They put a hand on Edgar's knee. "I was going to ask if you've ever tried an antianxiety."

Edgar's eyes went wide, and for a moment, he looked betrayed. Then he slumped.

"Yeah, once. It was... It didn't help. It was after Antoine died and I freaked out."

Jamie squeezed his knee, encouraging him to say more.

"He was the first ghost I saw on my own." Edgar reached for Jamie's hand. "I was... I loved him. He was the only person I ever..."

Edgar trailed off, but Jamie thought they understood. The first person Edgar had ever loved had died, and Edgar had seen it happen and then been haunted by his ghost. It was about the worst circumstances Jamie could imagine for a first love. And since that happened, Edgar became terrified of losing the people he loved and terrified of ghosts, the latter preventing him from developing relationships that might result in loss.

"I'm so sorry," Jamie said. "I'm so fucking sorry you had to go through all that."

Edgar sighed. "I didn't like how it made me feel. The medication. I flushed it down the toilet."

Jamie wanted to ask exactly how long Edgar had taken the medication, which one it had been, how he'd felt, anything to try and help Edgar understand that perhaps circumstances might be different now. That he had been a child, directly after a trauma, and not in control of anything in his life. That now he could work with a doctor, try different things to see what could help.

But this was not the time. They'd have that conversation when Edgar hadn't just been trampled by his brother and perplexed by his aunt.

"It kills me to watch you suffer," Jamie admitted for now. "It makes me want to burn the fucking world down to make it stop. But all I can do is be here for you in the aftermath."

Edgar squeezed Jamie's hand. They sat in silence for a while, and Jamie's mind wandered to the first time they'd done burlesque. It was strange to remember that there was a time only about a year before when the idea of revealing their body to a crowd was one of the scarier things they could imagine. And how after they rushed offstage, they had an adrenaline high that lasted days. They'd felt, for the first time, in control of something that had previously felt like it controlled them.

What if Edgar could experience something similar?

"When I first did burlesque, it was really cathartic for me," Jamie mused.

Edgar nodded politely, clearly unsure where this non sequitur was going.

"This is a little odd," Jamie said. "But how would you feel about *being* a ghost?"

Edgar blanched. "Um. Like. After I die?"

"No. Like while you are very much alive."

## 22

## Edgar

"How the hell did I let you talk me into this," Edgar groaned, looking down at the grayish-brownish makeup clotting on his skin. He was going for a light, jokey tone but didn't think Jamie was fooled. He didn't think Jamie was fooled by much.

They put both hands on his shoulders and looked at him steadily.

"Hey. If you don't want to do this, you don't have to."

When Jamie had asked him the week before if he wanted to be a ghost, he'd assumed they meant as a therapeutic tool. But no. Here he stood at midnight, just inside the abandoned Six Flags amusement park, costumed and made up as the very thing that haunted him.

Edgar smiled at Jamie. He knew that they meant it. If he said right this minute that he wanted to wash off the makeup, take off the wig, and leave Jamie and Amelia one ghost short for the night, Jamie would kiss him goodbye and bear him no ill will. Which just made him that much more determined not to let them down. After all, what was the worst that could happen?

"I'm good. You know, I came here once as a kid. About a year before Katrina. My mom was on this 'group activities' kick for Allie, Poe, and me."

Jamie scrunched up their nose. "Ick."

"Yeah. Allie joined choir, but I can't carry a tune."

"You really cannot," Jamie said tenderly.

"Poe found some group that, looking back, I think was probably churchy, but he didn't care. He just knew they were going to Six Flags at the end of the summer, so he got me to join with him. I don't think we ever went to the church part or did any of the stuff we were probably supposed to do, but come Six Flags day, we were in that van, ready to go. I don't remember what we told Mom, but I think Poe got money from her for snacks and games. Hell, maybe he took it from her wallet."

Jamie smiled as they continued applying Edgar's makeup.

"Poe was *so* excited. When we got inside though, he realized he wasn't quite tall enough to ride the big rides. He was a scrawny little kid. And he was furious. He used to throw these tantrums sometimes, and when someone would try to hug him or pull him away, he'd absolutely freak out. I didn't want him to do that in the middle of Six Flags so I left him alone. He went off and came back taller."

"What? How?"

"He'd gotten paper towel from the bathroom and wadded it up inside his shoes. Gave him that extra inch he needed."

"Wow, that's pretty diabolical for a little kid."

"Yeah."

His brother had always been good at getting what he wanted. He didn't have any qualms about getting in trouble or disappointing people, an attitude that seemed to allow him the latitude he needed.

"He wanted to go on every scary ride. I…didn't. But he would look up at me with this expression that—" He shook his head. Poe had been able to get him to do anything in those days. He'd been terrified to ride the big rides, but he hadn't wanted to disappoint Poe. "But when we got to the front of the line and I saw the sign that showed someone too short flying out of the ride, I was terrified. I tried to pull him out of line, but he just looked at me like I was crazy, and there were people all around so I couldn't really do anything. We sat down, and all I could think of was our car turning upside down on this roller coaster and Poe falling out and splatting on the ground."

Jamie winced.

"He was so excited though, and I didn't know what to do. So I held on to him for dear life the whole ride. I hooked my leg around his, and I held on to his arm. He was trying to push me off, but he couldn't. When the ride was over, I was so relieved that he hadn't died that I almost collapsed. Poe was furious and told me to stay away from him and ran off."

"Harsh," Jamie said, frowning.

Edgar frowned too. He hadn't thought of that in years. Had he spent the whole day chasing after his brother? Looking for him? Worrying about him? It was a blur, except for the van ride home when he'd been so relieved to see Poe unharmed that he'd pulled him into a hug. Poe had gone stiff and pushed him away, choosing to sit next to two kids he'd befriended after leaving Edgar behind. Edgar had sat by himself, frowning out the window as a sign instructed visitors leaving the park to *Have a Great Day.*

He pulled out his phone and snapped a picture of the abandoned park. It was nearing midnight, and the moonlight fell eerily, erasing some shadows and emphasizing others. The Ferris wheel stood, just visible in the chiaroscuro. He sent the picture to Poe.

**Edgar**: Remember when we came here with that weird group?

Since Poe was back in New Orleans, he responded to texts occasionally.

**Poe**: Have you been kidnapped and do you need assistance?

No, Edgar replied. I'm here of my own volition and in full possession of my faculties.

That's what a kidnapper would say, Poe replied.

Edgar was pretty sure he was kidding, but honestly he couldn't always tell with Poe even when they'd been close. Now? He hardly knew his brother at all.

Leave a million dollars in unmarked bills in the place you puked after we came here and find out, he replied.

A screen full of puking emojis filled his screen. He knew that if he texted again, Poe would not reply.

"Okay," Jamie said, stepping back to admire their work. "I think you're good to go."

The other night, when Jamie explained what Edgar would be doing in the movie, they had asked him to describe the scariest ghost he'd ever seen. *Exposure therapy*, Jamie had called it, and Edgar had agreed to try.

Jamie handed Edgar a mirrored compact. Edgar raised the mirror slowly, trying to prepare himself.

The eyes that looked back at Edgar were his own, but everything else had been transformed. His skin was the grayish brown of death, clotted and pinched into a contour map of scars and ridges. His chin appeared to be half gone, and his lip on that side gaped open, so part of his jaw and a tooth were visible. His nose now appeared to be crooked to one side, the tip bulbous and greasy. And his hair was replaced with a bald cap made up in the same way as his face, only brownish tufts clinging to rotting skin.

"Baby? You okay?"

Jamie slid a hand up his back.

Edgar made himself nod to reassure them, but he couldn't look away from his reflection. When ghosts appeared to Edgar, he was so startled and afraid that he only got an initial impression. He certainly never stuck around to peer at the ghosts' various injuries. Now though, Jamie had conjured the effect atop his own face, and Edgar was able to examine every detail.

He raised a clotted gray-brown hand to touch hair the texture of cobwebs. His fingertips hovered over the makeup on his face. He didn't touch it, not wanting to ruin Jamie's art, but he peered close and traced the pattern of scars and puckers with his eyes. He thought about what might have happened to his body to create the result he'd seen in that ghost. The crunch of cartilage and bone, the tearing of skin, the deprivation of light and air.

It would hurt. A lot. It would be traumatic, both physically and emotionally. But the ghost, when he'd seen it, had been single-minded. Counter to Aunt Alaitheia's theories about postdeath temporality, the ghost had pushed through Edgar. To get *somewhere* or to *someone*? Edgar hadn't thought about that part because he'd been so terrified at the time. Now though, he found himself imagining the urgency the ghost displayed. Had it been trying to save someone? Had it taken the shortest route to whomever it was trying to save, and that route had simply happened to be through Edgar?

What would he do if he woke up, confused and hurt and lost in time or space, knowing only that Jamie was in danger and needed him? He would take off at a dead run, needing to get to Jamie before it was too late. He wouldn't stop for anything or anyone, not until Jamie was safe. And if his need to get to them scared a random pedestrian, he wouldn't give it a second thought.

"Baby?" Jamie asked again softly. "Are you okay?"

There were so many things swirling in his mind at once that he couldn't even begin to untangle them. But he was, surprisingly, okay.

"Yeah. I'm ready to terrify some people." Edgar grinned, and the twisted gray face in the mirror grinned back at him.

✦ ✦ ✦

Amelia shouted, "Action!" and Edgar spun to his left as he and Leila had practiced. When Leila turned, he was right in front of her. Amelia's camera was close to capture Leila's expression. Her face twisted into a mask of horror, and she screamed and bolted from him. Edgar jerked backward.

"Cut!"

Amelia peered at the playback. Edgar's heart was pounding, and his ears were ringing. Never in his life had someone responded to him that way. He knew it was a movie, of course, but his body still felt the startle, still felt the actor's fear like it was real. He felt…awful.

Was this how a ghost felt when Edgar screamed or ran? This sensation of shame, guilt, and sadness that made up the ultimate rejection?

"You okay?" Leila asked breathlessly, jogging back toward him. "Hope I didn't shatter an eardrum or anything. Amelia told me to really go for it."

She grinned and smoothed the edge of her hijab.

"I'm fine," he assured her. "Just startled."

"Yeah, about that?" Amelia said.

She spun the camera toward Edgar and pressed Play.

Leila's terrified face filled the screen, and as she screamed, Edgar watched himself look even more afraid than she was and practically scramble away from her.

"Uh. Oops."

"Yeah," Amelia said gently. "If you can look a bit more…"

"Like I'm not terrified of the human I'm supposed to scare."

"Yup, that's the one." She patted him on the shoulder and called, "Reset and let's go again."

The second time Leila screamed in his face, Edgar tensed every muscle so he wouldn't move.

"Um, let's try you over here, Leila," Amelia said, setting up the shot so Edgar was only in the corner of it. This time, he had been trying so hard not to move backward that he ended up pitching forward, as if his ghost was drunk or clumsy.

They tried a few this way. "Better," Amelia said, but she frowned at the camera.

Jamie walked over to her, and they talked quietly. After a few minutes, Amelia gave a thumbs-up.

"Okay, Edgar, let's try it so that you turn and immediately run toward Leila. We'll shoot it from behind so we only see her face and the back of your head. No matter what, you just chase Leila, okay?"

"Okay," Edgar said. He was feeling more and more like this had been a mistake. Now he was ruining Amelia and Jamie's movie.

"It's all good," Jamie said. "This is totally normal. We don't know if a shot's gonna work until we try."

Edgar calmed a little. "Okay."

When everyone else turned back to their tasks, Jamie blew Edgar a kiss. Edgar felt warm beneath the heavy makeup.

As they set the shot up again, Leila leaned in. She was athletic and funny and had been keeping everyone entertained during their downtime. Now she said, "I don't know if it'll help at all, but what if you scream too? Or yell? They're going to add a sound for the ghosts, so maybe they can mix your scream in?"

It was worth a try, Edgar supposed. He thanked Leila, and she gave him a wink.

"I've been an extra in six movies, and Jamie's right. It's always like this. You're not fucking up."

Edgar's shoulders slumped. "You sure?"

"Yup, totally sure," she said. "So you think you can scare me? Cuz I'm not sure that you can." Her voice was a challenge, but her expression said this was all in good fun.

Honestly, Edgar thought that just seeing him made up like this should be enough to scare her, but she was clearly unimpressed.

"Um. What about this isn't scaring you?" He gestured to his makeup.

Leila cocked her head like a babysitter might, to sugarcoat

something for her charge. "Weeeeeeell, kinda everything," she said. "You're just—sorry, I hope you're not pursuing a career in haunting like Jamie or anything because your entire being is deeply unscary."

"No. I work at a cat café."

She put a hand to her heart. "Yeah, that seems much more your speed."

"But you don't even know me."

"No, but...I'm not sure I can explain it, but you emanate noncreepiness. It's a vibe, same as when you can tell someone *does* seem like a creep."

Edgar frowned. "But if you saw me unexpectedly. In an alley or something?"

Leila considered him.

"Yeah. If you jumped out at me in an alley, I'd be terrified. But I'd be terrified if a not-covered-in-ghost-makeup person jumped out at me in an alley too. Being startled is always, you know, startling."

Edgar nodded, considering.

He remembered all the times that he'd seen people he thought were living, but then the light had struck them in a certain way and he'd realized they were ghosts. When the figures were far away, there wasn't the element of immediate fear that he felt when a ghost appeared from nowhere near him. He wasn't scared of them after the initial jolt of recognition, because the startle didn't require action. No fight or flight, just walking in the other direction.

"Okay, places!"

Edgar stood on the tape *X,* and Leila grinned at him, two compatriots who'd hatched a mutual plan.

"I dare you to scare me," she whispered.

This time, Edgar didn't think about seeing a ghost.

This time, he imagined *being* the ghost.

This mortal couldn't hurt him. Nothing she did would affect him in any way. She could scream or throw things or shoot him, but he wasn't bound by mortal rules. He was free from judgment, free from consequence, free from fear.

*Can you remember a time when you* weren't *afraid?* Poe had asked him in their aunt's bar. *Even before the ghosts? Because I can't.*

Poe was right. Edgar had been afraid of a whole hell of a lot besides ghosts. Before ghosts had become the thing he'd focused all of that fear on.

Freedom from fear—what would that even feel like?

Edgar closed his eyes and imagined that he could sweep fear out of his life like cobwebs, collapse it in a tiny sticky packet, and wipe it from his fingers.

It would feel like ease, like relaxation, like part of him that had been working very hard for a long time was finally able to take a long, desperately needed rest. It would feel like a fog being cleared away from the window between him and what he might want in the world. It would feel like the ability to pursue those desires. It would feel like curiosity and wonder and experimentation.

It would feel like a chance, finally, to stand in the world, *of* the world, and see what all the fuss was about. It would feel like arguing for what he wanted and standing up for who he wanted. It would mean friends and a partner and maybe a family.

It would feel like love.

Because wasn't that what it all pointed to? Fear was keeping him away from all of it, and that meant being kept from love. Keeping himself from love.

Jamie stood behind Amelia's shoulder, pointing at something on the screen. As if they could feel Edgar's gaze on them, they looked up. They smiled at him, and it was a smile that cracked on his head an egg of joy that dripped down his neck.

*I'm so close to loving you,* Edgar thought. *I'm as close as I can be with all this shit in the way, and I* want *to get rid of it, please. I just don't know if I can, and I'm so so afraid that you'll give up on me before I get there.*

Jamie winked at him and turned their attention back to Amelia.

Edgar started to clench his fists, dig his fingers into his palms like he usually did to forestall the escape of inopportune emotion. But he stopped himself because it would ruin the makeup coating his hands. Instead he sucked in a deep breath through his nose and blew it out his mouth.

He was going to scare Leila. He was going to take all the fear that he held inside him, form it into a ball packed tight with rage and resentment, unfairness and grief, and he was going to launch it at Leila the second the camera started rolling.

"Ready, sound?" Amelia called, and someone shouted in the affirmative.

Leila mouthed, *I dare you,* and turned her back on him. Edgar was vibrating with intent.

"Action," yelled Amelia.

Edgar stepped to the side, and Leila turned. As the fabric of her hijab floated around her, Edgar let his face show everything he'd always tried so hard to trap inside. And when her eyes met his, her expression changed. The look of fear she had composed for the other takes shifted, crept up to her eyes. Her fear, it appeared, was real. She hesitated for a moment, like she couldn't tell what was real and what wasn't. Then, when she opened her mouth to scream, Edgar launched toward her, bellowing from the depths of his soul.

The sound spewed from him, a puke of fear and rage and desperation that echoed in the abandoned amusement park like the one-time screams of roller coaster passengers barreling full-speed downhill, wind drying their mouths but utterly safe in the certainty that the ride would end and their chosen beast would trouble them no more.

"Holy fucking shit, cut!" Amelia yelled.

She had to yell louder than usual, because both Edgar and Leila had sprinted halfway to the arcade entrance during the take.

"Omigod," Leila said, stooping to rest her palms on her knees. She was breathing hard. "You totally got me."

And Edgar, makeup cracking off his face, smiled peacefully.

"Yup, we got it," Amelia said. "That was exactly it."

She held up her hand to high-five Edgar, saw his hand was covered with makeup, and gave him an air fist bump instead.

"Are we—do we get to do it again?"

"I think we got—"

"Yes," Jamie said, loud and clear, wide eyes fixed on Edgar. "We get to do it again."

## 23

## Edgar

"I can't believe we forgot," Edgar mumbled.

Next to him, Poe made a pained sound of agreement.

They were doing something that any New Orleans native knew better than to ever do: try to shop while a festival raged.

Southern Decadence, sometimes described as Gay Mardi Gras, descended on the French Quarter every Labor Day in a flurry of glitter, feathers, body paint, beads, and a *lot* of intoxicated queers.

When Edgar realized he'd forgotten Allie's birthday in the chaos of Poe's return, the baby, and Jamie, he'd rousted Poe from Allie's couch and into the heat of the evening, hoping that because they were in the Irish Channel, they could avoid the hubbub.

Poe had run back inside for his leather jacket and sunglasses and glared at Edgar for the first few blocks down Magazine Street. He'd softened a bit when a street cat had wound around his ankles, and Edgar thought he'd invite his brother to come to work with him next week to hang out with the cats.

Stores on Magazine Street were closing early in preparation for Labor Day, so, gritting their teeth against the inevitable onslaught, they caught a bus into the Quarter.

"What should we get her?" Edgar mused, staring out the window.

"Dude, she's got a new baby. She wants a whole lot of something we can't give her."

"What? Help?"

"Her life back," Poe said.

"I know you're not Mister Baby. Neither am I. But she wanted a kid."

"Big mistake."

"Kids in general, or Allie's specifically?"

They hopped off the bus when it terminated at Canal Street and headed downriver.

"Whatever, let's just find something," Poe said, shading his eyes with his hand. "Thought that counts, right?"

It was something their mother used to say, but Edgar thought Poe was missing the spirit of the expression.

"Books?" Edgar suggested as they passed Beckham's, an orange and white tabby cat drowsing in the upstairs window.

"When will she have time to read?"

"A gift card for Sylvain's?"

"She won't be able to eat out for, like, twelve years."

"Uh, maybe some fancy mixers for cocktails?"

"She'll fall asleep immediately. Or drop her baby."

"Bath stuff?"

"Drown her baby."

"Well, could you offer some suggestions, please? Preferably something that won't result in the immediate death of our sister or her offspring?"

Poe snickered at the word *offspring*, and Edgar decided he wouldn't ask for his input anymore.

As they approached Jackson Square, the crowd thronged.

"Hey, I think that's Carys and Teacup."

In addition to her work as a tour guide, Carys was a math grad student by day and often set up in the square to perform calculations for the tourists and their money.

"Who the hell is Teacup?" Poe scoffed.

"Her miniature horse."

"I sure am back in New Orleans," he mumbled. "If you wanna say hi, I'm gonna wait here. Can't deal with the tourist mob."

But all thoughts of saying hello to Carys and Teacup fled Edgar's mind when he saw *something*. Something that dripped cold between his shoulder blades and down the back of his neck and sent a tingling across his scalp like insects skittering through his hair.

Edgar's breath came short. Surely it was just his eyes playing tricks on him in the heat?

"Poe," Edgar croaked out. "Do you see that?" He pointed a shaking finger.

"I see a bunch of drunk gay dudes and sunburned tourists staring at them."

Edgar shook his head, unable to swallow. He tugged on Poe's sleeve, and his brother sighed.

"What?"

"B-behind the band," Edgar said without looking away. "Antoine."

"Antoine who—Wait, *Antoine* Antoine?"

Edgar tried to swallow again. Surely, if he just concentrated, he could make his throat close and then open again. But it was as if all the systems that run him had shut down. He shivered then and couldn't stop. A mule-drawn carriage blocked his view for a moment, and when it passed, Antoine was gone.

Edgar staggered, trying to cross the street to the square. He was vaguely aware of Poe throwing an arm around his waist to keep him from falling, but he was already pushing toward the steps of St. Louis Cathedral.

He caught sight of Antoine again, drifting past a line of tourists clapping along to the brass band.

"There!" Edgar pointed, unconcerned about seeming rude. The crowd surged around him in every direction—revelers drifting in from the parade, tourists wrangling children, teens yelling to their friends, tipsy partygoers calling from windows and balconies above. The chaos scrambled his senses, but all he cared about was getting to Antoine.

Edgar had never run *toward* a ghost before. But if Antoine was here, Edgar *had* to speak to him. If Antoine was lost or scared or needed something, Edgar had to make sure he gave it to him. Because for all that he wasn't sure why ghosts were or how they were, he did know one thing: if his old friend was stuck here, in pain, Edgar would do anything to help him find peace.

Edgar reached blindly for Poe, intending to pull him along without losing sight of Antoine. But when his hand found Poe's, his brother jerked it away.

"Don't fucking touch me!" Poe yelled.

Edgar was so startled by the violence of Poe's reaction that he turned from Antoine and saw Poe cringing away from him. He had his collar turned up and was pulling his jacket around him like it was the only thing holding him together. He looked angry and scared and so, so tired.

"Are you okay?"

Poe set his jaw and glared. "I'm fucking *fine*. Now can we go?"

Edgar turned back to where Antoine had been. His friend was gone.

"No!" Edgar heard himself yell.

He rocketed through the crowd, shouldering aside a red-faced blond man and a woman with a triple-wide stroller. Antoine had been close to Pirate's Alley, so that was where Edgar went. If he could just catch up to him. If he could just make Antoine talk to him.

He ran, dodging people, until he tripped on the drainage ditch next to the path and stumbled. Poe caught up with him.

"Are you trying to get yourself killed?" Poe snapped.

Edgar wasn't hurt. He'd scraped his palms a bit when he caught himself, but the sting only served to focus him. Antoine was close. He could feel it. Edgar got his feet under him, but when he moved to stand, Antoine was already there, no more than ten feet in front of him.

"Antoine," Edgar mouthed. He grabbed Poe's leather-clad arm, then dropped it like he'd been burned as he remembered Poe's injunction.

They crouched there on the ground, Poe frozen at Edgar's side.

"Antoine," Edgar said again, his voice audible this time.

The ghost before them had been his best friend. The person he'd spent the most time with, with the exception of Allie and Poe. The boy who'd had the most infectious laugh Edgar had ever heard and the kindest heart he'd ever encountered. The boy who had been his first love as well as his best friend.

The boy he'd watched drown and hadn't been able to save.

Edgar's cheeks were wet.

"Poe. Poe, it's Antoine."

He didn't know what he expected from Poe, but his brother didn't respond. He was looking from Edgar to Antoine and didn't seem afraid. Then again, Antoine had been Poe's friend too.

Edgar rose slowly, afraid that any sudden movement or lapse in attention and Antoine would disappear. But he was still there when Edgar took one step toward him, then another.

Antoine's face was the gray waterlogged misery that Edgar remembered from when they had pulled his small body from the water. Bits of bayou plants and the insects that lived in them were caught in his hair. He was wearing the clothes he'd died in: blue jeans, an orange-and-blue-striped T-shirt, and his favorite red high tops. They'd been the same height when Antoine died, but now Edgar towered over him.

"Antoine?" Edgar said softly. "Is that really you?"

He imagined Poe rolling his eyes at the foolish question. But he'd never spoken to a ghost before. Well, except occasionally to yell at them to get away.

Antoine—no, Antoine's ghost—opened his mouth, and water poured out, evaporating before it hit the ground. Edgar winced but didn't look away. He stood just feet from the boy whose death he'd never really gotten over and watched the water that had killed him gush from his stomach and lungs and throat.

"What can I do? How can I help?"

The cloudy gray of Antoine's eyes cleared to reveal the warm brown that Edgar remembered. As they focused on Edgar, his heart beat faster, and tears dripped down his nose.

"Are you okay?" he asked, and other foolish questions.

Antoine didn't answer.

Edgar didn't even know if ghosts could speak. All this time, he'd thought about what they might do to him and why they scared him, and he'd never realized that they might not be able to answer even if he could get up the courage to ask.

Edgar reached out a hand. Slowly, he let his fingers come within an inch of Antoine. A chilly fug clung to him, like Edgar was reaching into a shaded cave or a cold spring, but it didn't feel frightening this time. It felt refreshing. He didn't get the sour taste in the back of his throat that he often got when ghosts appeared either. In fact, the fear he'd always felt—even of Antoine when he had first seen him—had drained away, leaving only longing.

"Antoine, what can I do for you? Do you have unfinished business?"

A derisive snort from behind him reminded Edgar that Poe was there. Edgar didn't turn though. He kept his eyes on Antoine's.

"Your sister's doing great," he told Antoine, not sure what else to say. "Cameron was Allie's birthing partner. Oh, and Allie had a baby."

He was catching Antoine up on his life as if he'd never drowned, never abandoned Edgar and all the plans they'd had: to draw a comic book, to sneak into the aquarium at night, to prank Cameron back. More. So much more.

"Poe finally came back to New Orleans. Oh yeah, you wouldn't know. Poe left when he was sixteen and never came back. Until now. Because of Allie's baby."

He couldn't be sure, but it seemed like Antoine was listening to him. His eyes glowed, and his skin had lost a hint of its grayish-green tinge.

"You gotta help me out, man," Edgar continued. "What *are* ghosts? What are *you*? Have you been here all along? Ever since you…" Then a horrible thought occurred to him. "You know you're dead, right?"

There was no gasp or heart-clutching from Antoine, so Edgar took that as a yes.

"Okay, back to the 'What are ghosts?' question, then."

No response. Antoine drifted a bit in the air, moving like a kite with the breeze.

"I don't know how you communicate," Edgar said, desperate now. Antoine couldn't disappear until he could figure things out. "Wait, please. Don't go. Talk to me. What do I do? How can I help you? What do ghosts want from me?"

Antoine looked directly at Edgar. Once, when they were eight, Antoine had broken his arm. He'd tried to be brave and pretend it didn't hurt, but Edgar had known it did. He'd distracted Antoine from the pain as Antoine's father drove them to the hospital, telling him stories of ghosts that his mother had told him. Antoine had stared into his eyes the whole time, like it was only Edgar's presence in the back seat keeping him from fear.

"I met someone," Edgar continued. "Their name's Jamie, and they're… Well, you'd really like them. They're pretty great. I think I might…" He shook his head and bit his lip. "We were too young, before. But I—I really loved you. Did you know that?

Like, I loved you as a friend and a brother. But you were the first person I fell for. And there hasn't been anyone since you. Not 'til Jamie. If I don't fuck it up."

Antoine's eyes were still fixed on Edgar's, but he'd begun to list more dramatically with the breeze. Now he floated close to the fence separating Pirate's Alley from Place de Henriette Delille.

Edgar was afraid he was going to blow away, like a child's let-go balloon. He reached out a hand, the same as he'd done all those years ago, when the water had closed over Antoine's head. He reached out, and this time—*this time*—he caught Antoine's hand.

A shock shot through him like cold electricity, leaving him shuddering in the twilight. For a moment, Antoine shimmered into solidity, and Edgar felt the brush of his fingers, his hand in Edgar's so small now.

Then, definitively, he was gone.

The sounds of the evening rushed back in, and the heat settled once again on his skin. Edgar's cheeks were wet with tears. He swallowed a thick sob and tasted apples. They had been Antoine's favorite food. His parents kept a bowl full, and Antoine would always grab one on his way out of the house. At some point during their adventures, he'd pull the apple out of his pocket and look at it with delight. And always, he would hand the apple to Edgar first, encouraging his best friend to share his favorite treat.

Edgar sank to the ground, back pressed to the unforgiving chain-link fence, and wept.

## 24

# Edgar

Edgar wasn't sure how long he sat on the ground in Pirate's Alley. He had his head in his hands, trying to block out the din of Jackson Square to his left, Southern Decadence to his right, and Poe prowling up and down in front of him.

At one point, he heard Poe say, "Dude, just come. He needs you, and I can't… Okay. Yeah, I will."

Then Poe was crouching in front of him.

"Edgar. I need you to stand up right now and come with me. Jamie's going to pick us up, but they can't drive down here with the parade."

At Jamie's name, Edgar looked up.

"Yeah. Can you get up?" Poe's hands were fists shoved in the pockets of his jacket.

Edgar pushed himself up. Now that the cold of Antoine's ghost was gone, he felt hot and shaky. His head was light, and his sinuses were clogged.

Poe led the way, looking back every minute or two to make sure Edgar followed.

Jamie met them at Canal Street, face drawn with worry. They tossed their keys to Poe and came to Edgar.

"C'mere, baby," they said and helped him into the back seat, climbing in after him.

Jamie stroked his hair and held his hand as Poe navigated traffic, swearing constantly and cursing a number of families into the tenth generation. He threw the truck into park outside Allie's place and unlocked the door.

"What the hell happened to you?" Allie asked when she saw Edgar. "Oh, hi, Jamie. Sorry, I didn't know you were here."

Edgar was shuttled to the couch, hands trembling and head swimmy from crying.

"What the fuck, Poe?" Allie asked softly.

"*I* didn't do anything," he shot back.

"I'm fine," Edgar managed. "He didn't do anything."

"Then would someone like to tell me what's going on?"

Poe snorted. "Got that mom tone down, eh?"

"Listen, you little shit," Allie said. "You show up here after six years of avoiding us like the plague. Ever since, you've acted weird, and now Edgar is…liquified. So shut your face about my tone, get me a fucking snack, and then sit down and explain yourself. Please. Thank you."

Poe glared, but he made Allie a peanut butter and honey sandwich without comment, and Edgar told her and Jamie about how they'd seen Antoine.

"Oh, shit." Allie took a bite and spoke through it. "Did he still look twelve?"

"He was thirteen," Edgar corrected automatically. "His birthday was two weeks before. We made an apple cake."

"Right," Allie said softly. "I forgot. How did he look?"

"Kind of…"

"Dead?" Poe offered flatly from his perch on the arm of the couch.

Something about the way he said it made Edgar look at him closely.

"How did he look to you, Poe?" Edgar asked.

Poe's eyes narrowed for an instant before he wiped all expression from his face. "Honestly, I was trying not to look at him."

That was reasonable. But something about his brother's voice made alarm bells go off in Edgar's mind.

"But you saw it when he liquefied into a puddle, right?"

"Yeah," Poe said. "Poor bastard."

Edgar's stomach dropped like he was on a roller coaster. Poe hadn't seen that because it hadn't happened.

Poe was lying.

But why?

Edgar ran through other options, seeking some reason—*any* reason—for the untruth. Maybe Poe had been too scared and really hadn't looked at Antoine. Maybe he'd seen how emotional Edgar had gotten and wanted to give him privacy. Could he be lying just to fuck with Edgar's head? Weird and cruel, but Poe had been gone since he was sixteen. Maybe Edgar didn't know him anymore. True though that might be, if Poe had wanted to mess with him, wouldn't he have been more likely to *disagree* with what Edgar said?

Hell, maybe ghosts looked different to everyone; what did he know? *Well, you know that Allie sees pretty much the same thing you do, because you've seen ghosts together. Same with Mom.*

But Poe had been there too when they were kids, and he'd seen them as well.

At least he'd said he had.

Edgar slowly became aware of Jamie's hand on his thigh. Someone had said something, but he couldn't track what. He ignored it and looked at his brother.

"Poe?" he asked softly. "Do you see ghosts?"

A muscle jumped in Poe's jaw, and he went still. It was a change so subtle that Edgar wouldn't have noticed it if he hadn't been looking for it.

"Not at the moment, no. You?"

"Poe. Have you ever seen a ghost?"

"We just saw one, like, five seconds ago. What are you talking about?"

"What *are* you talking about, Edgar?" Allie asked, leaning forward. She looked, in that moment, so much like their mother, and a longing rose in Edgar for the first time in years. To be enfolded in her arms as he hadn't been since he'd grown taller than her at fifteen.

"That's not what happened," Edgar said. His voice sounded thick and dull in his ears. "Antoine didn't liquefy. He floated away. And he didn't look dead. Well, he did at first. But then he looked…almost like he used to." He swallowed hard.

"I told you, I was trying not to look." Poe stood up, pulling his jacket around himself. Edgar stood too. He was a few inches taller than Poe and broader. Poe didn't raise his chin to look at him.

"You were really that scared?" Edgar asked.

"Yup. I'm a huge wimp," Poe said and rolled his eyes. "Now can we discuss the way—"

"I don't believe you."

It was something that Edgar had never said to another soul. Growing up with a mother who saw ghosts and a father who didn't believe in them and seeing ghosts himself when the world said they didn't exist…it all added up to a deep knowledge that there were a lot of things in the world he didn't know about or understand. And if someone said something was true for them, he always erred on the side of believing them rather than the alternative.

Poe flinched.

Edgar searched his face for any sign that Poe felt like he was being falsely accused and didn't find it. Something was wrong.

"Poe?" Allie said, her voice a gentle warning. Allie had always been their staunchest ally. Their fiercest champion. But when you fucked up, she would not hesitate to let you know exactly how much. "What's going on?"

For a moment, Poe seemed to teeter between fury and bravado. Edgar thought he might walk out the door, walk to his car, and leave New Orleans for another six years without telling them.

But then he squeezed his eyes shut and jammed his fists into them.

"*Fuck!*"

Allie and Jamie were watching them, wide-eyed, from the couch.

"Just tell us what's up, buddy," Allie said gently. Edgar hadn't heard her call him buddy since they were kids.

Poe swore a blue streak, running hands through his wild hair.

"I thought…when I was little, I thought you both were playing along with Mama. So I did too. When we'd be out, and she'd point and say there was a ghost and she thought it was from the 1920s because of this hat or that dress? I didn't even know what the 1920s were. And you'd both nod and say, yeah, you saw it too. So I said I saw it. And I thought…I guess I thought you were doing it so she'd feel better. Since Dad always gave her so much shit. I thought—"

Edgar's stomach flipped imagining little Poe, just trying to make their mom less alone.

"And I don't know, I thought maybe I *was* seeing the same things as you guys. I wasn't trying to tell some huge lie. But then—" He shook his head. "Dad left, and you still talked about seeing them. By then, it had all gotten so big I couldn't say anything. And I just…I didn't want you to think I was like him."

Allie was on her feet by the time he finished speaking, and she came at him with open arms, ready—always so ready—to comfort. Poe jerked away from her and pulled his leather jacket closer.

Allie looked hurt but gave him space.

Poe said, "There is just one more tiny thing." He laughed nervously.

"Oh shit," Jamie murmured and clapped a hand over their mouth.

Poe looked at them and shrugged. "I can see the future."

Silence. Blinking. Then a wail cut through the silence, and Allie sprang to attention. She stabbed a finger at them all. "Don't any of you say one single word until I get back, on pain of death."

Poe mimed zipping his lips and then throwing away a key. Jamie started to say something, then snapped their mouth shut.

Edgar was pretty sure they'd been going to ask why something that zipped would have a lock on it.

They all stayed still and quiet, like the world's most awkward tableau, until Allie returned, holding the baby.

"You can see fucking *what* now?" she said.

"It's not always, like, clear. But. Yeah."

"When you touch people, right?" Jamie said slowly, like they were putting a puzzle together. "Just like Phillipe Rondeau. That's why you wear that batshit hot jacket in the summer in New Orleans?"

"Better than being deluged with information about how people are going to die or the ways their relationships are going to fail or that their kids are never gonna speak to them again," Poe said.

Jamie made an expression of agreement. "Is it always negative things?"

Poe shook his head. "Not necessarily. A lot of the time, it's jumbled. I can't tell who anyone is or where. Or when."

"Stop, stop, stop," Allie said. She managed to be commanding without raising her voice above baby-approved volume. "Pause. Go back to the beginning. Like, *birth* beginning. And tell me everything."

Poe sighed and sat back down, settling himself on the floor. Edgar sat back down next to Jamie. Their eyes were wide, and they were practically vibrating with excitement.

"I didn't know what it was at first," Poe said. "In the beginning, it was just like, sometimes when someone would hold my hand, I'd get impressions of their life. I dunno how I knew that's what it was. But it made sense. I assumed it was like that for everyone. Like, that was why people shook hands and hugged or kissed when they first saw each other: to learn stuff about how their life was going. Kind of a tactile *How are you?*

"So I didn't think much of it. Then sometimes I'd make a comment based on something I'd seen, assuming it was common knowledge, and Mom or Dad would act confused. Once, I asked why Mr. Clark—you remember him, Eddie? Dickhead with the greasy mustache?"

Edgar sure did. The second-grade teacher had taught through terror, choosing a few people each lesson to make an example of.

"I asked why he wasn't teaching at our school anymore, and Mama and Dad were like, 'What do you mean? He's still your teacher.' But then a couple months later, he disappeared, remember?"

"Yeah," Allie said. "He molested a student. The school didn't want to fire him publicly because it would come out that they'd hired someone without due diligence, but then it came out anyway. It was a huge scandal."

"Right. So when that came out—I assume; I wasn't old enough to know what that even meant—Mom came to me all horrified that he'd molested me. She thought that's why I'd known he might get fired. When really, he'd just touched my hand giving me back a quiz or something."

Edgar couldn't look away from Poe. *How* had he missed this?

"At the time, it confused me, because I still didn't get what was happening or that it wasn't something that happened to other people. I think maybe when you're that age, you don't really experience time the same as when you're older and everything's settled in. Time seemed unclear to me then, so it took me a while to understand that what I was seeing wasn't happening in the present. Lots of times, if it was strangers I touched, I'd never see them again. So I never knew what I'd seen."

"When do you think you really knew for sure what was happening?" Allie asked.

Poe's eyes darted to Edgar's and then quickly away. "Um. I dunno if you wanna know."

"What? Of course we want to know," Allie insisted. The baby yawned hugely, less insistent.

But it was Edgar that Poe was facing. Even as he heard himself say, "Tell us," his stomach flipped. Like his body knew what Poe was going to say before it heard him.

"One night," Poe said, voice a bit rough, "Antoine and Cameron were sleeping over."

Edgar swallowed, willing his body to regulate itself.

"We were all sleeping out in the living room by the air conditioner, and we'd watched *Blood Mansion* before going to bed. I was scared of the big mirror over the mantel because of the way the lady comes out of there in the movie. Anyway, I was huddled close to you and Antoine because I was freaked. And that night, I had a dream where, uh, a boy drowned. And just at the end, right before I woke up, I realized it was Antoine."

Poe was hugging himself. "Eddie, I swear I didn't know. I didn't know it was real or that it would happen soon. I hardly even remembered it a few minutes after I woke up. Mama started making pancakes, and I just—"

His fists and jaw were clenched.

"Then that day—the day he—I had a strange sense of déjà vu the whole time and didn't know why. But when it happened. When he was slipping under." Poe choked on his words. "I realized it was his shirt. The striped one. It was in my dream. All of a sudden, it was exactly the moment from my dream."

Outside, a man was yelling, and a bus passed by. Inside, no one moved or made a sound.

Then a noise escaped Poe. A strangled sound that had once been a sob before it had been twisted by years of guilt into a plea.

"I didn't know," he begged, voice gone as small as a little boy. "I swear. Please, *please*, believe me. If I'd known it was real, I would have stopped him. I wouldn't have let him go in the water; please, you guys, you have to believe me." He put his head in his hands. "Fuck, I'm so sorry. I'm so damn sorry. It's my fault, I know that, but it was an accident."

Allie handed the baby to Edgar and knelt next to Poe. She wrapped her arms around him carefully. He jerked away.

"I'm not gonna touch you. Just your jacket. Okay?"

Poe slumped, the effort he'd been putting into staying remote and on guard only revealed when he let it go. Allie hugged him tight. Then she pulled back and looked at him.

"It's not your fault," she said fiercely.

Poe looked at Edgar then, and there was something familiar in his eyes. He'd seen flashes of it for years and years, but it had been hidden behind bravado, aggression, and a biting sense of humor. But now those had been stripped away, and Edgar could identify the emotion at the core: shame. Shame and the desire for an absolution he didn't think he deserved.

*Fuck.*

Edgar's mind was reeling from Poe's revelations, but although he had a million questions, there was one thing more important than all the rest.

"It wasn't your fault, Poe."

"*Obviously,*" Allie vehemently agreed. "He's exactly right."

"Because it was mine."

"Uh, nope, pause. Disregard. He is *not* exactly right." She took the baby back from Edgar as if his wrongness might infect them. "What the hell is wrong with both of you? Antoine drowned. It was a horrible, tragic thing, but it was an accident. *Everyone* said it was an accident. There was nothing any of us could've done."

Jamie put a hand on Edgar's lower back. It was a steady pressure that said, *I'm here if you need me.*

Edgar squeezed his eyes shut. Apparently this was the evening for the baring of family secrets.

"I liked him. Had a crush on him."

"Duh," said Poe, as Allie snorted.

"You knew?" Edgar asked.

"You used to watch him all the time. You'd smile like a huge goon whenever you saw him," Poe said.

Apparently someone was feeling better.

Edgar scowled. "Yeah, well, I was trying *not* to do precisely that when he fucking drowned."

Poe's eyes darkened, and Allie looked horrified.

"I realized I was staring at him. I didn't want him to know, so I turned my back on him. When I turned back around, he was too far away and the mud was too—" He swallowed hard. "If I'd just looked a *minute* sooner, I would've had time to get to him."

"Oh my god. Why are both my siblings such complete and total cabbages?" Allie bemoaned to the baby. "What am I gonna do with them?"

The baby made a strange face. Then they grinned a gummy grin, and an unpleasant smell wafted through the room.

"I couldn't agree more, frankly," Allie said.

"Not it!" Poe said instantly.

"Dude, you just told me you see the future, including people's deaths. You think I'm letting you touch my *baby*? Gimme the diaper bag."

Poe passed it to her and turned to Edgar. "It's not your fault, dude."

"Not yours," Edgar replied. Then, "That was his birthday."

Confused looks.

"The night he and Cam stayed over and we watched *Blood Mansion*. It was Antoine's thirteenth birthday."

"Oh, right," Allie said. "He got those new sneakers, and he was so excited."

"He was wearing them tonight. Same outfit he died in."

Silence fell over the room once more, but this time, it was lighter, easier. Edgar looked at Allie, then at Poe, then at the nameless baby who might inherit any number of supernatural abilities but who was, at this moment, bare-assed and blinking gummily up at Edgar. He smiled back.

"Is anyone else hungry?" Allie asked sheepishly. "I feel bad interjecting something so mundane into the conversation, but—"

"I'm famished, actually," Jamie said.

"I could eat," said Poe.

Edgar could too. "Do you have anything, Al?"

Allie gestured vaguely toward the kitchen and said, "Use whatever you find to concoct something edible."

"I'll do it," Poe said, standing. "I've been working in a restaurant lately."

"Was that a genuine sharing of information about your life?" Allie asked.

Poe stuck his tongue out at her and went to the kitchen.

"You know," Allie said as he rummaged through the cupboards. "Now that we know about the whole touching issue, you don't have to wear that thing inside anymore."

Poe tugged his leather jacket closer and looked at Allie as if she'd suggested removing his skin. Then he shrugged, shoulders almost to his ears.

"Yeah, okay," he said.

He peeled off the garment, draped it over the back of a barstool, and started pulling ingredients from the refrigerator. His arms were lean and toned against his black T-shirt. Scars crisscrossed his arms like a child's game of tic-tac-toe. He held himself as if he'd brutally punish anyone who asked about them.

Soon, Poe handed around bowls of pasta with lentils, feta, and capers, grumbling about Allie not having any fresh herbs.

"Grow some, then," she said.

Poe's childish, nonsensical comeback—"I'll grow you"—gave way to chewing and then murmurs of appreciation.

"Honestly, when you said you'd cook, I was expecting nothing," Allie said. "But this is damn good."

"Agreed," said Edgar.

"I don't know you well enough yet to have expected nothing from you," Jamie said lightly, giving a thumbs-up to the food.

Poe winked at that.

Edgar didn't know if he liked the idea of Jamie and Poe being friends. God knew what trouble Poe would get Jamie involved in. Then he reminded himself that his brother wasn't a child anymore, and Jamie could certainly take care of themself.

"Can I just go back to the previous topic for a minute?" Allie asked.

Poe rolled his eyes. "I suppose it was too much to expect that

I might drop the whole seeing the future thing and hope there would be no follow-up questions."

Allie said, "Because, okay, I suspected the ghost thing just a little bit, but—"

"Wait, you suspected?" Edgar demanded. "What? Why? How come you never said anything?"

"How'd you know?" Poe grumbled at the same time.

"Er, I mean, I didn't *know* know," Allie said. "But you never talked about seeing them until someone else did. And when you were little, you always wanted to do whatever Edgar and I did. So occasionally I wondered if you didn't see them but didn't wanna feel left out. And I suspected, a little, that was why you left. Because maybe it was easier if you didn't have to keep up the act."

Poe shoved food into his mouth so he couldn't answer.

"But what I don't get," Allie said. She looked at Poe, but he wouldn't meet her eyes. She looked at Edgar, and he could see how close she was to tears. "Is why you didn't tell us."

Poe shook his head.

"We were all so close," she went on. "We told each other everything. I thought." Her voice broke. "If you'd just said something—"

Poe sighed and looked at her. "Allie. I was a freak even in a family of freaks. And I couldn't tell you because you'd ask me to use it."

She stopped with her fork halfway to her mouth. "What?"

Poe rolled his eyes. "Sure, maybe not right away. Maybe you'd promise me it would never happen. But at some point, there comes a time when everyone thinks they'd be better off knowing what's gonna happen."

He looked haunted. How many people had promised him

they'd never ask, and how many of them had smashed that promise to smithereens?

"And if by some miracle neither of you ever asked me, then I'd end up seeing it anyway. By accident or in a dream. Or in some weird fucking *freak* way that I haven't even experienced yet because who the hell *knows* what I am."

The hand holding Poe's fork shook, and he put it down.

"If I wasn't here. If I wasn't around you. I thought it was less likely that I'd see your—"

"Futures," Allie finished for him.

"Deaths," Edgar corrected, the penny finally dropping. "You were afraid you'd see our deaths. That's why you left."

Poe nodded miserably. "Please don't make me," he said.

His voice was colored with fear and exhaustion and something that hurt Edgar in ways he didn't understand.

"No one's gonna make you do anything," Edgar said fiercely.

He didn't care how long Poe had been gone for, he would destroy anyone who pushed him to do anything he didn't want to do.

"Except cook more often," Allie said. "Cuz this is seriously good."

Poe ducked his head at her praise.

"Yeah, uh, cool. I…enjoy it."

Jamie caught Edgar's glance and raised an eyebrow, as if to say, *Poe unsarcastically expressed enjoyment?!*

Allie took another bite and eyed Poe with respect. None of them had ever been very good at expressing emotion; they'd never learned to. But Edgar thought maybe that could change. After all, it had already started to change for him, being in a relationship with Jamie.

"Well, don't just sit there," Allie said, wiping at her eyes. "Tell us what the hell you've been up to the past six years, you enormous freak."

Looking around the table, a genuine smile that Edgar realized he hadn't seen in years quirked his brother's lips. As if assessing the level of their interest and deeming it sufficient, he leaned in, eyes shining with six years of stories. Edgar felt something that had been tightly coiled in his belly all these years relax and go to sleep.

"Okay," Poe said, raising his eyebrows. He began to talk and didn't stop until they were all hungry again.

# 25

## Jamie

It was casting day for scare actors at House of Screams, one of Jamie's favorite parts of their job. They swung by to pick up Amelia on the way.

"Dude," she said as she hopped into the front seat and slung her bag in the back. "I think we've got a preliminary cut. Can you come over after work to watch?"

"Hell yes." They raised their hand, and Amelia high-fived it. "Sorry I've been so busy lately. The text thread with Emma and my folks has exploded."

Now that the wedding was drawing nearer, new problems or decisions cropped up nearly every day. Dozens of texts would greet Jamie when they took their lunch break, with links and pictures and words like URGENT at the top of every single one.

Jamie had told their family multiple times that if emergent decisions needed to be made, they shouldn't wait for Jamie to weigh in. It hadn't made a difference though. This wedding was a train chugging along the tracks, and god help anyone who got in its way.

"If I don't respond quickly enough, my folks call when they know I'm at work and leave sigh-punctuated messages about how I'll regret being selfish and not prioritizing my only sister's wedding years from now, because a wedding only happens once."

"Ew," Amelia expectorated. "Wait, wasn't your mom married before she and your dad got together?"

"Yeah, I dare you to try and bring that up with her."

"So would I be right in assuming my invitation to be your date to the blessed event is rescinded?"

Jamie sighed. "I haven't asked him yet."

"I thought it was going well?"

"Edgar's wonderful. But I'm honestly dreading the wedding. Even with the suit issue settled, I just… You've been to these family events where my mom is running a political shadow op while the rest of us eat macaroni salad. You know how it is."

Amelia snarled. "Yeah, every time your parents misgendered you, I wanted to scream. I don't know how you stand it."

Jamie's stomach hurt. "Hence my dread." They waved a merging truck in front of them as they slowed down to make the turn into the haunt. "So what do you think I should do?" Jamie asked, throwing the truck into park. "Should I go?"

"You don't have to decide now if you're gonna go to the wedding. But I think you should invite Edgar no matter what you choose later. I'd want to be asked."

"I would too," Jamie said, linking elbows with her as they walked toward work. "Thanks."

Amelia cupped her hand to her ear. "What was that?"

"I said you're right, my wisest and most trusted advisor."

"I know," Amelia said cheerfully.

"Your every crumb of sagacity is a blessing to my—" Jamie was interrupted by Amelia shoving a doughnut into their mouth.

"Mm, 's my favrt," Jamie said through a mouthful of delicious old-fashioned.

"You're the smartest, most correct person I've ever—" Jamie intercepted the second doughnut before Amelia made it to their face and held on to it for later.

"All right," Jamie said, in a much better mood now. "Let's go make a bunch of people scream."

✦ ✦ ✦

Jamie cued up the scene in Amelia's film and cast it to Edgar's television.

"It's not scored yet or anything," Jamie explained. "This is just a rough cut she gave me to show you."

"Good," Edgar said with a shiver.

Jamie pressed Play.

The clip was eight seconds long. It was dark, and the loop of the abandoned roller coaster soared through the fog in the background. In the fore, feet in yellow sneakers ran through the dark park, then skidded to a stop. The camera traveled up slowly, and Edgar came into view.

His hair was cobwebbed and skin cinereous, his eyes dark pits, his mouth wizened. The ghost onscreen opened its maw and screamed, darting forward to chase his victim out of the shot.

"Holy shit. That was really me?" Edgar asked, looking stricken.

"Yup. What do you think?"

"I'm...really scary," Edgar said slowly. "If I saw that ghost from across the street, I would definitely be terrified."

"Yeah."

Edgar's eyes were on the paused screen, his mouth down turned as he peered at ghost him.

"What're you thinking about?"

Edgar turned pained eyes to Jamie. "I've been a ghost."

"Yeah. You're scary as hell! It's awesome."

"No, I mean." He shook his head, and when he spoke next, his voice was thick. "I thought I was protecting myself. But you and Poe are right. I've been skulking around my own damn life, so scared of *being* scared that I just...hid."

He swiped angrily at his wet cheeks.

"I've done more stuff in the last month than in the last five years. And—" His voice was unsteady, but he fought to speak anyway. "Is this what my life could've been?"

Jamie's heart broke for him. They stroked his back and held his hand.

"I've been so scared for so damn long that I guess I didn't think I could *be* any other way. And now..." He hung his head. "My life's been so small. I've missed everyth-thing."

*Yes!* Jamie wanted to shout. *Yes, it could've been like this. It still can!*

They took Edgar by the shoulders. "Baby. You experience the world in a way most other people don't. Your fear is real and understandable. It's not your fault that you're scared. But it seems like you could be a little...less scared?"

Jamie didn't want to seem like they were expecting Edgar to stop being afraid. They just wanted him to see how much progress he'd made in such a short time.

Edgar shook his head. "I'm more scared now."

Jamie's stomach fell. *Well, that was short-lived.* "Oh."

"I've got more to be scared *of* now. I'm scared that Poe will leave in the middle of the night, like he did when he was sixteen, and I'll never see him again. I'm scared Allie's kid will see ghosts and be as scared as I've always been. I'm…I'm scared I'm gonna lose you." He wouldn't meet Jamie's eyes. "That you're gonna realize what a mess I am and how being with me isn't worth it. But now that I know what it's like to have you, it'll be so much worse when you leave, and I just don't know if I—"

He broke off, shaking his head.

"*When* I leave?" Jamie's heart clutched. *No, no, no, this can't be happening. I can't be thrown away again.* Their mind screeched to a halt at that thought. *Okay, whoa, slow down.* "Hang on, mister," Jamie said sternly, turning Edgar toward them.

Edgar blinked, his pupils dilating.

"That is a ton to talk about, and I'm excited to try, but I'm starting here: I don't want to lose you or be lost. I really fucking care about you. I like your weird family. I like *you*. Like, I truly, deeply enjoy you. Do you understand?"

They cupped Edgar's face, stroking his cheekbone with their thumb.

Edgar's lashes fluttered, but then he met Jamie's eyes, and the need there was fathomless. Heat sparked low in Jamie's belly. They wanted Edgar's need, his surrender. They wanted to tease him until he was so desperate he cried and then wreck him with pleasure.

Edgar said, "Me too."

"Good. All of those are normal things to be scared of. Maybe you were so focused on your fear of ghosts that it was easy not to notice anything else."

"So now I'm scared of natural shit as *well* as supernatural? This sucks."

Jamie smiled and ran gentle fingers through Edgar's hair. "Fear is the consequence of love. Now that you've registered how much you care about people in your life, you understand how horrible it would be to lose them."

Then Jamie realized what they'd said. *Love.*

"Like, for your brother and sister, I meant, not, um—"

They tried to scramble off the couch, got a leg tangled in Edgar's, and would've fallen if Edgar hadn't caught them.

Suddenly, Jamie was in Edgar's lap, looking up at his lightly stubbled chin.

*Damn him for being able to have naturally perfect stubble!*

"You okay?"

The rush of adrenaline subsided, and Jamie removed their fingers from Edgar's velvet stubble where they'd apparently migrated, unbidden.

"Ahem. Yes, I'm fine. Thank you." Jamie attempted to pull themselves together. "I got all in my head for a sec, freaking out at my awkward use of the word *love*. I'm good now."

Edgar smiled warmly. "Yeah, I got that."

"No need to look so delighted by it," Jamie said primly.

"It's nice for you to be the one getting flustered for once instead of me, that's all."

Jamie grumbled.

"I liked it," Edgar said thickly. "The word."

Jamie's heart hammered in their chest. "Cool." They grinned. "I like it too."

Jamie leaned in, still on Edgar's lap, and kissed him, hands in his hair. Edgar melted into the kiss and held Jamie closer. When they touched their tongue to Edgar's, they felt his cock harden. Lust shot through them, and they fisted Edgar's hair until he shuddered.

He broke the kiss and rested his forehead against Jamie's, breathing heavily.

"I wanted to, um, return to something you said earlier—"

"Is that right?"

Edgar's warm breath made the hairs on Jamie's neck stand up. "You said, *mister*. All stern and hot and, um."

He pressed closer to Jamie, and they groaned at the feel of his hard cock against their hip bone. He kissed their jaw, then beneath their ear.

"No," Jamie said sharply, and Edgar's head jerked up. "I *said*, Hang on, mister." They said it low and commanding and heard Edgar's breath catch.

"Jamie," he said ardently. "Do you ever—" He ran a hand down Jamie's back. "Do you ever like to be on the receiving end of sex? In whatever way?"

He kissed their neck, and shivers of desire ran down their spine.

"Sometimes, yeah."

"I just." Another kiss on their neck. "I would love." A kiss below their ear. "To make you feel good."

"You do," Jamie said. "You always do."

"Okay. Whatever you want, truly."

He nuzzled their cheek, and Jamie had the strangest sense that they were about to cry. But then that feeling bundled itself up, crawled back inside them, and got back to doing what feelings do when you don't let them out.

"Whatever I want, huh?"

Edgar's *yes* was endearingly enthusiastic. Jamie stood and

walked to the bedroom, confident Edgar would follow. They removed clothing as they went, glancing over their shoulder at Edgar, whose eyes burned hotter with each garment shed.

Jamie stood next to the bed in only their underwear. When Edgar turned into the room, he gawked.

"You're stunning. Just hot and gorgeous and handsome and sexy and—" He shook his head. "All the things."

Jamie grinned. "I'll take it."

"Do you wanna...?" He gestured to the bed.

Jamie wanted this. They were nervous, but they wanted this. "I like to be on top, or I like it from behind," they said.

Edgar watched them intently. He took a step closer, and Jamie grabbed his hand.

"I like it if you touch me here." They showed him. "But not inside. You can fuck my ass with abandon though."

They were getting turned on just thinking about it.

Edgar groaned, clearly in agreement.

"So you like to stick your cock in a hot ass?" Jamie asked. They'd been teasing, but mostly they were curious about Edgar's response.

Edgar nodded.

"Well then, get over here, mister."

Edgar shuddered, and then Jamie found themself on the bed, on top of Edgar.

"Whoa."

Edgar ran trembling fingertips down their throat, sending shivers in their wake. Jamie kissed him, hard. Edgar's mouth was sweet, his tongue yielding and his lips ardent, and they made out until they were both panting.

Edgar touched them worshipfully, then closed his lips around one nipple and sucked. Jamie jumped at the jolt of sensation.

Edgar stopped. "You okay?"

"Yeah, very."

Jamie pushed his head back down so his clever tongue could be put to better use. Edgar cradled their back and feasted on their nipples, their ribs, their collarbone, until he nipped at their neck and they groaned.

"You can bite me," Jamie murmured. A second later, Edgar's teeth sank in, and he sucked on their tender flesh.

The sensation was exquisite, and their neck throbbed like it had a direct connection to their crotch. They ground their hips against Edgar's, groaning at how hard he was. They felt swollen and tight with blood and need, and they thrust until tiny frissons of pleasure built deep inside them.

"Fuck me now," Jamie said. Ordinarily, they'd add a *please*, but Edgar seemed to really get off on being ordered around.

Edgar groaned and swore as his pants got stuck on his feet. When he was nude, he cupped Jamie's face.

"Where do you want me?" he asked, clearly eager to obey.

"Behind me, leaning over the bed."

They slid over until they were in the right position and looked back over their shoulder at Edgar.

"Fuck me hard, mister," they growled, and Edgar obliged. He slid on a condom and slicked lube down his length, eyes closing in pleasure at his own touch. "No," Jamie said. "That's mine."

Edgar whimpered. "Yes, sir. Do you want my fingers first?"

"No."

Jamie slicked themself quickly and pushed their hips backward, demanding to be fucked.

Edgar's erection felt like steel, and Jamie breathed through their nose, reminding themself to relax their muscles.

"Oh my god," Edgar whispered worshipfully as he slid fully inside.

Jamie waited for the moment they knew was coming, when their brain sorted out the sensations and got on with feeling amazing. Two deep breaths later and it came, sliding from *too full* to *exactly right* in the space of a second.

Edgar was strong and hung, and he did just as Jamie had instructed: he fucked them hard.

The thrusts rocked them both, and soon Jamie couldn't keep their footing. Edgar hauled them up the bed, pushing them forward so he could get back inside. This time, the moment of penetration felt exquisite, and Jamie knew they weren't going to last much longer. The liquid, full feeling was leaking all through their guts in a way that left them overwhelmed and out of control.

Jamie didn't like to be out of control ordinarily, but this? *This*, they did love.

Jamie's arms couldn't hold them up any longer, and they collapsed onto their stomach, cheek on the pillow and ass in the air, getting deliciously pounded. They had just enough wherewithal to snake a hand between their legs and stroke themself as Edgar fucked them.

"Jamie, fuck, god."

"Don't stop," Jamie demanded. "I'm so fucking close."

Jamie could feel Edgar gather his strength to keep fucking them, and they groaned their appreciation, fingers flying between their legs.

The pleasure was hot and deep. When they cast a glance over their shoulder, Edgar looked like something torn from their deepest, most potent fantasies, holding their hips and fucking into them like a god.

"Jamie," Edgar gasped. He thrust hard and deep and stayed there, rotating his hips so they stayed full of him, so full they could almost choke. His hand came down to their own, and he groaned. "Fuck, you're wet."

He gathered the slick moisture and stroked between their legs with featherlight touches. It still felt so fucking good, the delicate, gossamer strokes meeting the deep, thick joy of penetration.

Jamie throbbed and leaked, caught right on the edge.

"Move," Jamie gasped. "You'd better fucking *move*, and fuck me, Edg—"

Edgar thrust deeper, each slide accompanied by a moan so desperate and involuntary that Jamie knew he was holding on by a thread.

They pushed his fingers down to rub harder and lifted their ass, spreading themself apart.

"Oh my god," Edgar said, then he sank a tiny bit deeper, and Jamie felt like they were spiraling apart.

Splayed on the bed, at the mercy of the thick cock inside them, Jamie came in rolling waves of orgasm that twisted them up inside and then released with such force that for a moment, they lost track of their body in space. The pleasure racked them, destroyed them, and they buried their face in the bed.

Edgar's fingers bit into their hips, and with a final flurry of thrusts that fanned sparks of their orgasm into fire again, he came with a roar.

"God, fuck," Edgar groaned, burying his face in Jamie's neck.

He was heavy, but the weight felt good.

Jamie moaned in satisfaction.

"Was that okay?" he asked, kissing Jamie's jaw and chin, seeking out their mouth.

Jamie forced their orgasm-trembly body to roll so they were facing Edgar.

"It's so hot that you like to be told what to do, and I'm definitely gonna do it again in the future. You fucked me into oblivion."

"Yeah?" Edgar said and grinned.

Jamie guided his hand between their legs and shivered when he touched them with worshipful fingertips.

"Oh, fuck," Edgar groaned into their neck.

Jamie felt utterly at peace. They were exactly where they wanted to be, with exactly whom they wanted to be with, and they never wanted it to end.

"Would you be my date to my annoying sister's extremely annoying wedding?" Jamie asked.

Edgar pushed himself up onto his elbows. He was smiling softly.

"Yeah? I didn't think you wanted me to come," he admitted.

Damn it, Amelia really *had* been right. Jamie felt awful.

"I'm sorry, Edgar. I never meant to make you feel that way. I just wasn't sure I'd even go to the wedding if my family was going to treat me like shit. But I want you. I always want you. I should've asked you sooner."

Edgar kissed Jamie so sweetly.

"Is that a yes?" they asked.

"You better believe it, mister," Edgar said.

## 26

## Edgar

Edgar got to Allie's with beignets and coffee by 9 a.m. to find a note on the door. *If you ring this bell, you will be haunted for all eternity.*

"Okay, then." Edgar knocked softly and whisper-yelled, "Allie?"

The door opened, but it was Poe on the other side, and he was making wild hand motions for Edgar to get the hell out of here.

"What the—"

Poe had a black bandana tied around his face. "Save yourself," he croaked, then darted back inside.

Edgar followed him inside. "What the hell is wrong with you?"

"Oh god, it's everywhere," Allie groaned from the bedroom. She appeared in the doorway, holding both hands away from her.

Suddenly the smell hit Edgar, and he stepped backward toward the door. "What on earth…?"

Allie turned tired eyes to Edgar. "Save yourself," she groaned.

"Too late," Edgar muttered, pulling his shirt up over his nose. "What are you feeding that kid?"

The smell was bad. Very bad. Edgar was used to cleaning out litter boxes and wiping dingleberries from unfortunate cats' backsides. But this was a whole other kind of reek.

"Edgar. My child is a demon," she said. "The family's range of abilities expandeth."

"Nameless Bebe shat all over themself in their sleep, then wriggled around in it, and then all over the bed," Poe explained.

"Poe, do you have any other useful superpowers you wanna share? Like the ability to burn a bed without catching the apartment on fire?"

"Alas, sister, I have not the ability," he said formally, placing his hand over his heart.

"Er," Edgar said, backing toward the door. "I seem to have come at a bad time." *For me.* "Maybe I'll just—"

"Edgar Vincent Lovejoy," Allie said in the tone that had stopped him in his tracks since childhood. "If you take that coffee away from me, I will never forgive you. Put it in the kitchen before you go."

Edgar was looking at his siblings. Allie, both hands held aloft; Poe, bandana covering his face and his sleeves rolled up to the biceps. They looked like they were battling some radioactive alien species.

He snorted, put the coffee and beignets on the counter, and walked into the bedroom.

The baby lay in their crib, naked, kicking their fat little legs at the ceiling and drooling.

Allie's bed was, admittedly, a disaster. But Edgar scooped the blanket and top sheet into a garbage bag to take to the laundromat, sniffed the mattress gingerly and, finding no remaining smell, concluded it had been a surface-level explosion.

He put a diaper on the kid and took them and the garbage bag back into the living room. "These need a wash, then you're good to go. Maybe consider a waterproof pad for your bed if you're gonna have Smoosh on there," he suggested. "Coffee?"

Allie—who had cleansed herself of her offspring's foul offering in the meantime—crossed to him and put her arms around him awkwardly. "Bless you."

"You know how to change a diaper?" Poe asked.

"I changed *your* diaper," Edgar informed him.

Poe took a huge bite of beignet, seemingly in an attempt to stop himself from responding.

"So," Allie said, helping herself to a coffee. "What brings you here? Other than saving my life."

"I need your help."

"Er, much as I deeply want to help you," Allie began.

"Not yours. Poe's."

Poe, who had been concentrating on pastry said, "What now?"

Actually, what he said was, "Whfnm?" because his mouth was full, and he blew powdered sugar when he spoke. But Edgar was pretty sure that was what he meant.

"I want to cook a really nice dinner for Jamie. Can you teach me?"

"How to cook?"

"How to cook something fancy."

"When's this dinner happening?"

"Um. Tonight?"

Poe looked to the heavens and pursed his lips. "Yeah, sure, I can teach you how to cook in one day. What could possibly go wrong?"

✦ ✦ ✦

Everything, it turned out.

"Listen," Poe said three hours later. "Jamie's rad and I like them a lot. And that is why I simply cannot allow you to feed them anything you cook."

"I can cook!" Edgar insisted, frankly a bit indignant. He had, after all, lived by and cooked for himself for years. "Just not this kind of stuff."

"Edible stuff," Poe said under his breath.

"Maybe you could take them out to dinner?" Allie suggested.

Edgar shook his head. "I want to do it. That's the whole point. I wanna show them I'm committed and, and—"

"That you're completely fucking hung up on them?" Allie grinned.

"Well. Yeah. Kinda."

"Awww, you really love them, huh?" Allie asked, her eyes warm and her smile peaceful.

Edgar choked on the bite of unpronounceable sauce that Poe had just been trying to show him how to make.

His cheeks grew warm.

Poe circled him, eyes narrowed. "Are you—are you *blushing* right now?" he asked, incredulous.

He and Allie exchanged *aw* looks.

"Shut up," Edgar muttered, as he'd done so many times as a kid.

"He does!" Allie and Poe crowed together.

"Jinx, bitches," Edgar said. But they didn't seem to care, too busy grinning like fools.

"Dude, come on," Allie said. "Our family is straight-up cursed, and it's a relationship ruiner. Give your poor loveless siblings some hope that things can end happily."

"Hey, what makes you so sure I'm loveless?" Poe said.

"Your personality," Edgar said.

Poe sniggered.

"You literally won't let other people touch you, so." Allie shrugged. "Must put kind of a damper on things?"

Poe flipped her off, but a shadow bloomed behind his eyes.

Edgar's phone rang, and he slid it from his pocket with the hand that wasn't massaging collards with garlic.

"It's Jamie," Edgar said. Poe and Allie exchanged kvelling expressions, and Edgar felt his cheeks heat as he answered.

"Hey," Jamie said. "Okay, super last-minute, I know, but are you free tonight?"

"Ummm. As it happens, I was going to invite you to come over for dinner tonight."

Poe did a facepalm and mouthed, *You didn't even invite them yet?*

Edgar had to admit this was a significant oversight.

"That sounds so lovely, but any chance I could take a rain check? Because remember how it's the Burlesque Festival this week?"

Edgar cringed, ashamed to realize that he'd forgotten, though Jamie had mentioned it. "Um. I forgot. Sorry."

"Well, anyway, Helen got tickets to one of the shows tonight from someone who—actually, they were super unclear on how they got them. I think they're legit though. So I have *two* tickets—"

Edgar's heart sank.

"Any chance you wanna venture out and be my date to queer burlesque?"

*Crowds, unfamiliar locations, could be ghosts anywhere. Small talk, claustrophobia, being forced to smile, everyone wondering what vibrant, gorgeous Jamie was doing with him.*

Allie and Poe were staring at him and making indecipherable gestures.

*This was what tonight's dinner was supposed to be about anyway—showing Jamie that you can be a real boyfriend to them. A real partner.*

"Um. Hello? Edgar? You there?"

*Jamie's sweet voice, glorious scent, the firm press of their shoulder to his, the way their lashes swept down, how they rested their fingers against his pulse point.*

"Hey, yeah, sorry, I'm here."

An epic eye roll from Poe.

"Uh, yeah, yes. I'd love to go on a date with you tonight."

✦ ✦ ✦

Edgar was waiting for Jamie outside the Luna Lounge, feeling less interestingly dressed by the moment as he watched people in amazing and outlandish fashion enter the club.

He'd worn the too-small T-shirt that Jamie had liked so much when he tried it on at Magpie Vintage and was self-consciously tugging the hem down any time a breeze hit the thin strip of bare skin between his shirt and jeans.

That was what you were supposed to do on dates, right? Look nice so your date knew you cared about them and had made an effort?

But when Jamie turned the corner, looking absolutely amazing and flanked by Helen on one side and a tall blond stranger on the other, Edgar found himself tugging his shirt down once more.

"Hey!" Jamie called when they saw him. Their eyes lit up, and they gave that private smile that was only for Edgar. "You look hot."

They elbowed Helen, who looked him up and down and agreed, one eyebrow raised.

"I say, Edgar," they said. "How you've blossomed since our last burlesque meeting."

And although that would've made him cringe from anyone else, Helen managed to convey nothing but delight with their comment.

"Thanks," he said, cheeks heating.

"This is my friend Max," Helen said, gesturing to the stranger. "She/her. Max, this is Edgar, he/him."

Max swept blond hair over her shoulder and narrowed her eyes at Edgar. "You don't want to be here at all. Thank god. I needed someone to snark with, as I also do not want to be here."

Edgar blinked.

*Wait. You're allowed to come right out and say you don't want to be someplace that you are, in front of the people who invited you?*

"What? Come on," Helen wheedled. "You wanna be here."

"No. I want to see the performances. I do not want to be in the place the performances occur."

"Fair," Helen said.

The night breeze caressed Edgar's waist, and instead of pulling his shirt down, he let himself enjoy how nice it felt.

*Kinda grim to learn at the age of twenty-five that you value strangers' opinions of you over your own personal enjoyment of the world.*

"Fuck me," Edgar said under his breath.

"Don't give me openings like that if we're gonna be snarking together," Max said.

"No, I just..." He trailed off, because he'd realized something.

For the first time in years and years, Edgar was more worried about social awkwardness with Jamie's friends than that he'd see a ghost.

*You have a whole new set of terrible anxieties! Oh god. But also, hooray!*

"I want to spend time with Jamie and make them happy. I don't want to be in the place this occurs either," Edgar said.

Slowly, he raised his eyes to Jamie's. But they were smiling warmly.

Edgar laughed in relief. Part of him wished Jamie were performing tonight, so he'd get to see them dazzle the crowd, but Jamie didn't perform during haunting season, so he'd have to wait.

Helen wanted to get a table close to the bar, so they went to claim one.

Jamie took Edgar's hand. "Thanks for wanting to spend time with me," they said.

"And make you happy," Edgar murmured.

Jamie's hand tightened around his. "You do." They caught his shoulder and turned him. "You make me really happy."

Edgar's chest tightened, and he swallowed hard. "You make me really happy too," he tried to say, but it didn't quite come out.

Jamie's soft smile said they'd gotten the message. They leaned in and pressed a kiss to Edgar's cheekbone, then another to the corner of his mouth.

"Is there anything I can do to make your experience any less horrible?" Jamie asked.

Edgar dismissed the idea automatically, then stopped himself. Jamie's question had sounded sincere. And... *was* there?

He ran through the slide show of dread, looking for improvements that could be made.

"Maybe, um." He shook his head. "I don't wanna tell you what to do."

"Please tell me what would make your time better. I'll make my own choices."

"I know you want me to be involved in the conversation. But, uh. When you prompt me, I can feel everyone looking at me, and my brain shuts down. I can't think of any words, and then I panic."

"Shit, Edgar, I had no idea."

"Yeah, I... Sorry?"

They squeezed his shoulder and ran a palm down his back. "No problem. You've got it. What else?"

Edgar let out a breath of relief. "I don't know," he said truthfully.

"Okay, well. Pay attention to what you hate and tell me later?"

They kissed him on the lips, and then they walked to the table where Helen and Max sat.

"First round's on me," Helen announced and took their orders to the bar.

People snaked around the tables, meeting and greeting, admiring outfits, clinking glasses, and scrolling on phones. Edgar let his eyes blur slightly so he could scan the crowd for any nonhuman beings. The multiple disco balls in combination with smoke machines made it difficult, light refracting strangely off particles in the air, shapes flickering to life in one instant only to fade into the background the next.

"Hey!" Jamie cried.

Amelia was walking toward them, brandishing a table lamp with a peacock feather shade. "Look what I just found!" Amelia said.

Amelia, Edgar knew from Jamie's stories, was constantly picking up things she thought might make good props in the future.

Then she turned to Edgar, and her eyes got wide. She exclaimed, "Ghost!"

Edgar froze, and his heart began to pound. How could he have been so oblivious to the world that one was able to sneak up on him? And—wait, Amelia could see ghosts too?

Then Jamie was squeezing his arm, and his heart rate went back to normal as he realized what Amelia was talking about.

"Wait 'til you see what a great ghost he is in the film," she told Max and Helen, who was returning with their drinks.

Max lifted one eyebrow conspiratorially, and Helen said, "Huh. I can't see it, to be honest, but I guess that's why they call it acting."

"He was amazing!" Jamie enthused. "He—" But then Jamie cut themself off, seeming to remember Edgar's earlier request, and just smiled.

Amelia began describing the effects, and the attention shifted from Edgar. His breath came easier.

"Jamie did an amazing job with my makeup," Edgar said. All eyes turned to him, but he didn't let panic worm in. "They made my skin look like it was sloughing off."

Helen waggled their eyebrows. "Awesome."

And just like that, they were part of the conversation by choice.

When the lights dimmed and the show began, Edgar found that he was having a surprisingly good time, and that was more than he'd ever thought possible.

## 27

## Jamie

"Try it now!" Jamie called, clawing sweaty hair out of their face.

From above, the chain saw roared back to life.

"Got it!" Randall yelled back.

Jamie pulled themself out of the tiny control room concealed beneath the stairs and closed the hidden door.

"Alright, are we good?" Marty called. "Shut up, please! Quiet! Are we all good?"

"I need two minutes," someone called.

"Okay, everyone *stay put*."

Jamie slipped their phone out and took a selfie of their sweaty, dust- and paint-streaked face and sent it to Edgar.

**Jamie**: T-minus 1 hour til we open the gates!

How do you look so good even covered in disgusting filth? Edgar replied. Congratulations, baby—I know it's so great and scary.

Warmth flooded Jamie at Edgar's words. It was happening a lot lately.

Jamie's phone buzzed again, and they looked at it eagerly. But it was just a message from their mother on the family text thread, which conjured the opposite of warmth.

I know it's still early to think about this, but your aunt Michaela will need to be picked up from the airport before the rehearsal dinner. Be a dear and get her, Jamie?

Sorry, I can't. I'll be at work.

"As you know," they muttered.

Their mother typed for a long time and then apparently deleted the message.

Well can you at least take her to the hotel after the wedding, came Blythe's eventual reply.

Jamie didn't have time for this right now.

I'm sure we'll have no problem getting Aunt Michaela back to the hotel that everyone is staying at. Gotta go, it's opening night of the haunted house and the doors are about to open! They added a ghost emoji, a skull emoji, and a pumpkin emoji, and sniggered as they slid their phone back in their pocket. The last time they'd dared to mention their job on the thread, it had gone dead for six days. Which would be absolutely perfect about now.

✦ ✦ ✦

This was Jamie's fourth October first opening night, but the rush was as exhilarating as it had been the first three times.

Jamie had worked as a scare actor on the first two haunted houses they'd helped create. Observing people's reactions throughout the haunt was crucial to designing them better the next time. Jamie had loved it. The theatrical anticipation of the darkness before visitors came through, the sense of camaraderie with the other performers, the intimacy of seeing people vulnerable in their fear—it was intoxicating and always made them want to go out and party after work, shaky with adrenaline and hunger. But it was also hot, cramped, bad-smelling, exhausting work that fucked up your whole schedule for a month and sometimes got you punched if you jumped out at the wrong person. So when they'd gotten the opportunity to move into Carl and Germaine's guesthouse last year instead of needing to pay rent, they'd stopped working double duty as a scarer.

Now, instead, Jamie changed into clean clothes, grabbed their branded clipboard, and surveyed the line of waiting ticket holders: What buzz had the visitors heard? Where did they learn about the haunt? What had this friend or that friend reported when driving past last week?

People waited at the exit with clipboards and questions of their own: What was everyone talking about? How did they look? When someone chased them after they thought they were safe, what percentage of them screamed in thrilled terror and what percentage muttered? It all helped inform what they'd keep and what they would abandon.

As if the universe was colluding with the haunt, it was the first semicool night of the year, and the moon was a dim waning crescent. The smell of rain was on the breeze, but that wouldn't deter this crowd. They were abuzz with excitement, and some of their costumes were elaborate enough to be in the show themselves.

Jamie leaned against the fence and watched the waxing anticipation. Nearly everyone had their phones out, taking pictures of the sign at the gate, the crowd, themselves. Jamie added their own phone to the mix, filming the crowd as a voice thundered out of the loudspeaker.

They risked a glance at their phone, which had vibrated several times while they'd been working, hoping Edgar had texted. He had—a cute picture of the baby grabbing Edgar's nose. But their mother had also replied. Jamie sighed but decided to get it over with.

**Jamie's right, it'll be fine,** Emma had responded.

**Slight change of plan,** their mother wrote. **We'll actually need you at the rehearsal dinner at 2, Jamie.**

Jamie blinked at the text, heart rate ratcheting up. What the hell?

**Jamie:** I can't be there at 2. I can be there at 5, like y'all originally told me.

Jamie stared at their phone furiously. Their mother always did this! She found ways to punish anyone who didn't do what she wanted.

"YOU ARE ABOUT TO ENTER HELL," growled the amplified voice, signaling they didn't have time for this.

"Already there, buddy," Jamie muttered.

A text from Emma came through to Jamie directly. Just come at 5, that's fine.

"Thank fucking god," Jamie said.

The dots that said Blythe was typing—a screed, no doubt—appeared on the screen, but Jamie just thanked Emma quickly and put their phone on Do Not Disturb. There would be plenty of time to deal with whatever she had to say later.

"GET OUT WHILE YOU CAN. ENTERING HELL IN TEN. NINE. EIGHT—"

As the voice counted down, the crowd chanted along with it so that when the voice said, "TWO. ONE. NOW!" a cheer exploded. The gate swung open. The line began to move.

Jamie watched people who loved haunts as much as they did get ready to appreciate what they'd worked for the last six months to create. They allowed themself a single moment of self-pity, that instead of coming to see Jamie's work, their family was texting them about wedding shit. But then they shook it off and let the pride replace it.

✦ ✦ ✦

Jamie was riding high when they got to Edgar's. It was late, so they knocked softly, but Edgar kept hours just as late as they did and answered the door with excited anticipation.

"Well?" they asked.

"It went so well!" Jamie said, then they were caught up in Edgar's strong arms and crushed to his chest.

"I knew it would," he said softly and kissed Jamie's hair. "You smell like... What do you smell like?"

"Er." Jamie sniffed at themself tentatively. "Maybe the smoke machine? But also maybe general haunted house ick? It's a particular funk."

"Come in. Tell me all about it," Edgar encouraged, waving Jamie into the living room. "Want something to drink?"

All Edgar ever had to drink was water and ginger ale, and Jamie needed something a bit more potent.

"Do you mind?" Jamie held up a tin of edibles.

"Please," Edgar said.

They settled on the couch, and Edgar got Jamie water anyway. Edgar dug strong thumbs into their left instep. Jamie groaned.

"God damn, that's amazing."

"Good," Edgar murmured.

"Dude. It went so well! At first, everything was going wrong—of course. But it came together at the last minute, like always. It's so wild how two hours before opening, we can be a total shambles, but then it all gets done."

As Edgar rubbed their feet, they told him about the anticipation of the crowd, the satisfaction of hearing the screams and curses as people went through, trying to guess which frights had gotten which person. They told him about the videos already making the rounds on social media, declaring House of Screams the best haunt in Louisiana.

"We're sold out for the next three nights, which is awesome because Marty gives us a bonus for every fifth night we sell out."

They tried to paint a picture of the night for Edgar without sharing any details that would scare him. This meant Jamie found themself saying things like, "And then this enormous, hairy, er—kitty jumps out while they're looking in the triptych mirror, and they can't figure out which way to run to get away from it."

Quickly though, it became clear that Edgar didn't need the details. He was just proud every time Jamie said something went well. Jamie was pleasantly stoned at that point, able to relax for the first time in what felt like weeks.

"The only bummer… Never mind." Jamie waved it off.

"What?"

"More texts from my parents and Emma. Wedding stuff. They probably didn't even know it was opening night, but…"

But Jamie knew their mother drove to work directly past a billboard advertising the haunt. She'd probably seen it every day for the last month.

"Would you want to invite them?" Edgar asked.

Sweet, innocent Edgar.

"I have. The first year, I was working as one of the actors in the haunt, and I put tickets aside for them at will call for opening night. I texted them two weeks before to let them know."

Jamie couldn't believe they'd ever thought their parents or Emma would go through a haunted house. It was laughable now. But that first year, they'd still had hope that their family might be happy for them. After all, they were getting paid to do what they'd always wanted. But when Jamie had gone to the ticket booth at the end of the night, the envelope of tickets remained untouched.

Jamie bit their lip. "Ugh, let's be done talking about this now. It went great, so. That's good."

Edgar opened his mouth like he wanted to add something but closed it. He redoubled his efforts at foot massage.

Jamie let their head droop over the armrest like a morning flower heavy with dew and let themself drift away on a sea of comfort, safe in Edgar's hands.

Edgar had been acting strange all weekend. Jamie had asked if anything was on his mind, and he'd said no, but the tension set Jamie on edge as they drove out to the haunt on Monday afternoon. Maybe Edgar's mood was just down to their screwy schedule, and things would go back to normal when the haunt wrapped. But a worm of doubt had been burrowing in all weekend.

Fortunately, a tricky problem distracted Jamie immediately upon arrival. One of the swinging sandbags between the dining room and the tight hallway passage that led to the stairs had sprung a leak and was trailing sand everywhere. It took Jamie and their coworker Dante until just before opening to fix it and clean up the mess.

When Jamie got outside for some fresh air and looked at their phone, they had fifteen missed texts and calls.

Their stomach clenched with worry until they read the first text from Edgar: **Look about halfway back in the line, and you might see some familiar faces.**

Jamie didn't even look at the rest of the messages before heading for the line.

"What the…?" Jamie said softly when they saw.

Standing with Edgar were Carys, Greta, Veronica, Helen, and Poe.

When Edgar and Jamie locked eyes, a hopeful smile bloomed on Edgar's lips.

"What are y'all doing here?" Jamie said, throat tightening with emotion as they approached the line.

"I'm here to have the shit scared out of me," Poe said. "What else?"

"Same," said Carys. The others agreed.

"Goddammit, don't make me cry at work," Jamie muttered, turning away from a chorus of *aww*s.

Edgar came behind them and wrapped an arm around Jamie's chest.

"Did you do this?" Jamie asked, even though they knew he had. They turned around and wrapped him in a hug. "Thank you," they said into Edgar's neck.

Edgar squeezed them tight. "You're welcome."

"Wait, hang on. Why are *you* here?" Jamie asked, pulling back to look at Edgar.

Edgar swallowed hard. That was when Jamie looked at him a bit more closely. In the dark, with only floodlights casting deep shadows and the red light leaking from the signs, they hadn't noticed how pale Edgar looked. How…green?

"Edgar," Jamie warned.

"I'm going through the haunted house," he announced. "I want to see all the amazing work you've done. This is your passion, and I want to support you. All of us do." He gestured to the group.

"Baby," Jamie said, heart overflowing. "You should *not* come in the haunted house. Thank you so much for bringing our friends to be here. But I don't want you to be scared, and I really think you will be."

"But I want to support you," he said again, and Jamie realized what this was all about. Edgar was trying to make up for their family's lack of interest and support with his own. It was incredibly sweet. Also misguided.

"Sweetheart, you *do* support me. You support me in every way that matters. You don't have to do this to prove it to me. In fact, I'm asking you not to."

"But—but I—"

Jamie pulled Edgar close and covered his mouth. Their heart was brimming with a weightless, hopeful anticipation that felt a lot like love.

"Shut up, you gorgeous, infuriating…" Jamie's speech devolved into fond muttering as they made a quick plan.

Jamie grabbed Edgar's hand, and they turned back to the group.

"Edgar's going to put his ticket back in circulation," Jamie said. "Thank you all for coming. I can't wait to hear your thoughts on the other side."

"Thank god," Greta said. "That was gonna be hard to watch."

Veronica, Helen, and Carys all nodded emphatically.

Poe looked like he'd received news of a death in the family. "Aw, come on, Edgar," he said.

Jamie winked at him. "Make some new friends, Poe." Then they took Edgar's hand and led him away. Edgar followed easily. "Where are we going?"

"There's a way you can watch the haunt on video." Jamie squeezed his hand. "But you don't have to see anything you don't want to. You interested?"

"Yes," Edgar said without hesitation.

Jamie opened the door to the trailer behind the haunt. There, a bank of monitors revealed every room of the haunted house from multiple angles. The cameras were equipped with a combination of regular and night vision lenses, and they were recording the whole time the haunt was open to make sure staff could intervene if there was a medical incident, an altercation, or if someone got too scared and needed an emergency exit.

"Hey, Trent," Jamie said. "I'm going to take over watching for a bit. Would you tell will call to add a ticket to the wait list pile and reverse the charge for it to Edgar Lovejoy's card? He bought one more than he needed."

"Yeah, no problem," he said and left Jamie and Edgar alone in the cramped trailer.

"We can watch them go through on here." Jamie pointed to the monitors. "But there's no sound, and the picture's really dim. And if you want to look away, I'll tell you anything weird Poe does so you can tease him about it later."

Edgar smiled and tucked a lock of Jamie's hair behind their ear. It was a tender, familiar gesture, and Jamie leaned into him.

There was only room for one chair in the small space, and Jamie patted it, indicating Edgar should sit. When he did, Jamie settled onto his lap. Edgar's arms enfolded them, settling them firmly against his chest.

He kissed the back of Jamie's neck, and warmth radiated from the spot.

"Mm, that feels too good right now," they murmured.

They felt Edgar start to get hard. He buried his face in Jamie's hair and mumbled something that sounded like reticent agreement. They stayed like that for a few minutes, basking in each other's physical comfort.

✦ ✦ ✦

When Jamie saw familiar faces on the first camera, they sat up.

"Okay, they're going in."

Edgar rested his chin on Jamie's shoulder to watch. Jamie

tapped on the first screen, where Poe was pinning a large white button to the front of his leather jacket.

"That means he doesn't want to be touched by any of the performers," Jamie explained.

The haunt was set up in four zones, and Poe and Carys led the group into the first zone. Veronica, Helen, and Greta followed, holding on to each other and looking deliciously nervous. The interior of the Victorian home showed all the signs of being first abandoned and then repurposed as a haunted candy factory. The dining room table was laid with lavish china and platters laden with food. Food that was rotting and crawling with insects.

"Oh my god," Edgar murmured.

To experience Edgar seeing their work live, even though they didn't *want* to frighten him, was unexpectedly gratifying.

"That's the chandelier you came with me to get," Jamie said, pointing at the cobweb-swathed twist of metal above the dining table.

"You *made* this?" Edgar asked.

"Well, not just me. But yeah."

"You built a whole dining room. A whole house?"

"Yeah, we did this room in sections that we could move in when we came to this location. Then the staging all happens here. We figured out how to get the effects to work in the warehouse, but you can't know exactly how an effect will play out or how much detail is required to make it work properly until you do it in situ. There's a lot to consider: direction of traffic flow, how close people are likely to get to each element, the time they spend in the space, what mindset they're bringing in from the previous zone, and how much time or attention the new element will require before they can shift gears. So—"

Edgar turned Jamie's face to his and kissed them softly on the mouth. "You're brilliant."

"Aw, well. It wasn't just me. I work with great haunters," Jamie insisted. But they glowed at Edgar's praise.

On the monitor, their group rounded the table. Veronica reached out a hand toward a rotting turkey carcass. Jamie grinned when she jerked back in disgust.

"What is it made of?"

"It's a latex cast made from a real turkey—we have to have a lot of the things people can touch in case they get messed up. Then we covered the latex in a mix of Vaseline, wax, and baking soda that feels like congealed fat and grit."

On the monitor, Poe, Greta, and Veronica startled.

"That's the clock striking midnight."

Carys ran a palm up the flocked wallpaper that led to the stairs, and Jamie leaned in to see if she would—

"Yes!" Jamie exclaimed, as Carys' hand slid from the flat of drywall into sudden squish and give. Her hand sank into the wall, and she stumbled forward, then snatched her hand away.

"That was my idea," Jamie let themself brag.

"You're terrifying and hot," Edgar murmured, but he kept watching, chin on Jamie's shoulder, hugging them. "What's happening in that part?"

There was no camera monitoring this hallway because it was packed with heavy forms that blocked any view of people moving through.

"It's pitch-black, and there are these sandbags chained to the floor and ceiling. You have to push your way through them. It's perfectly safe, but it kinda feels like you're being crushed to death."

Edgar shuddered. "Jesus. And people *like* this."

"Hell yeah, they love it." Jamie grinned.

When everyone in the group made it through and appeared on the next monitor, Jamie warned Edgar of an upcoming jump scare, and he buried his face in Jamie's shoulder.

A figure wrapped in rotting gauze and doused with seeping blood jumped out at Carys and Greta from behind a metal gurney. They both jumped and cringed, but Carys stepped in front of Greta, ready to defend her.

"It's over," Jamie murmured.

Poe stalked warily at the back of the group now, looking from side to side.

"Okay, so Poe is what we call an anticipator. He's constantly looking around to try and minimize the scares by feeling like he's in control of the space. Those people are harder to surprise because they're paying really close attention. But they're also the most satisfying to scare."

"Hmm, what about the others?"

"Carys and Veronica are explorers. They're looking in crevices and around corners to see how things work or to admire the detail. Explorers are satisfying because they're more likely to see all the hard work we put in. But they can also be a problem, because they sometimes try to go off the path or, in extreme cases, ask questions of the performers."

On the next monitor, the group wound through narrow tunnels made to look like caves.

"I love this one," Jamie murmured just before one of the haunters pressed the button and wet Spanish moss dropped from the ceiling to dangle in their faces. Helen dropped to her knees, while Poe and Greta clawed at the air around their heads, but the vegetation was pulled up again before they could grab it. Veronica, looking up to anticipate more vegetation, was the first to notice that the ceiling was sloping down. The group had to crawl on hands and knees through the dark to escape the room.

"I think Helen and Greta fall in the tagalong category. This isn't necessarily their vibe, but their friend or date or kid invited them, and they came along for the ride."

"What's the fourth category?" Edgar asked.

"The thrill seeker. Those are the people who go to dozens of haunts a year, watch horror movies, and are generally here to test the scare factor. They *want* to be terrified, but since they go to so many, they rarely are. They're the ones who come out at the end and are comparing the haunt to the twenty-eight others they've already been to and discussing which haunt did which elements better."

Veronica was at the front of the pack as they got to the vortex tunnel that would deliver them into the fourth and final act of the haunt. The tunnel was white, and she shaded her eyes. A quick glance showed her no way to the doorway before them but to cross an openwork metal bridge. She stepped onto it, blinking against the brightness.

Suddenly, the tunnel was engulfed in darkness and then transformed to give the illusion that the space they were walking through was spinning 360 degrees.

"Wow," Edgar said.

It was a truly mind-blowing effect. The second the view changed, Veronica grabbed for the metal handrails. Even though she had *seen* the bridge before, she couldn't keep her balance.

Carys, Greta, and Helen followed Veronica across the bridge, each of them walking the exaggerated, heavy staggers of the drunk, all clutching at the handrails to drag themselves forward as if the gravity had shifted as well as their footing.

Poe stepped onto the bridge, paused for a moment, then walked forward as easily as usual.

"What the…? How'd he do that?" Edgar asked.

"He might have closed his eyes. The bridge isn't really moving, and people who can't see the projection can walk fine. Spoilsport," they added.

"I didn't realize how many elements of the haunt *weren't* scary," Edgar mused.

"Yeah, a lot of it is about maximizing people's emotional or sensory states. It makes their minds play tricks on them. And the mind is the most potent source of fear." Jamie tapped the next monitor. "Speaking of, the transition here is cool."

Through the nucleus of the vortex lay a blank and empty hallway, one that was wider than others, allowing more guests to enter together. As they staggered out of the vortex tunnel, the group struggled to find their footing on this new, solid ground. After two or three steps though, they stood tall again.

And just as they thought they were on solid ground, they all stumbled. The floor gave way with no warning, suddenly tipping them off their feet. Then the light began to strobe.

"What?" Edgar leaned forward and peered at the monitor.

"It's a layer of sand over the floor, covered with layers of thick rubber, so for just a *moment*, it feels like you suddenly fell through the floor. And then—"

The lights strobed on, that moment of illumination revealing a horrifying figure. Then the lights went off again. When they strobed on again, the figure was closer to the group than before.

"Oh my god, that's so scary," Edgar said worshipfully.

Then, *strobe* and the figure was between Greta and Carys. Then disorienting darkness. *Strobe* and the figure was gone, leaving their friends grabbing for one another and Poe running for the exit.

Edgar grabbed Jamie and manhandled them around. He looked deep into Jamie's eyes and spoke with utter conviction. "Thank fucking god you didn't let me go in there!"

Jamie laughed and wrapped their arms around Edgar, breathing in his scent. He was here. Even though he could see *actual* fucking ghosts, he was here, watching a haunted house through a video monitor in order to better appreciate Jamie. Poe and Greta and Carys and Helen and Veronica—all of them had accepted Edgar's invitation because they wanted to support Jamie. Even without Emma and their parents here, they had all the support they needed.

They held each other tightly.

"I've got you, babe," Jamie said.

## 28

### Edgar

It was the last week of October, and the Crescent City was ajangle with Halloween spirit. Krewe of Boo, the Zombie Run, and dozens of other Halloween-related events were taking place all over town. Artfully arranged gourds and corn plants had appeared on the steps of hotels and historical buildings. Balconies dripped with spiderwebs, glittering skulls adorned porch steps, and the occupants were even more likely to be in costume than they were on an ordinary day.

For most of his adult life, Edgar had spent October searching the decorations for threats that could lurch from behind the scarecrows or burst out of the caskets. He was leery of Christmas trees and Mardi Gras floats for the same reason. Over the years, he'd developed a habit of only leaving his apartment when absolutely necessary during those seasons.

But this year, everything was different. This year, Allie had a new baby, Poe was back in town, Edgar had seen Carys, Greta, Helen, and Veronica multiple times socially, and, most amazing of all, Edgar had a boyfriend who enjoyed doing things like leaving the house.

Of course, they weren't getting to do much of that, since their work schedules were out of sync now that the haunt had opened: Jamie left for work at 2 p.m. and didn't get home until ten, while Edgar usually began work at the cat café at 9 a.m. and finished delivering for Lagniappe Lemonade around five. It had left them with little time over the last few weeks for anything but sleepy late-night cuddles, Jamie letting themself into Edgar's apartment with the key he'd given them and crawling into Edgar's bed, the smell of smoke machine juice clinging to them even after a shower.

But Friday was Halloween, and that would be the final night of the haunt, as well as one of New Orleans' biggest party nights of the year. After that, Jamie would have to strike the set, and then they'd have a month off before their holiday bartending gig began. Edgar couldn't wait.

For the moment though, he consoled himself with cats. There was truly nothing like them for comfort when you were lonely. Before he'd opened the cat café that morning, Edgar had spent half an hour lying on his back on the rug the cats liked best, letting them nuzzle him, bunt him, curl up in his various angles, and lick his hair. Now, as he unlocked the door and flipped the sign to *OPEN*, Edgar wondered what he should do for Jamie to celebrate the haunt closing.

As he was contemplating this, the door tinkled its opening, and Allie pushed a stroller through the door, Poe close behind.

Allie had been making an effort to get out of the house with the baby every day, and Edgar and the cats had been the delighted beneficiaries. Poe hadn't joined them before though.

"Morning!" Allie called. "Baby, say good morning to your uncle and a whole lot of cats."

"Morning," Edgar said. He crouched beside the stroller and wiggled his fingers at the baby. "Hi, Smoosh."

The baby blinked large brown eyes up at Edgar and followed his fingers intently. Raven hair feathered over their forehead. They wore a black onesie with a white skeleton on it. They looked adorable.

Poe stuck close to the stroller, not acknowledging Edgar.

"What's up, Poe?" Edgar asked, attempting to elicit some reaction.

"What's up," he mumbled.

Then he did something Edgar didn't expect. He pulled on black leather gloves, tucked the sleeves of his long-sleeved shirt into the cuffs, wrapped a scarf around his neck, and bent to lift the baby out of their stroller.

"C'mere, Bones," he said and cuddled the baby to his chest.

Edgar cast a look at Allie that asked, *What the hell?* Last he knew, Allie wouldn't let Poe touch the baby, for obvious reasons, and Poe had assiduously avoided it.

*I know*, Allie's expression said. *I guess this is happening?*

Poe bounced the baby as he walked around the café. Three kitten siblings had recently been dropped off by a lady who lived down the street and found them inside her garbage can. They were adorable, fluffy white things with blue eyes and extremely sharp claws that allowed them to climb Edgar and stick to him like burrs. They tended to do things in a pack, and now they began to chase after Poe's feet, batting at the shredded denim where his boots had rubbed the hem to strings.

The baby made a sound between a gurgle and a coo, and Edgar couldn't help his own mew in response. He and Poe locked eyes in mutual cute appreciation. Then Poe's expression changed, and he sniffed the baby.

"I've got it," Edgar said at Poe's wince and took the diaper bag off Allie's shoulder.

"I got it," Poe said and snatched the bag from him.

Edgar certainly wasn't going to argue about that. Allie gave him a look that said, *See? Watch!*

Poe took a box of rubber gloves from the diaper bag and snapped them on over his leather gloves. He laid the changing mat on the floor and the baby on the changing mat and unsnapped the skeleton onesie. He changed their diaper efficiently, snapped their onesie up, and took off the rubber gloves as if he'd been doing it for years.

"Um."

"I figured it out. Me and Bones have an understanding. Don't worry about it," Poe said. "Right, Bones?"

The baby gurgled, and their eyes rolled wildly. Edgar and Allie raised amused eyebrows at each other.

Then Edgar got back to work, happy to let his family entertain the cats, and didn't notice anything amiss until Poe let out a surprisingly tiny *Eep*. Edgar looked over to see that the three white kittens had climbed his jeans and were now attempting to crawl the rest of the way up on the thin material of his shirt.

"This little shit almost pulled out my nipple piercing!" Poe said, making no attempt to remove the kittens.

"That's William Fitzwilliam," Edgar said as Allie exclaimed, "You have a nipple piercing?"

But Poe was too busy unsticking claws from his torso to answer. Finally, he scooped the kittens inside his jacket. When he flashed them the lining, three white fuzzy heads protruded from three pockets.

"Allie, take a picture. Poe, don't move," Edgar added preemptively. "I need this for the shop's website."

Poe glared but let her take the picture.

Two of the kittens soon extricated themselves from Poe's pockets, but William Fitzwilliam curled up and went to sleep. Poe got to his feet.

"Gotta go. Sis, you can take the truck home. I'll be back later."

Allie held her arms out for the baby.

"I like this place," Poe said softly to Edgar, looking around. Then he shoved his phone in his back pocket and turned to leave.

"Poe."

He looked over his shoulder, eyebrows raised.

"Are you *shoplifting* that kitten?"

"No," Poe said. "He *wants* to come with me." Poe was glaring, but he pulled his jacket close. Something about it hurt Edgar's heart.

"Do you want to adopt him?"

"No. I don't know. Maybe. What would I have to do?"

They'd never had pets growing up, though Edgar, Poe, and Allie had all loved animals. When they'd beg for pets, their father would always tell them that cats were unreliable sociopaths, dogs were pathetic brownnosers, and their mother was allergic. But Cameron and Antoine had always had cats, rabbits, dogs, and sometimes lizards around the house. Their father had been a veterinarian and also an epic softy, and Poe would pick a different animal each time to cuddle with every time they'd go over.

"You just have to fill out a form and promise that you can care for the animal." He slid the form across the desk to Poe.

"Um. Allie?" Poe drawled.

"Yeah?"

"Uh. Can I have a kitten at your house?"

"Will you take one hundred percent responsibility for it no matter what?"

"Yeah."

"Like, I want to experience all the cute advantages of the kitten and none of the work or annoyance."

"I understand."

"That means that if the kitten wakes the baby, you're responsible for the kitten and the now-awake baby. *Any* consequences of this creature's behavior are on you."

"Yeah, I got it," he said, nostrils flaring.

"Then, okay," she said. She peered at the tiny white head sticking out of Poe's pocket. "It really is adorable."

"There's just one thing," Edgar said. "Kittens really need a friend. They're much easier to manage when they can get attention, support, and comfort from another kitten. So you could take Cormac—"

"You want me to adopt two of them?"

He eyed the floor where Cormac and Mingus Fitzwilliam were twining around his ankles. "Yeah. Except then Mingus would be left behind…"

"You want me to adopt *three* tiny white kittens? What the hell am I gonna do with three of them?"

"What were you gonna do with only one—crown a new Highlander?"

Poe glared. "What is that, a Scottish thing?"

"Maybe y'all should think about the logistics for a few days?" Edgar asked. "Buy a litter box and cat food, and get some old towels to make them a bed. Maybe make a vet appointment and—"

"Whatever, just give 'em to me." Poe scooped up Cormac and Mingus before Edgar could, tucking them back into his inner coat pockets. "Allie?"

"Same rules apply," was all she said. She looked like she needed a nap.

Poe pulled a ballpoint pen out of a different pocket and filled out the form in handwriting Edgar could only decipher because he'd grown up reading it.

"I'll get all their stuff. Don't worry about it."

"Okay, but don't you want a box to carry—"

"I've got it. They like it in there." Grudgingly, Poe held open his jacket, revealing three slowly breathing pockets.

"That's adorable," Edgar said. "But what if they wake up before you get home? It's safer for them if you carry them in a box."

For a moment, it looked like Poe might concede. Then he pushed the form back across the counter to Edgar with one finger, zipped up his coat, and left, bell echoing in his wake.

"Well, he's just a little ray of sunshine, isn't he?" Allie said flatly.

"Can he talk to animals in addition to seeing the future?" Edgar mused. "Not like he'd have told us. Maybe he's been communing with gators and crows and freaking earthworms this whole time."

Allie laughed. "Poe in conversation with an earthworm."

"Right? He'd be like, *Don't let these fuckheads step on you. Their puddle is your pool.*"

"*What does it feel like to get cut in half and then grown into another one of yourself? Can you think for both of you then?*" Allie said in a good imitation of Poe's flat, aggressive tone.

"Whatever, he better not let anything happen to those kittens."

"He won't. Poe's…Poe, but he'd never hurt a helpless animal."

"I know he wouldn't on *purpose*. But he just adopted three animals and left with them in his *pockets*. And I *let* him."

Edgar knew he shouldn't've, but the truth was, even after he'd been gone for so long, Edgar still trusted his brother in his deepest, unwavering places.

Allie said, "When you don't let Poe have his way, he takes it anyhow."

That was also true.

"Yeah. He should really go to therapy."

"We all should."

"Yeah. That's probably true."

"I have." Allie said it casually, but Edgar could tell it was important.

"Yeah?"

"Yeah. I started when I got pregnant. There's a lot of stuff to think through when you go from being someone's kid to suddenly being someone's parent. Especially since our parents were…uh…"

"Yeah," Edgar agreed. "Has it helped you?"

"Oh good *lord*, yes." She put Smoosh down on their back on the changing mat. "When I told my therapist that Poe can see the future and has been lying about seeing ghosts this whole time?"

Edgar did a double take. "You told your therapist about…the ghosts?"

"Well, yeah. I could hardly explain anything about my life without that bit."

Edgar had always imagined telling a therapist you saw ghosts would be a one-way ticket to a mental hospital. "Mom always said…" He trailed off when he considered the source.

"I know."

"Did your therapist believe you?"

"Yeah, of course. I mean, I don't know if she personally believes that ghosts are real. But for the purpose of our sessions, she takes that as fact. Otherwise, she wouldn't be able to help me."

"I never thought about that," Edgar said. He'd just pictured the pitying look someone would give him the moment they realized he was tragically delusional.

"Also, a lot of people believe in ghosts. You know how I feel about the secrecy shit."

This had been Allie's perspective since they were teenagers: that talking about it normalized it and encouraged other people to talk about their own experiences. Secrets were an unnecessary burden. She'd been right: whenever she brought the topic up, there would be someone who said they believed, had experienced something, or knew someone who had. Nothing like what the Lovejoys experienced—mostly shadows in their peripheries or dark figures at the ends of their beds. But knowing she wasn't alone had helped Allie, so Edgar would never argue with her. At her urging, he'd even tried a few online forums, years before. But unlike Allie, it had made him feel even more alone to understand the gulf between his experiences and those of even other people who'd seen ghosts.

And that isolation had only gotten more habitual.

*It doesn't have to be like that anymore. It's not going to be.*

Edgar put a hand on Smoosh's belly, soothing himself with the warm, dependable rise and fall. The baby cooed, and Edgar turned to see them awake and looking at him.

"So I've been thinking," Allie said. "About a name."

"Oh yeah?"

"Mama chose Lenore for herself because it sounded a bit like Nora." Nora had been their mother's given name. "So I was thinking of the name Nour. It honors Mama in both ways. And it means *light*." She paused for a moment. "I guess I feel like this little weirdo has been a light for me, showing me what I want for the future. For me and for us. And illuminating a lot of shit I've struggled with for a long time. I feel as though I can see what I should do more clearly now that they're here."

Edgar swallowed around the lump in his throat.

"Bah, cornball alert," Allie said, rolling her watery eyes. Then, after a moment, "But, um. What do you think?"

"I think it's beautiful," he said. "And I think it's good you've picked something, because my first thought when Poe called them Bones was that it was cute and maybe I should start calling them that too."

"Dear god, I've acted just in time. Although actually, I think Bones is a pretty wicked name too."

"Don't tell Poe," they both said together and laughed while Nour bobbed their little fists at the nearest cat in pure joy.

# 29

# Jamie

"I told you, I don't drive!" Edgar said, as he swerved and barely missed hitting a parked car.

Edgar, dressed to the nines, had agreed to lift his moratorium on driving this once so he could pick Jamie up from work and speed them to the art museum while they changed their clothes.

"Yeah, but," Jamie said from the back seat, where they were wriggling into their pants, which looked amazing but were inconveniently snug for changing in a car, "I assumed that was in case a ghost startled you, not that you were a menace more generally."

"I'm sorry. I'm nervous!" He blew out a breath for the dozenth time since he'd picked Jamie up and shook out his hands.

"Listen," Jamie said. They reached around the armrest and

squeezed Edgar's shoulder. "I wish I could say they're gonna love you or not to worry about it, but the truth is they're assholes, so just…try not to take anything they say or do personally. Okay? And I'm sorry in advance."

Edgar snorted as if that were inconceivable, and Jamie crossed their fingers that their family was on their best behavior. Or at least so preoccupied with the rehearsal that they didn't pay any attention to either of them.

Edgar screeched into a parking spot, tires spraying gravel into the lush grass.

"Jesus, remind me to procure a Dramamine from Great-Aunt Marge in case you have to drive home."

Jamie extracted themself from the back seat and opened the driver's side door for Edgar. He looked amazing. Jamie hadn't had a chance to fully appreciate him while they were running toward the truck trying to shave precious seconds off their commute. But now? He was clean-shaven and his brown hair curled over his forehead, grown out enough since Jamie had first met him that they could now twine it through their fingers when they were watching movies together and wrap it in their fist when he begged them to.

He wore a navy linen suit that Jamie had never seen before, and he smelled like a dream.

"You look incredible," Jamie said, palm to his lapel. "Damn."

Edgar ducked his head and smiled. "I wanted to look nice for you."

Jamie kissed him, loving the crush of Edgar's sweet lips beneath theirs.

Inside, they were directed to the rehearsal hall, and Jamie patted their pockets and collar to make sure everything was in place, took a deep breath, and held their hand out to Edgar.

When the doors opened, all eyes snapped to Jamie and Edgar. Their parents made a beeline from one end of the room, and Emma did the same from the other.

So much for everyone being too preoccupied with wedding plans to notice them.

"*There* you are," Jamie's mom said.

Jamie had checked their watch a minute ago and knew they weren't late.

"Mom, this is my boyfriend, Edgar. Edgar Lovejoy, I'd like to introduce you to my mother, Blythe Wendon."

"So nice to meet you," Edgar said and held out his hand.

"Lovely to meet you," Blythe said, giving Edgar a hawkish once-over. "My husband, Hank Dale."

His parents had a whole bit they did whenever they met anyone new, and Jamie tracked Emma's approach while the familiar script played out. She looked happy, if a little stressed. Her betrothed stood with a group of guys who looked just as beefy and privileged as he did.

"You're here," Emma said as she reached them. She sounded relieved, like maybe she thought they weren't going to show up.

"This is Edgar," Jamie said, taking his hand. "Edgar, this is my sister, Emma."

"Congratulations, Emma," Edgar said. "Thank you so much for including me."

Did Edgar google *how to greet your significant other's sibling at her wedding?*

*Fuck, he's so cute.*

Emma smiled and shot Jamie a look that seemed to say, *Surprisingly good choice.* Jamie raised an eyebrow to say, *I know.*

"I could have used you here an hour ago," Jamie's mother said resignedly. "We need to practice everyone walking down the aisle."

Jamie swallowed down everything they wanted to say, plastered a smile on their face, and squeezed Edgar's hand. Edgar squeezed back.

"No problem," Jamie bit out. "Will you be okay hanging out here for a bit?" they asked Edgar.

"Yeah." He slid an envelope from his jacket pocket and took out some crossword puzzles and a pencil. "Cameron's grandma hooked me up."

Jamie grinned. They were thrilled that Edgar and Poe were reconnecting with their childhood friend now that she was back in town for the near future. Talking about Antoine with Cameron was healing for them all.

The second they were out of earshot, Emma slid her arm through Jamie's.

"He's attractive," she said accusingly.

"I agree," Jamie said happily.

"The bathrooms are that way," Blythe interrupted. "If you need to change."

Jamie forced themself not to react. "This is what I'm wearing, Mom. Let's go ahead and rehearse." They walked toward the front of the room where Dave and the rest of the people were standing.

"Hey, Dave," Jamie said, giving their future brother-in-law the half wave, half salute that they had never used with another living soul but that burst from them any time they greeted Dave.

"Jamie, my dude!" Dave called and returned the gesture. That was a pleasant surprise.

"God, he's already drunk. Ignore him," Emma said.

Someone corralled them into their places, and they practiced walking down the aisle.

"Just promise me you'll be here on time and dressed appropriately on Saturday," Blythe said when Jamie sank into the chair next to her.

"No one said anything about a dress code for the rehearsal," Jamie hissed. "I'm wearing a suit. I'm wearing dress boots. What is not appropriate about this?"

Blythe *tsk*ed, as if she couldn't possibly enumerate all the transgressions.

"And I wasn't late," Jamie muttered. "I was right on time. I made sure."

"Fine, just be here by two at the absolute latest," she warned.

But that wasn't what Emma had told him all those months ago. Emma said to be there an hour before. The wedding was at six.

"I thought I had to be here at five," Jamie said.

Blythe's eyes flashed with barely concealed fury, and she grabbed Jamie's arm and marched them into the hallway.

It had always made Jamie feel like they were in trouble. In fact, Jamie had spent the first twenty years of their life feeling like they were in trouble all the time. Now though, Jamie realized their mom couldn't pilot them the way she once had. She was counting on Jamie to help her make them feel like shit.

So they stopped.

Blythe had always been a few inches taller than Jamie, but now they were the same height.

"What's going on, Mom?"

"This is your sister's wedding," Blythe said.

Jamie waited for the rest of the sentence, but nothing seemed to be forthcoming. "Yup."

"So you will be here at two on Saturday, dressed appropriately and ready to help out."

"Mom. I usually work from ten to ten on Saturdays in the fall, since I, *you know*, create a haunted house. I got off at four thirty by promising my boss I'd work three extra shifts at no overtime pay. So I'm really sorry that you're disappointed, but I can't be here until five. That's the time Emma told me, so that's the time I have."

Rage flickered in their mother's eyes and was quickly controlled. "I would think you'd care a bit more about your sister's big day," she sniffed.

"Yeah?" Jamie finally snapped. "I probably care about as much as you cared about me when you thought you'd have a dress made for me in secret in case you were able to guilt me into wearing it instead of something I'd feel good in."

Blythe opened her mouth, but Jamie barreled on.

"I probably care approximately the same amount as you cared about my presence or my life when you scheduled this wedding right after the one month out of the year that I work Saturdays." Jamie drew in a ragged breath. "So yeah. Looks like I don't care either."

Their mother's nostrils flared, and her lips pursed as she arranged her face into rigid neutrality. If they hadn't been in public, Blythe would've ended Jamie. They turned around to head back inside.

Emma was standing between them and the door. Her face said she'd heard everything.

"Shit, Emma, I didn't mean—"

"Whatever," she said patting her hair. "Just, can y'all come back in? It's time for dinner."

† ✦ †

Dinner was at a single long table with Emma and Dave at the head. The wine flowed freely, and several of Dave's friends made speeches, as did Emma's real maid of honor.

"Sister of the bride!" someone called, and everyone else raised a cheer.

Jamie's stomach tightened, and they ignored the cheer, turning to Edgar instead. No one had mentioned anything about preparing a speech. But their parents were both glaring pointedly at them. Jamie swallowed the anger and awkwardness down and did what they always did at family gatherings: they acted like a good sport so they wouldn't make anyone uncomfortable.

"Oh, me?" they said, rising and accepting the microphone.

They straightened their tie and gulped champagne. Emma's tight smile pleaded with them not to embarrass her. *It must be really stressful to need people's approval this much*, thought the part of Jamie that would once have needed to say, *I'm not her fucking sister*.

"My sister, Emma, has always known what she wants," Jamie said instead. "I admire that about her."

Emma's smile turned more genuine. Their parents' faces relaxed into pleasant masks.

"When we were kids, she had a crush on this boy, Nathan Jones. She said she loved him and was going to marry him."

People chuckled, and Emma, relaxed now, made obliging *aw shucks* gestures.

"I asked Emma how you knew you were in love, and she said that it was when you couldn't stop thinking about someone, when you wanted to be around them all the time. What was the third part, Em?" Jamie vamped. "Oh yeah, when you want to smell their hair."

Emma's bridesmaids laughed, and Emma rolled her eyes congenially.

Jamie glanced at Edgar to see he was watching them intently. "I hadn't been in love at the time. But now, um, I know she was right. And what better way to be around someone all the time than to pledge forever to them? Emma, I'm so glad you found someone you want to make your life with every day." A chorus of *aww*s and murmurs of assent came from up and down the table. "And," they concluded, "I do think Dave is the wiser choice—even though he doesn't have much hair to smell."

Dave ran his hand over his buzz cut and grinned, color high on his cheeks. His groomsmen pounded him on the back.

"Because I think Nathan Jones ended up playing hockey in Canada, and you could not deal with the weather up there." They held up their glass to gratifying chuckles. "So congratulations, Emma and Dave. I wish you all the happiness in the world together."

They quaffed their champagne and sat down to a chorus of cheers and congratulations. Edgar slid a hand onto their thigh and squeezed. When Jamie looked up, Edgar's warm brown eyes burned intensely, and Jamie felt an answering warmth burning just as bright inside.

✦ ✦ ✦

After dinner, people moved more freely, making the rounds to socialize, and Jamie hoped they'd be able to make a break for it soon. Edgar was starting to get the wild-eyed look that beset him after too much social interaction, and Jamie was exhausted. They glanced at their watch. It was close to nine. Surely things couldn't go on too much longer? Then someone wheeled out the dessert table.

Speeches from another bridesmaid and groomsman, and then Emma took the microphone. On the table amid platters of desserts was a large covered platter. Emma removed the dome to reveal a cake, and cheers erupted from Dave and the groomsmen. At first, Jamie couldn't tell what it was supposed to be, but finally they realized it was a set of golf clubs.

"I'll save the mushy stuff for Saturday," Emma said.

"Wouldn't want to accidentally show people how much you like your husband," Jamie joked, bumping shoulders with Edgar.

Edgar didn't respond, and Jamie had a moment to think grudgingly, *You're right. I guess I shouldn't audibly make fun of Emma at her own wedding event.* But then they looked up. Edgar was looking at something over Jamie's shoulder, and he looked terrified.

"Baby, it's okay," Jamie said. "I'm here. I won't leave you."

"I need to..." Edgar pushed his seat out slowly, but his trembling made the chair scrape against the flagstone floor.

Emma stopped whatever she'd been saying about golf, and everyone turned to look at them. Jamie tried desperately to tap into any lingering sibling frequency to communicate to Emma that she should keep talking and distract everyone from Edgar.

"Are you okay?" Emma said into the microphone instead.

Jamie gave a nothing-to-see-here wave and slid their arm around

Edgar's waist, supporting him upright. Murmurs arose around them, and Jamie could feel their mother's eyes on their back.

Edgar was shaking violently, and as soon as they pushed the doors open, he pressed his back into the wall, slid into a crouch, and curled up tightly, covering his face. Jamie wrapped their body around him, holding him, as he took deep, shuddering breaths. His hair was wet with sweat, and Jamie rubbed knots out of his clenched shoulders until slowly he began to relax.

"Fuck, Jamie," he said as soon as he could speak. "Fuck, I'm so sorry."

"Don't you dare be sorry for that," Jamie said fiercely.

Edgar buried his face in Jamie's neck. "I just wanted one night," Edgar said softly, and Jamie could hear his exhaustion, his mortification. "Just one night where they'd leave me alone and I could be a normal boyfriend. Someone you could bring as the date to your sister's wedding and meet your parents, and not…"

He sighed.

"Do you want to tell me about it?" Jamie asked.

"No, I just… I'm sorry, I just really wanna go home."

"Of course, let's go home."

Edgar shook his head. "Stay. I'm gonna ask Poe to come get me."

"I want to come with you. Make sure you're okay."

Edgar kissed them, and Jamie tasted salt. "Don't leave in the middle; you'll freak out your family. Go smooth things over with them. Have some cake."

Jamie snorted. "It's probably pretty good cake."

Edgar held up his phone. "Poe's coming."

"Okay. I'll walk you out."

Jamie helped Edgar up, and they walked slowly down the hallway to the exit.

Outside, the wind was cool, and a sharp crescent moon rose above the trees. Edgar tipped his head to the sky and sucked in a deep breath. Jamie stroked his back. He'd sweated all the way through his coat.

"I don't suppose…" Edgar said.

"Hmm?"

"That your family will ever give me another chance?"

"If they don't, then they're not people you wanna have in your life anyway," Jamie said fiercely.

Tires crunched the gravel in the roundabout, and Poe's truck pulled up.

"What did your weird family do to my brother?" Poe asked, then cackled to himself.

"Thanks for coming," Jamie said.

"Eh, I was out anyway. Bones will only sleep in the car seat this week," he explained.

Jamie opened the door for Edgar and saw Nour asleep in the back seat. Jamie patted Edgar's chest and kissed him gently. Then, from the corner of their eye, they saw a small furry white kitten head pop out of the middle of Poe's chest.

"Oh my god," Jamie said. They kissed Edgar again. "I feel good releasing you into these capable paws."

Edgar looked into their eyes for the first time since they'd left the dinner. "Will I see you later?" he asked hesitantly.

Jamie smiled. "Definitely."

✦ ✦ ✦

Inside, the cake had been served and the champagne cleared, and things seemed to be winding down. Dave's contingent was leaving for a bar, and Emma's was going back to the hotel, where they were preparing a spa night for Emma. Dave's mother and Jamie's dad appeared to be settling up with the caterers. Jamie headed for the dessert table before it was wheeled away, giving the area where Edgar had seen the ghost a wide berth.

They took a piece of cake with part of a white golf ball of frosting. The frosting was grainy with sugar and too sweet, but the chocolate cake was rich and moist, and Jamie commended Edgar's judgment.

They managed to avoid their mother while everyone said their goodbyes, at the cost of getting caught in a conversation about mortgage lending with Dave's mom. But the second everyone had filed out, Blythe rounded on Jamie.

"Honey, please." She sounded concerned. Jamie had anticipated anger and hadn't prepared for this approach. "That man seems kind, but he is clearly not a suitable partner for you."

"Why is that, Mom?" Jamie asked through gritted teeth.

Their father joined the conversation, drying his hands as he approached. "He's clearly unstable," Hank answered. "Come on, sweetie. You don't—"

"He was falling down drunk at your sister's wedding," Blythe finally exploded.

"He wasn't drunk, and he's not unstable," Jamie said. But of course, they didn't have any other explanation. So they decided to leave it at that. "Did Emma leave already?" they asked instead.

"Listen, dear," Blythe said, toying with their tie. "Don't bring him on Saturday, please. It's not about me or you. It's about your sister. Let's make sure she has a perfect day."

*And how many other people have to suffer in order for that to happen?*

Rage boiled over, and things that Jamie had never been able to say on their own behalf flowed from their mouth as they defended Edgar. Kind, gentle, sweet Edgar who always fucking tried his best, even to his own detriment. Who was always thinking about Jamie, even while having a panic attack. Who'd welcomed Jamie with open arms into his heart and into a family just as complicated as their own but far more generous. Who'd insisted on coming as their date tonight, even though Jamie had warned him repeatedly that it would be a drag. And who was now, as a result, being speculated about by people who didn't even know him.

"Not one time did either of you ask if my boyfriend is okay. You thought he had a problem with alcohol, and you recognized he has an anxiety disorder, both things that mean someone needs help. But neither of you care about helping anyone."

Jamie broke off. They had seen what they needed to see. Jamie had spent so long feeling like their parents hadn't truly valued and respected them. They'd spent so long wanting to gain their respect, to convince them via excellence to reevaluate their opinions and beliefs.

But now Jamie realized that need was gone.

They didn't want the approval of people they didn't respect. They didn't want to be well thought of by people whose judgment they didn't agree with. And they didn't want to constantly put themself in the position of shoving down great swathes of themself so that those people could feel more comfortable. In fact, now that they could see this clearly, there was a shift—like their entire being took two steps to the side—and Jamie couldn't believe they'd held back this long.

Blythe's mouth was pinched, generally a sign she was thinking about how to annihilate the enemy, but Jamie didn't care. What could she say to them that they hadn't felt every instant they spent in her presence?

"You know," Jamie said, "I've been dreading this wedding. Not because I'm not happy for Emma. If this is what she wants, great. But because I knew that the two of you would find some way to make me feel like I was ruining your perfect picture just by existing. And I accepted that, because it's what you've always done. But what I won't accept is you treating my boyfriend like shit. He's amazing and sweet, and he went through a lot just to be here. He really wanted to make a good impression. But you don't care about any of his amazing qualities. Because the only way to make a good impression on you is to be exactly like you, isn't it? And no fucking thank you!"

"Are you quite through?" Blythe asked coldly. Their father looked on, aghast.

Jamie wasn't, but now their heart was beating fast, and their ears were ringing with anger.

"You have been free to live your life as you wish," their mother hissed, as if even alone in a huge empty room, she wouldn't raise her voice loud enough for her political enemies to overhear. "But when it comes to a family event, there are ways that things are done. And if your little boyfriend can't even make it through a dinner without humiliating himself, then it is appropriate for us to ask him not to attend the wedding that everyone has worked so hard to arrange."

Jamie saw red. "Humiliate himself?! He—I—we—"

What would happen if they told their parents the true reason Edgar had left the rehearsal dinner? They could imagine what their folks would say. *You managed to find someone who's as much of a freak as you.*

"Jamie," their father appealed. "Your mother's colleagues will be at the wedding. Understand how it would look."

They understood perfectly. Really, they always had. But now, finally, they accepted that it wouldn't change.

"It would look like you care about your kid more than you care about appearances. So I understand that it'll never happen," they said, resigned.

Their parents hesitated, as if they had expected protest.

"Here's the thing," Jamie continued, taking advantage of their silence. "I care far more about my boyfriend's feelings than I do about appearances. And I care more about myself than I do about what you think of me."

As soon as they said it, it became true. Jamie stood taller.

"So I'm not interested in spending time with you guys if I have to compromise who I am to be accepted by you. I'll be polite in public, of course. Haven't I always? But you guys go ahead and give me a call if you ever decide that you'd like to know me. *Me.* Not the kid you hoped you'd have or the adult you hoped that kid would turn out to be."

Their parents looked at each other, as if unsure how to proceed in this new dynamic.

"Good night," they said and walked away before their parents could reply.

Heart pounding, Jamie didn't slow down, even when they realized they were walking the wrong way; they kept going until they found doors to burst through, and then they burst through them.

"Whoa." Emma jumped out of the way to avoid a collision. She was smoking a cigarette and drinking a glass of red wine.

Jamie swore. "Sorry. Shouldn't you be at that spa thing?"

Emma rolled her eyes. "I can't be around people for one more second tonight." Her speech was softly slurred. "Is everyone gone?"

"Mom and Dad were still in the room."

"I'm avoiding them," she said conspiratorially.

"Oh yeah? Why's that?" Jamie asked, amused.

"Because they're driving me fucking crazy, why else?"

"Cheers to that," Jamie said.

Emma passed them the wineglass and sat on a marble bench. Jamie followed.

"Was your boyfriend okay?" Emma asked.

"Yeah." Jamie sighed. "Listen, I'm sorry. For disappearing earlier. He needed me. Good cake, by the way."

"Dad picked it."

"The frosting was shit."

Jamie passed the wine back and took a joint out of a case in their pocket. They'd rolled it with rose petals in a silver paper and dipped the end in keef. They lit it and offered it to Emma.

"I haven't smoked weed in so long," she said on the exhale. "Dave says it makes me paranoid."

"Paranoid about things he might be doing that you don't like?" Jamie asked.

"Why do you always have to criticize him?" Emma said, standing up. She took another hit. She looked like she wanted to flounce away but offered the joint to Jamie instead. "You criticize everything."

"A lot of things are shit," Jamie said. "But I'm sorry if I made *you* feel that way. I'm sorry you overheard me. Earlier, with Mom? I didn't mean to hurt you."

They handed the joint back to Emma. The temperature

seemed to drop five degrees from one breeze to the next. Autumn was truly in the air.

Emma inhaled appreciatively too, and Jamie remembered that once, they had shared a love of this time of year. She plopped back down on the bench next to Jamie.

"You didn't hurt me. Of course I knew you didn't care about this wedding. I have known you, like, most of my life. I...I wish we were close, but we're not. It is what it is."

They passed the joint back and forth, and then Jamie crushed it under their boot heel, a tiny sparkle of silver like a fallen star.

"It's not that easy for me either, you know," Emma said after a long silence. "With Mom."

Jamie straightened back up. "You never said. You always acted like you wanted to be exactly like her. Follow in her footsteps. Have her same haircut." They elbowed her in the ribs.

Emma whirled around. "I do *not* have her haircut!" She shrieked, patting her hair.

Jamie laughed. "Emma, come on. It's identical."

"That's not even funny, you little shit," Emma said, scrambling to grab her phone from her bag at the base of the bench. "She has a frozen old lady wig, and I have a French bob."

But she was stoned, and her balance was off, so she just succeeded in pushing it farther away and gave up.

Jamie bit their lip but couldn't keep from laughing.

"Yeah, well. I don't want to be her. It's easier to go along with her until she burns herself out. I save my energy for battles I care about."

"Like what?" Jamie asked. They hadn't realized Emma had any battles with their parents.

"Can you keep a secret?"

"From Mom and Dad? Of course."

Emma looked around cautiously, as if Blythe or Hank might be lurking behind a topiary or urn.

"We're going to move next year. After Dave's contract is up." She rolled her eyes fondly. "Dave wants to open a winery. And I don't really know what I want, but I'm going to figure it out on my own."

Jamie's mouth fell open. "You're not joining the political legacy?"

"Nope."

"And you're gonna be a…vintner? Is that the word?"

Emma raised an eyebrow. "Guess so. Until I figure out what else I want to do."

Jamie's mind was reeling. "Shit, Em. I really know nothing about you either, do I?"

Emma looked like she was going to make a joke and laugh it off, but sadness flickered in her eyes. "Probably not," she said.

"Dave must be really loaded, huh?" they observed.

"Yeah. He's gonna tell his parents about the move after the wedding, but I don't think I'm gonna tell Mom and Dad until right before we go. It's just easier."

"Easier in some ways, harder in others," Jamie said.

"Probably. But I don't have your knack for confrontation."

Jamie was surprised. "I don't have a *knack* for it."

"Okay."

"No seriously," Jamie said. "I don't like fighting with anyone. But if I don't stand up for myself, who the fuck else will?"

They'd meant it rhetorically, but Emma drooped as if she'd taken it personally.

They sat in silence for a while, then Jamie slung an arm over her shoulder.

"Just because Mom and Dad are…the way they are, it doesn't mean we have to be, you know. We could try and be…" They searched for the right word and found nothing.

"Okay," Emma said. "You're right. Yeah. We could just *be*."

"Speaking of having or not having a knack for confrontation," Jamie said. "I kinda told our parents to fuck themselves just now."

Emma's eyes widened. "When I wasn't there to hear it?" she demanded. And then, "I fucking told you."

"They were horrible about Edgar. It's not acceptable, and I won't have it," Jamie said simply. "Which is what I told them. Among other things."

"Damn." She sounded…impressed?

Jamie didn't know if it was the weed that made them ask the question or the fact that they had finally told their parents what they really thought of them, but suddenly it felt possible.

"Emma? Why didn't you ever take my side? With Mom and Dad?"

It was something Jamie had never planned to ask her, though they'd wondered it a thousand times. But nothing about this conversation was going the way Jamie expected.

Emma stood up and went to the railing of the balcony. In her dress, with her hair dancing in the breeze, she looked like an art nouveau princess.

"Because I'm a bad sister," she said.

For a moment, Jamie thought she was being sarcastic and braced for the kind of self-righteous defense of their parents they'd received in the past. But Emma just looked sad.

"Because if I used up Mom and Dad's goodwill by picking fights over you, then they wouldn't've had any left for when I had to pick my own fights with them. I'm sorry."

Jamie swallowed hard, shocked. As they processed what Emma said, they realized that they hadn't expected a real explanation. Clearly, Emma had thought about this though.

"Thanks for telling me the truth," Jamie said, voice only a little thick.

"You deserve it," Emma said. Then, "Do you have any more weed?"

She seemed appropriately ashamed, so Jamie decided to let it go for the moment and handed her another joint instead. They passed it back and forth, smoking in silence for a few minutes.

"This is beautiful," Emma said, holding up the joint. The silver paper sparkled in the moonlight. "Everything you do is beautiful."

"You really stoned there, Em?" Jamie asked, amused.

Emma nodded but continued. "Really though. Your clothes, your hair, your life. It's all…" She looked at Jamie searchingly. "You make everything specifically the way you want it, and you don't compromise just 'cause it's easier. It always annoyed the shit outta me 'cause it was like nothing was good enough for you the way it is."

She took a deep drag and exhaled a plume of white.

"But it's 'cause things *aren't* good enough the way they are, are they?" she said.

Hope, as fresh and green as a new leaf, bloomed in Jamie's heart.

"No," they said, leaning in. "They really aren't."

Emma turned to face Jamie on the bench and grabbed their hand. "You know what?" she said. "You shouldn't come on Saturday."

Jamie stared at her. They couldn't be hearing this right.

"I'm serious," Emma insisted. "Mom and Dad will be awful to you and Edgar. And honestly, I wouldn't want him to even meet Dave's other friends."

She made a mortified face, and Jamie began to hope that she might be serious.

"What about Mom and Dad?"

Their parents would be furious, and the last thing Jamie wanted was for their parents to ruin Emma's wedding because they were so angry Jamie wasn't there.

Emma blew smoke heavenward and handed the joint to Jamie. "I'll talk to them. Honestly," she said sheepishly, "I owe you one."

"You owe me so many," Jamie said. But they were feeling a strange sense of jubilance. Not just about Emma but *for* her.

"You're right," she said. "I do. So. Take Edgar out on a date in your beautiful new suit instead, and don't worry about it."

Things felt vertiginous with Emma, and this was all moving quickly. Jamie's instinct was to dismiss the offer automatically. Their parents would be furious. And what if Emma looked back on it later and felt it was a mistake?

"Are you *seriously* telling me not to come to your wedding?" Jamie asked.

"What do you want, a formal disinvitation?" Emma joked.

"Yeah, actually, is there an e-card company that handles disinviting people to your wedding while stoned on a balcony?"

"Probably," Emma said.

Jamie's heart was beginning to flip with excitement, like it was jumping up and down for joy in their chest. They wouldn't have to white-knuckle it through hours and hours of being referred to as Emma's sister. They wouldn't have to fake smile politely as extended family said, "A *haunter*?" and whatever followed every time they were asked what they did for a living. They wouldn't need to take pictures with their mother in her politician pose that she'd sort through later to use on her website. And Edgar—kind, loving, beautiful Edgar—wouldn't be subjected to any of it.

"If you're serious, I would absolutely fucking love to not go to your wedding," Jamie said.

"I'm very serious," Emma confirmed.

Jamie felt light enough to drift up into the sky and float among the stars.

"I just have one more question," Jamie said.

"Oh god," Emma said. "Okay, let's just get all the ways I'm a shit sister over with at once."

"Are you scared to lose your virginity on your wedding night?" they joked.

Emma ducked her head. "Okay, listen, you can't tell *anyone*. But I am kind of scared." She turned wide, terrified eyes to Jamie.

Jamie's mind went blank with guilt, and they stammered. They'd never thought… They'd just assumed…

Now it was Emma's turn to elbow Jamie in the ribs. "Kidding." Jamie snorted with laughter and relaxed back on the bench.

"So anyway, your boyfriend's really hot," Emma said.

"That he is," Jamie agreed enthusiastically. "That he is."

## 30

## Edgar

Edgar stared miserably out the truck window as Poe drove.

"Are you okay?" Poe asked after a while.

"No."

Edgar was not in any way okay. His wonderful Jamie had invited him to be their date, and he had utterly failed them. He'd wanted one night, just one, where he could stand next to Jamie and make them proud. Where he could prove that he could be a partner to them. And his fear—his exhausting fucking fear—had made it impossible.

"I'm so goddamn sick of this," he said. "I'm so sick of being scared all the time. I—it was okay when I was alone, but—"

"No, it fucking wasn't," Poe said.

He spun the wheel and pulled into an empty parking lot. The

baby gurgled in the back seat. Poe threw the truck in park and turned to Edgar.

"So glad you pulled over just so you could glare at me more effectively," Edgar muttered.

"Brother," Poe said. "This isn't about Jamie. It isn't even about the ghosts. This shit is about you. Please listen to me. I'm not trying to be a dick. I'm just…fucking bad at talking to people sometimes, okay?"

He raked a hand through his hair frustratedly but looked right at Edgar.

"It fucking kills me to watch you," Poe said. "I can't even imagine how Jamie must feel. You're…you're a fucking prince, man. You're smart and kind, and you manage to put up with dipshits like me. This isn't any fucking way to live. You have to listen to me, please."

Edgar couldn't remember the last time he'd heard Poe say please to anyone, and now he'd said it twice in the span of a minute. He was desperate. And he was right. It wasn't any fucking way to live.

"You're right," Edgar said.

Poe immediately opened his mouth to protest, then registered what Edgar had said. "Wait, what?"

"You're right. It's no way to live."

"Oh. Well then. Good."

The germ of an idea tickled Edgar's brain. Tonight was the end. It was easier to think of it as being about Jamie. But Jamie was not the reason; they were the reward. Getting to have a life with them. Getting to have a life at all.

"I'm gonna fix it. Now."

"You're…what?"

Yes, this was right. "Can you drop me off at Lafayette Number One?"

"It's closed by now."

"I know," Edgar said.

✦ ✦ ✦

The cemetery was six blocks from Edgar's apartment, and he'd avoided even walking past it ever since he moved in. Now he was seeking it out for the same reason he'd always avoided it.

Poe pulled up in front of Commander's Palace, the cemetery gates looming, and Edgar got out.

"Do you want me to come with you?" Poe offered.

Edgar was sorely tempted to take him up on his offer. Just imagining Poe holding a baby and a kitten was enough to make seeking out a ghost seem less scary. But this was something he had to do on his own.

"No, thanks. I'll be okay."

Poe raised a hand, like he wanted to reach for Edgar, then let it drop back into his lap. "Do you want me to wait?" he offered.

"Now who's scared?" Edgar teased. He tried to hit Poe with a reassuring grin, but his teeth chattered.

"Text me when you get home," Poe said, sounding a lot like Allie.

"I will."

Edgar closed the truck door quietly so as not to disturb Nour.

"Bro," Poe called as he turned away.

When he looked back, he saw something new in Poe's expression. Now, in addition to the concern he tried to hide, Edgar recognized something he thought might be pride.

"I love you," Poe said.

Then he screeched away before Edgar could respond.

Edgar tried to hold on to the positive feeling as he turned toward the cemetery. The air had cooled a touch. Lights were on in the houses that faced the cemetery, but the streets around Lafayette No. 1 were quiet.

The breeze rocked the skeletal branches that reached above him into the sky, making them sway. Edgar knew he'd find a ghost near the cemetery as surely as he knew how he felt about Jamie. Just like those feelings, he didn't know *how* he knew, but he was certain.

He turned the corner as a peal of laughter rang out from a balcony nearby. He hoped Jamie was managing to have a good time with their family. He hoped he hadn't ruined that for them.

*Click clack, click clack,* his heels drummed as he walked the second block that surrounded the cemetery. He'd walk the perimeter as many times as it took until he found one.

He put his hands in his pockets and whistled, pretending not to have a care in the world. It seemed that ghosts appeared to him more when he was least expecting it. Here, wearing a suit and strolling slowly, he had to seem like the perfect mark. One of them would find him.

His footsteps echoed even louder around the next corner. Maybe it was in his head? No. There it was, the familiar sensation of sounds swelling and then bleeding together right before—

A cold, viscous sensation prickled at the back of his neck and slid down his spine.

There it was. Somewhere up there.

Edgar forced himself to keep walking even as he started to tremble and sweat. He got halfway down the block when it oozed out of the cemetery and stopped in the glow of the streetlight before him.

Edgar froze.

The ghost had once been a young man, perhaps around his own age. But now, what had been a slicked-back coiffure was mangled and bloody. What had once been broad shoulders were twisted strangely in on themselves.

Edgar shuddered as the thing turned blank bluish-gray eyes toward him. They quivered like jelly.

"Fuck, fuck, fuck," Edgar chanted.

He told his foot to lift off the ground and move forward, but it didn't obey him.

He sucked in a breath through his nose and blew it out slowly through his mouth, attempting to get his body under control. Every single instinct he had was screaming at him to turn and run. To get as far as possible from this unnatural creature that caused nothing but terror.

*Can you describe it?* Jamie had asked when they were planning the makeup they would use to transform Edgar into a ghost for Amelia's film. And when Edgar had said he usually tried not to look, Jamie had asked questions. *Can you tell how it died? Can you tell when it was from? What does their skin look like? Their hair? Their fingernails?*

Now, Edgar risked a look at the ghost in front of him and began with the smallest details. He wasn't close enough to see the ghost's fingernails. He took a step closer. The ghost didn't move. Another step closer, and now he could see in the glow of the streetlight. Its nails were buffed to a smooth shine. In fact, its hands could have been living hands if they hadn't been so pale, so still.

It wore a gold band on its ring finger, polished to a twinkle.

Edgar frowned and took another step forward, eyes on the

ring. The ghost had been married. When he'd died, someone had mourned him, as Edgar had mourned Antoine. There had probably been a funeral, maybe a second line. The man's family and friends would have gathered to comfort one another in their loss.

Edgar imagined how he would feel if he lost Jamie. If it was Jamie whose fragile human body had been torn apart by violence.

He choked on it.

The ghost's head swung in Edgar's direction, as if it could sense his sadness. But still, it didn't move toward him.

Edgar's gaze followed its hand up its arm to its shoulders. They had been crushed toward each other somehow, giving the ghost a hunched silhouette. It must have been excruciating, whatever had caused such strong bones to crunch. Edgar winced, imagining what it might have been: a car accident, mishandled farming equipment, a plane crash? He took another step toward it, trying to find answers.

Wondering slowed his heart and made his breath come easier. When he looked for answers, he focused on details. It was the opposite of focusing on what his own body was doing in response.

Curiosity was the opposite of fear.

This, he realized, was what Jamie had been trying to help him do when they asked him to look at himself as a ghost. But no one could do this for him.

Edgar took another tentative step toward the ghost. He was now twenty feet away, and the ghost stayed put. At ten feet away, Edgar could see everything.

He could see the small wire-rimmed spectacles that had perched on the man's nose before he died. They'd been smashed, the glass digging in around his eyes. Blood seeped from the wounds as if he had cried crimson.

Edgar's hand went to his own face. The ghost's hand drifted up in a strange echo of Edgar's gesture. It touched the bits of smashed glass and the blood around its eyes. Its eyebrows drew together.

Edgar took a step closer. He touched his hair. The ghost touched its hair, fingers exploring the wound that mangled its head. On its face were confusion and pain. Edgar would know the expression anywhere.

"Fuck, I'm so sorry for whatever happened to you."

Edgar didn't realize he'd spoken aloud until his voice startled him in the dark quiet.

The ghost didn't respond, but its arm dropped back to its side.

Edgar took one last step toward the ghost. He was now standing closer to a ghost than he ever had, except when one blasted through him, like on his first date with Jamie. Usually he fled long before they had the opportunity. He was still trembling slightly. But his feet were beneath him, his head functional. He couldn't believe it.

Antoine's ghost had floated away from him. Why wasn't this ghost? Was it tethered to the cemetery? Did it like the light?

"Why are you here?" Edgar asked. "Do you know you're dead?"

The ghost just stared. Not *at* Edgar exactly, but around him.

"When did you die?"

The ghost didn't respond. Edgar supposed he hadn't really expected it to.

"What do you want with me?" This was the real question.

The ghost's gelatinous eyes blinked, but it said nothing.

Edgar slumped against the cemetery gates. It had been wishful thinking to imagine a ghost would have any answers for him. This had been stupid, and he was angry with himself that he'd thought it might change things. Suddenly he wanted to tear the ghost limb from limb. How dare it just stand there staring when it and ones like it had ruined Edgar's life?

"Why won't you leave me alone?" Edgar yelled at the ghost.

Edgar's words echoed around them, and he punched the stone wall surrounding the cemetery. Fuck, that hurt, and Edgar roared his pain out into the uncaring night.

He blew out a furious breath and looked at the ghost. It had moved. Edgar watched as it took a step away from him, then another.

"Are you…?"

Edgar's brain supplied a truly hilarious thought: *The ghost is afraid of you.* But that was absurd, right?

He stood tall once more and yelled at the ghost again. Again, it stepped away from him.

"Wait," Edgar said. "I'm sorry. I didn't mean to scare you."

The ghost stilled.

"I didn't even know ghosts could get scared. See, I don't really know much about y'all, even though I've seen you my whole life. It's not your problem, I realize. I just really need to get over this fucking terror."

*Great, now I'm making a ghost my therapist.*

It did feel good to talk to someone though. He'd talked to Allie about it, sure, and even Jamie. But always there was the pressure not to worry them. To keep them from knowing how utterly undone he was by fear, because if they truly knew, then they would understand that he was beyond help. Beyond hope.

But the ghost just listened. Or not. Who could tell? But it stayed. And Edgar poured his heart out.

He didn't know how much time had passed before he'd

exhausted himself talking. But when the tears came, he let them fall. The ghost stood in the pool of light once more, and Edgar lifted himself to sit on the wall of the cemetery across from it.

Now that Edgar had gotten used to the particulars of the ghost's configuration, they lost some of their grotesque impact. He was able to imagine what the man's face would have looked like when he was alive. Handsome, probably. Blue-gray eyes a little like Jamie's. Dark hair a little like his own. About their age when his life was ripped from him.

"Thanks for listening," Edgar said.

Still, the ghost said nothing. But they both stayed there, looking at each other for a long time. Something like peace settled around Edgar.

He'd done it. He'd faced a ghost directly. He'd spoken to it—hell, he'd *yelled* at it. And here he stood. The ghost hadn't harmed him. His fear hadn't killed him.

Now he could walk away.

He eased down from the wall and addressed the ghost for the last time.

"I'm gonna go home now. Maybe you can go wherever you belong too. Or if not, maybe I'll see you around sometime."

The ghost's expression was neutral now, and Edgar did something strange. He reached out his hand and offered it to the ghost. The ghost slowly raised its own hand. Edgar reached for it very, very slowly. When his fingertips touched the ghost's, a cool, minty sensation crept up his wrist. They clasped hands.

Edgar got a flash of confused thoughts that felt like a different texture than his own and feelings that felt just like his: fear, sadness, the desperate desire to be with his love. Then Edgar let go, and it was all gone. He was only himself.

The ghost—no, no. His name, Edgar realized, had been Benjamin—looked different now. Less…mangled? Or was it simply that Edgar had gotten used to it?

No, Benjamin looked *less*. Less mangled, less corporeal, less everything. He looked like he was fading away.

Edgar was overwhelmed with sadness and relief. Maybe ghosts were just looking to be witnessed. To be truly, accurately seen.

After all, wasn't that what most people wanted?

He stayed until Benjamin was gone. Gone where, he didn't know. Back inside the cemetery or somewhere else in the city or perhaps nowhere at all. It wasn't for him to know.

Then Edgar Lovejoy dusted himself off and walked slowly toward home.

# 31

# Edgar

"Congratulations!" Edgar swept Jamie into his arms. Jamie had a week of strike ahead of them, but the haunted house was officially closed for the season, which meant Edgar would get far more time with them. Jamie was elated to have finally confronted their parents and had been gratifyingly proud of Edgar for confronting a ghost. Add how well he and Poe were getting along, and Edgar was feeling dangerously close to being in the Halloween spirit.

"Thanks! I'm so glad to be done until next year." They kissed him, lips a sweet promise for later. "So are you feeling up for the party?"

Edgar was still learning what it meant for him to be up for a party at all. He'd spent most of his adult life afraid to leave his house, anxious whenever he did, and desperate to get back to his safe haven so he could deal alone with whatever feelings he had incurred.

Spending more time with Jamie, who had a large circle of friends and several who were quite close, it became clear to Edgar that he had a lot of shit going on. Antoine's death at thirteen hadn't just been traumatic for all the obvious reasons. It had shown Edgar that when he cared about someone—when he *loved* someone—they disappeared from his life.

Cameron's parents had sent her to boarding school the year after Antoine died, needing space for their own grief, so he'd lost her then as well. His father had left a year later. His mother several years after that. Then Poe.

Edgar had wrapped his strangeness around himself like a blanket and hidden away from the world, convinced that anyone he might care about would think he was too much of a freak to love him back. Certain that if they did, they would inevitably leave.

"There are so many people who like you and wanna hang out with you!" Jamie had told him more than once over the past few weeks, referring to Helen and Veronica, Carys and Greta, Leila and Amelia, and more. "And they would like you just as much if you told them the truth."

More and more recently, Edgar had begun thinking about changing everything.

Sitting with Benjamin hadn't magically cured him of fear. What it had done was show him that anything, *everything*, could change.

And how could he not take that seriously, since his whole life had changed since meeting Jamie? Now, there was one final piece missing in the puzzle that was Edgar's life.

*What if you didn't have a secret anymore?*

It was a question so bright and overwhelming that Edgar only dared to look at it sidelong.

Edgar agreed to go to Helen, Veronica, Carys, and Greta's Halloween party, even though it was at the time by which he usually made sure to be inside his apartment.

"Yeah?" Jamie grinned and gave him a once-over. "Awesome. I want to show off my sexy boyfriend."

Edgar flushed hotly and loved every second of it.

✦ ✦ ✦

"You came!" Helen called excitedly across the room when they walked in. Edgar assumed they were talking to Jamie, but it was *him* they threw their arms around. "V, look, Edgar came!"

"I see that," Veronica said, but she smiled and squeezed his shoulder. "Glad you're here."

It was the first party Edgar had been to since high school. The crush of people, the bumping music, and the constant addition of new voices made Edgar's head spin, so after a little while, he wandered onto the porch to get some air.

Greta was out there, and she was talking with two men Edgar didn't recognize. He tried to duck back inside, but Greta saw him before he could escape.

"Oh, Edgar, I'm so glad you came! This is Truman," she said, indicating the smaller of the two, who had soft brown curls and eyes that looked like they saw everything. He waved, expression friendly. "And this is Ash."

The second man was uncommonly attractive, with messy blond hair and stubble. He nodded somberly in welcome.

"Guys, this is Edgar. He—"

"I see ghosts!" Edgar blurted.

While Jamie had been at the haunt the last week, Edgar had been thinking about telling them. During Emma's wedding rehearsal, Edgar had been thinking about telling them. He'd been thinking so much about how he was going to tell his friends that it had popped right out of his mouth at this total stranger. A wave of mortification broke over Edgar, but Ash just looked around and calmly asked, "Where?"

Edgar cleared his throat. "Just, uh. In general."

"Really?" Truman asked, looking fascinated. "I have so many questions."

"Wait, wait," Greta said. "You can see ghosts and you've, like, never thought to mention that? Tell me *everything*. Also, can I tell Carys?"

"Um. Yes?"

Three faces looked at him with interest, eager to hear—what? A ghost story? A secret? Some insight told to him from beyond the grave?

Edgar swallowed, mouth suddenly dry.

"My mom says she sees a ghost. In her house. But she's not living in the present sometimes." That was Ash.

"She has Alzheimer's," Truman explained.

"She's convinced though," Ash said. "Kinda makes sense that you'd be able to see things out of time more clearly if you're also living out of time."

"My younger sister thinks life and death are happening simultaneously because all time is happening at once. It's just that our puny brains are too simple to process it," Greta chimed in. "Wait, we've gotta get Helen and Veronica out here."

She stuck her head inside and yelled something that was inaudible to Edgar. Helen and Veronica came outside a moment later.

"What?" said Veronica.

Greta turned to Edgar expectantly.

In an attempt to be smoother this time, he said, "What are your thoughts on, um, ghosts?"

Helen's eyes widened, and Veronica's snapped to him.

"Totally believe in," said Helen.

"My gran saw ghosts," Veronica said. "She used to tell me her son—my uncle, who died when he was nineteen—came and told her secrets in her sleep and when she was hanging out the laundry."

Truman chimed in, "I've never had an encounter with one that I know of, but that doesn't mean they're not real. I mean, I haven't personally seen lots of shit that I know is real, so."

Carys came outside then, looking for Greta.

"Dude," Greta told her. "Edgar can see ghosts."

Carys raised an eyebrow. "Somehow that doesn't surprise me," she said, nodding at Edgar. "Hey, can you come help me with the pumpkin bread?"

Reluctantly, Greta followed her inside but turned at the last moment to point at Edgar and say, "You *are* gonna tell me more about this later, right?"

He nodded, not able to speak.

The conversation naturally moved on, and Edgar tried to force his heart to beat in a normal rhythm and his muscles to unclench. He tried to understand the words his friends were saying, but he couldn't track them. Someone asked if he wanted a drink. He didn't. The next thing he knew, he was alone, his head swimming.

The final fault line in Edgar's heart had opened up, and now it was broken.

No one had cared. He had told them his deepest secret, and it had gone *fine*. *Well*, even. As well as it *could* have.

Edgar had been wrong. He'd been so wrong for so long. And it had cost him friends, lovers, support. It had cost him a life. *Fuck*.

He walked around the block, trying to clear his mind and figure out how things could've gone so differently than he'd pictured all these years.

Jamie found him a few blocks away, sitting on the bench in a park where once the ghost of a stooped woman carrying something unrecognizable had sat beside him, terrifying him when he'd looked over to say good morning and been faced with its dead eyes.

"Hey, baby," they said softly, crouching in front of him.

"Hey," he said weakly. "Sorry I abandoned you."

"No worries. I was talking with Muriel—she's such a delight—and Veronica said I might want to come find you. She said you looked a little… Well, anyway. Are you okay?" They rubbed warm palms up and down Edgar's tense thighs.

"You were right," he croaked. "Turns out. Have I…? Could I have…?"

Jamie stood and sat next to him on the bench, lifting Edgar's hand to their lips and pressing a kiss to his knuckles. As always, his body relaxed automatically with their touch.

He tried again. "It didn't have to be like this," he whispered. "It could have been better. All this time."

"Oh, baby." Jamie folded him in their arms and held him tight, stroking his hair. There was nothing to say, really. It was a good, joyous thing. But like every new good and joyous thing in Edgar's life lately, it highlighted the opposite choices he'd made before and all that they had cost him.

Edgar didn't want fear to cost him anything more. Not ever again.

He swallowed hard and cupped Jamie's face.

"Jamie, I love you. I love everything about you. You're my best friend, and I think you're amazing. That…that's all."

Jamie's face did something complicated and precious. "I love you too," they said right away. "I respect you so much. Your kindness and your generosity. The way you always expect the best of me. Also did I mention how brave and handsome and incredibly sexy you are?"

Edgar pulled them close.

"I love you," they whispered and kissed his cheek. "I love you." A kiss to his jaw. "I really fucking love you."

"What a night," Edgar said. Then he started to cry.

# 32

# Jamie

MARDI GRAS, FOUR MONTHS LATER

The thing about having Edgar Lovejoy for a boyfriend was that Jamie was constantly getting sneak attacked by things that turned their heart to absolute mush.

Unpredictable tiny things, like when he made Jamie a birthday cake. It had been delicious, and Jamie had said so. What they didn't find out until later, from Poe, was that Edgar had been over at Allie and Poe's place five days in a row practicing how to make it.

There was the time he bumped into a bush while they were walking to get coffee and absently murmured, "Oops, sorry," without breaking stride. The way he ducked his head when Jamie opened a door for him, surprised and pleased by the courtesy. How he'd introduced Jamie to his coworker at the cat café by saying, "This is my…Jamie," and hadn't noticed.

The time he'd texted Jamie, **Do you want to come fuck me, please?**, got immediately self-conscious, and texted the follow-up, **Yikes, is that weird? If so I am totally kidding**, and a string of emojis that Jamie could only parse as a pictography of shame. Edgar's request and uncertainty had tingled deep in Jamie's gut, and they'd made sure that Edgar would never doubt himself about sending similar texts in the future.

There was the way he mumbled in his sleep, as if even in dreams, he didn't want to disturb anyone. The way he sometimes gasped an "Oh!" of surprise at the pleasure Jamie caused him. And how he fell asleep in Jamie's arms, head heavy on their shoulder like Edgar trusted they could take his weight.

At Jamie's request, they'd decided not to celebrate Christmas with Jamie's parents, but Jamie had made plans to meet up with Emma in the new year. Although Jamie knew their parents were hurt and offended by their decision, it had led to the nicest Christmas they'd had in some time, celebrating Christmas Eve at Allie and Poe's, quaffing champagne and playing an old version of Trivial Pursuit that Allie took from Magpie Vintage. Even Edgar had sipped a glass, resulting in an adorable tipsy confidence in his incorrect answers that Jamie wished they'd taken video of.

But that night, in bed, after Edgar'd fallen asleep, Jamie had felt a dislocating sadness that they pulled around themself like a blanket and huddled in. And Edgar had known. He'd known Jamie would feel bittersweet about their first Christmas without the Wendon-Dales, and he'd planned a new tradition to replace the old. He had curated a movie marathon of holiday romantic comedies and prepared a cheese plate to go with them. Jamie had burst into tears on the spot and found themself cuddled under a blanket and a large man who kissed their face and held them close.

When Jamie was ready, Edgar bundled them into the living room, put the cheese plate on the coffee table, pushed Play on the first movie, and cuddled Jamie close. It was two in the morning.

There was the time Jamie had been a guest on a haunting podcast and Edgar had texted everyone they knew to tell them to listen.

Then there was their first fight. It had been a silly nothing of a fight—stress plus exhaustion caused Edgar to snap at Jamie, and Jamie had snapped back. They'd both apologized later, and Edgar had said in a serious but shaky voice, "I don't like when I'm not at my best for you."

Jamie wanted to ask Edgar if he wanted to move in together. They loved Edgar and were sick of missing him on nights when they were too tired to drive over. They hated that when they weren't together, Edgar woke from his nightmares all alone.

They were ready.

But unlike Jamie, who'd been living with five other people when they got the chance to live in Germaine and Carl's guesthouse, Edgar had always lived alone, by choice. His home was his sanctuary, and Jamie wasn't positive he'd want to share it. So Jamie decided to compose a love letter for Edgar in the form they knew best: a haunt. Only this was no ordinary haunt.

This was an *un*haunt. The opposite of something that would scare or startle, this would be a place that soothed and comforted, a place that inspired happiness.

It would be Jamie's way of showing Edgar what their home together could look like if he wanted it.

✦ ✦ ✦

The streets had been teeming with Mardi Gras celebrations all week, and Jamie had picked up extra shifts at Le Corbeau, where they had started working, alongside Poe.

Alaitheia Rondeau was, for Jamie, a revelation. They knew the Lovejoys found her frustrating, but her stories about the New Orleans of a different time captivated Jamie. The history of the building, which had been a brothel and a restaurant before it was a jazz club, was palpable in the bootlegging tunnels and storage rooms that she showed them.

In fact, if Jamie didn't know her ability was seeing ghosts, they might've thought she had a bit of other magic in her.

She probably did have at least a *touch* of magic to have convinced Poe to work at Le Corbeau now that he was—tentatively, as he kept insisting on reminding everyone—staying in town.

Poe's presence behind the bar at Le Corbeau drew the attention of many a thirsty patron, and the leather gloves he wore only heightened his sense of mystique. Jamie knew from long experience that brooding white men could be all kinds of rude, dismissive, and self-centered and still have scads of patrons vying for their attention. But never had they seen it work to this extent.

People fell over themselves to talk to Poe (he wouldn't). They asked him to recommend something (he recommended they look deep within themselves and figure out what they wanted to drink). They came on to him in every possible way (he ignored it). Once Jamie even saw an older woman slide a hundred-dollar bill across the bar and give Poe a knowing look. He'd pocketed the money and said he assumed it was a tip for his exceptional service.

When Jamie asked Poe if he was worried that being dismissive would be bad for Le Corbeau's business, Poe just snorted, winked at his aunt, and said, "We're not worried, are we?"

She had raised a knowing eyebrow. "We are not," she replied. After that, Jamie decided to stick to pouring drinks.

✦ ✦ ✦

Jamie led Edgar through the fence and around the back of Germaine and Carl's place, enfolding them in quiet and softly twinkling fairy lights.

They had the place all to themselves, as Germaine and Carl were spending a few days with Muriel, doing their annual Mardi Gras *something*. Germaine and Carl would never tell Jamie exactly what they did. All they knew was that the year before, the couple had been gone for three days, and when they returned, they seemed happy and rejuvenated. Did they bathe in the blood of virgins? Dance naked in the moonlight? Get blasted and eat fancy cheese all night? Jamie had no idea.

"What are we doing, baby?" Edgar asked when they got to the glass French doors of Germain and Carl's parlor.

Suddenly, Jamie was hit with a wave of nerves. They'd donned the suit that had been Emma's gift, wanting to look as good as possible for Edgar. The fabric was luscious, and it was tailored perfectly. Jamie smoothed their vest.

"So, um, I made you something. It's an *un*haunted house."

At the entrance to the unhaunt stood a balloon arch tall enough to walk through, in terra-cotta and dark gray. The colorful sign that hung above it announced, *Unhaunted House—Enter at No Risk to Yourself.*

"Wait, what?" Edgar uttered in shock. "You made a haunted house? Just for me?"

"No. I made an *un*haunted house just for you."

Edgar took Jamie's face in his hands and kissed them with the drowning sweetness that had made Jamie fall for him in the beginning.

Edgar took Jamie's hand and stepped through the balloon arch.

It had been an interesting project: deconstructing the characteristics of a haunt in order to figure out how to create the opposite feeling.

The first unhaunt was a wooden bench like the ones in City Park. It sat on a carpet of moss and greenery and had a view of the live oaks, the lake, and all the animals that could be found there. The fabric drop of the view alone had taken them a full day to paint.

"You can sit on it if you want," Jamie murmured, not wanting to disturb Edgar's experience.

Edgar sat on the bench, and Jamie sat beside him. The scents of water and trees came from the oil diffuser they'd hidden among the mosses. A low soundtrack of birdsong, bicycle wheels, and the distant sound of families picnicking played in the background.

"If you open that drawer…" Jamie pointed to the top drawer of a dresser.

Edgar slid it open to reveal a tiny cup of coffee and a beignet.

"You once said that you wished you could be a normal person who could go read on a bench in City Park while you drank coffee on weekend mornings but that you could never relax enough to do it. Because you're always on the lookout for ghosts. So now you can."

"You…you *made* this?" Edgar gaped.

Jamie nodded.

Edgar traced the boughs of the oak trees and put his finger to the beak of a brown pelican Jamie had painted in flight.

"Holy crap. You're amazing." Edgar was looking at them with wide eyes. "I mean, I knew you were amazing. But this is *amazing*. This is a realistic landscape painting. It must've taken forever."

Jamie smiled, blooming under Edgar's appreciation. "It took a little while. The coffee's real, if you want some. But I just gave you a little 'cause it's so late. If you don't want the beignet, I'll take it off your hands," they teased.

Edgar handed them the pastry and inhaled the chicory scent of the coffee. Then he took a tiny sip and closed his eyes.

"It even smells real," he murmured, expression serene.

And in that moment, Jamie Wendon-Dale made a promise to themself that someday, Edgar Lovejoy *would* enjoy a relaxed morning in the park, goddammit, even if they had to bring Allie along to keep watch.

"We can sit as long as you want."

Edgar seemed torn. "I want to see everything. But then maybe we could come back here at the end?"

*Just wait 'til you see what's planned for later. We'll see if you still want to come back,* Jamie thought with relish, but they nodded.

The birdsong and scent faded as they reached the next unhaunt zone. Six different monitors set at varying heights streamed cat videos, one of which was the camera Edgar had set up to watch the cats in the café. Guessing Edgar's password—*cats1!*—hadn't been difficult.

Furry little faces peered at them; furry little paws knocked things off counters and made biscuits on people's faces.

"I love cats so much," Edgar murmured.

Jamie grinned.

After they watched cat videos for a while, Jamie hooked their elbow through Edgar's and led him to the next unhaunt, in the spare room. They pressed the remote in their pocket, and then Edgar's recorded voice said, "I feel different." Then, after a long pause, awe audible in his voice, "I feel wonderful."

On the wall, Jamie had hung stills from the film they'd shot: different angles of Edgar as a ghost, blown up to eight feet tall. The audio had come from the end of the final take Amelia had done with Edgar. Though he'd absolutely nailed it on the take when he'd first scared Leila, Jamie had insisted they do three more, because they wanted Edgar to experience the catharsis he'd clearly felt during that amazing take. After Amelia called cut and told Edgar he was done, Jamie had asked him how he felt.

His answer, at the time, had disappointed Jamie just the tiniest bit. They'd wished, they supposed, for a bit more detail. Later though, when they were watching the footage, they'd been able to pay attention to what they could hear in Edgar's voice. Without any other distractions, they'd been able to hear the awe, the wonder, the threatening tears.

They'd been able to hear that Edgar truly had released something that day.

Edgar gazed into his own eyes as the audio played again.

"Can't believe I did that," Edgar said. "I know I didn't say anything, but I was so freaked out."

Jamie chose not to tell Edgar that it was clear to anyone who'd looked at him, talked to him, or stood in his general energy field that he had been petrified.

"I feel different," Edgar of the past murmured through the speakers to Edgar of the present. "I feel wonderful."

"Are you ready for the last two unhaunts?"

"I'd follow you anywhere," Edgar said.

Jamie started to laugh, but something in his voice stopped

them, and instead they took Edgar's hand and led him out the door to the yard.

The fairy lights they'd strung through the branches on the walk to the guesthouse glowed in pastel shades. On either side of the walkway were easels, each one holding a large photograph. First was a picture of Edgar and Allie with their arms around each other's waists in Magpie Vintage, from the night he'd tried on clothes. He was looking at the camera with a little smile quirking his mouth, but his eyes shone bright with love. She was midlaugh, head tipped back and eyes on Edgar.

Next was a picture of Edgar and Poe. They were mirror images of each other, each sitting cross-legged on the floor of Allie's apartment, each leaning in, each resting his chin in his hand. They appeared to be having a deeply personal conversation, but in fact, Poe had been in the middle of emphatically insisting that Smoosh was the one who had farted.

Edgar laughed and touched Poe's face with his fingertips.

"He's obsessed with the Scottish cats," Edgar said fondly.

When Edgar had texted Jamie to tell them Poe had adopted three kittens and left with them in his pockets, Jamie had demanded proof. Later that evening, Edgar had sent a photo he'd snapped without Poe's knowledge, in which he lay on the couch with the three kittens on his head and neck. He looked like he wore a living balaclava with claws, but his eyes were closed, and his bare hand rested on his chest, as if he'd fallen asleep petting the little fuzz balls. It was the only time Jamie had seen Poe look even close to happy.

"Who wouldn't be?" Jamie asked.

In the next photograph, Edgar lay on his stomach on the rug in Allie's living room, and Nour lay on their stomach atop him.

They fit precisely into the curve of his spine, and their rosebud face was turned toward the camera, helpless and trusting in sleep.

"Oh lord," Edgar said when he saw it. He laughed, wiping at his eyes.

"So good, right?" Jamie said.

"So good." Edgar scrubbed at his eyes with his sleeve. "Look at that little nose."

"It's so fucking tiny."

The final photograph stood on its easel just before the door to Jamie's house. It showed two generations of Lovejoys piled on top of one another on Allie's couch. It was a little blurry since they'd been in the process of falling *off* the couch when Jamie snapped the photo. But they all looked joyful, even Nour, who looked like they might have been in the process of pooping when everything went down.

"They all love you so much," Jamie murmured.

Edgar pulled Jamie close. They could feel the tremble in his deep breaths and squeezed him tight.

"Damn," he exclaimed thickly. "This is the best unhaunted house in the whole world."

"There's one more bit. Um."

Jamie swallowed hard, throat gone tight with nerves, and led Edgar to sit on the bench under the crepe myrtle tree spangled with fairy lights while they tried to get their nerves under control.

Now that it came down to it, Jamie realized how desperately they wanted Edgar to say yes. How much they wanted their life together to start now.

"Edgar." Jamie took his hand and cleared their throat. "I love you so much, and I want to spend all the time with you that I can. I know it can be a huge deal to share your space with someone, especially for you, since it's your sanctuary. But I promise you that if you would consider living together, every day, I would—"

Jamie found themself swept up in Edgar's arms and in his lap.

"I didn't really finish my—"

Edgar kissed them.

"I have points to make," Jamie said.

"Yes," said Edgar.

"Okay. First of all, I know that—"

"Jamie, *yes*. Yes. I want to live with you."

Then Edgar kissed the hell out of Jamie, and they forgot the speech they'd worked so hard on.

"Holy shit," Jamie said when Edgar let them go, weak with adrenaline, relief, and excitement. "I can't believe this is really happening."

Edgar gaped back at them, appearing as overwhelmed as Jamie felt. Then he kissed Jamie softly and got them both to their feet. It was getting cold.

"I can't believe you did this for me," Edgar said as they walked back past the photographs on their way to the guesthouse. "I do have one complaint though," Edgar said.

"Oh, okay, sure," Jamie said, trying to switch their mind out of addlepated schmoop mode and into editing mode.

"You didn't include the biggest unhaunt."

Jamie ran through all the ideas they contemplated and discarded as imperfect. "Which one do you mean?"

"Jamie." Edgar pulled them close. "There should be pictures of *you* everywhere."

Jamie bit their lip and closed their eyes, overwhelmed by the pulse of love that suffused their entire body. Then Edgar kissed them, and they decided not to think anymore.

# Epilogue

# Edgar

TWO MONTHS LATER

It was the day Jamie was moving in with Edgar, and Jamie had sent him to Allie's for the day so he didn't have to deal with people tramping in and out of the apartment, for which he was grateful. Allie had made pancakes for breakfast, and he'd spent a pleasant if overstimulating day hanging out with Nour, Poe, Allie, and three kittens hell-bent on world domination.

Allie had just lain down for a nap with Nour, and Poe was making marinara sauce in the kitchen. Now, Edgar was awaiting the all-clear text from Jamie that meant he could return to his apartment—*their* apartment.

"So what're you thinking?" Edgar asked Poe. "Are you going to stick around?"

Edgar and Allie had discussed Poe, and while they both

wanted him to stay in New Orleans, neither of them could tell if he would. Poe had been suspiciously nice lately, and Edgar couldn't help but think that soon the other shoe would drop.

"For a while," he said noncommittally.

"How long's a while?"

"Why, you sending out wedding invitations or something and don't wanna waste a stamp?"

This comment had done something funny to Edgar's stomach, but this wasn't the time to interrogate it.

"I was just wondering if I should get used to having you around or if you're gonna disappear again," Edgar said.

Poe tasted the sauce, the tomato scent thick with herbs, then put the lid on. The timer went off, and he swore, silencing it immediately and glancing toward the bedroom where Allie and Nour were napping. They both stayed silent for a moment, listening. When no crying (Nour) or embittered swearing (Allie) was forthcoming, they relaxed.

Poe slid a sheet of scones out of the oven. They steamed temptingly on the counter.

"I was thinking about it," he said. Then, slowly, "Auntie mentioned I could have more hours. Cook at the bar, maybe. They used to have food, but she lost her chef a few years back, and he did all the ordering and everything, so…" Poe trailed off, as if it would violate some personal ethos to express any more than the bare minimum of enthusiasm about anything, ever. "Anyway. Maybe."

"It seems like you and Nour have been hitting it off," Edgar said. Casual again, *so* casual. The imp of the perverse was strong with Poe.

His brother stirred the sauce, the picture of disinterest. "Yeah, I mean. Bones is cool."

"That'd be so clutch for Allie to have more help," Edgar said. "Jamie was talking about picking up more shifts at Le Corbeau too. They worship Aunt Alaitheia."

"Allie doesn't mind the kittens," Poe said as his knife flew through an onion, mincing it in seconds. "So maybe I could stay a while."

Onion hit the hot pan and sizzled, and Edgar's phone pinged with Jamie's text.

✦✦✦

Edgar juggled the front doorknob, his key, and the lasagna pan that Poe had shoved into his arms on his way out the door.

"Hi, honey. I'm home," Edgar said under his breath and smiled.

He put the lasagna on the square of countertop not covered in boxes and went in search of Jamie. He found them on top of a ladder, cursing the high ceilings they'd only ever praised before. Not wanting to startle them, Edgar moved right behind them before saying, "Hi."

Jamie startled anyway, measuring tape going flying as they tried not to fall off the ladder. Edgar grabbed them easily from behind, and Jamie startled again.

"Sorry, babe." Edgar set them gently on the floor, and they pressed their palm to their chest.

"I can't get like a *Hi, honey, I'm home* or something? Jesus, if you don't wanna live together, just say so instead of *murdering* me."

"I'm so sorry. I didn't want to startle you from across the room. I wanted to be ready to catch you. And, uh, I did say that. Just. Very quietly."

Jamie made the face they always made when they thought Edgar had said or done something adorable and they thought they weren't showing it.

"How's the family?" Jamie herded him into the kitchen.

"Good. Allie had a brilliant idea. She's gonna hire a hybrid babysitter and clothes seller at Magpie Vintage so that she can have Nour in the shop. When they're awake, the babysitter can help out with them, but when they're asleep, the babysitter can do stuff around the place."

"That is a good idea," Jamie agreed. "Now, where's my lasagna?"

Edgar looked at the counter where the dish lay. "How'd you know Poe made us lasagna?"

"Because I requested it." Jamie looked at him like he'd asked something strange. "He asked what we wanted for dinner on move-in day."

"He texted you? He offered?"

"Yeah. He offered so we wouldn't have to cook, and I said I wanted lasagna." Jamie was speaking carefully, as if concerned that the simple concept was evading Edgar.

But what had evaded Edgar was something else entirely: Poe had changed. He wasn't sure when it had happened or if it had been too incremental to notice until now, but the Poe Lovejoy who had shown up the night Allie went into labor was *not* someone who would offer to make lasagna from scratch so someone else wouldn't have to cook. He wasn't someone who adopted three kittens or lived with his sister. And he *certainly* wasn't someone who would've described a kid as *cool* and been excited to hang out with their aunt, cooking food in the city he'd once sworn he would never return to.

It was a day full of so many firsts that Edgar was a bit

overwhelmed. But he forced himself to put any uncertainty with his family out of his mind and took Jamie's hands.

He gazed into their eyes and brushed a piece of hair from their forehead. This was his person. This was his home.

This apartment, where once Edgar had retreated from the world alone, was now a home that he and Jamie shared.

"We live together now." Jamie screwed their face up into an adorable expression.

"We do," Edgar said. "I kind of can't believe it."

They both stared at each other.

"Can I show you something?" Jamie asked, holding out their hand.

In that moment, Jamie could have led him a hundred miles away to the top of a volcano, and Edgar would have followed them.

As it happened, they only led him to the closed bedroom door.

"Okay, I hope you don't mind," Jamie said. "But you said you were sick of it. And obviously if you don't like it, we'll change it."

Jamie seemed to be having an internal argument about whether to include any more caveats, then fell silent and opened the door.

Four years ago, Edgar had run home and slammed the door behind him, desperate to be safe from the ghost of a little girl who had followed him from the bus stop. Its eyes had been black voids, its mouth a hole of jagged teeth, and its hair leucistic snakes. (Later, when he'd calmed down, he'd realized that it'd *had* no eyes, its jagged mouth was that of someone caught between baby and permanent teeth, and its white-blond hair had been in braids.)

That night, door shut and double-locked firmly behind him, he had ordered paint, rush delivery. He'd stayed awake until the package came the next morning, dragging it inside with one hand while the other shielded his eyes from the sun, a rat heaving its treasure back into the sewers. Then he'd stayed up until every inch of his bedroom was painted, ceiling to windowsills to floors, with haint blue in a piteous, desperate, wretched bid for safety.

Now, he stood in the doorway of that same bedroom, but it had been transformed.

Gone were the gray rug, a hand-me-down from Allie, the heavy dresser that had been in the apartment when he moved in, and the storage trunk—a yard sale find that had never stopped smelling like crayons.

In their places, Jamie had set a light modern dresser on each side of the closet and laid down a gorgeous rug that Edgar thought he recognized from Germaine and Carl's house. It was warm shades from deep wine and terra-cotta to the lightest petal pinks. Hints of midnight blue played beneath it all, grounding the color. The linens were the colors of champagne and mushrooms.

His mother's painting had been rehung above the bed, and now Edgar could see Jamie's inspiration for the palette for the room.

There wasn't a speck of haint blue in sight. The walls were now a delicate peach color that was warm in the lamplight. When the morning sun filled the room, Edgar knew, it would positively glow.

Edgar walked in slowly, wanting to look more closely at everything.

The white blinds had been replaced with gauzy curtains the color of saffron. Where the serviceable (but distinctly nipple-shaped) ceiling light used to be hung a fixture with a light and a sleek ceiling fan that would make sleeping much easier on the hottest nights. And on a small shelf next to the mirror stood several framed photographs of Jamie and Edgar, Poe and Allie and Nour, and the kittens.

"What do you think?" Jamie's arms came around his waist from behind, and he leaned into them.

"It's absolutely amazing. I don't know how the hell you did this in one day, but it's…it's like being inside a sunset."

*Jamie, in Edgar's T-shirt, hair tousled and eyes soft, asking him his favorite color as they held hands over cereal.*

"I can't believe you remembered," murmured Edgar, overcome.

"Course I did. I remember everything about you." Jamie's arms tightened around him; their breath was warm on the back of his neck. "These colors are warm and intense and comfortable. Just like you."

For a moment, Edgar thought they were teasing. He turned around in Jamie's arms to look at them. "Is that really how you see me?"

"Among other things, yeah." They winked at him.

"Oh yeah?" Edgar's cheeks heated. Jamie's compliments always made his stomach turn to goo.

"Yup. I haven't even mentioned your awesome family, your superior ability to see ghosts, or your exquisite taste in boyfriends," Jamie teased.

Edgar grinned. His heart felt like it would overflow his chest. "I do have all those things, don't I?"

Jamie reached a hand out to Edgar, and he took it. "We should see how it looks from the bed, right?"

Edgar agreed, and they climbed into bed, curling around each other.

"What do you think, gorgeous?" Jamie asked. The compliment warmed him from the inside.

"It's perfect, Jamie, really. And these sheets feel like heaven."

"Germaine and Carl gave them to us, and I'm sure they're fancy as fuck. They'd been sitting in their linen closet since the Nixon administration, according to Carl."

Edgar smiled.

"Rug's from them too. And the dressers. Your old one was untenable."

"I don't know why you'd be so quick to dismiss something just because three of its drawers collapsed when you tried to open them."

Jamie snorted. "Three *of four*."

Edgar grinned. A wave of exhaustion closed over him, and he sank into the fluffy, luscious embrace of rich people's cast-off linens.

"Mmm, so comfy," Jamie said against his shoulder.

Edgar pressed a kiss to their hair. He was on the edge of falling asleep, and everything he'd ever wanted was in his arms. "Love you."

"I love you too, sweetheart," Jamie said.

"Jamie?" Edgar murmured. "I want to get a cat."

It was time.

Jamie chuckled softly. "I think that could be arranged. I know a guy." They kissed him softly.

"Yay," Edgar said against their lips and let sleep creep in.

Edgar wouldn't have any bad dreams that night. He wouldn't wake afraid or alone or lonely. He would not see a ghost or feel a ghost or hear a ghost. That wasn't to say that in the future he would not have bad dreams. That wasn't to say that he would never again wake afraid or alone or lonely. And that was not to say he wouldn't see or feel or hear ghosts again.

But at least for tonight, he would sleep well, part of him always touching Jamie, in their champagne mushroom sheets, in their sunset of a room, in their gem of a city, surrounded on all sides by life and death and the living and the dead—and frankly, a lot of people in between. He would sleep until the first tentative rays of sunlight fell through saffron linen and lit the walls and the ceiling and Jamie's hair and eyelashes a brilliant, hopeful gold.

He'd watch, Jamie's head cradled against his shoulder, their arm in a tight embrace across his stomach, their breath a sweet whisper in his ear, as the sun rose higher and brighter, spangling rainbows over the bedclothes from chandelier crystals hanging in the window, and made the room glow, happy, safe, connected.

# Hungry for more Roan Parrish? Don't miss *The Holiday Trap*, available now.

**FROM A COZY NEW ENGLAND HAVEN TO THE HEART OF NEW ORLEANS COMES ONE HOLIDAY THAT'LL CHANGE THEIR LIVES**

Greta Russakoff loves her tight-knit family and tiny Maine hometown, but they can't seem to understand what it's like to be a lesbian living in such a small world. When an act of familial meddling goes way too far, she realizes just how desperately she needs space to figure out who she is.

Truman Belvedere's heart is crushed when he learns that his boyfriend has a secret life including a husband and daughter. Reeling, all he wants is a place to lick his wounds far, far away from Louisiana.

Enter a mutual friend with a life-altering idea: swap homes for the holidays. For one perfect month, Greta and Truman will have a chance to experience a whole new world…and maybe fall in love with the partner of their dreams. But all holidays must come to an end, and eventually these two transplants will have to decide whether the love (and found family) they each discovered so far from home is worth fighting for.

# 1

## Greta

Snow fell in fat, picturesque flakes, fairy lights twinkled around the stage, and the hum of excitement and cheer that always attended the Owl Island, Maine, Holiday Fair electrified the town square.

Greta Russakoff stood in the center of it all and contemplated precisely how she would murder her entire family one by one.

It had begun as the Holiday Fair always did: Valentine Johnson, the mayor of Owl Island, turned on the lights that illuminated the town square and all the businesses that lined the four streets creating it. She called the Holiday Fair to life amid cheers and whoops from a familiar crowd. And then she called up the volunteers for their annual charity auction.

This year, the charity was the Owl Island Library, and the

auction was for a dinner date at Francesca's, Sue Romano's Italian restaurant.

Only this time, after Valentine had called up the usual suspects, another name rang out.

"Our final volunteer is Greta Russakoff. Come on up!"

The smile of holiday cheer died on Greta's lips, and for one tremulous moment, she thought she'd simply misheard. After all, there were six other Russakoffs in town. They stood all around her: her parents and her four sisters.

But that hope died the same death as her smile when she saw the faces of her mother and her eldest sister, Sadie, who were looking at her with twin expressions of satisfaction.

Her father was pointedly avoiding her eyes, as was her older sister, Tillie, the peacemaker. Her twin, Adelaide, blinked in horror at her but didn't say anything. Her youngest sister Maggie's mouth dropped open, and she mouthed *Oh, shit*, the words swallowed by the murmurs of the crowd.

"What," Greta bit off between gritted teeth, looking between Sadie and her mother, "Did. You. Do?"

"Greta, are you here?" the mayor crooned into the microphone. "Remember, this is for charity."

Valentine was beloved on Owl Island. She had increased tourism and revenue for small businesses, including the Russakoffs'.

Greta added the mayor to her kill list.

Her heart sank as people began to reach out and pat her on the back and smile.

"Go on, Greta!"

"Get it, Greta!"

"Greta, yeah!"

Could you murder an entire town?

"Go get 'em, kiddo," Sadie trilled, and Greta wondered, not for the first time, why Sadie gloried in messing with her more than with anyone else.

*You could just leave*, Greta told herself. *Just turn around and walk away. You're an adult now, and this isn't the damned hunger games. They can't make you.*

Greta squared her shoulders and cleared her throat. "I didn't volunteer," she said confidently and prepared to leave.

Only her words came out as a croak, and she *didn't* leave.

She turned to Adelaide, looking for a rescue or help or… something. But while Addie looked horrified on her behalf, she just shrugged, an I-don't-know-what-to-do gesture familiar from every awkward situation of their childhood.

"Dude," Maggie said to Sadie. "You're such an asshole."

"Greta, go," her mother hissed. "It's for charity!" Nothing scandalized Nell Russakoff like a lack of performative generosity.

Owl Island was a small town. Leaving would mean answering questions for weeks. Which would mean offending people about the auction, a beloved town tradition. Which would mean even more talking to people who'd known her since she was a child and still treated her like she was one.

Greta gritted her teeth so hard she felt a headache threaten and walked stiffly to the stage, taking care not to meet anyone's eyes lest she perish from mortification or reveal previously unknown Medusa-like powers. She stood next to the other volunteers with what she hoped was dignity but would see in pictures later was the pose of someone who desperately needed to pee.

One by one, the volunteers were bid on.

Greta had attended this auction since she was old enough to

remember, and since she was old enough to remember, it had been her least favorite part of the holiday festivities.

Still, she went every year because it was a family tradition and because she loved the rest of the Holiday Fair that first December weekend. The auction had even been the occasion of her coming out five years before.

She and Tillie had been in the booth their family ran every fair. The handmade items they were selling changed with the whims of their mother's crafting. One year it had been quilted oven mitts, another it had been felted table decorations, and that year it had been knitted hats and mittens. Tillie and Adelaide were the most enthusiastic crafters and usually made the bulk of the items alongside their mom. Sadie liked to sell things but not make them. Maggie would start one of whatever they were making that year and quickly lose interest. And their father concerned himself with all elements of display, providing snacks, and cheerleading, but didn't have the dexterity for most crafts. His attempts were generally hilarious, though, and every year, they had him try to make one and enshrined it on the shelf above the piano, which now held two decades of misshapen crafts.

In the family booth, Tillie had been showing Greta how to knit a hat for the third time, her attempts at mittens having proven hopeless, and Greta had sworn bitterly as the whole thing slid off her needles.

"Watch your language," her old math teacher Mr. Sorensen had said as he walked past. "Men don't bid on young ladies with potty mouths at the holiday auction."

Greta, home for the holidays from her freshman year of college and high on the freedom of her first months away from her family, had snapped back, "Well, this young lady has no interest in men or being auctioned off to anyone, so that'll work out great for all of us."

Tillie and Greta's father, who'd returned with hot cocoas in time to overhear the exchange, had turned to her with identical hazel eyes—her father's wide and Tillie's smiling. Tillie raised an eyebrow. "Yeah?"

"Yeah," Greta said, starting to shake with nerves. Her whole family—strike that, the whole town—would know in a matter of hours.

She shoved her woeful knitting at Sadie and got to her feet. As she walked past her father, he caught her shoulder and squeezed. When she looked up at him, he smiled and nodded just once. Then he let her walk away to be alone with her thoughts.

Now, she wished desperately for a similar exit strategy, but she was onstage in the middle of the town square with nearly the entire population of Owl Island staring at her.

Just as she was telling herself that it couldn't get any worse, she caught sight of Tabitha Ryder. Greta winced.

Tabitha's smooth blond bangs and elfin face were framed by the faux-fur-lined hood she had pulled up against the Maine winter. She held mittened hands with Jordan Laverty, who was handsome and too infuriatingly kind to loathe the way Greta would have liked.

Hey, at least Greta had a perfectly self-deprecating story to tell when the topic of first loves came up. Not everyone had confessed their love to their best friend and then puked on her shoes. (Although, Greta found out, more had than you might think.)

Tabitha's blue eyes grew wide when she saw Greta onstage,

and Greta braced herself for the utter carnage of her heart that would follow if Tabitha smirked at her pathetic misfortune.

But Tabitha didn't smirk.

It was so much worse.

Tabitha, curse the kind soul that had made Greta love her in the first place, gave Greta a look of such pity that Greta felt her insides fold like a paper bag. Gone was the urge to murder. Now, with Tabitha—beautiful, happy Tabitha—looking at her while holding the hand of her new love, Greta simply wished to disappear.

✦ ✦ ✦

Greta allowed herself one hour of furious shower wall punching and postshower cringing at the memories of the day before she pulled a wool hat over her damp hair, stepped into her boots, zipped up her heavy coat, and stormed over to her parents' house three streets over, where the whole family always gathered on holidays and Saturday afternoons.

*Close* was the word Greta always used to describe her relationship with her family. Occasionally, as she got older, *tight-knit*. But it wasn't until her friend Ash had returned to Owl Island after leaving for a few years that someone had finally looked her dead in the face and said, "Dude. Your family isn't just close. It's codependent. And weird," he added under his breath as Greta squirmed.

And, okay, she'd always known her family did more things together than lots of people's, but they had a whole *thing* going on, and usually it was great. Her family was lovely and fun. Her sisters—especially Adelaide and Maggie—were her best friends (since Tabitha wasn't in the picture anymore), and she loved having a built-in support network, no matter what happened. But then there were moments like this. Moments when they were intrusive and possessive and infuriating and—

Greta took a deep breath before she opened the door, steeling herself not to give an inch. She couldn't give them a chance to explain, because there was *no* acceptable explanation. She couldn't hear them out, because *no* motivation could justify it. She just had to storm in there, set her jaw, and start yelling. It was the only way to be heard over six other people.

Tillie was just inside the door.

"Are you mad? You're mad. Okay, listen, I can talk to Mom. I think Sadie told her you'd think it was funny, and—"

"*Sadie* told her that?"

"Well, I don't know exactly. I just think—"

"Duuuude," Maggie said, skipping down the stairs. "You looked like you were about to turn into a flock of crows and peck out everyone's eyes up there! Did you see Sadie yet? I bet—"

But she fell silent as their mother walked in from the kitchen, drying her hands on her apron.

"Hi, honey," her mom said with a smile.

"That's what you have to say to me after earlier?" Greta demanded.

"Well, what do you want me to say? That I'm happy my daughter stood up in front of the whole town and glared at everyone?"

"I *glared* because you and Sadie put me in a position where I'd have to do something I hate or publicly offend the whole town. What, did you think I'd be, like, excited about it?"

"Don't be such a baby, Grotto. It was just a joke," Sadie said as she walked in from the kitchen. She took a loud, crunching bite of an apple and cuffed Greta on the shoulder.

"It's not a joke!" Greta seethed with a deep, trembling kind of anger that made her voice come out thin and reedy. "That's what shitty incels and rapey frat boys say when they realize whoever they're talking to isn't going to let them say horrible things. Don't tell me it's a joke to put your sister on a fucking *auction* block for someone to *buy* the right to a dinner date."

"Pshh, it's for fun. It's a holiday tradition," Sadie said.

"Fun for *who*? Not for me, certainly. And I'm *not* going out with Nicholas Martens."

"What do you mean?" their mother broke in, frowning. "You can't not go. It's for charity."

Greta spluttered.

"And you're cool with this," she said to Sadie finally. "I know we fuck around, but you actually think that I should go on a *date* with a *man* who *bought* time with me. Come on."

"Not like you've got any other dates," Sadie muttered. "Whatever, take the free dinner. Nicholas isn't that bad." She waved her hand in dismissal.

Greta took a step toward her. Sadie was only two inches taller than Greta but around ninth grade had decided that she would never lower her chin, so she seemed even taller.

"Fuck you," Greta said. "I *know* you don't think this is cool. You would never do it to anyone but me."

Something flickered in Sadie's eyes, but she just sniffed and the moment was past.

"Now, girls," their mother said. "Stop this. Greta, I'm sorry you're upset. We just thought it might be nice if you gave someone a chance who you ordinarily wouldn't look at twice."

Greta goggled.

"Someone I ordinarily wouldn't…do you mean, like, a *guy*?"

Nell shrugged. "Love is love, isn't it?"

"Yeah," Greta said. "It is. And if I happen to fall in love with a man, then fine. I mean, I probably won't, because I'm a *lesbian*. But you don't get to throw those words around like a flotation device to redeem you from doing something shitty. You *knew* I would hate that. You knew I would've hated it even if it was all women who were bidding on me! I can't believe you!"

Unlike with Sadie, where all strong feeling eventually got expressed as anger, with her mother Greta finally felt tears threaten. It was a betrayal, plain and simple, and while the sisters all messed with one another from time to time, the thought that her mother either honestly didn't know her well enough to understand how much this would upset her or, worse, didn't care was enough to make her cry.

Their argument had brought her father to the living room as well. Always the last to engage, he looked at Greta with sympathy, but she'd long ago stopped thinking of him as an ally. What use was someone who agreed with you if they weren't ever willing to risk discomfort to say so?

Tillie started to chime in with her typical placations, but Greta was done arguing. She wanted her mother to admit what she'd done—even Sadie had done that—and then she wanted to get the hell out of this house.

"Did you seriously not get that I would hate that?" she asked her mother point-blank.

Nell Russakoff's face was the picture of aghast innocence.

"Darling, no. I would never do anything to upset you. I just thought maybe a little push... You can't want to stay single forever. And it's not as if there are many other lesbians on Owl Island..."

But Greta knew. The slight flick of her mother's gaze to the left told Greta that Nell had been perfectly aware how Greta would respond.

"Okay, cool. Great," she said sarcastically. "A push. Well, that sounds great to me. Yup, a push actually sounds like exactly what I need. The hell away from here."

And without another word, she turned on her heel and walked back into the snow.

# Acknowledgments

This book has been a long time in the making and I'm so grateful to all the readers who have remained excited about *The Holiday Trap* and this world while I brought it to life. I'd like to thank my agent, Courtney Miller-Callihan, for all she does. My editor, Mary Altman, for her clear vision in helping to make this book the best version of itself. Jillian Goeler for capturing its spirit with the absolutely beautiful cover. And the whole team at Sourcebooks for their care with this manuscript. Most of all, I'd like to thank my partner for her endless encouragement and excitement about this project, especially when I was feeling a bit haunted myself.

# About the Author

Roan Parrish lives in northern New York where she is gradually attempting to write love stories in every genre.

When not writing, she can usually be found cutting her friends' hair, meandering through whatever city she's in while listening to torch songs and melodic death metal, or cooking overly elaborate meals. She loves bonfires, winter beaches, minor chord harmonies, and self-tattooing. One time, she may or may not have baked a six-layer chocolate cake and then thrown it out the window in a fit of pique.